Caermaellan Palace

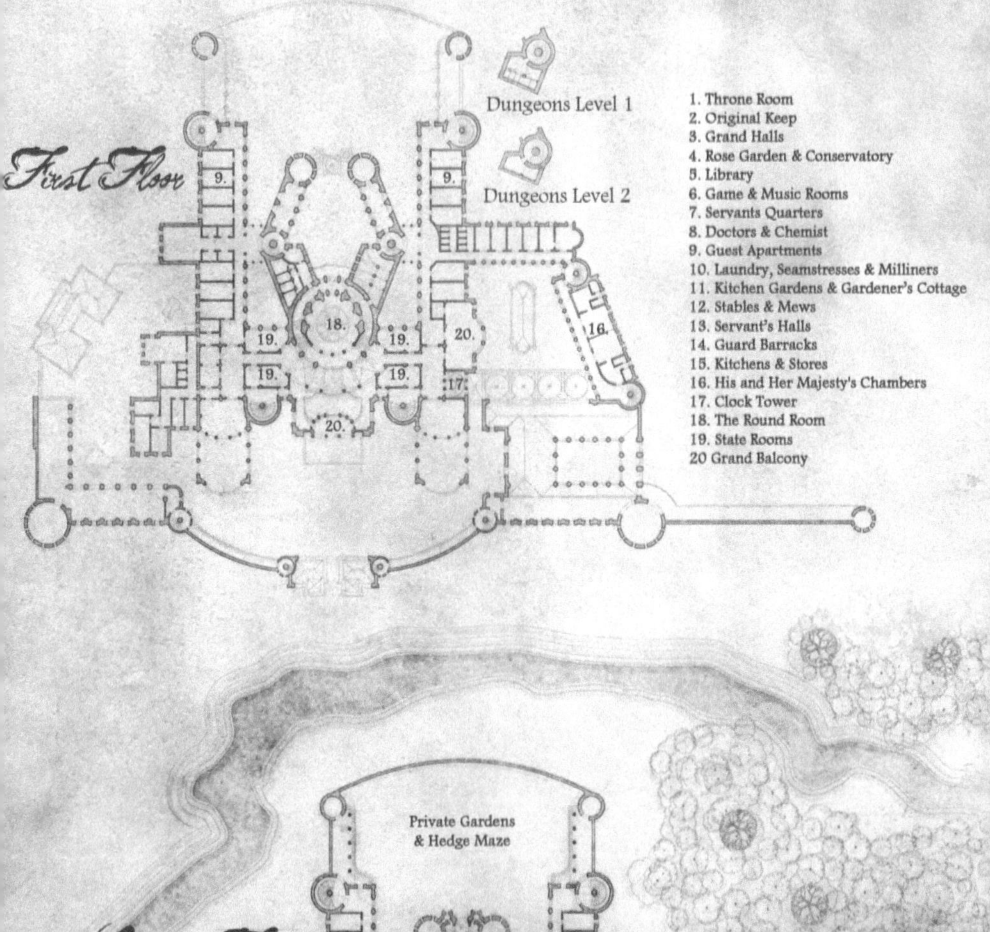

Ground Floor

Private Gardens & Hedge Maze

Horse Paddocks & Fields

Hunting Grounds

Main Gate & Public Gardens

First Published May 2013
Paperback ISBN: 978-0-9871511-9-3
Hardcover ISBN: 978-0-6487080-7-0

THE MEMORY'S WAKE TRILOGY

Book One - Memory's Wake

Book Two - Hope's Reign

Book Three - Providence Unveiled

www.memoryswake.com

HOPE'S REIGN

SELINA A FENECH

CHAPTER ONE

Living in the castle with her friends wasn't turning out to be the Happily Ever After that Memory thought it would be. With skirts hitched up and heart fluttering with adrenaline, she bolted across the lawn and pushed through a gap between dense hedges and the garden wall. A final glance back showed a page, handmaiden, and guard stumbling down the palace steps, bewildered at her disappearance. Spying through the leaves, Memory grinned. If she knew it would be this easy to lose the entourage, she would have done it sooner.

Life had become an ongoing parade of public appearances, formal dress, legal documents, rehearsals, posing for portraits, fairy representatives, and the mighty task of rebuilding the kingdom of Avall. It gave Memory the distinct sensation of drowning. No time was left to just be herself. Whoever that was.

Moments ago, escorts had come to chaperone her to yet another meeting. *Yet another meeting. I couldn't stand another meeting!* Something snapped and she just dashed off when they were looking the other way. A tactic they obviously weren't expecting. And she'd become well practiced at running away from people since returning to Avall.

Memory slowed from a jog to a relaxed walk. Light rain misted the air, weighing down her pale hair and the wide-skirted gown better suited to a ballroom. A carpet of muddy leaves sloshed under foot, and the hem of the dress was already stained, but Memory didn't care. Water beaded on soft ferns and she caressed the fronds, like wet velvet under her touch. *Silence.* She listened and smiled. *I've missed you.*

Memory wandered farther into the long strip of woodland that spread into the distance on the eastern side of the palace. Hunting grounds, left wild and ancient and full of life, including one new resident. Or at least Memory assumed Will now lived somewhere in these woods. Neck arched, she peered into the rain-blackened branches of the sturdy oaks but saw no sign of him. She frowned. *Mental note- must find out where and how Will lives.* Memory wondered if she'd come this way with the hope to see him, or just because being lost in a forest still seemed more familiar than the gold-leafed walls of the kingdom's finest castle. With Will, there was no pretense, no pandering. He was her only link to a forgotten past and distant life. She wished he'd visit more often.

Memory felt like the kingdom's newest toy, getting propped up next to Eloryn on display as the visible face of change for Avall, while behind the scenes Hayes and the Wizard's Council dealt with pulling the kingdom back together. The Council kept the information about where Memory had been on strict lockdown, letting people assume she had been with Eloryn and Alward the whole time, but rumors of how she defeated Thayl spread fast. The twin with the strange hair, name, and behavior was the hottest topic in Avall. The most people gossiped about Eloryn was to say "how lovely" she was.

Hayes and his cronies also treated Memory like some sort of arcane oddity to be studied. Her first visit with them, which had been advertised as being friendly and social, turned into a civilized interrogation full of questions she couldn't answer about things she didn't understand. Where did she get her powers, where had she been, what did Thayl's ritual do to her? They wanted her to use magic for them, to observe her. She didn't want anyone studying her too closely, worried about what they would see.

Memory swore as something sharp jammed into the side of her satin slipper. The stupidly big skirts prevented her from even seeing her own feet and the source of pain. Memory glared at the lacey gown, now woven with twigs and leaves. She was not dressed for this. *Run-away-and-plan-the-rest-later proves yet again to be a bad fallback strategy.*

Trying to settle the voluminous skirts, Memory sat on a nearby fallen trunk and brought the injured foot up into view. A sharp stick had wedged itself into the sole of her shoe. She pulled her knife from where it had been stashed in her corset, flicked the blade out, and levered the stick free with the point. *Eloryn would probably be able to just ask the stick to remove itself, not that she'd be hanging out with me in a forest anymore.* Memory sighed. Why did she think things would remain the way they were? Just her, Eloryn, Roen, and Will looking after each other. They'd bonded under extreme conditions, and now that they were safe, Memory could feel the group drifting separate ways.

The princesses' every minute was managed, and when Memory thought things couldn't get worse, Hayes sprung a new surprise on her. On top of the stress of the upcoming coronation ceremony, he insisted she had to go back to school. To that horrid land where bullies teased her hair colors and the only place to reliably skip class smelled like a urinal. She always hated school. She...

Chewing gum smooshed into the back of her head. The horrified disgust on her face when she turned around made the pointy faced boy behind her laugh. Gus. He was so getting unfriended.

"What's the problem? It's the same color as your hair anyway," he said.

Her hands became fists. "Nice one. By that logic I guess it means you won't notice when I stick your head in a toilet because you're just a piece of—"

Opening her eyes, Memory clutched at the rough bark of the log to steady herself. The flashback was far too vivid to have been only imagination. Gus's weasel-like features were still clear, and she could almost smell the dirty-sock scent of the school corridor. A shiver danced through her limbs simply by knowing what these were. Memories.

She replayed them like hitting the previous chapter button over and over on a remote, savoring them. She could remember something. School. Just a tiny fragment, but it was there, and it belonged to her. A low giggle started huffing its way out of her mouth, growing as excitement took over. She had to get back and tell Eloryn. A wide grin cracked her face. She closed the knife and jumped up to head back to the palace.

Memory skipped over woodland debris, ducking under dripping branches and trying not to slip in haste when she ran face first into something hard. A sharp sting shot through her nose, and she clutched at it with both hands. Eyes watering, she stumbled backward, only to hit something behind her. She blinked, trying to see what blocked the way, but found nothing. With arms outstretched, she tried all directions. The air seemed to spring back, like pushing on a firm mattress.

"Look what I caught," an ethereal voice whinnied through the cool air. "Pretty as a princess."

Creeping from behind some trees, a creature approached Memory. From a distance it looked like a little girl, but as it drew near Memory could see it wasn't human at all.

The creature moving forward twinkled from rain, which formed pearls on the fine layer of white fur that covered a feminine body. Bovine ears and curled horns protruded from a head of wooly hair, and long animal-like legs ended in cloven hooves. Was there even a little tail swishing to and fro? The creature stared straight at Memory with two nebulous black eyes and grinned.

Black eyes… does that mean unseelie fae? But she's so beautiful. It must have been some type of fae, something that had a classification, a name, a place in either the seelie or unseelie courts. Eloryn would know. Memory just knew the creature was gorgeous and terrifying.

She held her breath, remaining still as though movement would provoke it. Would the Pact protect her from this? Maybe it was time to start paying more attention to the politics of Avall.

"So, hi," Memory said. "Nice to meet you, I guess. I'm just heading off that way, as soon as I can move again. Are you causing that? Are you allowed to do that?"

The grin on the furry fae spread wider, and she tilted her head down to the ground. Memory's gaze followed.

Stupid skirts. She hadn't even noticed past all their ruffles that she'd walked directly into a fairy ring. She'd heard that wasn't a good thing to do. Memory pushed against the force that encircled her where the white-spotted red toadstools poked from the ground.

The fae giggled and danced around the circle. "My fairy ring, my territory. You're mine, mine, mine."

"Look, let me go, and I'm sure we can work something out. I'm, like, someone important here in Avall. And we're both reasonable,"

Memory paused, "people, right?"

The fae stopped and looked her up and down.

"I know who you are," the fawn sang like a nursery rhyme, "Little ticking time-bomb came home from Hell."

"What do you mean? And how do you even know what a time bomb is anyway?"

"We fae, we travel, see many things. Or we did, before the human plague poisoned the world." The fae grimaced. "Now, I could keep you as a pet," she began, stroking her furry chin, "but humans are so greedy and unclean."

The snowy fae poked Memory in the shoulder. Memory startled, flicking the knife in her hand open again and holding it up protectively.

The fae snorted. "Cold iron. You stink of it. That knife will get you into trouble, princess. Just try and use it on me, I'll Brand you faster than lickety-split. My territory means no Pact for you." The fae bent in close. Memory could see her face reflected in the creature's wide black eyes. "No, no, no. We'll find a use for you. You look like you could dance well. I could make you dance for eternity. Dance, dance, dance so beautifully."

Gulp. Time for an escape strategy. Memory took stock of her assets and disadvantages. Corset strung too tight. Skirts too big. Rights under the Pact lost. Unable to use her fae-burning knife or be Branded. No one actually knew where she was. Will hadn't seemed to have noticed his Memory-is-in-danger cue. Veil doors took too long to cast. Other magic was unpredictable and scary. *Assets, where are you?*

Memory made a display of putting her knife away.

"I'm sorry. I'm new here and don't know how things work yet. Is there any chance you can just let this one time slip, and if you ever catch me again I'll be yours for reals? What harm could there be in letting me go?"

"What harm?" the fawn cried, sounding like a whinny. "This from the girl child who pointed an *iron* knife at me? A jest! Stinky, ticking time-bomb means no harm!"

The fae straightened up to her full height, just taller than Memory's five-foot-nothing stature. "Perhaps, perhaps I will turn you into something harmless. That would be the best thing for everyone."

Okay, magic it is then. Memory hated using magic, the way it burned through her and left her empty and singed. But she had to get away. She prepared herself as the fae seemed to come to a decision.

"I'll turn you… into a flower!" The fae lunged forward, grabbing Memory's shoulders tight. She flinched backwards, lifting both fists as a shield. Releasing the flame of magic, she closed her eyes and hoped for the best, the only technique she'd mastered so far.

Magic exploded. Gusting winds and the disconcerting feel of the Veil pulled at her, but Memory kept her eyes squeezed closed. She waited, breath held, and after a few moments she couldn't feel the fae's grasp anymore. *And I don't think I feel like a flower, not that I'd know what being a flower felt like.* She peeled one eyelid open, and the sight made the other eyelid snap wide alongside it.

"What the…"

CHAPTER TWO

She was back in her room. Back in the castle.

Memory doubled over, breathing through the shock and pain of the instant, and unexpected, Veil transportation. *What in the holy horse balls was that?* That was not what she meant to do, but then her magic had always been as predictable as it had been explainable. The Veil door was something that she could do if she concentrated to control it, but to do it instinctively, or worse accidentally, made her stomach contract.

A shiver built in her back and shuddered out through her limbs, bringing with it a cold sweat. *Calm down. You're okay, you're still here,* she told herself firmly, but panic kept debating that with her. What if she wasn't? Was she even in the same time? What if she got lost in the Veil again for another sixteen years?

She straightened up and analyzed the room. *My room*, she reminded herself. It looked the same as it had that morning, still a total mess. Eloryn had ended up in Loredanna's well-maintained suite, and the pristine, ornate setting suited her, but Memory couldn't handle it. It felt like stepping right into the shoes of a mother she'd never known.

Instead, Memory took the adjoining chambers, which would have been the king's, her father's. She knew less about him than she did her mother. The royal bloodline was through Loredanna, and he was just some sorry soul whom the Wizard's Council picked to be her husband, and he only lived another nine months after that. His chambers had not been well kept. Shards of broken vases covered the patchy rug and torn paintings, shrouded in cobwebs, sat where they'd fallen off the walls. This entire wing of the castle had been closed up during the sixteen years of Thayl's rule, with only Loredanna's chambers being cared for by Thayl himself.

The debris had been cleared out by servants, and the castle steward argued that room should be properly renovated before Memory moved in. She preferred it like this though, a clean slate. She intended to decorate the room with personal mementos, make it her own, but so far her only belonging was her old wallet that Will had returned to her.

No one had snuck in and renovated the room, or even made the bed, so she guessed she managed to come right back. But this was something that needed to be confirmed. She needed to see her sister and tell her what had happened, both the good news and the bad. How to share the news was another matter. *Hey, I remembered stuff, but then got caught by a furry fairy and Veil doored back to my room without meaning to! Yay?* Memory doubted her twin would take this new installment of weird very well.

She walked to the corner of the sitting room and heard muffled murmurings coming through the patchy wallpapered wall. She knocked hesitantly and the sound stopped. A second later Eloryn called her welcome. Her voice sounded tiny.

"Lory, you won't believe what I've got to tell you." Memory opened the doorway that looked like a section of wall, joining their chambers. It wasn't really secret, just designed to fit in. Nerves twinged as she thought how to share the news with her twin, but the sight in the room chased the idea out entirely.

Eloryn's neat and pretty chambers were now cluttered with wooden chests of all shapes and sizes. Some were open, showing folded clothing and books. Mostly books. Eloryn sat on the floor, surrounded by the boxes, her face splotchy red and wet.

"What happened?" Memory stood frozen for a second then managed to step through the boxes and kneel in front of her sister. Eloryn squinted through tears.

"Hayes arranged to have it all brought here. That's what the meeting you missed was about. All of our belongings, mine and Alward's." She held a man's shirt, hands like claws, gripping it tight.

"It's... a lot of books." Memory bit her tongue. She had to do better than that, be a better friend, a better sister, but felt so awkward.

"It's not even all of them. They kept everything that falls within the Council's legal domain - books on magic, the speaking mirror, and all of Alward's research into the Veil. I understand that the mirror and books had belonged to the Council to start with. Alward took them with him when he went into hiding. I'm not ungrateful. It's so moving that they went to such trouble to bring this all to me, but I would have liked to see Alward's research again. I wanted to see his handwriting again." Eloryn's small body shook as a loud sob ended her sentence. She covered her eyes with a forearm, blonde hair shimmering as she shook with silent sobs.

Memory had so many things to ask her twin about accidental magic, the fairy ring, and the black-eyed fae. She wanted to celebrate her memories returning. She paused for a moment and looked at her sister.

Memory leaned forward and wrapped Eloryn in a tight hug. The fabric of their skirts rustled against each other and puffed out like they were sitting in clouds. Eloryn put her head on Memory's shoulder and wept quietly.

"Mem, why is your dress all muddied? What did you want to tell me?" Eloryn mumbled.

"Nothing to worry about." Memory squeezed Eloryn and let her cry.

It was like some kind of cruel joke, but she was there, really there, standing right in front of Thayl's cell.

Memory's lip twitched in confused anger. She hadn't known where Thayl was being kept. She didn't want to know, as long as he was kept away from her. She had just been wandering the castle, and her traitorous feet led down the cold stone steps into the wisp-lit depths of the dungeons. Guards nodded as she walked by, unlocking gates, watching curiously but not daring to stop her. She just walked and found herself there.

She stood and glared. Thayl sat on a cot in the furthest corner of the room, back against the rough cut wall, hunched over, face hidden by dark wavy hair. Memory could see he'd been unable to shave. His right hand hung down on one side. *Right arm,* Memory corrected herself. Thanks to her, he no longer had a hand there. It was still bandaged, blackened by blood and dirt from the cell. A thick, rotting stench filled the space. His clothes, the same he'd worn the morning she'd cut off that hand, looked grey now, not the rich blue and gold they once were. *Hadn't he been given anything else to wear?* She cringed off a feeling of sympathy, twitching it away like a spider crawling up her arm.

Thayl reacted to the movement, his head jerking up. He stared at her for a moment then rested his head again on his knees. "Come to gloat? I guess this was inevitable. Say your worst, demon."

Caught off guard, Memory rambled, "I'm not. I didn't come here for anything. I didn't mean to come here at all. I was looking for Roen."

"I don't think you'll find him down here."

"I mean, I went to try and see Roen, but Isabeth says he's not here, gone off on some trip all of a sudden without telling me. I couldn't find him and then I... I ended up here." *Why am I telling him this? What am I doing here? Why am I not leaving?* Memory looked to the stone stairwell then back to the cell. This was the only cell down these stairs, separate from the rest of the prison. A private high-security dungeon for the most hated man in Avall. Thick gridded copper squares let her see in clearly to the simple stone room. A wooden tray had been slid under a small gap at the front, with just one piece of bread the size of her small fist. She wondered if he'd eaten the rest, or if this was all he got.

Thayl sounded tired, any bait in his words overwhelmed, making him almost seem interested. "Surely you have other people to see. What about your sister? Or that savage pet of yours?"

"Will's not savage! And it's your fault how he is now. He wouldn't

have had to grow up like that if it wasn't for you." Memory shivered. It wasn't only Thayl's fault. She couldn't help but feel guilty too. "He hasn't been around much. Being around too many people freaks him out."

She had thought of looking for Will, but it seemed he could only be found when he wanted to be. She knew he was still around, on guardian angel duty, but she hadn't exactly been in any danger lately, until the furry-fae encounter, and then he didn't show. He'd only visited a few times these last weeks and seemed to be getting more withdrawn. His sprite friends were also still hanging around, keeping an eye on her. Memory tried talking to them once, but they treated her like toxic waste. And Eloryn was always so busy, much like Memory should have been if she wasn't dodging handmaidens and duties. She needed someone to talk to, someone to share her big news, and found no one to turn to. But that didn't mean she wanted to talk to Thayl. She balled her hands into fists.

"Like you can talk anyway, you're not far from savage yourself. Doing what you did to the woman you claimed to love."

Thayl half smiled, as though he were expecting this. The smile didn't reach his eyes, still as dark and sad as when she'd first seen them at Duke Lanval's estate. "Not just one."

"Not one... who what now?" Memory's raised voice faltered in confusion.

"Not just one woman I loved, but two." Thayl shook his head, the oily mess of his dark hair glossy in the low light of the cell. "It's not surprising you were drawn here. You don't know, but when you were born I had a sixteen-year-old sister. Another beautiful life sacrificed as part of the ritual to take your power. That bloody ritual. That's why you're here."

Memory shook her head, not understanding, not sure she wanted to understand.

"The ritual bound us together, you and I. I barely feel it now without my hand, but I know it's still there." Thayl tapped his chest. On the same place on Memory's body, a disfiguring scar twisted the skin. "Even if you won't acknowledge it, it's bringing you to me."

Memory stood frozen for a moment before a growling grunt of disgust burst out. "Connected to you? Make me want to barf my skin off. I wasn't drawn here, I just got lost! How could I be connected to someone who would kill his lover *and* his sister over revenge?" Memory breathed hard, snorting the anger out, but her feet remained planted.

Thayl spoke again after a long pause. "Does it help that I didn't know? I didn't kill either of them. And I didn't know they would die."

"Why should I believe you? Why are you even telling me this? You let them die. It was your fault. My mother died because of you, and you sent me away!" Memory screamed at the top of her lungs, not caring how far the words carried up the stone stairwell into the rest of the dungeon.

"It wasn't my fault!" Thayl's voice rose in return. "I made such a fool of myself in court, begging Loredanna to be with me. She refused me, in front of everyone. The Wizard's Council was so cruel. I vowed revenge on them all right there. That night the witch came to me, said she saw what happened, and that she could help. She promised me enough power to take my revenge on the Wizard's Council. Looking back, I don't know where I thought such power would come from. I should have known the cost would be so great, but I had no other way, not enough power to do anything on my own. I didn't know what my deal with her would entail. All I did was take Loredanna, my beautiful Loredanna, to the witch, and then..." Thayl's last words shook from his mouth. He turned away.

"All you did? Then, killing my father, hunting the wizards, banning magic, and generally being evil for sixteen years, who was that? You won't even admit it, what you did to her, what you did to me! You screwed up my whole life. I hate you! I hate what you did to me!" *You stole my soul. You broke me. I'll always be broken!* Her mind kept screaming as her voice failed, and she turned away from the cell and dashed up the stairs and away from the man who took everything from her, making her as much a monster as him.

It took days for Memory to calm down after seeing Thayl. Her hands shook every time she thought about it. The worst part being that it was her own stupid fault for going there like that, talking to him. Saying she couldn't control her own actions, that it was some magical connection compelling her, made it both better and worse. She hated the idea that she wasn't in control, but being able to put the blame elsewhere brought some comfort. But the comfort had a bad aftertaste. Just like Thayl, not accepting the blame. She kept returning to what he said, wondering what was true, and denying the morbid desire to go back and learn more about the dark ritual that changed her life.

Memory thought through all of this instead of paying attention to the meeting currently underway. Her entourage had become wise to her escape tricks, and she hadn't managed to avoid this one. She sat beside Eloryn and did her best not to put her head down and fall asleep. Eloryn was engaged in the conversation, but Memory's mind roamed. The meeting room, which she'd heard called the Round

Room, was part of the oldest section of the castle, the ancient stone keep the rest of the palace was built around. The high ceiling had a stained glass design of a glowing sword and light shone through, down onto the enormous ring shaped table they all currently sat around. She traced fingertips over the smooth, worn wood of the table where the colored light fell. The table looked like it had seen centuries of use.

Hayes shot her an unimpressed look at her blatant disinterest. He, Waylan, Madoc, Lambeth, Bors, and a bunch of other gray faces with names attached she hadn't managed to remember talked at her. They all wore the same style of suit they wore when they'd first met. Rich black satin, floor-length coats with stiff collars, purple lining and trim, but the suits were new now, not aged and ragged as they had been before. They were saying something about school again. *Fantastic.*

They had explained that Thayl destroyed the university the Wizard's Council used to run in Caermaellan, Avall's capital. The university had been the place where they trained and taught future wizards, some of which became part of the Council, while others were assigned to townships to offer services throughout the islands. Other non-magical higher education was also offered there. The school was the only university of its kind in Avall before Thayl razed it to the ground as part of his hatred of all wizards.

Hayes had a strange, constipated look on his face as he announced that they would be reopening the university in the large Women's Finishing School that still operated in the city, taking over much of the grounds for their classes in magic, math, politics, and sciences.

"Your Highnesses." He nodded to Memory and Eloryn together, looking down at them over his hooked nose. "We hope to be ready for classes right after coronation. Your attendance at the school will be a sign to the populous of the return to normality and restored peace in Avall. And an opportunity to fill out any shortfalls in your own educations, of course."

Hayes didn't even try to be subtle in directing the last comment toward Memory.

"What about Will? Can he go as well?" Memory asked, trying to show interest.

"I'm not sure it would be the best place for him. The university is only open to those of noble blood," Hayes said.

Memory pursed her lips. "Will's not *NOT* noble. He's just, different. I think it would be good for him to be around more people again. He's been alone for so long. And maybe his parents where he came from were royalty? Huh? What then?"

"Mem," Eloryn spoke in her calm, quiet voice. "It would be lovely to see more of Will, but do you really think it is something he would want? We must encourage his reintegration into society but also be sensitive to his needs and undertake the process at his pace."

Memory sighed. *My sister, always right.*

"Fine, but if he wants to go, he should be allowed," Memory said. "Same with anybody. Noble or not, shouldn't everyone have a chance to learn? Come on, guys. Thayl banned everything but really basic magic for all this time, right? Now he's gone you're still not going to let everyone use magic?"

"Respectfully, if everyone had access to higher forms of magic, what kind of world do you think this would be?" Hayes said in a mocking tone as though she could barely understand the concept.

"That's not the point. You're saying you want to limit the use of magic based on the title someone has. That's not right."

Eloryn spoke up again, and Memory hoped it would be to take her side. "It's not only about title. It's in honor of the heritage of

magic. Noble families are the ones with the right to the education because it is their families who established the studies of magic, who did the hard research to confirm the wording of behests throughout history."

Memory's mouth hung wide. "I can't believe you're with them on this. It's not exactly like we've been brought up noble. I wasn't even brought up in Avall!"

"It's still in your blood. You should be eager to begin learning again. Eloryn at least had some education from Pellaine," Hayes said. Eloryn cringed slightly as Hayes continued to use Alward's old name. "It will serve her well after her coronation as queen."

"You mean Memory's coronation," Eloryn said.

Around the table, everyone froze so still it seemed as though time had stopped, apart from eyes darting from person to person, blinking through the silence.

"Memory is to be crowned queen, is she not?" Eloryn asked the room.

Hayes frowned sympathetically. "We thought it was an obvious outcome, considering your pasts. You will be crowned queen, and you will be a fine queen."

Eloryn paled, clearly shocked.

"It's okay," Memory spilled out, directing her words to Eloryn and ignoring the prickle of tears. "I don't mind. I mean, I'm not exactly queen material. I know Eloryn's got her head screwed on better than me." She should have known. It was an obvious decision. Not even a decision. It's just how things were. *What kind of queen would I be anyway? Lory already sounds like a queen.*

Eloryn shook her head and spoke firmly. "Memory is the legal heir before me. She was born first, is the elder, and was Thayl's stated heir as well."

Hayes took over again. "Memory may be legal heir for all our human reasons, but do not forget your deal with the fae, Princess Eloryn. You are required to rule, and renew the pact with them, or the consequences could be dire for all of Avall."

Eloryn dropped her head. Memory could see she hadn't thought of that.

"It is important now more than ever to maintain peace with the fae," Hayes said. "So many are leaving Avall, and those remaining are stirring, upsetting the order, acting out. They will not accept Memory as the ruler of Avall. Not the way she is."

"Then could we not both rule? We're twins. We should be together. We can do it, rule equally." Eloryn turned to face Memory, a strange desperation in her expression. *Is she scared to do it alone?*

Hayes's eyes shifted side to side, seeking his words. *Oh,* Memory thought. *They really, really don't want me as queen.*

"Of course we considered this," Waylan spoke up, kindness in his voice instantly more sincere than Hayes's. He rested his hands on his round belly as he talked. "Never before has such a thing happened, and with reason. Having two figureheads essentially divides the power, weakens the throne. Power needs to lie within one hand, a strong, unilateral decision maker who the people believe in." Waylan looked apologetically towards Memory as though the words were harsher than he'd meant. He offered her a small smile. "Memory will still be crowned and recognized officially as princess of the realm at the coronation ceremony. She can be with you and help you when you need her. This would also officially place her as heir to the throne, until as queen you have your own children as heirs, of course."

Nods around the table marked the end of the meeting, and the Wizard's Council departed. Hayes left last. Although he was the youngest of all the wizards, he carried a dragon-headed walking cane that he didn't seem to need, other than to thump on the ground as he disappeared down the hall. Eloryn and Memory remained in their chairs for a while after, silent together. Eloryn seemed to be trying to say something, but after a while she left Memory alone in the room.

Memory ran her hands over the ancient table's surface, wondering how something she didn't even want hurt so much for being taken away. *It's because no one believes I can do it. Not even me.*

CHAPTER THREE

Eloryn stood next to Roen, trying to be as quiet as possible. They'd just sent for Memory and waited in Eloryn's sitting room, watching the door. She felt more nervous than she had need to and kept glancing over at Roen for reassurance. He'd just returned from his trip and hadn't changed out of riding clothes, knee-high boots and tight leggings slightly marked with mud and caramel hair still windblown. The loose-fitting shirt he wore revealed his collarbones and strong angle of his shoulders. Eloryn's heart beat faster, and she quickly turned back to look at the door. It opened and Memory walked in.

"Happy birthday!" Eloryn and Roen shouted together, enjoying the shocked look on Memory's face.

"Happy what the... what?"

"It's our birthday." Eloryn smiled.

"Surprise," Roen added.

Memory raised her eyebrows. "Surprise the amnesiac. Fun game."

"We thought we could celebrate tonight, just the three of us. It's actually our birthday tomorrow, but tomorrow is also a day of mourning because, well…" Eloryn trailed off, not sure how to finish the sentence.

"Oh right. The whole massacre thing," Memory said.

Between Memory's lukewarm reception and the reminder of the past tragedy, there wasn't much celebrating occurring. Eloryn really wanted to do this for Memory, do something to make her happy and feel wanted. The recent meeting with the Wizard's Council was awful, and Eloryn hated that Memory had been denied so much in her life. She wanted to give her sister something, even something small. Eloryn tried to stay positive.

"There are presents!" she said cheerfully.

Roen gave Memory a quick hug and laughed. "Just a couple of small gifts. You get the rest tomorrow. I don't know how you've missed the river of presents flowing into the castle. Still avoiding your staff, I assume?"

"Like they were itty bitty plague rats," Memory said.

Eloryn bit her lip. It was obvious Memory hadn't had any handmaidens or staff around to help her. Her pale hair was loose and barely brushed and her gown's fastenings hadn't been done up properly at the back. She was worried about how well Memory was adjusting to this world that should be her home. *Although considering I had handmaidens spend three hours this morning using hot irons to set my hair into perfect ringlets and cycle me through three gowns each day, I can understand the allure of keeping them away.* The plum velvet off the shoulder gown they had picked for her evening attire stood out as far too formal compared to Memory or Roen's outfits.

Memory kicked Roen softly in the shin. "When did you get back, anyway?"

"Only moments ago. I didn't mean to be gone so long. I went to Duke Lanval's, and he insisted I stay and travel with him when he came to Caermaellan."

"Lanval's here too? I never know anything! And don't you tell me it's my fault because I don't want a million maids fussing around me all day." Memory jabbed a finger at him.

Roen held out a large silk-covered box to her like a peace offering. She stared at it like it might bite her, but soon reached for it and a grin split across her face.

"Well, hopefully you at least know what to do with that box." Roen smirked.

Memory made a scrunched nose grin and headed over to the lounge. She sat down with the gift on her lap, tugging at the satin bow that imprisoned the box.

After pulling the lid open, an audible gasp wheezed through Memory. "My stuff? My stuff! You found my stuff!" She plunged her hands into the open box, dragged out her strange shirt, and rattled through the jewelry she used to wear in her face. She bounced a little on the edge of the seat, and looked like she could leap up and hug Roen, but became too engrossed in rediscovering her belongings. "I have stuff! That's mine!"

"Even Isabeth's dress she lent you is in there, not that you have a shortage of fine dresses now, but she wanted you to have it. I thought you might want your belongings back and was sure Lanval would have kept them safe somewhere after what happened that night."

Memory's bouncing stopped. Some dark emotion past over her face then cleared quickly. A smile returned, but the bouncing energy didn't.

Memory's words came out raspy and quiet. "Thank you."

"You're most welcome." Roen put his hands in his pockets and leaned on the wall, a bashful look on his face. Eloryn watched the whole exchange between the two of them, wishing she could have the easy friendship they had.

"He also brought back my bag I left there, and my mother's, I mean, our mother's medallion." Eloryn stumbled over the words. She'd barely had a month to get used to having a sister after a lifetime of thinking all her family were dead.

"Oh. Of course he did." Memory's face dropped again.

Eloryn fidgeted her fingers. She'd said the wrong thing. She looked across the room where the medallion of gold and rubies sat on velvet in a glass jewelry case, a priceless artifact of the Maellan family. "I'm sorry. It is ours, and if you wish for it, I'd not hesitate to let it be yours."

Memory rolled her eyes. "No, it's yours. I know it is. Always has been."

"Well, I have a gift for you, something new that can be yours," Eloryn said, biting her lower lip. She reached behind the chair and brought out another pretty box.

Memory's mouth flickered into only a slight smile this time. "Damn. I'm an idiot. We're twins. It's your birthday too, and I don't have anything for you."

"What more could I need than my friend and sister to celebrate with? Open your present, I hope you like it."

Memory pulled a well-worn book as large as her chest from the box and flicked through the pages with raised eyebrows.

"It's a history of Avall." Eloryn paused, seeing her present wasn't getting the excited reaction Roen's had. *She doesn't like it.* "I thought

you may be interested to read about our history and family, and learn some more about how the kingdom operates."

"Yeah. It's good," Memory said. "All the better to not keep embarrassing myself, right?"

Eloryn tried to stay enthusiastic, but an awkward silence descended over them.

Memory stood up and shrugged. She didn't appear to have enjoyed herself. In fact she looked sadder than Eloryn had seen for a while.

"So, I have this thing. A headache, kind of thing happening. Thanks for the birthday surprise, but I'm going to take an early night. Sorry." Memory sat the book on top of the box of her old belongings and left, apologizing again on the way out.

Eloryn sighed and looked at Roen who offered a sympathetic smile. He reached for something in his pocket.

"I have another present for you," Roen said.

"You shouldn't have. You went so far to collect our possessions back for us."

"Well, I thought Mem would be excited by her present. Her clothing is part of who she was." Roen paused, hand still in his pocket, half smiling. "Close your eyes."

Eloryn took a deep breath and let her eyelids drop. She could hear Roen approach as he kept talking. He sounded nervous, words running fast.

"It was no trouble to collect your items from Lanval's as well. And I knew the Council was bringing you your other belongings, but I believe many of your possessions have sad pasts. So I wanted to get you something new." Roen's voice caught at the end.

Eloryn felt the warmth of his hands on hers, bringing them up and placing something soft onto them. Her eyes opened and saw a gold embroidered pouch. With a nod from Roen, she tugged the drawstring open, fingers shaky from her pounding heart.

A small teardrop of rare jade on a thin strand of silver poured from the pouch into her palm. It was still warm from being kept close to Roen's body.

Roen shrugged. "Just a small token. It reminded me of your eyes."

Eloryn looked from the pendant up at him with her lower lip between her teeth. "It's beautiful."

Roen cleared his throat, looking across at the fist-sized medallion of gold. "I understand it's not a grand piece as fitting a lady of your rank, but I hope I chose something you may find occasion to wear."

Eloryn shook her head. "I'll wear it all the time."

She undid the clasp and brought the chain up around her neck, her hair getting caught as she tried to do it up.

"May I...?" Roen moved forward, reaching to help pull her hair back. Eloryn scolded herself internally when the clasp clicked closed and he moved back away again. Frustration bloomed red in her cheeks.

The long silver chain was like a strand of hair, glimmering when the light hit, but almost invisible otherwise. Roen's eyes followed it down, the pendant disappearing down into her chest. He quickly looked the other way. Eloryn saw a faint glow of red on his high cheekbones, which made her blush more.

"Thank you for inviting me to share gifts with you and Memory tonight. I will take my leave. My parents will wish to see me now I've returned."

Eloryn grasped for more to say, wanting the conversation, her time with Roen, to continue. "Are your parents well? I've not seen them lately. Silly I know, since they are so close in quarters."

"Yes, both well." Roen hovered for a moment then bowed stiffly, pausing at the bottom. Eloryn heard him curse softly before he straightened up. She'd requested he wouldn't bow to her anymore, at least in private. She frowned, knowing how much trouble he went to for her.

Roen left and Eloryn curled up in an armchair, holding the pendant in her hand. She spoke words of magic to it, asking it to hold onto the warmth it had drawn from Roen's body, to keep it always, the way she wished she could but knew she couldn't.

Roen leaned on the closed door to Eloryn's chambers, grinding his teeth. The evening had not played out well. It was significantly easier getting along with either of the twins when they were running for their lives. He constantly fought down feelings for Eloryn. He couldn't be with her, nor did he deserve to be. But he now worried even for the friendship they'd tied between them. He could feel those bonds slipping loose.

Out of habit he felt for the edge of the blade he used to keep within the seam of his work pants and found it missing. He no longer carried the tools of his old trade.

How life has changed. Memory and Eloryn never once brought up the subject, that they were the only people to know the truth of the criminal he used to be. He never raised it either, never asking for their silence or secrecy. He wasn't sure whether it was because he trusted them or some guilty part of him hoped they told.

It was enough that they knew. No matter that they didn't seem to care. He could never outrun the shame of that.

Roen rubbed his forehead. And that silly gift he got for Eloryn. He had almost said out loud how he wanted to buy it for her properly. He could have stolen her something that would have taken her breath away. His family had no real income while they were being housed here in the castle, with no estate or lands of their own anymore. They were given most of what they needed, but Roen spent some of his time at Lanval's working. Honest work. Earning money rather than taking it. Funny, given his new reputation as friend to the Maellan twins, he found a job much more easily than in his days as a sparkless nobody. It was enough to buy the small pendant for Eloryn, but he couldn't tell her any of that, without reminding her again of what he had been.

Tonight, seeing Eloryn dressed so finely, she reminded him of the portrait of her mother, Loredanna, that he'd seen as a child. She somehow seemed so fragile, even though she wasn't nearly as brittle thin as her identical twin. Was it just who she was, the pureness in her? Or was it a hangover from the trauma they'd suffered just weeks before? Everything about Eloryn made him want to protect her, from everything. Even himself.

Roen brushed back the fall of hair from his face and looked down the hallway to see a shadowed shape slip suspiciously around the corner. Roen straightened up, shifting from discomfort to worry. His need to protect Eloryn took control.

Muscles running up the backs of his legs worked hard as he moved silently down the length of the hallway. He closed the distance quickly. The man he'd seen didn't look like a servant. Servants in this castle didn't skulk. It was prestigious work, and they were almost as arrogant as the nobles. He reached the corner so quietly that the man had no idea he was there, which was evident when he peered around the corner again to spy down the hall, finding himself face to face with Roen.

Roen moved fast, grabbing the front of the man's shirt and pinning him against the wall. "What are you doing?"

The man stuttered, and Roen saw he looked familiar, wearing the black and purple of the Wizard's Council.

"Bors? Why were you spying on the princesses' chambers?" Roen growled at the man, who stared back at him with as much outrage in return. No guilt showed in his features at all, and Roen released his tight grip on his shirt, worried he'd over-reacted.

Bors straightened out his clothing and re-buttoned his coat. "It is important to know the virtue of the princesses isn't being compromised."

Roen took a step back as though he'd been struck.

"I would never..." Roen's words ran to nothing, knowing full well he'd once taken advantage of Eloryn, after he'd gotten her drunk no less. Even with how bashful Eloryn could be, the three of them felt so familiar together with everything they'd been through. Now life had reclaimed some normality he'd never realized how improper his behavior had been. He shouldn't even be seeing them like this, these private, unchaperoned visits to their very chambers. What if he had been wrong about everything? What if the reason Eloryn was so uncomfortable around him was because of what he'd done when they were alone together at Elders Bridge Inn? Roen stepped back again, and the man smiled.

"The Council understands you have some relationship with the princesses, but these inappropriate evening meetings won't be tolerated. Don't think we haven't checked on your past. We know of your exploits with more common women. The princesses are no common women." The man stepped forward, so close Roen could smell his stale breath. "Know you've been warned."

Memory found her chambers empty. A week ago they would have been swarming with maids, turning down the bed, fluffing pillows, trying to help her change clothing. She'd been so standoffish, to the point of actually hiding from them, that they had stopped showing up.

Memory pushed aside her newly tailored gowns and squeezed the box of old clothes into the bottom of the wardrobe. Thinking about what had happened the night of the masquerade ball stole all happiness from the gift. Not that she'd be allowed to wear any of her old things anyway. Jeans and t-shirts didn't seem to go down very well in Avall, and she'd been trying to fit in. Guilt weighed on her. She had considered at times trying to tell the others what she'd done that night at Lanval's castle, how her actions got them so close to being captured, that she considered selling Eloryn out to Thayl. But fear gave her excuses. Why should she tell them? She didn't actually do anything. They're all okay. It all worked out fine. It was all just a mistake. Excuses on excuses.

Memory gave the box a swift kick, denting the silk covered side. A noise distracted her and she turned around.

The diamond glass doors to the balcony stood open as always, Memory's way of letting Will know he was welcome. A peach-tinted sky changing to night over the forest silhouetted Will as he climbed easily over the balustrade. The fires inside her already burned, and when she saw him there, they sizzled more, fueled by guilt. He tried

to save her as a boy, and for that he got sucked into another world where he lost his whole life growing up like an animal in the woods, waiting for her. She only wished she could do more for him, but he hadn't even accepted a room here in the castle. The weather had started to grow icy, moving from autumn into winter, but Will still wore the strange collection of old torn clothing and furs, lashed on with leather strapping. Most of his back and chest were still bare. The thick layer of dirt that darkened his skin when she first saw him in the forest, confusing him for an animal, had been cleaned away. His skin was a lot paler than she'd thought, making his lightning blue eyes glow against dark brows and hair.

"Hope." He smiled at her, remaining perched on the balustrade where overgrown ivy and rose vines tumbled over and curled onto the balcony.

Will was the only one who knew her real name and hearing it made her feel odd, a remnant of a past self that she could barely recall.

Memory rolled her eyes. "Please don't call me that. So typical for people to give such a lame name to an orphan. I'm Mem now."

"Sorry." Will looked like a struck puppy.

"Crap, no I'm sorry. I'm not in a great mood. And it's good to see you no matter what you call me. But don't take that as an invitation to go name crazy."

He mumbled, turning away so she could barely hear him, "Why didn't you tell me it was your birthday?"

"Geez, learn to eavesdrop better why don't you? I didn't know myself!" Memory's voice became shrill. She dumped herself down onto the bed, and the book Eloryn got her poked into her backside. She pushed it angrily out of the way. "You probably know more than me with my whole month worth of memories. And if you want to know something you should just come and ask me instead of lurking around listening in like that. Not like I could tell you anyway since you're never around!"

Memory glared at the book, and when she turned back to the balcony, Will was gone. *Right, first time all week he shows up and I yell at him and scare him off.* Memory cursed seven times and hurled the heavy book at the wall. It made a satisfying thump, dislodging some old wallpaper before it fluttered down onto the floor.

Memory stared at the ceiling and took a deep breath. *Calm.* She'd been so worked up ever since seeing Thayl, as though seeing him again flared up every wound inside her. She could still hear the words he said to her that day in Kenth: *The ritual to steal your power was interrupted, leaving you like this, this shell. But I can end your suffering. I can finish taking the rest of your soul.*

No one but Thayl and her knew. The others knew he took her memories and magic, but nothing else. Memory wondered how it could work, how she could still live, breath, talk, and move with only part of a soul. Maybe she couldn't, not well anyway. No wonder she couldn't keep her friends, why she kept being such a monster to everyone.

The tantrum slipped straight into a dull depression. She stepped across to the wall and squatted down to pick up the book, wondering if Eloryn would notice the new dent in the cover.

The book lay open on the floor, its ruffled pages showing an intricate illustration of a majestic sword. *Oh, pretty.*

Memory picked the book up and drifted across to the armchair in the corner, staring at the sword. The caption called it Caliburn, sword of Arthur Maellan. Memory wondered if he might be one of her ancestors. Memory flicked to the next page, skimming over the text, looking for more information.

She couldn't believe she'd never shown a proper interest in the history of Avall, when that meant the history of her family. She tended to take a lot for granted and not ask questions because after a while it just became easier not to know when the sheer number of questions overwhelmed her.

Memory turned another three pages, absorbing information about Avall before she turned the weighty tome back to page one with a thud, ready to start at the beginning. *Damn it, Eloryn, this* is *interesting.* Memory pulled her knees up onto the chair and balanced the book on top of them, her mind swimming with the words.

And how Avall suffered through those darkest of times. The beginning parts of the book were sparse, indicating a history rooted in despair. Stories about people starving to death, invasions, and slavery; horrors from some 1500 years ago from what Memory could tell from the timeline.

And the magical creatures from beyond the Veil didst warn mankind of the approach of a greater Hell that would consume all.

Arthur Maellan appeared again in the text, and Memory read on to discover whether he was related to her. He was a commoner from Avall who had "a talent for tongues." Able to speak with the fae, he had a friend called Myrddin who was half human and half unseelie fae.

It was through Myrddin that both courts of the fae approached Arthur with a deal. The fae would save Avall, removing it from the rest of the world, bringing it into the Veil to become a safe haven for man and fae alike. In order to make Avall a sanctuary for the fae, all iron would have to be removed and in return the fae would bestow upon the humans of Avall the Spark of Connection, allowing them to use magic.

Lo, Avall was saved and the rest of the world thus lost. Arthur took this offer to the king, Uther Aurelianus, who accepted and the Pact was formed.

Memory frowned. *So Avall was separated from the world way back then and progressed on its own ever since?* According to everyone she had met in Avall, no other land outside Avall still held life. They only spoke of Hell beyond Avall or the land of the fae beyond the Veil. But the rest of the world must still be there. She'd grown up there. Will too. The land of big buildings and cars and grimy old orphanages. Memory shook her head, not understanding. She read on.

The great Purge was begun, the great sword Caliburn drawn from the stones of Avall. The fae were serious about removing iron from Avall. Not only did they have the humans ship every piece of forged iron off the islands before the separation, but to guarantee no more iron could ever be forged, Arthur and Myrddin worked magically to draw all iron ore from the land. The ore was smelted into an enchanted sword – the one from the illustration – which became a symbol of the human rulers' solidarity and strength, the one tolerated item of forged iron

in the land.

The very presence of the fae in Avall made the land fertile and prosperous. Uther Aurelianus had no heir of his own, and so made Arthur Maellan his heir as reward for saving Avall. Memory whistled. The Maellan bloodline went back so far.

Memory considered her knife. If such effort had been taken to remove iron from the land, it only seemed right that she respected it. She pulled the knife from her corset and held it like a pet.

"I understand you want to leave," a voice in Memory's head echoed.

She was in an office with the blinds pulled down. In front of her was a figure that she couldn't quite make out.

"But what do you expect me to do, Hope?" the man said. "We tried to get your fostered, Jesus, we tried. But you always end up back here." The figure stood up and paced, silhouetted by what little light came through the blinds. "Same old story. We find a nice family for you, get you settled, and then there's a fire. The cops say there were no signs of arson, but these accidents just keep following you around."

The front door opened with a quiet creak, and Memory looked up with a start, drawn out of the vision from her past. No one had knocked, but a tall figure walked in. The room was dark and the fire had all but died, leaving just a spluttering candle to light the room. The serving staff treated her request for candles very oddly. Surely a Maellan heir could create their own light? Memory squinted from her chair at the approaching figure.

The person stopped in the middle of the room, looking her way. They seemed as shocked as Memory.

"Your Highness, forgive me. I expected you slept," said a breathy female voice.

"What time is it?" Memory looked around. The sky outside was

pitch black, and the moon had risen high. The doors to the balcony were still open, rushing icy air inside. *How long was I reading for?*

"It is well past midnight. As you're awake, do you mind if I light the room?"

"Sure."

"Àlaich las."

The serving girl stood awkwardly next to a light fitting that now glowed with a soft golden light. Tall and buxom, she had wavy red hair and a peachy complexion. She wore the neat gray maid's uniform of the castle and carried a copper tub with cleaning tools hanging around the edge. She curtseyed deeply. "I can see to my duties another time if I am disturbing you."

"No, it's okay. You just surprised me. I thought I'd scared all my staff off."

The girl almost smiled at the joke, but stopped, looking unsure as how to react. "I'm newly assigned to your keeping, Highness. The other servants warned... I mean... told... I mean..."

The girl blushed and winced. Memory smiled to try and comfort her. "Yeah, whatever they said was probably true. So you do this work at this time of night?"

"We must keep the fire warmed for you during the night as winter closes on us, it would be poor form to have our royalty waking to a cold room." The girl eyed the dying embers and wide open bay doors. She briskly swung the doors shut and locked them, drawing the heavy curtains. The room felt instantly warmer, and Memory reminded herself to unlock the door next chance she had.

Memory detected a hint of scolding in the maid's tone. "I'm sorry. Is there anything I can help with?" Memory left her book and knelt next to the girl who had put her tub down near the fireplace. She was sifting through the embers with a poker, drawing up the still

glowing few and speaking behest words to them that brought them to greater light.

The girl stopped, rigid for a moment. "I'm new to the castle, but I am capable in my duties, Highness."

"It's no problem. I'm wide awake anyway."

The girl paused again, midway to putting a log onto the coals. She gave Memory a look that though friendly, bordered comically quizzical. "That's not... You really wish to help?"

"I'm not exactly great with this stuff, but if you just tell me what to do I pick things up quick. Sorry, what's your name?"

The girl looked completely dumbfounded. "Clara, your Highness. But your Highness, this is not clean work. It wouldn't be well for your Highness—"

"Less of the Highnesses already!" Memory rushed her words out in an exasperated sigh. "Just call me Hope."

Memory's brain froze in confusion. "No, I didn't mean that. I meant..." Memory frowned. She stood back up, moving towards the bedroom. "Don't worry about the fire. I'm fine, I don't need it. The room is fine how it is."

"But your... Hope—"

"Clara, please, just go."

CHAPTER FOUR

The next morning, the shock of getting her name wrong still affected Memory. She sleepwalked through the birthday-celebrations-cross-remembrance-day, her thoughts too busy to pay attention to the lines of visitors offering gifts and condolences. Sleep deprived and confused, she couldn't understand how she could slip up on something so fundamental as her name. With some of her past returning, was she becoming Hope again? And if so, what would happen to Memory? Did she even want to be Hope again? Both of them had been pretty rude to people lately.

Memory added Clara to her list of people to apologize to, along with Eloryn and Roen for ditching them despite their birthday plans.

Will made the top of her list, and she hoped he'd also have some advice on how she could get rid of her knife appropriately, since he was in with the fae. Actually finding Will was the challenge. She grew hoarse calling his name in the forest, carefully avoiding fairy rings, until he showed up.

Memory apologized and then asked if he'd help her find a place to hide her knife, and the very next day she found herself with Will again. He led her into the hunting grounds to a spot just out of sight of the hedges that marked the end of the manicured palace gardens.

"Are you serious?" Memory looked skeptically at the subsided well he had brought her to. In front of her, the ground buckled and sunk into a black pit, the stones that once formed the well lay strewn like a breadcrumb path down into the darkness.

Will nodded from where he leant against the mossy trunk of a tree. "I'll go with you."

"Of course you bloody will. I'm not going down there on my own." Memory felt for the purse at her side and the hard weight of her switchblade inside.

"It's what you asked for. A good place to hide your knife. The only place I know that the fae never go."

"I'm not surprised. I don't know why anyone would go down there, except maybe the insane, like me." Memory sighed. This had to be done, but she didn't like it. Being someone important in the hierarchy of Avall meant she simply couldn't be in possession of something as controversial as cold iron. She had to get rid of it, in a way that wouldn't further insult the fae who already seemed to hate her.

She moved toward the sink hole, and Will stepped in front of her, going first. Ahead of them, the ground sloped down then quickly dropped away into a black rip in the earth.

"Is it even safe? How far does it go?"

"Not far. I checked yesterday. We should leave the knife at the end. Don't worry, I won't let anything happen—"

"I know, I know." Memory hitched up the rust red skirts of Isabeth's old dress. She had almost worn her jeans for this expedition, but didn't want to be so conspicuous since she had to get away on her own again. Isabeth's dress proved to be a good disguise since it was less formal than her new princess wardrobe. It was the plainest gown she had, no bustles, frills, or hooped petticoats. Still, it wouldn't be easy scrambling down into a cave in floor-length fabric. At least she got away with wearing her skater shoes. They felt like old friends on her feet.

Will squatted down at the edge of the hole then stepped off into the darkness. Memory panicked when she didn't hear him land, worried he'd fallen into a bottomless pit, and knelt down to look over the edge. His face was right in front of her, an arm out to offer her help. *Silent bastard.*

Memory wriggled around so her feet dangled off the edge, then slid down over it into the hole. Will caught her around the waist and eased her descent. She put her hands on his shoulders to balance and felt the tight chords of muscle moving under his skin. The instant her feet hit the ground he let go of her, acting like he'd done something wrong. He paused for a moment, looking concerned.

"I can do this without you. Let me take it," he said.

Memory shook her head. "This knife almost feels like part of me. I feel weaker without it. I know it's dumb, but I have to say goodbye to it properly." *What an odd, morbid funeral this will be,* Memory thought, *crawling into the depths of the earth for a little piece of metal.*

Memory surveyed the tunnel, a dirty crevice hanging with tree roots lead down, back in the direction of the castle. Dark brown and blue fungi grew on the walls, and a thin layer of mucus gave the rock a slick sheen. It sounded like water was running in the distance. It looked like a fairly smooth descent, and she'd hardly have to duck. Will, on the other hand, stood nearly two feet taller than her and twice as wide. He turned toward the tunnel, pushing through sideways. Memory winced and hoped he wouldn't get stuck, but looking at the powerful shape of his back, she figured he could probably dig his way out if he did. She would still feel guilty since he was only doing this for her. But at least he was talking to her again, interacting with something other than Mina and the trees.

The tunnel quickly became claustrophobic. Memory drew deep breaths of the cool earth-flavored air.

"Are we there yet?" Memory joked. They were running out of natural light, and she wondered how far they would go, how deep the tunnel led, when she ran into Will's back.

"Yes," Will said. Memory thought he was smirking, but there was barely enough light to tell. Ahead of them was a dead end. "This is as far as it goes."

A strange sensation passed through Memory. Something warm and welcoming.

"There's something…"

Memory pushed past Will, and he squeezed awkwardly out of her way. She didn't put down the knife. Something drew her forward. She put her hands against the end of the tunnel. It shifted under her fingers. Memory looked to Will and without a word he moved to help, pushing at the dirt wall. Earth and stones crumbled out of the way leaving a dark hole of a tunnel that led much farther, deeper than expected.

"We shouldn't go in. I haven't checked it's safe past here, and it's too dark," Will said.

"Scaredy cat. I want to keep going. Look at this wall, these were bricks. Besides, I came prepared."

Memory pulled a candle from her purse and struck a match against a nearby rock. It hissed alight with the smell of sulfur. "I don't suppose you can cast that light behest?" Memory asked, lighting the candle with the scarily spluttering match.

"Only people born here get magic. That's what Mina says," Will said. "What does it feel like? Having the connection to magic?"

"Like a bonfire burning me away from the inside."

Will frowned.

"And not good for much when I can't even cast the light spell. You know I saw a three-year old cast it the other day." Maybe she should wait until Eloryn could come with them, but crawling into dirty holes somehow seemed below her majesty these days. Memory took another candle from the purse, lit it with the first, and handed it to Will.

Memory looked at Will, the candlelight reflecting in his eyes. "Did I ever use magic back in our world?"

"I never saw it." Will hesitated then took the candle and stepped through into their discovered tunnel.

Memory blinked as his candle light disappeared to the side, then realized the tunnel had opened wide, wide enough for him to stand to full height and step out of her way. She crept through the last of the earthen tunnel, pushed through a web of tree roots, and tripped over a brick on the ground. Will grabbed her arm, and she pivoted around and ran into his chest. Memory felt a jagged scar, smooth and raised, under her fingertips. Her heart ached. *So many scars…* Will stepped back, running into the wall, and half way through an apology he hissed as hot candle wax spilled on his hand.

Memory turned away to see where they were and to hide the blush on her cheeks. They had stepped through the broken-down wall

into a manmade tunnel. Rough-cut square stones of mismatched sizes formed the ancient walls. Will used his candle to light a crumbling torch on the wall, and its light illuminated a long hallway sloping down, disappearing again into darkness at one end, and the signs of a spiral stairwell at the other leading up.

"Do you think we're under the castle? Could this be part of the castle?" Memory muttered, her voice low as though someone might hear.

"Maybe, close at least. Up or down?"

The warmth Memory felt grew strong, coming from the downwards direction, pulling at her. "Down. That way. We have to go that way."

The stone hallway was only just wide enough for them to walk side by side, and Will seemed to be making an effort not to brush his arm against hers. Memory wondered what problem he had with her, knowing how touchy feely he was with his sprite girlfriend Mina. Not that she wanted to be all touchy feely with Will, but she didn't want to feel like an untouchable. Memory's teeth ached from being clenched, and she shook off the frustration and tried to get her mind onto a different subject. She had important questions to ask Will after all, and what better time than when he couldn't dash off into the trees.

"So I was reading this book," Memory started.

"Since when do you read books?"

"Since shut up."

That quiet smirk in reply again. The tunnel took them a long way, down slippery stairs covered in slime where moisture dripped in from above. A thin glaze of limestone coated the walls like milk where the water ran.

"I was reading this book," Memory started again. "About the Pact, and how the fairies said the rest of the world was going to become

Hell, and so they just took Avall off the map, like poof, gone. That's why everyone here thinks the rest of the world was Hell. But it wasn't, was it?"

Will huffed, almost a laugh. "Not Hell. Hell wouldn't have the internet. But different from here. Normal, not all old fashioned. No magic or fairies. Do you remember..." Will paused. Memory could almost hear his teeth grinding in the silent subterranean pathway. "Back in our world, there were lots of stories of lost lands. Whole cities, islands, or countries that disappeared. Like Atlantis. Things are different here, but a lot is the same, even the language. When I ended up here, for a while I thought I'd just gotten lost, until I saw fairies. Might make sense if it used to be part of our world."

"So we're in Atlantis or whatever, and the rest of the world is still okay out there too, so what's the deal? Why did old King Arthur make the pact with the fairies?"

Will stopped walking. "King Arthur? Like King Arthur and the Knights of the Round Table?"

"I dunno. I just know Arthur Maellan was my ancestor who made the Pact. But you know the castle totally has a round table, I kid you not."

Will shook his head. "Avall isn't Atlantis. It must be Avalon. From what I remember of the stories it fits, even the name. And Caermaellan, it's like Camelot."

"There are really stories about Avall you remember from the other world? Could you tell me more about them? The more we can understand about this place, the better, right? We might work something out between the two of us."

Will's voice grew quiet. "I used to think maybe this was an alternate Earth. Like there could be infinite Earths, and you could be in any of them, lost anywhere."

Memory bumped his shoulder with hers, a small gesture of comfort. "Sounds to me like it's just Avall and the rest of the world."

"And the fairy world. It's different again, very different to here."

Memory's jaw dropped. "You've been to the fairy world? Get out! What's it like?"

Will just shrugged then started walking again. "You're descended from King Arthur. I can believe that."

Memory was about to question him some more, since this was the most words she'd gotten out of Will, ever, but the sensation she'd been feeling spiked.

The last flight of stairs opened into a room so large the dim light of the candles didn't show the ends of it. Memory saw another old torch and lit it.

The ground wobbled in front of them, sparkling with gold flecks of the torch light. Memory took a step toward it before seeing that it was water, some kind of underground lake. The manmade tunnel had come to an end, and they were in a massive underground cavern.

"Hope," Will said from behind her as she stared out across the midnight water.

Memory spun around, glaring, but saw what Will pointed at and refrained from complaining about her name. A stack of wooden crates and chests stood against the wall, on top of which sat a silver-colored metal dagger.

"Is that iron?" she asked.

Will picked up the dagger and hit it against the stone wall. Sparks flew. "Too hard to be silver."

"What are these doing here? Is this why the fae don't come here?" Memory brushed her hand over one of the boxes and cracked it open, finding what looked like the head of a hoe lying on a bed of velvet. *Weird.*

"No way they'd come close to this much iron."

"Maybe when they got rid of all the iron from Avall, they missed some and stashed it here?" Memory puffed out a long breath. She put her hand into her purse and pulled out her own small knife. "I should leave my knife here then, too. I guess this is goodbye."

Memory placed it on the top of the boxes.

The buzz of hot energy rushed through her, and she could feel her eyes closing.

"Hope?" she heard Will ask, his voice different, high and clear. "Hope?"

"It'll be so cool," she said. She sat at the head of an unmade bed, on yellowed pillows. In front of her sat Will, but much younger, wearing flannel PJs, his hair cut short and neat. He was hiding how scared he was in the completely obvious way that little boys do.

"Won't it hurt?" he asked.

"Well, yeah!" she said. "But once it's done it'll be forever. That's what it means. Friends forever." Memory held out the paper with the draft design on it, tracing the symbol of eternity with a swirl through the middle. Next to the bed was a small table that had a lamp, a ballpoint pen, a needle, and a lighter on it. The room was dim, grey. A wisp of moonlight shone through thin curtains.

"Forever?" he asked.

"Yeah. You and me against the world. Together forever." Memory examined her wrist. "I think we should do them here. It's okay, I'll go first. Scaredy cat."

"Hope?"

She had completely zoned out. Will called her name a few times, but got no reply. She just stood there, eyes closed, with a hand still on the knife on top of the boxes. Will reached to touch her, to see if she'd respond but decided against it.

"Memory?" he tried. He struggled to think of her by a different name.

"What?" She opened her eyes and looked at him, blinking a couple of times. "Sorry, wow, I spaced, huh?"

"We should get out of here. You probably need fresh air."

A frown pinched her eyebrows, and she reached out and took his hand, turning it palm up to see the tattoo they shared. Her hands were so small around his, cold fingertips sending thrills up his arm. Will tensed and Memory let go, clearing her throat.

"Yeah, some fresh air would be good, but can we check out where the rest of the tunnel goes? I bet you it goes into the castle. Could be a short cut."

Will looked around for Mina out of habit, but knew she would never come for him here with all the iron. He had plenty of time. "Okay, we'll go up."

The passageway up proved to be slow going, with narrow stone tunnels and winding stairs. Memory began complaining that she'd neglected to bring food with her.

Will smiled. It was nice seeing her eat. She was still so thin, but at least she ate now. Eating seemed to be one of her new favorite things.

Hunger crept up on Will as well, urged on by Memory's descriptions of what she planned to eat the moment she got back to the castle.

"They even have two chefs just for making cakes. Can you believe that?" She puffed as she talked, sentences broken up by heavy breathing. The stairs were steep and unevenly cut, each step often as

high as Memory's knees. *It must be hard for her.* Will almost offered to carry her, but decided against it. He'd broken the rules enough. He would only make exceptions when it was necessary to keep her safe.

Will worried more about the lifespan of their candles. He tried to carry one of the old torches, but it broke apart when he pulled it from the wall, too fragile to be moved. The tunnels must have been ancient.

Up ahead, the hall ended in a heavy wooden doorway. It looked solid, and no sound or light travelled through it. To the best of his judgment, they should be in the castle, somewhere, but he lost most of his ability to track distance and direction when not under the open sky.

"This had better be the way out, or I might have to just eat the door instead," Memory said, peeking over his shoulder as he carefully pulled at the handle, worried it might break like the torch had.

The wood of the door felt solid, newer than anything they'd passed so far. Will stopped with the handle half turned, pausing to think. Everything except the boxes of iron objects, he realized. Many of those seemed new, not covered in dust or the grime of centuries.

"Any time now," Memory said.

Will pulled at the door, sensing the weight of it, but it glided open smooth and silently. On the opposite side, the door was rendered in stonework to match the walls around it.

Memory followed him through into another long, skinny corridor where enough natural light fell to let them douse their remaining candles. "We're in the servant runs. I used these yesterday to lose my shadows but ended up getting caught out by Clara. She said they're for the servants to get around the castle fast without bothering the nobles, which seems silly to me. The halls out there are wide enough for everyone."

There were slits in the wall every dozen paces that showed the

main hallway running parallel to them. Memory turned back and closed the secret doorway behind them and wedged her small stump of a candle into a gap in the rocks next to it. "I don't know if anyone else knows about that tunnel, but I want to be able to find it again."

Will heard voices and put a finger to his lips, not wanting to be found there. Along with the men's voices, the rhythmic thump of a walking cane could be heard.

Memory pushed past him to look through one of the peep holes. She always was the game one, breaking rules, daring risks.

She said in a breathy whisper, "That's Hayes. I want to hear what he's saying."

Memory stood close to Will in the small space, so she could press her ear to the hole. He put his back up against the wall, shivering as he inhaled the scent of her, rising from her hair. Blood and crushed flowers. The scent of hair dye she used to always carry had left now that her hair was its natural pale blonde again. She had changed in so many ways; the loss of a whole life's memories did a lot to her. But in others, she was still Hope. Impulsive, brash, and fragile. He breathed her fragrance again, and let it take him back to when he was young and idolized her, and never dreamed she'd ever see him as anything other than a little boy. Now he towered over her, and she seemed so delicate as she brushed against him in the confined space. The desire to wrap her in his arms, bury his nose in her hair, press his lips onto the soft skin of her neck, rolled over him with knee weakening force. He denied the desire. Even if he wasn't a boy anymore, he still remembered the rules.

Will could hear the conversation clearly through the wall without moving closer. His time with the fae had improved all his senses.

"Plans for coronation and surrounding celebrations are going well. Princess Eloryn has undertaken her rehearsals with diligence."

"That's Bors, too," Memory whispered.

"She is perfectly amenable, is she not? What of the other one? That scamp can't even be kept track of half the time."

"She does as she wishes, sir, completely wild. We're no closer to understanding her in any way, not her upbringing or her magic."

Memory grunted. "Yep. That's me they're talking about."

Hayes continued. "I had hoped schooling would add some needed structure to her life, but she's already resistant to that concept. We simply need something to keep her entertained to which she agrees, and once occupied she will stay out of our way and out of trouble. I have a thought or two on that matter."

Their voices carried out of range as they left that area of the corridor.

"Pfft, I doubt I'd find anything they chose for me entertaining," Memory said. She looked through the peephole again. "I think we're in the old keep, near the Round Room. Oh, do you want to see it?" Memory asked.

Will looked through the hole above her head. A number of nobles in well-tailored and spotless suits were wandering through. Will looked down at his fraying clothing and furs. "Can you find your own way through the castle from here? I think I'll go back out the tunnel, the way we came in."

Memory also seemed to be assessing how he looked, then looked down at her dress, spotted all over with powdery dirt and slime.

"Okay, maybe it's not the best time for a tour, but I hate that you feel like you can't be in the castle." Memory folded her arms tight around her chest. "We can probably make it most of the way to the gardens in these servant halls, then if you want you can leave from there. But my rooms are pretty close too. We could do a runner and no one will see us. I mean, if you didn't mind. I'd like to spend some more time with you."

Will enjoyed these times he had with Memory, getting to know who she had become, but the more time he spent with her, the more terrified he became. He knew how easily, how quickly, everything in his life could be taken away, his parents and whole family lost in one tragic natural disaster and then his whole world in an entirely unnatural way. *I only just got Hope back. Not Hope, Memory,* he reminded himself, trying to get her new name right. He'd only been able to be with her while Mina wasn't demanding his company, something she had been demanding more and more often lately. Mina had always been possessive, but the more time he tried to spend with Memory, the more possessive she became.

Memory put her hands together like she was praying and made a puppy dog face.

Will smiled. "Okay, let's go."

Memory dashed into her chambers, startling Clara as she tidied

up.

"I don't even want to know where you've been." Clara raised an eyebrow at Memory's dirt-covered dress. Then something cheeky flashed in her eyes. "Or maybe I do? Did it involve a man?"

Memory had managed to apologize to Clara the night before, and Clara had received the apology as an invitation to take over all of Memory's maid's duties. She'd become downright feisty since Memory gave the order to be free with her words and opinions.

"Clara, could you come back later? I'm expecting company."

Will chose that moment to emerge over the top of the vines on the balcony. He'd refused to come through the last small stretch of palace with Memory, so she agreed to meet him there.

Clara studied Will up and down.

"Oh my. Now I understand why you leave your windows open," she said. Memory's cheeks flooded with hot blood, and she imagined she must match Clara's hair. Will looked ready to bolt, but too stunned to move.

"Clara, this is Will. He is my friend, from when we were kids. It's a long story. Clara, since you busted us anyway, would you mind helping us get cleaned up?"

Memory still found it hard asking for help for everyday tasks. But she had to be honest. She had so much trouble getting changed and looking after the antiquated chambers on her own, she needed someone. She couldn't even take a hot bath on her own. Water came out cold, and people expected her to use a behest to warm it.

"Anything, Hope."

"How about calling me Memory now?"

Clara smiled and answered as she went to draw the bath. "Unless you're taking back your order to let me speak my mind, I'll stick with Hope. It's such a pretty name, and I can't be changing what I call you every time you ask."

Memory had no other response than to stick her tongue out, so she went and dragged Will in from the balcony.

Clara eyed him again. "Would you like me to fetch some clothing for Master Will?"

Memory thought back to the last time she'd offered clothes to Will, and they were left untouched. "Okay. Maybe between the two of us we can wrestle him into wearing something clean."

"Oh, I like the sound of that." Clara giggled and left the chambers

to find something for him.

"And bring us some food!" Memory yelled after her.

Will was giving Memory a look.

"What? I should have said please, right?"

"Maybe I should go." He looked catastrophically uncomfortable.

"You said you'd stay for a while. Come on. Let me do this for you. Everyone likes a bit of pampering, right?"

"Just worried about your idea of pampering. You painted my nails hot pink once. Got me picked on for months."

"Just a hot bath and some clean clothes this time, promise," she said, swiping an X over her heart.

"A hot bath… that would be nice." Will half-smiled.

Memory put her hands on her hips, appraising him. "And a haircut. Let me cut your hair, please?"

There was a lot of grumbling, but Memory soon had Will on a chair and worked at removing the largest of knots from his hair. She had a plan to make Will more presentable, so he'd fit in at the castle, but with scissors in hand, she realized how much she liked his hair how it was and became scared of doing something that changed it. She didn't take much off, just trimmed the roughest parts out to make it a bit more manageable.

Clara returned with clothes for Will and sent him into the bathroom where the tub had filled and warmed. She put down a tray of neat sandwiches in a range of cut shapes and rolls, and Memory grabbed three.

Stuffing them in her mouth, Memory took the chance to kick off her muddy shoes, leaving them in the middle of the floor while she went to the closet for a clean dress.

Clara picked them up, pouting. "I'm happy to assist you in whatever way I can, but that's no excuse to be a slovenly. Watch out, or I'll have to call in extra help again."

Memory smiled at the motherly tone. "And I sure don't want that."

Clara inspected the muddy shoes. "You two look like you've been on quite an adventure."

"You know me, anything to get out of the castle."

"Funny when so many people would do anything to get into this castle."

Memory pawed through her current selection of dresses. Only a dozen or so filled the wardrobe, but these were exchanged and refreshed every few days so she was never seen in the same dress twice. Each one looked like it would take a month to create, with delicate beading and embroidery, and so many layers of fine fabric folded to create bows and roses. "That's just the thing, Clara. Look at this stuff. This isn't me. Or maybe it is, but the point is I don't know yet. I'm a diary full of blank pages. I went from nothing, to forests and fear for my life, to crazy opulence. I feel like I've missed a few steps in between. I want to know more about the normal people of Avall, what their lives are like."

"It's a fine sentiment. But after all you've been through you may find us quite dull."

"If everyone else is anything like you, I doubt it. Is there any chance… Could we go out somewhere? Into the city, just for a night?"

Clara pouted a cheeky smile. "You know the whole of Avall has been celebrating. It's a shame you're stuck in here on your own while the celebration is so much for you. You have me scheming now. I think we could do it. Oh, partying with the princess! My sisters will be so jealous when they hear!"

It will be good for Will too, to get out with some normal people, Memory thought. "Can we go tonight? Will isn't around much, and I want him to come with."

"We'd better get you changed then. One of the coachmen is a friend, but his shift ends soon."

In just moments, Memory leaned against the thick carved post of her four-poster bed as Clara tugged at the lacings of her corset. "Oof, really? Aren't I skinny enough?"

"Might as well flaunt it," Clara said.

"Skinny is over-rated. I want curves like Lory. Do you think I'll get boobs if I eat enough, or have I permanently stunted my growth?"

Memory reached for the silk bolero to match the gown Clara had chosen for her. The smoky purple skirts fell in a neat bell shape with a small bustle, and the shrug jacket buttoned over a simple square topped corset. Classy but unassuming, Memory liked it.

After she was dressed, Clara set to work on Memory's hair while Memory threw on some make up. Memory flinched and twitched as Clara poked through her hair with fingers, combs and pins. She was growing fond of Clara but still not keen on having other people dress her, touch her. But her hair was one of her most recognizable features, and there was no way she could do something with it herself to disguise the modern cut. She'd been trying to let it grow out, but a month hadn't gotten it much longer.

Clara managed to create a style that completely hid her ragged haircut. With a few strategically placed braids and curls, it looked like her hair was a lot longer than it really was.

Just as they finished with Memory's hair, the bathroom door opened slightly. They turned around, but Will didn't immediately emerge.

"What's up? Come on, I've got a surprise for you!"

The door opened fully and Will stepped out. Memory got her own surprise. She fumbled behind her for a chair but found nothing, so put

extra energy into her legs to make them keep holding her up. *Oh dear god, he's gorgeous.*

Will had been a bit cleaner lately than the day she first saw him, but she'd never seen him like this. His hair, Memory saw with relief, looked great. Still wet, he must have finger combed it back from his face, and it fell in neat waves to around chin length. There was nothing animal about him anymore, the furs and skins replaced with a neat pair of trousers, a black shirt and vest and a deep blue knee length overcoat that his shoulders were just a bit too wide for.

He held a tie of some kind in his hand. "I don't know what to do with this."

"Oh my, I could volunteer a few ideas," Clara muttered, fanning herself with a hand. Memory elbowed her.

"You look great, really." Memory beamed. Her comment caused an obvious blush on Will's high cheekbones. Or maybe it had been Clara's comment. "We're all ready then. We better get going!"

"Going where?" Will asked.

"That's the surprise."

CHAPTER FIVE

Clara left them briefly to get changed from her maid's uniform and arrange for their exit from the castle. Memory spent the time convincing Will that he looked good enough to go out in public.

As the three of them climbed into the carriage, Clara gave the coachman a sly grin. He tipped his cap in return, and the horses broke into a trot.

The cool night air blew softly in through the windows as the carriage clattered along the road, and a sense of freedom exhilarated Memory. Caermaellan castle lay just on the outskirts of the city and before long they were being driven through narrow cobbled streets, full of revelers and the subtle smell of wood-smoke. It had been explained to Clara that Memory suffered a form of amnesia and was

relearning everything about Avall, and Clara took pride in offering as much information as she could. She pointed out various important buildings they passed, including the finishing school the twins would soon be attending, and sprinkled her information with juicy bits of gossip.

Memory asked if they could stop, to get out of the carriage and continue on foot. The coachman pulled up near a watering fountain for the horses and agreed to wait for them there. Memory hopped down from the carriage, wanting to run off in every direction at once. The city was so enticing, full of misty secrets and winding pathways to explore.

The lively sounds of a busking fiddler filled the air. Men in top hats and waist coats and women in dresses much like hers surrounded them. Clara had chosen her outfit well. The utter volume of people passing by made Memory feel completely anonymous. She found comfort in that. The pebbled pavement under her feet felt real compared to the silky marble floors of the palace. She kept checking on Will to see how he was managing the crowds, and he seemed more intent on keeping an eye on her than worrying about himself. She smiled. *He's doing fine.*

To cater the city-wide street party, food vendors had set up on nearly every corner. Some roasted chestnuts and whole potatoes in small ovens. Others offered boiled sweets and candy apples. The sweet smell intoxicated Memory, but she could see that not everyone was benefiting from the business taking place on the streets. Next to nearly every stall that sold food there was a child or teenager begging. And where there weren't stalls there were yet more people hunched together, either sleeping or pleading for alms.

"Who are these people? Are they homeless?" Memory asked Clara.

Clara grimaced unpleasantly. "I guess you could say that. They've nowhere else to be. They're beggars."

"Why are there beggars? I thought Avall was supposed to be all prosperous and rich."

"Oh, it is," Clara said. "But I've heard some of the older folks say that things are changing. That there are less fae in the world these days, and it is the fae that turn Avall from barren to abundant. There are stories of some land becoming infertile and dead like in the olden times."

"Like Kenth?" Memory shocked herself in having information to offer the conversation.

Clara nodded. "And when a township cannot grow food any more, folk must look for work elsewhere and often go missing, and the children who are left behind find their way here, looking for help."

"Are they not finding it? Why isn't anyone helping them?"

"I'm not sure anyone knows quite what to do with them. This has never been a problem before. Some say it was Thayl the fae disagreed with, but others say it started earlier. Anything I know is just gossip and rumors of course, I mean there has even been wild talk of beggars being found drained of every drop of their blood. Vampires, some say it is, but I don't prescribe to such superstition."

Superstition? In a world full of dragons and fairies?

"Well this is a terribly depressing topic of conversation for your night out on the town. Shall we find something more entertaining to do?"

"How about we go there? It looks good." Memory indicated a busy looking tavern across the road from them called "Beyond the Veil."

"Oh fun! They welcome the fae there, and boy do the fae know how to have a good time!" Clara grinned.

Will had been following along a step or two behind the girls as they chatted, but moved up close beside Memory now. "I'm not sure that's a good idea."

Memory hesitated. "Yeah, isn't that dangerous?"

"Dangerous? Pish. It's all fine as long as one adheres to the usual precautions when dealing with fae."

"What, like don't piss them off?"

"Indeed. Also remember that although they may sometimes appear human, always be on guard," Clara warned. "Never accept food or drinks lest they've been spiked with fae-food. Always purchase at the bar. And certainly don't agree to do anything for anyone. If in doubt about whether someone is really a human, offer to share some bread or some salted food. They won't touch the stuff. That's a sure way of telling whether or not they're fae. Just follow my lead, you'll be fine."

Memory looked up at Will for confirmation. He frowned, but shrugged and nodded.

Inside, the tavern was alive with energy. The décor was lush, with red velvet furnishings and dark, oaken walls. Memory could see fae mingling with humans throughout the room. A lithe woman with green skin and leaves sprouting throughout her white hair lounged in an oversized armchair and a circle of entranced men surrounded her. Smaller sprites, bright as stars, socialized in the rafters and a couple sat on a chandelier, making the crystals shoot bright spots of light around the room. From what Memory could see, none of them had fully black eyes. That made her a little more comfortable.

As she moved through the room, the fae watched Memory suspiciously. She almost walked straight into the bare chest of a tall fae man with elk horns, and he hissed and pushed through the crowd to get clear of her.

"The fae keep such a distance from you," Clara observed.

Memory shrugged. "Yeah, they don't like me very much. Vessel too full, gonna spill and spoil everything or some fairy nonsense. Guess we didn't need to worry about avoiding them after all."

Most of the fae and human patrons were engrossed in some sort of play being acted out in the center of the room. A large table formed a makeshift stage, but nothing else about the performance seemed makeshift. It all looked far too fancy for being performed on a table in a pub.

Clara must have noticed Memory's disbelief. "The fae use their glamour to change the player's appearance and dress the stage. Looks wonderful, doesn't it? I love these. We can watch it, if you wish?"

Without responding, Memory sat down at a table, with Clara and Will following suit.

Clara pouted and stood back up. "Oh, I've seen this one. And it's nearly over. You watch. I'll get some drinks."

Nearly over? To Memory, the play seemed in full swing. Arthur Maellan was locked in armed combat with another man. Or at least, some actor glamored to look exactly like Arthur from the illustrations Memory had seen.

"Ooh, he's using Caliburn." Memory told Will, recognizing it also from her book. "You know he and his fairy friend Myrddin drew up all of the iron ore in Avall to make it with?"

Will looked thoughtful, his eyes on the play. "In the stories I know, Arthur drew a sword from a stone, but it was way more literal."

The swordplay intensified, and the men lunged upon each other, swords bloodied, piercing through each other's torso. Memory gasped. It looked too real.

The men fell apart, both lying still when they hit the ground. Another man ran onto the stage, distraught. He looked human, but his eyes were solid black orbs. He tried to revive Arthur, and cried beside him when he could not. With a look of resolve, he stood, took Caliburn from the ground, and vanished into thin air.

The dead men on the ground lay still, as dirt and grass grew up over them. A creature of powerful beauty walked in, calling for Myrddin. Tall and built like an Amazon goddess, this fae woman wasn't waif-thin like sprites Memory had seen. She had the all-black eyes of the unseelie fae and matching black hair that was not so much hair as swirls of pure darkness that caressed her figure, flowing down to her heels. She wore regal gowns, but where her skin showed it rippled like tree bark and shone silver with the scales of a serpent.

She continued to walk, calling Myrddin's name, as the graves beside her feet turned white, covered in snow, then sprouted fresh blossoms which withered into dust and blew from the stage. She fell onto her knees, called out for Myrddin one last time, and then collapsed into tears.

The audience stood in applause. The fae glamour faded, revealing a cast of normal human actors who looked nothing like the roles they played. Even the female fae was played by a man. They stood and took their bows.

Clara returned with glass goblets that held some kind of pink-blushed cocktail in them, and Memory thanked her. She had got one for Will too, who accepted it but sniffed it suspiciously.

"Did you enjoy the play?"

Memory grunted. "Damn spoilers. I hadn't gotten that far in my book yet. I didn't know how Arthur had died."

Clara waved off the comment with her hand. "This is just one version of events, a dramatization. King Arthur and his nephew Mordred were indeed found dead together, and Myrddin, who had been King Arthur's closest companion, was not seen ever again after

that time. Playwrights have come up with the rest on their own."

"Who was the fairy woman, at the end?"

"Lady Nyneve. She was Myrddin's lover. Some say she still looks for him and still mourns him. It's a sad tale, but they love to show it in taverns. I think it makes people drink more," Clara said, taking a swig as proof.

Memory brought her own goblet up to drink from, glancing around as though she could still get in trouble for drinking alcohol. She was the youngest person in the tavern. Even Will and Clara were older than her. She guessed Clara might be twenty. She had done the math and worked out that Will should be eight years older than her, but he looked much younger than that, closer to her age. Must be a lifestyle thing.

"You're not drinking. Don't you like it?" Clara asked Will, pouting slightly.

"It's very sweet. And pink," Will said. He still acted so much like a boy, too.

"Not man enough to drink a girly drink, huh?" Memory challenged, hammering her own drink on the table with a slosh.

"I'm sorry," Clara said. "I'm not used to buying drinks for men. Normally it's the other way around. I have to head back to the bar anyway as I appear to have finished mine. I'll get you something else." Clara stood back up. "Do you have a request?"

Will shook his head. Memory doubted he went out drinking much.

Memory offered Clara some of the money she'd brought, but Clara refused.

"No, this is my treat! In return for getting to party with the *you-know-who*."

With a very conspicuous wink Clara headed to the bar. Memory watched as she went. She seemed so natural, talking to people on the way and giving the occasional flirty smile to men. After a few moments, she returned with drinks on a copper tray. Two more pink cocktails and a monstrous jug-sized mug filled with something brown and frothy. She heaved the mug onto the table and pushed it towards Will.

"Here is something you might like better," she said.

"Clara, are you trying to get Will drunk?" Memory said.

"Me? Why never," Clara said in her breathy voice that made everything sound sexy.

The three of them continued to drink and enjoyed some of the music that was being played. It was a mixture of human and fae musicians, with two human fiddlers and a flautist and the fairies singing in voices that reminded Memory of birdsong. Clara dragged Memory up to dance, showing her a set of moves where they clapped hands and spun each other around. Memory got the sequence wrong half the time, turning the wrong direction and laughing all the while. Some men approached the girls on the dance floor to request a dance, but the girls both refused through giggles, having far too much fun together.

Memory and Clara returned to the table rosy cheeked and all smiles. They each took Will by a hand, trying to drag him up to dance. They couldn't budge him, but a smile broke on his face at their efforts. The girls gave up and returned to their seats. Memory was happy Will seemed to be fitting in. He wasn't doing much more than sitting and watching, but that was a big step up from hiding in nearby bushes and watching.

"How about I get this round?" Memory offered after looking into an empty glass. She left Clara and Will together, a little worried of what Clara would do with the opportunity. Memory would have to break it to Clara later on that Will already had a girlfriend. Or girlfae. Or whatever he called Mina.

As she waited to be served at the busy bar, a thin man with slicked back hair and oiled moustache approached and stood far too close to her. A friend hovered behind him, looking over his shoulder with a dopey smile.

"My lady," the thin man said, holding a cup in a spidery hand and pausing for a sip. "That was a fine display of dancing you gifted us with before."

"Yeah, right. Me and my two left feet don't know much about dancing."

"Would you be interested perhaps in some private dance sessions?" he suggested with a smarmy smile.

Oh gross. Memory held up a hand between her and the man. "Sorry, mister, not interested."

"Come now, don't be like that. This is a time of celebration and free spirits."

The man ran his finger down the length of Memory's lifted arm.

Memory recoiled in disgust, but before she could react more, something hit the skinny man. His head hit the bar, his arm twisted behind his back, held down by Will.

"Will, stop!" Memory shouted. Everyone nearby fell silent, and Will withdrew his grasp. The thin man took his wrist in his other hand and rubbed it. His friend fawned over him. Another group of men hurried to their side.

"You brute. I was just speaking with the lady."

Will growled.

The thin man shivered, but his voice rose in outrage. "You've made a big mistake. Don't you know who I am? I'm Count Delaney, you fool! And I'll see to it that you hang for this."

Clara pushed through to the middle of the confrontation, wobbling slightly and red faced. "Don't you know who this is? Do you not recognize your princess when you see her?"

"Clara, shush!" Memory said, too late.

Clara's voice was only a little raised, but the entire tavern stilled, everyone looking their way.

Count Delaney looked amused for a moment, but his eyebrows started twitching as he looked at Memory again. He quickly took to a knee. Half the tavern followed him, the other half whispering and gossiping. Memory was glad no one here had camera phones, but already knew how fast gossip in Avall could spread.

"Hayes pulled me up in front of the whole Council for what had happened at the pub. Talking to me like I was a little kid, like they could ground me or something."

Memory ranted, pacing back and forth. The space was small with grimy beige walls, spotted with old sticky tape, and a single bed made of metal framework that looked like a flattened cage. She could hear the noise of cars and a busy street outside. Thayl stood near the small window and looked out through the bars that covered it.

"Where are we? I feel I'm still in my prison cell."

"This is where I grew up. Where you sent me. Trust me, it gives me the creeps too." Memory folded her arms and dumped herself down on the bed with a huff. The mattress springs screeched.

Thayl assessed the dreamscape with a serious expression. "I'm sorry," he said, simply.

"Sure you are." This was the first dream they shared since she'd cut off his hand, which, she noticed, he had grown back in dream form. Until now she wasn't sure it was still possible to share dreams, but whatever was linking them together had brought him into her head again, into her dream. They were still connected, just like he said. She wasn't sure why it happened now, but he proved to be a sympathetic ear for complaining about the Wizard's Council.

Disembodied voices carried through the room.

"This is not behavior befitting a princess of the Maellan line."

"It is an embarrassment to your sister, the queen to be. We cannot have this sort of scandal on our hands while we try and reestablish a trusted ruler for Avall."

"You can't play dress up with him and think he's a man. That boy is an animal, and the sooner you realize it the better. He is not proper company for a princess."

Memory swatted at the air like the voices were flies that she could bat away. She grunted. "They don't want me to see Will anymore. They have no right to tell me who I can and can't be friends with."

"They would disagree. They think meddling in other's relationships is exactly their duty when it comes to the Maellan bloodline."

"Right. You and Loredanna," Memory said. "Wow, they haven't changed at all. Talk about learning nothing from past experience."

Thayl nodded grimly but kept his eyes on the cars passing by on the street below. Memory wondered what he must think of them.

"Would you laugh were I to say I have learned? You know, I told Loredanna we were running away together, that night, but instead I lured her to the witch, so her unborn child could be part of the ritual. I have learned, and could I have my time again I would have run away with Loredanna as I promised and forgotten my revenge. But my mistakes have all been made and paid for."

"You knew I'd be part of the ritual? You would sacrifice a newborn baby for your revenge, but you expect sympathy from me that things went wrong for you?"

Memory gripped the edge of the bed, anger rising. The smell of smoldering plastics filled the room and small wisps of smoke rose around her, forming the shapes of carved runes.

"To me, back then, the offspring Loredanna carried were nothing but another man's spawn. How could you know what it feels like to have another man's children grow within your beloved? I despised what you were and fooled myself into thinking that justified the terrible ritual." Thayl turned away from the window and looked at Memory, right into her eyes. "But now, I see you not as another man's, but as Loredanna's. You are so clearly the daughter of the woman I loved. In you I see her fire, her spirit, her natural compassion. You are a constant reminder of what I lost, the mistakes I made." Thayl held his ghost hand up in front of his face. It flickered in and out of existence.

"Just because I'm blonde now," Memory muttered.

An awkward silence spread between them, broken only by the dull roars of a dragon, competing with emergency sirens in the distance. The dragon often haunted her dreams.

The smoke cleared. The urge that came to Memory to comfort Thayl irritated her. He deserved whatever he got, and she reminded herself of how he ruined her life, her soul. She was the one who deserved comfort and answers.

"And you're a reminder of what I've lost," Memory said. "I need to know more, about what you did to me. Like how, or why, are some of my memories coming back now? Could my soul be coming back, too? I have to find some answers. Can you tell me more about what happened, how the ritual worked?"

"I could. But why would you believe me?"

"Because I'm asking you, because you owe me. You owe Loredanna. You've got a lot to make up for and not much else to lose."

Thayl laughed wryly. "You are right there. But you might be disappointed in what I can tell you. I know nothing of magic. In my youth I never studied the lore. I was never a talent. The only power I ever had was what I stole from you through Providence's ritual, and I used it like a weapon. Your raw power was all I required. I didn't try to understand it."

"You've got nothing for me? What about Providence? Would she know? Where is she?"

"You don't want to meet her. At first I thought her just an old woman," Thayl scoffed. "I could not conceive she could hold such evil. It took me a very long time to realize that she was more than she seemed."

"Then show me. Do your flashback thing and show me what happened," Memory demanded, not sure if she really wanted to see.

Thayl turned back to the window, head shaking slightly. "So be it."

A scene emerged in front of Memory, but Thayl kept his back to the vision. It showed the forest clearing the ritual took place in. Bodies lay scattered on the ground, including her mother's. It must have been just after Memory had been dropped through the Veil and Alward and baby Eloryn had fled. A young Thayl knelt with his hands clasped around his face. Behind him stood a hunched figure, covered in robes so nothing showed but undulating skeletal fingers spotted with blood.

"You still thirst for revenge? You would do anything for it?" An old woman's voice came from under the robe's heavy hood. The witch, Providence.

"I would do anything, give anything. My need for vengeance is now tenfold." The young Thayl lifted his head from his hands, stood and looked squarely at her.

"With this knife," Providence drew a blade. Memory felt a pang of pain in her chest. The serrated edge was still wet with blood. *My blood.* "We do sacrifice."

A girl was brought out. She was tied and blindfolded, being hauled by two men wearing cloaks like Providence. The girl looked similar to Thayl with bundles of wild dark hair and handsome face.

"No," Thayl shouted. "No, I will not!"

Providence raised the knife. More of her men moved to hold Thayl back. "It has already begun. You have given your permission and made your bargain."

"But why? Why her? There must be another way."

"No other way. No other chance. She is the only link that will enable you to venture into Hell and steal the power of the mature Maellan girl. The power you'll need to gain your revenge."

Thayl sobbed, looking over at his sister. The girl, blindfolded, recognized his voice and was begging him for help. Providence uttered words that Memory didn't understand, like the words Eloryn used for her magic, before slitting the throat of the young girl in one smooth, brutal motion. Blood flowed from the gaping wound as she choked and the men held her upright. Memory had to look away. When she looked back, young Thayl sat staring blankly at the girl's limp body as Providence carved symbols into his hand with the twice bloodied blade.

She spoke technically, as though the explanation would console him. "The doorway must be tied to the Maellan child. We cannot tie it to a place. We do not know what the hellish lands beyond Avall

look like to do so. With the child's blood, your blood and your sister's blood all tied, we can focus the doorway to find the Maellan child when she is older, the age of your sister, when her magic has grown strong, ready to steal."

The doorway opened, and the young Thayl, feral in his loss and anger, stepped through with determination.

The older Thayl finally spoke again and let the vision fade. "When I stepped through that Veil door, I didn't know what I would find. I barely trusted the witch's words and hoped I would die myself. I welcomed Hell. But instead, I found you as promised. My hand was drawn to you and the feeling of the flow of power as I stole your essence, I cannot explain it. Then your boy showed up."

"Will. He stopped you, before you could take all of… me."

"If he hadn't, I wonder if I would have been more powerful. I may have been able to defeat all of the Wizard's Council much sooner. There would have been more death, more destruction, and I am sure that I would have achieved my goal. Then have had that power set to Providence's goal."

"What was her goal? What did she get out of all this effort and bloodshed?"

"There was a covenant, a debt," Thayl said. "She would help me destroy all of the Wizard's Council for my revenge, and then I would repay the debt to her."

"Repay it? How?"

"I never discovered what I was to do for her. Some of the Wizard's Council still lived, so she had not fulfilled her side, so I had no reason to follow through with mine."

Memory tried exercising her dream control skills and summoned a vision of the witch back into the room. She stood frozen like a mannequin and Memory walked around her, trying to peak under the hood to see who was underneath. The shadowed face just revealed a normal-looking old woman, with a spatter of blood on her wrinkled lips.

"She's one scary old lady that's for sure. I bet she would have answers for me, but I'll be damned if I want to be in the same room as her."

Thayl looked from Memory to the frozen vision of Providence with a frown. "I am sorry that I don't have answers for you. Though there is one thing Providence told me that you should know. If you travel through to Hell, there is no guaranteed way to return. She would say it is easy to get from here to there, but not the other way around. The only way I managed to come back was because Providence maintained the gateway at this end."

Memory shrugged. "I haven't really thought of going back since I don't really remember it there. My home, family, friends – they're all here now."

"Just keep in mind, if you ever change your decision about going back to this world you grew up in," Thayl gestured to the room around them, "Be sure it is what you want, as you might not be able to return to Avall."

CHAPTER SIX

"Mem, it's *Bron-marbh Ai-leadh.*" Eloryn enunciated each syllable carefully. She knew the Branding spell would have no effect unless used in a situation where the Pact rightly allowed it, but saying it aloud still made her uncomfortable.

"Bron-marf Allalee. Oh pfft." Memory sputtered out, obviously aware how far off her pronunciation was. Eloryn frowned at Memory's inability to articulate the behest. She should have learned the Branding spell by now, and Eloryn felt neglectful that it had taken this long to find time to teach her. Hearing about Memory's recent run in with an unseelie fawn made the lesson more urgent. She'd only just told Eloryn about being trapped in a fairy ring. The thought of losing her sister to an unseelie fae terrified Eloryn almost as much as the fact that Memory had taken so long to tell her about it.

Both Memory and Eloryn's guards and handlers trailed a few feet behind as they made their way to the Round Room, acting as though they couldn't hear or had no interest in the girls' conversation. Memory kept glancing at them like she was embarrassed to be getting this lesson here. She folded her arms childishly. "Damn it. I can't get it. I don't even understand how it's meant to work anyway,"

"That's all right. I've never used it myself and hope neither of us ever need to. To be honest, the Brand is more of a punishment than a defense. It can only be used if a fae has already acted unjustly toward you, even a small act of violence. And you must remember it's a death sentence. Not only does the Brand itself kill the branded within twenty-four hours, but the Brand is also a sign that the fae, or human, has violated the pact and can be hunted and killed by anyone. But it's important to at least know the words, so you have the option of threatening its use as a deterrent. Try one last time? Bronmarbh Aileadh."

"Bron-marv Allay-ay," Memory repeated.

"Almost." *Not quite.*

"Why do I have to come to this meeting anyway?" Memory moaned. "It's not like I was invited."

"I want you to be there. It's important to me." Eloryn felt like she hadn't seen much of Memory recently. The growing gulf between them made her stomach ache. Her time had been almost completely consumed with rehearsals and planning for the upcoming coronation. She'd been hearing rumors of how her sister had been spending time without her, from fairy rings to public taverns, and it increasingly concerned her. She refused to admit it also made her jealous. At least Memory was accepting some help from palace staff now. Her new handmaiden was doing a good job of keeping Memory presentable,

looking like the princess she was. Her hair was almost always up now in a style that disguised the short cut, and she wore elegant gowns Eloryn was sure Memory wouldn't have picked herself, like the shimmering aqua dress with a giant bow for a bustle she had on now. Eloryn knew how some people talked about Memory and was happy to see her fitting in even a little bit more. "I want to help you to understand magic and your connection with it. I'm sorry I haven't been able to do that yet."

"I'd love a chance to talk to you about that stuff too. There are things I have to tell you and haven't had a chance. But we're not going to get to do that at Hayes's dumb meeting, or here," Memory said, glaring back at the following guards again.

As the twins approached the entrance to the Round Room, they heard angry shouting. Their bodyguards reacted swiftly, breaking from their position behind the girls to run forward and create a wall in front of them. Peeking between the bulk of their guards, Eloryn saw Hayes in heated conversation with a red-faced man who she didn't recognize. The rest of the Council surrounded them, muttering amongst themselves.

"It can't be allowed. The kingdom shouldn't be ruled by some little girl who's been who-knows-where for who-knows-how-long! Not at such a fragile and crucial time," the man shouted, each word a short, sharp bark.

"I don't like this guy already," Memory whispered.

Hayes lifted his hands in a calming gesture. "We have invited you here to allow a reasonable discussion. If you will not be reasonable then there is no more to discuss. Should you calm yourself you could meet with Princess Eloryn and see what a fine young lady she is, and you should have confidence that we the Council and our knowledge and experience stand behind her."

"In a role that is not yours. Running the government is not the role of wizards." The man waved away Hayes's gesture. "I don't need to remind you how powerful my family name is. We are the ones who should be ruling, and I'm willing to fight for that right should the need arise."

"Quiet yourself and think twice before making such rash threats. Perhaps if you spent some time with the girls. They are, after all, family and becoming close to them could prove beneficial, providing you with the power that you desire."

"From what I hear those girls are nothing but harlots. I want nothing to do with them. At least my family maintains its dignity."

"Then might I remind you, Sir Ewain, that you in fact have no rightful claim to the throne? You may quip about the pedigree of the sisters, but unlike you they are of Maellan blood and are therefore the heirs. Be warned you speak of treason."

Eloryn thought to her studies on the family trees of Avall nobility. From the name Ewain and the crest he bore on his vest, Eloryn made a swift guess at who this man was.

Eloryn pushed through her bodyguards, ordering them from her path and strode in to join the conversation.

"Dear Uncle," she began.

The man snorted in disgust and pushed past both Memory and Eloryn on his way out. Their guards stepped in and moved to apprehend the man for the insult, but Eloryn waved the order to free him, and he stormed off down the corridor.

"Uncle?" Memory asked. She and Eloryn moved into the Round Room where the tension of the argument had everyone on their feet.

"Yes. Your father's brother." Hayes moved over to the table where he took a seat, motioning for the sisters and the rest of the Council to do the same. He ran a hand over his short cropped salt and pepper

hair. He seemed tired, making him look as old as some of the other Councilors. "He's hotheaded and believes that his family has a right to the throne. Whilst there's no legality to it, they could still pose a threat should they gain popular support."

"First I've heard of any uncle," Memory said. "Do I have more family I don't know about?"

"None of Maellan blood," Eloryn answered. "Yet there are some on our father's side. I'd hoped to welcome them as beloved family. I had no comprehension they had such ill feelings toward us."

"I'm sorry they are not the family you've hoped for, princess," Hayes said. "I've been in talks with them to try and settle the matter, but it seems they resent your family's bloodline for what happened to their son and their brother, King Edmund."

"That's not exactly fair," Memory said. "It's not as though Loredanna was the one who picked him as her husband."

Hayes, who already looked worn from the argument with Ewain, glared at Memory. Eloryn wished Memory wasn't so blunt sometimes.

Waylan spoke up from across the table. "I would have to agree with Princess Memory in this case. We the Council do have much to atone for, and our taking on so many roles in rebuilding Avall is clearly agitating people. I understand the need for our guidance at this time, but we need to start putting the normal order of government in place. Ours is the role of guardians and teachers of magic in the land, not of ruling and politics. Seeing the Council step back from that may placate Ewain and his family."

"And when should I step back, Waylan, now? While rash families are hovering the throne awaiting any mistake by our young princesses?" Hayes said.

"Their rage is misdirected. Perhaps the execution of Thayl will calm their boiling blood," a Councilor from the far end of the table

suggested. Lambeth, Eloryn reminded herself, still teaching herself the names of all the Councilors "After all, he is in fact the one to blame."

Memory rose to her feet in an abrupt movement.

"Whoa, whoa, whoa, what are you guys talking about? What execution?" she asked.

"Having been found guilty of high treason, murder, and numerous other crimes, Thayl is to be publically executed not long after coronation as part of ongoing celebrations," Hayes explained.

Memory shook her head. "You're using the words executed and celebrations in the same sentence here. Have I just gone to crazy land? You're not really talking about killing Thayl in public?"

Lambeth spoke up again, his voice crackly and dry with age. "The sentence for Thayl's crimes is to be hung, drawn, and quartered. Crime in our lands is treated very seriously, perhaps unlike in the lands where you have been."

Memory glared at him, mouth hanging open.

Eloryn stood up by her sister's side. "I must admit, Council, the sentence does seem ghastly. Avall suffered many years of such terrors under Thayl's rule. Perhaps we should reconsider, so that Avall's new beginning is free from such bloodshed."

"What would you have us do? Have him go unpunished?" Bors scoffed from the other side of the table.

"You think having your hand cut off and rotting in a cell for the rest of your life is 'unpunished'?" Memory replied.

Eloryn felt torn. The man had been the cause of great sorrow for her, but she couldn't find it in her anymore to wish for his death. She had once, and when sharing her sister's body, she almost took his life herself. She was glad she did not, and it felt odd to have spared his life then only to see him executed now.

"I agree with Memory. I do not need to see this man's blood on display," Eloryn said.

Bors stood to respond and Hayes stood as well, giving him a firm look which quieted him. "I understand that executions aren't a pleasant idea for a heart as gentle as your own, but the people of Avall expect this. Why should the murderer of your mother be treated differently than any other criminal?"

Memory huffed. "But he didn't kill our mother. That was an accident."

Eloryn winced. The man who raised her like she was his own daughter was the one who committed the deadly accident.

Memory looked at Eloryn as though she were sorry to have reminded everyone of it and then continued. "Besides, Thayl was being manipulated by someone else, a powerful witch called Providence. She was the one who gave him the power and encouragement to do what he did. It wasn't all his fault."

"Princess, we can see you are concerned, but your sympathy for this man is unhealthy. The bailiff informed me of your visits to Thayl's cell. Undoubtedly, you have become emotionally attached to this murderer, and he is manipulating your sympathies for this very purpose of trying to spare his life."

"Memory?" Eloryn looked at her sister. Memory's face turned pink, and she looked away. Eloryn felt ill. "Memory, you've been visiting Thayl?"

"So what? I was looking for some answers. That's no crime," Memory snapped.

"What is more," Hayes said, looking down at Memory, "we've no knowledge of this woman 'Providence.' Indeed, no women have a high enough learning or understanding of magic to do what she is said to have done, except, perhaps, those of Maellan blood. Princess

Memory, these are nothing but the tales of a man attempting to shift the blame.

"The public expect, no, *need* Thayl to be executed. They need to know he is gone for good. Your highness," Hayes said, pushing a piece of paper towards Eloryn. "I implore you to sign his death warrant. It is the only way that we can secure the safety of the kingdom. He could still be a threat."

"He's not a threat. He's just a poor man in a cell. He can't do anything." Memory looked from the paper to Eloryn. "Lory, please, you can't do this."

"Mem," Eloryn said quietly. "You didn't have to experience it. The things he did. You escaped it all. The murders, the torturing, the decay of the land. The banning of magic put a strain on everyone, you can't imagine. Something as simple as sending a message to a friend was almost impossible, and there was no magic to heal the sick. Thousands died. You can't imagine the suffering this man caused."

"I escaped it all?" Memory's face scrunched up. "How can you say that after what I've been through?"

"It's for the best." Eloryn held her breath and signed the death warrant. Her chest pounded. She felt faint. Hayes took the paper from the table.

Memory looked at her sister in disbelief then turned and ran out of the room.

"And that is why you will make a far better queen than your sister," Hayes said.

Eloryn could tell that he was trying to be nice, but she wasn't sure she believed him. *What have I done?* Her legs wobbled beneath her. She fell onto the chair, put her head on the table, and started to cry. Hayes knelt beside her and excused the rest of the Council from the room, leaving him and Eloryn alone.

"My dear, my dear, I know it is difficult. But it takes a true queen to do what you have done today."

"I can't do this," Eloryn implored. "I can't say who lives and who dies."

"I understand. Your role is not an easy one. But know we of the Council are here to advise and assist you in any way. It is traditional for a monarch to delegate their duties, for to carry every responsibility alone would be a weight enough to crush any man."

Eloryn wiped her eyes and looked up at Hayes. "Could you? Would you take this horrible task from me?"

Hayes paused, as if considering, then nodded. "By granting me the power of court legislature you won't have to sign another piece of paper like this again. Perhaps it would be more appropriate for me to see to the matter of death sentences. Living through what I have, I am more equipped to deal with such dreadful decisions. Such matters should not be the realm of children."

But they are the realm of a monarch. How can I be that person? Eloryn shook her head. Maybe she couldn't be that person because she couldn't put her name on a piece of paper like that again. "Yes. Please have the appropriate documents written up to transfer this role to you. Thank you, Hayes. Thank you for being here for me."

Memory ran all the way from the Round Room to the dungeon, her dress swishing around her like an aqua tide. Her heart hammered. Her face burned in anger at her sister and the Council. Her anger also turned inward. Maybe she did she have an unhealthy connection to

Thayl. But she still thought everything about an execution was wrong, no matter who was being executed or why.

Memory stormed past the bailiff, giving him a filthy look for ratting her out. She wondered if as a princess she had any hiring and firing powers. After passing the first floor of cells, she took the final flight of stairs to Thayl's solitary confinement.

On her approach, she heard the sound of hushed conversation, but as she stepped in front of the bars she saw only Thayl, sitting alone, chained up as before.

"They're going to kill you," she stated. Her face turned redder, embarrassment mixing with her rage for the fragile and desperate tone of her voice.

"Of course," Thayl responded. "You didn't know till now?"

Memory shook her head. The cell was cold, but Memory burned inside and out, the flames inside her threatening to burst through her skin, kindled by her emotions. She leaned against the damp stone walls in an attempt to cool herself down. "I tried to stop the execution, but no one will listen to me. Hung, drawn, and quartered. Does that mean what it sounds like?"

Thayl nodded slowly. "It is the traditional punishment for treason. What would the people think if they changed it for the likes of me?"

Memory's stomach clenched at the thought of the punishment and she bent forward.

"Why does this matter so much to you?" Thayl said. "After all I did to you I thought you would be pleased to see me gone."

"Not everyone thinks blood for blood is cool. It's wrong to kill people like this. And there's got to be more you can tell me, about Providence, or my mother, or…" *Or I'm making excuses. I just don't want him to die. Could I have gotten that close to this monster? What does that make me?*

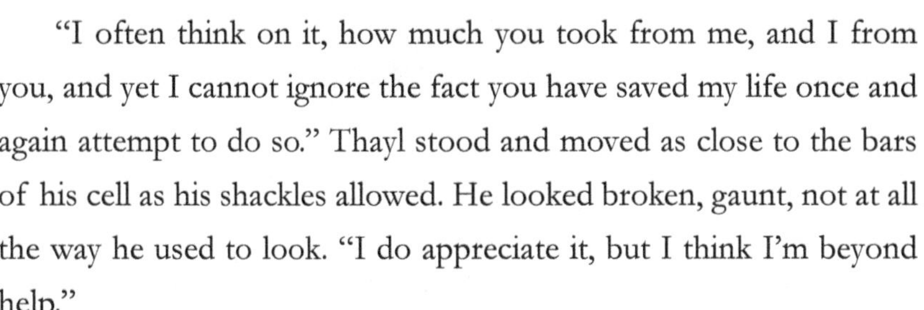

"I often think on it, how much you took from me, and I from you, and yet I cannot ignore the fact you have saved my life once and again attempt to do so." Thayl stood and moved as close to the bars of his cell as his shackles allowed. He looked broken, gaunt, not at all the way he used to look. "I do appreciate it, but I think I'm beyond help."

Memory's eyes watered. "They can't kill you."

Thayl looked blankly at her, but then gave a smile with the corner of his mouth.

"Do you remember that trick you played on me, when you told me that you were my daughter?"

Memory just nodded.

"I'm glad that you're not," he said.

Appalled, Memory fled the room.

CHAPTER SEVEN

"I don't even know what this thing is," Memory said, lifting a strange golden utensil from a silk-lined box. Clara giggled and showed her the finely crafted tea set it accompanied, making the item some kind of tea strainer. Memory sat by her dresser while Clara worked on her hair, incorporating stuffing and wirework into the structure to build volume, and lacing strands of pearls into twirling braids. They were up before the sun had risen, and the elaborate hair style was almost complete, but Memory still sat in her bed-clothes. The flowing chemise was light and draped in silky falls over her body, but a roaring fire across the room kept her warm. Clara had already mentioned three times how much faster she could prepare Memory for this day with some extra help, and how she'd gone out of her way to convince the

designer to let her prepare Memory on her own. Apparently dressing up for a coronation was even more of a big deal than normal. Memory couldn't bear the idea of more people buzzing around, touching her. She'd been dreading this day since it was announced. Not only did it mean suffering the embarrassment of being paraded around the city streets like a carnival float, but it was also the day before the execution of Thayl, the bloodbath her twin had sanctioned.

"We've got plenty of time," Memory said again, secretly hoping they would be late. She pushed the boxes with the tea set and implements of tea making over into the Do Not Want pile. It was already much larger than the Want pile.

Clara put a bobby pin back in her mouth and shifted the set into the Want pile. "Those are from Duke Lanval and Duchess Marian de Montredeur. You may want to keep them for when they visit you. You really should read the cards."

Memory rolled her eyes. A knock on the door and four servants entered with more stacked presents. She'd already been through this for her birthday, and here she was again, getting buried in finery.

"Just put it all over there," she told the servants, indicating the Do Not Want pile.

Clara tsked and put a new box in front of Memory to open. "Can we at least see what's in them? It's so exciting."

"It will be more exciting to see all this stuff go to a good cause. When I told Hayes I wanted to help those homeless kids, he allocated me some 'promotional funds.'" Memory dropped her voice to a mock imitation of Hayes's. "A handful of coins to give out on the street, smiling and patting babies on the head. He said it was a good idea, good for improving my image. It was nice, but I didn't have enough to give all of them. Not even close. Hayes won't increase the funds. He's got no idea of what's going on out there, so I figure I'd make some

money myself, right? I just hope this crap sells for lots." Memory lifted a vase, decorated with a sculpted scene of lilies and frolicking otters. It looked made of gold, but was almost transparent and icy to touch.

Wide eyed, Clara took the vase carefully from Memory like she cradled a priceless newborn. "This one will fetch a fine price indeed. True fairy gold!"

"I thought fairy gold was a bad thing?"

"The broken scraps of it are worthless since humans can't work it. Only the fae can, creating masterpieces like this, or weapons. It is almost as brittle as glass, but makes deadly sharp blades. A beautiful thing."

"Beautiful and useless. Over with the rest."

Clara pouted, but put the vase carefully back in its padded box and onto the Do Not Want pile. "You might not understand it, but the people do love you, Hope. You are the one who defeated Thayl. They want you to have these fine things."

"Yeah, I'm sure those orphans want me having golden strainers while they are begging for food."

Clara paused and smiled. "You have a good soul, highness."

If I even have a soul. Memory shrugged. Soul or not, it was just common sense.

A racket of marching feet and clattering weapons came from the hall and the door burst open. Peirs rushed in followed by a huddle of guards among which Memory could barely see Eloryn and Roen. Eloryn, already in her dress for the big day, barely fit through the door with the sheer volume of her skirts and oversized lace collar fanning out behind her.

Memory knew that Peirs, who previously led the resistance against Thayl, had been made Captain of the Guard at Caermaellan castle, but the place was so big she hadn't seen him since the morning they defeated Thayl. Peirs did a quick check of the rooms, and the guards averted their eyes from Memory when they saw she still only wore her silky undergarments.

"Okay. What's going on? You lose something?"

Roen squeezed through the crowd filling Memory's sitting room. He hugged her briefly. "Thank the fae, you're all right."

"It's Thayl." Eloryn ran up to her sister and held her as well, shaking. "He's escaped."

Clara did a dramatic cross between a gasp and a squeal. Roen took and squeezed Memory's hand.

Peirs returned from checking her bedroom and offered a brisk salute and bow, followed by the lopsided smile she remembered. "Sorry for the intrusion. We feared he may try to come after you. It's good to see you're safe."

People kept talking around her. Peirs arranged soldiers to stand inside and out of Memory's chambers, and Eloryn explained how they hadn't been able to track Thayl through magical or non-magical means and had no idea how he had got out of his cell.

Memory's head was shaking softly from side to side and she chewed her bottom lip, the news sinking in. She mumbled, mostly to herself, "He won't come here. That would be crazy. He hasn't got any power anymore. He must be trying to get away, but where could he hide?" Her words were lost under the other conversations.

Roen kept looking to Eloryn, the worry on his face clear. A plan formed in Memory's mind. *They'll be safe here. But this might be the only chance to avoid the execution.*

Memory raised her voice over the crowd. "I'm just going to chuck some clothes on."

Approaching the bedroom, she gave the guards in there a look.

"A little privacy please? And, Clara, I'll manage by myself, thanks."

Memory smiled in a way to indicate she was calm and coping and closed the double doors to her sitting room, leaving her alone in the bedroom. She dashed across to the wardrobe and yanked out the box she'd stuffed in the bottom. A minute later, she'd wriggled into jeans and pulled on the t-shirt and shoes.

She stepped out onto the balcony and scooted up onto the balustrade. Looking down, she swallowed. It was a long way, but the only way she could get out of here alone was Will style.

She began to lower herself, taking care to hold tightly onto the vines. Thick, ancient ivy intertwined with woody rose stems. She inched her way down, managing to grab the thorny option more than once and her hands bled by the time she had her feet on the grass below. Memory cursed at her stinging hands. *Will makes it look so easy.*

The palace grounds were clear of people except the occasional group of guards. Memory waited behind some bushes for a patrol to pass and tried to work out what to do next. She only had one option, walk, and hope whatever connection she had with Thayl led her to him, or vice versa.

She ended up heading into the northern wing where Thayl had lived during his reign. The area had been closed up since his defeat, as there hadn't been time yet to properly dispose of his belongings, and no one was keen to move into the same rooms as he'd been in anyway, as though they were tainted. The rooms she wandered into were small, more the size of the castle's guest rooms than the sort of chambers made for the monarchs, which Memory and Eloryn now inhabited.

A wardrobe had been raided, and the old, gray rags Thayl had worn in prison lay on the ground. This was the right place. Memory could hear Thayl up ahead, arguing with someone about debts. Memory reached the stairs to the far tower and crept up them. The tower was large, with round rooms between the spiraling flights of stairs. Memory went up two stories, trying to listen in to the conversation above her, but her rubber-sole sneakers squeaked on the marble steps, and the conversation ended.

"Memory?" Thayl's voice bellowed. "I know it's you."

"Who are you talking to?" Memory called back from halfway up the flight. "Is Providence there with you?"

"She's gone. You can come up. I won't hurt you."

Memory stepped up into the tower's highest room. It seemed to have been turned into storage, mostly full of disused furniture, a pile of old mattresses, and gold framed paintings stacked against the wall. Thayl wore clean clothes, standing by an open window. Memory almost fled again when she saw his remaining hand had been freshly cut, covered in the runes and markings like the one she had dismembered.

"What are you doing?" Memory pointed at his hand, keeping her distance, circling Thayl in the round space. A pigeon fluttered in the conical roof above them and Memory jumped.

Thayl raised his hand, examining it as though he'd forgotten what it meant. "Don't worry. I'm not going to be part of that witch's plan any longer, although letting her help me escape will serve a purpose."

"I wanted to help you, let you get away, but that hand, how can I trust you?"

"You don't have to. Thank you, but I don't need your help. I hadn't even expected to see you again." Thayl seemed so eerily calm, it scared Memory more than if he were angry. "But I guess that is good too. I can tell you now that I fear you misunderstood what I last said to you, when I said that I was glad you aren't my daughter."

Memory scrunched her nose, angry at the sting there threatening to cause tears.

"What I meant in truth was that I am glad you didn't have me as a father. I'm not worthy to be father to someone like you."

Memory moved closer to him, but he motioned for her to keep her distance, stepping back so he pressed against the small balcony outside the open full length window. From this height, Memory could see the hedge maze, garden wall, the river that encircled the castle, and green pastures spreading into the distance. It felt like she could see half of Avall.

"Thayl, the execution doesn't have to happen. We can get you away from here," Memory said. "I could open a Veil door to where I came from. You can escape for good, start a new life."

Thayl shook his head. "I am still such a problem for you. You don't wish me killed, but you must know I have to die. There is nothing else left for me."

Memory refused to listen. Instead she tried to focus her energy, to concentrate on the room in the orphanage she now remembered clearly and open a door to it, but nothing happened. A force pressed back at her as she tried to open the Veil, like pressing against stretched fabric.

She grunted at the failure. "No, there's got to be another way."

Memory started pacing, trying to think but was distracted by a strange sight. On the path she'd walked to reach where she stood now, glowing footsteps lit up like made of sunlight, following her trail. *Some kind of magic, some spell?* Memory drew a sharp breath. A spell to track her.

"Memory!" Eloryn's voice echoed up the stairs, and Memory could hear the approach of armored men. Her sister, Roen, and a small division of soldiers in bronze armor ran up into the room, immediately surrounding Thayl and forcing him against the low balcony wall at weapon point.

"Leave him alone!" Memory rushed forward, but Peirs and another guard held her back. "Let go! Lory, Roen, stop this! They're going to kill him!" Memory yelled as the guards lifted her by her arms.

"Memory, please, it's all right," Thayl spoke calmly. He looked into her eyes as he stepped backwards, elegantly raising himself onto the balustrade.

"Remain still!"

"Not another step!"

The soldiers yelled, and the sound of more people charging up the stairs filled Memory's ears.

"What are you doing?" she mouthed, barely a whisper.

"Removing a problem," Thayl replied. His soft words reached her clearly over the shouting men.

"No!" Memory screamed.

There was no grief in Thayl's face, merely resolve. Only his brow suggested that he felt anything at all, curled and pained. He stood up straight, almost appearing as his former self, darkly handsome and charismatic, and looked around at those in front of him. Then he let himself fall backwards from the tower and to his death.

The guards ran to the edge to peer down. Peirs sent men to ensure Thayl's demise. Roen blocked Memory from looking herself. Eloryn tried to hold her, but she wouldn't be held. Memory's head swam and she felt about to explode, her insides boiling. It seemed like the tower trembled. Old frames clattered beside her.

The Wizard's Council arrived, armed with scrolls and loose leaf pages of spells at the ready.

The guards beckoned them over to the edge and Hayes looked down.

"What happened here?" he asked. He approached Memory and

began to shake her. "What happened?"

Memory put her arms up, clawing away his grasp on her. Eloryn stepped between them. "Memory had nothing to do with this. She merely tracked Thayl down."

"The people are robbed of their execution," someone said.

The world blurred and Memory realized she was crying. She couldn't deny it or make excuses anymore. She'd grown close to Thayl. No matter what he was or what he'd done. Maybe because they were both broken and wrong inside. Memory couldn't believe what she heard, disgusted that this death meant nothing to anyone else but the loss of their bloody execution. How could a life mean so little to these people, any life?

She pushed everyone away, stumbling toward the stairs. Eloryn called after her, but no one followed.

Memory stopped running only when she neared her room. Someone was up ahead, staring down the stairs. The figure stood in shadows, obscured, blurry, but familiar.

"Eloryn?" Memory called out, wiping her eyes clear.

"It's your fault, all your fault," was the hissed reply.

Memory charged forward but found no one there. She turned to look back the way she'd come but found herself alone.

A tap on her shoulder sent Memory jumping back against a wall. Clara, who had tapped her also jumped about a foot with a squeal.

"Highness!" she gasped like it was a curse word. "Are you all right? I was told what happened and sent to find you."

Memory gave a hollow laugh. "Am I all right?"

"No, I suppose not by the look of you. Such a horrible thing, and you, young lady, running off like that! What were you thinking? Come, let's get you cleaned up and into your dress. At least your hair is still decent."

"Decent enough to curl up and sleep for the rest of the week?"

"Oh, Hope, no. I've been instructed to prepare you for the coronation. It's going ahead."

CHAPTER EIGHT

A set of eight white horses pulled Memory and Eloryn along in a gilded, open-top carriage. They drove through the streets of the city lined with billowing pennants, accompanied close behind by another open carriage carrying Hayes and key Wizard Council members, followed by battalions of soldiers and dignitaries. Massive crowds lined the streets and rooftops, trying to get a glimpse of the Maellan twins. The people of Avall had hoped for an heir of the Maellan line to return for so long, and now they had a matching pair. Her whole life had become a surreal side show in which the twin sisters were the biggest crowd pleaser, and folk from every corner of the known world came to watch. The people were so jubilant. Maybe Clara was right, and Memory just didn't understand how much this meant to them and the hardships they had gone through under Thayl.

Despite the crisp coolness of late autumn, the sun shone warmly, making the carriage and her over the top coronation dress sparkle. It was a beautiful day, but Memory couldn't focus on more than keeping her tears in. She struggled to breathe in her - she could hardly call it a dress, it was more like some kind of bizarre artwork. Folds and frills wrapped and tied into place so tight she couldn't move or bend her back, the silver fabric covered in so many fine gemstones it weighed more than she did, and a huge filigree collar fanning out behind her.

Memory couldn't believe what had just happened on the castle tower, and that this supposedly joyful scene could happen straight afterwards. She tried to take a deep breath and it came out more like a sob.

Eloryn, her dress matching but in rich gold tones, took Memory's hand and gripped it tightly as she waved to the crowds with her other. Memory could feel her shaking. Eloryn kept smiling to the people around them, but it looked strained.

"I'm sorry for what happened with Thayl," she said, while still looking out at the crowds, keeping up the happy monarch impression.

"For how you were going to have him killed, or how you didn't get to because he killed himself?"

"I didn't want for either outcome." Eloryn gave Memory a pitiful look before quickly returning to the smiles and waves.

"It doesn't matter. It's over now." As much as she wanted to, Memory couldn't blame Eloryn. She could only blame herself for caring too much for a man that everyone else thought of as a monster.

"Look at them all, Mem. Look how happy they are. We owe it to them to do our best by Avall." Eloryn obviously had the coronation on her mind. As much as Memory didn't care for the day, it was a much bigger deal for her sister, about to become queen. She sounded so nervous that Memory squeezed her hand back.

Occasionally amongst the exuberant crowds Memory saw small faces she recognized. The homeless children she had given coins. When she saw that they were cheering just as hard as the more well off people on the streets, she found herself actually smiling back. She spent the rest of the parade making her plans to visit them again soon with more alms and whatever she could get selling off her presents.

Eventually the cavalcade returned to the palace. The massive front yard leading to the castle was also crowded, filled with the nobility of Avall. As Memory and Eloryn were driven up to the front steps, fireworks streamed into the sky, hissing and exploding in the twilight. *Is it that late already?* Memory thought, looking blearily at the multicolored lights blazing like living flame in the sky, enhanced with behests to form sparkling representations of the twins and Maellan crest.

The carriage stopped, and Hayes helped Eloryn dismount, leading her up the palace steps that had been lined with red carpet. Another Councilor that Memory couldn't name did the same for her. This wizard looked like the oldest of the Councilors, and Memory took baby steps to help him keep up pace with her.

The entrance hall and the public throne room that it led into had been decorated for the coronation. Banners hung from the ceiling and massive floral arrangements spread like gardens across tables. Wisp-lights hovered throughout the room, dancing around crystal chandeliers, casting a golden glow. Near the furthest wall, a grand throne stood the height of three men with a smaller throne beside it. They would have been the king and queen's throne, but for now would be the queen's and princess's.

Eloryn and Memory took their seats. Clara appeared at Memory's side, standing half hidden behind the throne. She offered a supportive smile as she did a quick adjustment of Memory's hair. Memory tried to get comfortable, but the torturous dress didn't allow it. It didn't look like the night would come to an end any time soon and Memory groaned.

Following Memory and Eloryn into the room were delegates and representatives from all over Avall. Dukes, counts, earls, and the monarchs of the fae courts queued up to pay their respects to Eloryn. Clara indicated to Memory who was who, whispering in her ear as the guests greeted Eloryn, so by the time they turned to recognize Memory beside her she knew who they were.

The first to approach the throne was Aine, the seelie queen. She appeared as everything Memory expected a fairy to be. Her translucent skin emanated a comforting glow. Auburn hair that ran down the entire length of her back and a few feet along the floor behind her was woven with flowers and framed a too perfect face and eyes that shone like stars.

Next to Aine was Lugh, a handsome man, all in shades of bronze, who carried a golden spear twice his height. *Fairy gold*, Memory noted. He appeared human, and Clara confirmed as much with her gossip.

"Aine took a human lover, and just look at him, you can see why! He's been with her for decades, some say nearly a century, but doesn't show it. They say it's the fairy food and spending time in the land of the fae, it makes a human ageless like the fae. Wouldn't mind some of that medicine myself."

Memory thought of Will, wondering how his time with Mina had affected him, but she didn't have long to think on it before the procession continued and two creatures with the all black eyes of the unseelie fae approached.

"It's her, the one from the play," Memory whispered to Clara.

"Lady Nyneve, yes, she's daughter to King Finvarra of the

unseelie court."

Memory stared at the raven-haired Amazon goddess. She was as stunning as in the play, but there was something unsettling about her. Her hands were delicately clasped together, and she wore a dress woven from black cobwebs, as though she were still in mourning. A huge sword hung from an ornate belt about her waist, as though it were jewelry. It seemed the fashion for the fae to be seen with fairy gold weapons. Memory wondered if they were just status symbols or actually put to use.

Nyneve and her father bowed to Eloryn. Where Aine was the picture of feminine beauty, Finvarra was a skeletal mess of geriatric masculinity, hunched and angular. He appeared withered like a dead tree and his fingers looked more like talons. When he opened his mouth a set of gleaming sharp teeth could be seen. His mouth held a permanent scowl, which seemed to stretch into a more grotesque anger when he turned to Memory. Nyneve put a hand on his shoulder and it seemed to calm him enough to continue on, muttering under his breath.

After the fae came the nobility of Avall, starting with Duke Lanval and Duchess Marian, followed close behind by Roen and his parents, Isabeth and Brannon. Seeing them brought a brighter moment in a long and difficult night. Both groups expressed great joy for the twins, but could only speak for a moment before the seemingly never ending stream of people had to continue. The twins' uncle was conspicuously absent.

The rest of the ceremony became a boring blur of speeches, etiquette, and a lot of standing up and sitting down. At some point Eloryn was crowned queen, but Memory couldn't be sure when since it seemed to be mentioned so many times. The solid gold masculine crown just seemed to appear on Eloryn's head at some point when

Memory wasn't looking. It appeared to be the very same one Arthur Maellan once wore, and she wondered if it was a replica or the real thing.

The girls were herded from their thrones into the ball room. The center of the room remained clear and some folk were already dancing to a softly playing string quartet. Around the edges of the room, great tables stood, piled with towers of food. Memory longed to go to them, desperately needing to eat, but Hayes interrupted her by handing her a sheet of paper.

"What is this? This had better be something I can eat." She waved it vaguely.

"You will be speaking after Eloryn. Don't worry. We kept your speech short."

Public speaking? Kill me now. Memory wondered why she hadn't been told about this earlier or given a chance to read what she was meant to say, but she probably would have if she'd actually attended the rehearsals. Memory glared at Hayes as he herded her back to another dais and two smaller ceremonial thrones to sit beside Eloryn. Hayes drew the attention of the room. Clara had followed and took her place again just behind Memory's seat and explained to Memory that Eloryn now had to read out and confirm the renewing of the Pact, which is something that every new ruler must do.

"It's really more out of tradition than anything else." Clara kept gossiping to Memory straight over the important words Eloryn spoke. "The only real way the Pact could be broken was if an act of war was committed, and even then, only if the offended monarch wished for it."

Memory tried to listen to both Clara and Eloryn, and it sounded like Eloryn was doing a good job. Her voice seemed so small and shy, but she spoke every word perfectly, having memorized the whole thing. At the end of the speech, Aine and Lugh both nodded their heads, and Finvarra just sneered.

Hayes took over again. In his speech, he explained that ordinarily the various representatives of local governments and regions would confirm recognition of the new monarch, but as the Wizard's Council was temporarily overseeing all governmental functions at this time the re-establishment of the government would be unfortunately delayed. This caused a few murmurs in the crowd, and Hayes thumped his cane on the ground to silence them and smiled gleefully.

"I also wish to share some good news. By the wishes of our Queen, Thayl Vaircarn was put to death in a private ceremony earlier this week."

Memory's head swung around in slow motion to stare at Hayes in disbelief. *He's really going to lie to everyone about how Thayl died and pretend it was all their plan?*

"Her majesty rightly felt that the tyrant needed no fanfare to his death, and the sooner he was removed from the land the better. We were, of course, happy to carry out that request." He chuckled, as if he had made a joke. The crowd joined in, applause building through the laughter.

Memory's inner fire raged. The sum of the day's events caught up with her. She tasted bile. Memory didn't think puking on the dais would make a good impression and stood to make her exit. Hayes smiled at her as she did and opened for her to begin her speech. Memory stood stunned for a moment, blinking at the roomful of people staring at her. So many expectant faces. Her gaze settled on Eloryn, who looked at her with an encouraging smile. *Crapness. I'm really going to have to do this damn speech.*

Memory cleared her throat and stared at the written notes. Her hands sweated, smudging the ink, and trembled so much she could barely read the words.

"People of Avall," she stammered. There were a few claps and cheers. "I speak to you today not just as a princess, but as one of you. A daughter of Avall, joyous to once again be free, delivered from the blight on our land." Memory skimmed over the script. *What is this bullshit?* She'd never say these things. Making it sound like she'd grown up in Avall and that she was ecstatic that Thayl was dead. More lies from Hayes. Memory crumpled the paper in her hands. If she was going to say anything they would be her words, and something meaningful. Something she believed in. *And if it pissed off Hayes at the same time? One stone, twice the value.*

"And as princess of Avall, I want to announce that the new Wizard's University won't be restricted to just nobles. The study of magic will be open to anyone, no matter who they are."

Memory swore she heard crickets. Some muted applause from a few individuals was covered by Hayes, stepping beside her quick as anything and laughing over her announcement.

"Of course commoners are welcome to join the university," he said. "If they can afford the entrance fee!"

The room roared with laughter again, as though they were putting on a funny skit together. Memory looked at Eloryn for support, but Eloryn just looked embarrassed for her.

Memory stepped off the dais, pushing angrily through the gaudy crowd. These were the people she was expected to live around? People that laughed at jokes about people being killed and the poor being unable to pay for their education? Memory dug fingernails into her palms to distract herself from imminent tears.

Clara trotted after her. "I think what you said up there was amazing."

Your fault.

Memory turned on the spot, looking for the source of the voice. Clara smiled back sympathetically. "Although I think you chose the wrong crowd for such an announcement, being as everyone here was eligible to go to the university anyway and probably don't want the likes of commoners attending beside them."

Unnatural.

From behind her again.

"Did you hear that?" Memory pushed through the crowd haphazardly. Her head ached. Her whole body ached. She was so exhausted she was probably delirious. Hissing whispers came from all around her in the crowd, dizzying her. She searched for their source, grabbing people as she went. Some laughed, others were diplomatically shocked, all were confused.

"Hope, are you all right? You're white as a ghost." Clara kept after her but was swallowed up by the crowd, unable to keep up with Memory's wild rush.

Murderer.

The word hit her like a freight train to the chest. She pushed her way out of the ballroom and ran.

Memory was an emotional wrecking ball. She stumbled down long hallways, each step shaking under her and a sound like distant thunder filling her ears. Decorative suits of armor along the wall rattled as she passed them. She felt unstable, her insides steaming out. In her mind she kept seeing Thayl step backwards off the ledge and disappear. Over and over. She was far from the celebrations now but still heard the voices whispering. *Your fault. Murderer.*

Memory tugged at her hair, pulling it free from its cage of bobby pins. *Did I drive him to kill himself by making him talk about the ritual so much? Did he do it for me, so I didn't have to see him executed?*

Her body jolted, faded. She was slipping, the Veil tugging at her.

Passing a stairwell, she clutched onto the banister as though holding on to it would keep her anchored. The banister shuddered.

Someone walked past, a shadowed shape. Memory caught a look at the face.

"Lory? Help me, please." Memory reached out, but the figure continued without pausing.

Memory let go of the banister, stumbling after. The person's body was blurry, shadowed, but Memory saw small glimpses of the figure's face, reflected in darkened windows as it walked ahead. It was her sister's face, for sure.

"Eloryn? Stop it, this isn't funny."

The figure turned a corner up ahead, and Memory broke into a wobbly jog. The rattling of armor and light fittings around her became more intense and curtains swirled and fluttered unnaturally.

Memory turned the corner and gasped. Herself, she saw herself, face to face in a full length mirror framed on the wall. And standing next to her, right behind her, reflected in the mirror was a second Memory. Not Eloryn at all, but her, Hope, how she used to look, complete with the dyed hair and piercings. She even wore the same clothes that Memory had on when she had arrived in Avall, the same striped long-sleeved shirt, broken heart tee over the top, and torn jeans.

Memory stared at this other self. Her other self smiled back.

Holding her breath, Memory turned around. Horror ran like ice water in her bones.

The other her wasn't just a reflection. She was there.

Memory stepped back.

"Don't be afraid," the other version of herself said.

"Who are you?" Memory asked, her lips quivering.

"Hope."

But I'm Hope. No, I'm Memory. This is not real. I'm losing my mind.

"I'm you. And you're me. The broken pieces of our self." Hope looked at Memory, a vacant, sad look in her eyes. "I'm here to be with you. Nobody can ever like us and nobody else will ever understand. Those idiots won't take long to figure out you're not a whole, *real* person. What do you think they'll do when they realize the monster you are? Still pretend to be your friend?" Hope spoke vehemently, but then softened her tone. "But I'm here now. *We* can be together, you and me, like we should be, and I'll make things better for you."

"No, you're not real. Not real!" Memory screamed out loud, shutting her eyes tight. The rattling intensified and a great cracking sound came from the mirror at her back. Shards of glass shot out around her, in every direction as though projected out from her own body, which remained untouched. The sound of smashing glass was only overpowered by her shattering scream.

CHAPTER NINE

Will could hear her screaming. Over the fireworks and oohs and aahs and giggles of nobles wandering the castle grounds enjoying the celebrations, he could hear her.

He ran over the soft grass of the gardens, keeping himself within the shadows cast by tall hedges. He still wore the shirt, vest, and pants Clara had given him but knew he wasn't presentable compared to the standards of those around him. He looked through an open door and quickly ducked inside.

The long halls of this part of the palace were fortunately quiet. His bare feet padding on the cold marble echoed back to him. He broke into a full run, no longer keeping to shadows, only worried about getting to Memory as fast as possible.

He found her curled against a wall, surrounded by broken mirror.

He wanted to go to her, scoop her up, and keep her safe in his arms. His first step brought a bright burn of pain. A small sliver of mirror cutting into his heel.

Will growled in frustration. His feet would be cut to shreds to reach her. He almost went anyway. After a deep breath to calm himself, he took off his vest and used it to clear a path to Memory, pushing the sharp shards away.

Memory turned her head, acknowledging his presence.

"Are we alone?" she asked.

Will frowned and nodded. "You can get past the glass now," he said, indicating the path he'd made. "Are you okay? How did it break?"

"It's okay. It wasn't real." Memory mumbled and made little sense. Tears still wet her cheeks and her makeup ran. He hadn't seen her this bad since back in the other world.

Memory stood up and stared at the path, making little effort to move.

Will coaxed her. "Come on. I've got something I want to show you. Come with me?"

Memory looked up at his face and after a moment a tiny smile appeared, and she walked clear of the broken mirror. "I'm sorry. God, I must be such a mess. I've had a pretty rough day." A sob broke the end of her sentence.

"It's all right. We can have our own celebration, just us, okay?" Will nodded for her to follow him. Memory dried her eyes with her wrists and followed.

Will had been wanting for a while to show her the place he'd found while roaming the palace grounds, but there'd never been a good time. Now also didn't seem good, but he needed something to distract Memory with and maybe make her happy. He led Memory

through the quiet halls, up towards her rooms. Then he detoured, taking her up the spiral stairs of the tower at the eastern end of the palace. He hoped this way would work. Normally he'd come here from the outside of the building.

After reaching a window on the second landing, he opened it. Memory gasped and shook her head, but he smiled and stepped out onto an old section of the castle walls. It looked like it had been abandoned and built around at some stage when the palace was expanded. As she followed him out the window, he held Memory's hand, so she wouldn't fall due to the monstrous dress she wore. He would break the rules to make sure she stayed safe. She didn't seem to mind, and held his hand back tightly, and he could feel her shaking despite that she'd calmed down and no longer cried. She gave him a wry smile like she agreed how ridiculous her dress was for climbing around like this.

Ahead of them a massive mound of overgrown ivy sprawled like a sea monster, leafy tendrils like tentacles reaching out in every direction. Memory had told Will how this wing had been closed off during the sixteen years of Thayl's rule. The plants had completely grown over this end of the roof.

Parting a section of vines, Will revealed a secluded entrance and motioned for her to go inside.

He gestured to the room they were standing in. "It's sort of a late birthday present," he said. "A secret place, where you can just be yourself."

The room must have been an old lookout or birdhouse. No longer part of the main castle walls and without easy access, it had become disused and forgotten. It was small, with just enough room for two stone benches that sat under windows without glass but screened by ivy, letting in just a little moonlight and the flashes of fireworks.

Across the courtyard they could see the clock tower lit up, about to strike midnight.

"Thank you, it's amazing," she struggled to speak. "A place to be myself. Hopefully not to be with myself."

Memory laughed strangely then seemed to notice they were still holding hands and let go. She stared at his wrist where he had the tattoo they did together.

"Will," Memory's lip trembled a little. "Something is happening to me. I've started to… remember things."

Will's heart jarred. Too many painful things for her to remember, things he wished she wouldn't ever have to know again. Like so often, he wanted to hold her, comfort every pain she had. He wanted to protect her from her own memories.

He made the mistake of moving forward, his body drawn to her.

Memory made a half cough, half laugh embarrassed noise and moved away. Will stepped back too, cursing silently.

"Don't look like I'm dying or something. Getting my memories back is good, right?" Memory hugged her arms around herself.

"I'm sorry," he said. "And I'm sorry that I haven't always been able to help, that I can't always be here for you."

Memory perked up. "Hello bright idea! How about we spend some time together here, every day? How does that sound?"

"Sounds great," Will said.

"Right, we'll meet here at six every day. Spit promise!" Memory hocked into her hand and held it up to him. The way she used to, when he was a kid and she wore jeans and they sat in the dirt together throwing rocks. Seeing her do it now when she wore something fancier than any wedding dress he'd ever seen made him smile broadly.

"Promise," Will said. He would try, for her, but he knew that this was a promise that he couldn't keep.

CHAPTER TEN

In the school's dining hall, a long table had been laid out with crisp white linen, silver cutlery, and an arrangement of arum lilies, lending a feeling of elegance to what was otherwise a mess hall playing dress-up. Ladies' classes now only occupied a small portion of the large finishing school grounds since the Wizard's Council had requisitioned the rest of the space for their displaced university.

Memory sat at the table, wondering why she and Eloryn had been sent into the finishing school section, rather than the university classes run by the Council. Her first day here and she'd already sat through a morning of lengthy lectures about the proper way to curtsy, stitch tiny flowers, and other 'womanly arts.' Memory thought it was fair to say she could do with improving her manners, but Eloryn was meant to be queen. Surely there were more important things for them to be learning than how to bend perfectly at the waist. It felt insulting to them both, and there was also the fact Memory was bored out of her mind. And hungry. *This is ridiculous.* Memory looked at the plate of rapidly cooling crepes in front of her. She was starving but hadn't been given the all clear to begin eating.

Memory glared in disbelief at Mistress Ursula, the teacher instructing her on the intricacies of how to eat, something she thought that she could do pretty well already. The way Mistress Ursula's waist had been cinched in so small under her all black, high-necked dress, Memory doubted her expertise on the subject.

Memory wore a plain gown and jacket combo similar to the one she'd worn out with Clara that night, but something about the cut or quality of the fabric still made her stand out compared to the other girls' simple lacey frocks. Around the room almost all the girls stared dumbstruck at Memory, Eloryn, and the crowd of Eloryn's bodyguards standing at attention in the background.

Ursula tapped what looked like a conductor's baton on the table and asked, "Can anyone tell me the correct amount of food that a lady should consume?"

"As much as possible?" Memory smirked at the girls around the table. A few smiled politely back, but the slight look of confusion in their eyes kept the tone flat.

"That is incorrect, your highness," Ursula said, her voice flat. "A lady should only consume a portion the size of which would befit a child. The correct amount is one-third of what is on your plate – and not a bite more!"

"Any chance we could get bigger plates, then?" Memory asked.

Beside her, Eloryn snorted, covering the laugh by coughing politely into a napkin and giving Memory a small kick under the table.

"Wouldn't bigger plates be lovely?" A girl with a mop of auburn ringlets piped up, looking so cheerfully at Memory and Eloryn it made Memory's teeth ache. *Suck up.* "They would make us look so charmingly petite in contrast."

Ursula's head twitched, shaking her mound of perfectly piled gray curls, but her face remained impassive.

"The size of the plates is more than sufficient." Ursula sat at the head of the table and brandished her own knife and fork in demonstration. "Remember that each forkful must be no larger than the end of your little finger, and you will place the food in your mouth, place the cutlery back on the table, and chew slowly and swallow before cutting your next piece."

Memory sighed, staring at her plate of food. *Dear crepes, you smelled fantastic and look so cheesy, but if I have to eat you under these conditions I shall go insane. We were not meant to be, my love, so I bid you farewell.*

Memory took her napkin from her lap and folded it with as much sarcasm as she could muster. "Mistress Ursula, I require the use of doth little girl's facilities yonder and was wondering, per chance, if I could be excused temporarily forth hence?"

The openly mocking tone appeared to be lost on the teacher. "Certainly, your highness. But don't be too long. We have to discuss desserts and the correct way to use a spoon." She smiled as if the prospect was exciting.

"Can't wait." Memory gave two thumbs up, tucked in her chair and left the dining area, breathing a huge sigh of relief.

A cartoon escape sound effect played in her head as she slipped out the door and off to find an interesting place to kill time. The room was on the ground floor of the hollow rectangular building, and Memory looked longingly through the windows at a group of boys in the central courtyard. They were lined up, performing some matching exercise routine that Memory didn't know the purpose of. Whether it was spell casting or aerobics, it seemed way more interesting than her classes. Down the hall Memory caught sight of Hayes, who was making his way around the building with the finishing school's headmistress. Memory felt the need to express her concern over the nature of her education. Surely, as a princess, she shouldn't have to go to school if she didn't want to? She knew she'd hate school, even before she realized that it included such bizarre forms of torture as sitting her in front of food that she wasn't allowed to eat.

Memory waited until Hayes and the headmistress had finished and approached him.

Hayes's eyes narrowed when he saw her, but his expression quickly changed to a welcoming smile. "Your highness, how are you finding your first day of school?"

He says like it's the only time I've been to school ever.

Memory matched his agreeable tone, trying to stay on his good side. "That's kind of what I was hoping to talk to you about. Do you have a minute?"

The corridor had a few passersby who nodded or bowed to them both. Hayes indicated a nearby vacant office which they entered. He pushed the door closed behind them with the end of his walking stick.

"You have some problem with your classes?" Hayes snapped, rubbing the bridge of his hooked nose. He stared down at her, making her nervous and Memory felt a ramble coming on.

"Well, yeah. Are they really necessary? I mean, it just seems a bit silly learning how to sip soup when I'm meant to be heir to a kingdom. There's just so much other stuff I don't know that I could be learning. And Eloryn too, although she already knows lots."

"Are your etiquette classes necessary? Well, that depends, *your*

highness," Hayes's voice became a grumbling hiss. "Are you ready to conduct yourself accordingly? As a princess? It's clear you don't even know how. We know that your background is… questionable, but it's high time you started learning how things work around here and stopped behaving like a wild girl."

Hayes stepped forward, looming over Memory with barely any space between them. Hayes glanced at the closed door then back at her with a sneer. The close proximity shot a disgusted shudder through Memory's body, and she tensed at the ill feeling in her stomach. Memory wished they weren't alone. He'd never speak to her like this in front of Eloryn. Her face heated with shame, and she bit back at him in outrage.

"I do want to learn how things work here, that's my whole point. But not all this girly rubbish. Real things about how to run the kingdom."

"The Council and I are managing all of the affairs of the kingdom. These are not duties for women or girls. If you can't carry out the simplest task of attending *charm lessons*, why should I think you deserve to study subjects that are of the realm of men? The fact is, *princess*, that you may not think that what you're learning is fun or interesting, but you will do what you're told if it has any chance to prevent you from causing further embarrassment to the throne."

Hayes yanked the door open and left, obviously finished taking advantage of the privacy for his tirade.

Memory was stunned into silence. Yeah, she'd made some mistakes, but she wasn't wrong about this. *Realm of men, my ass.* Memory kicked a cabinet and one of its glass doors swung open. It caught her reflection, and the reflection of Hope, just beside her.

Stumbling back out of the office into the hall, Memory tried to straighten up and act normal when she drew the attention of a group of passing students.

Great. Hayes was right. I'm embarrassing myself again already.

Memory found a seat on the low windowsill across from the dining hall and waited for the class to end. She didn't have anywhere else to go, but refused to go back inside as her own form of protest. She also needed a moment to recover after seeing Hope again. The glass was cold against her back, and she let it calm her boiling insides. She wondered if witnessing Thayl's death could really have tipped her over the edge into full-blown psychosis. The first time she saw Hope she was emotionally and physically exhausted, delirious, so she could write it off as a mental hiccup. She had no excuses for this time.

The lesson ended and Eloryn was first out, escorted by her intimidating entourage. Memory imagined that it must be difficult to constantly have a small battalion of soldiers trailing you around. The girls that followed looked torn between a bursting desire to befriend the young queen and white-faced terror at the prospect of doing it in front of heavily armed men.

Memory stood up and started walking beside Eloryn. "I miss much?"

"No. It got even more boring after you left." Eloryn gave Memory a sideways smile and blushed as if she had said too much.

"I bet you knew all that stuff already anyway, right?"

Eloryn's blush deepened. Memory figured that was a yes.

"Can we go eat some food like real people now?"

Eloryn gave her head a small shake. "I don't think we can fit it in before our next class- Posture and Perambulating."

"Perambu-what?" Memory grunted. "Maybe I should attend that one. I don't think I even know how to perambulate."

Eloryn giggled, and the sisters continued to walk. The long corridors were lined with arched windows showing the inner

courtyard on one side, and along the other side, portraits of past school headmistresses were spaced between the classrooms. Memory didn't appreciate the sour-faced glares most of the women held, staring down at her like she was offending them just by being there. They passed by open double doors, revealing a large hall where two men fenced before a substantial crowd of girls.

Memory bounced on the spot. "Let's watch, let's watch, let's watch!"

Eloryn frowned. "We'll be late for class."

"We can learn to perbamuwhatever any old time, come on."

Memory pushed Eloryn into the room, and the two struggled to see over a crowd they were mostly shorter than. As the girls around them started to realize who the newcomers were, they hastily moved aside and Eloryn and Memory ended up with a front-row view.

The two men in matching padded jackets and mesh masks lunged and parried, moving backwards and forwards like crabs. One of the men moved very formally, and the other fenced with a swift fluidity that won him more gasps of admiration from the watching girls.

The formal fencer struck at his opponent, but in an effortless twirl the blow was dodged. The other man continued the graceful move and struck back in return. The point of his sword embedded into the padded jacket above the first man's heart and flexed into an arch.

That seemed to mark the end of the fight, and the combatants bowed to each other with their swords to their chests. The girls in the audience sighed and giggled when the winner took off his mesh mask and shook out his ruffled tawny hair.

Roen.

Memory grinned and gave a loud wolf whistle which drew a little more attention than she intended.

Roen noticed and smiled at the twins. He gave his sparring partner a solid handshake and a few words Memory couldn't hear.

"He's pretty good, hey?" Memory asked Eloryn.

Eloryn's cheeks had lost all their color. Her whole face paled. With a small nod, she took a step back. "We'd better get to class."

"I'm going to go say hi. Come with, I'm sure he wants to see you too."

Eloryn's mouth twisted and her head dropped. With a small shake of her head, she ducked back through the crowd and left the hall, surrounded by her handlers.

Roen was already headed their way, and Memory noticed the hurt look on his face when he saw Eloryn leave.

"She has a class now," Memory covered, more to save Roen's feelings than whatever was going on with Eloryn.

"You don't?" He smiled warmly, but a small frown still marred his expression.

"Nope. Free as a thing that's free," Memory lied. "That kicked ass, by the way. You were like a fancy ninja."

"Thanks, I think." Roen started heading out to a side door and motioned for Memory to follow. Around them, girls stared with open jealousy and gossiped to each other. Memory wondered what they thought Roen's relationship with her was, which made her wonder what it was as well. She felt a little satisfied to be walking out with him while he barely acknowledged the throng of smitten girls he left behind.

"What's up with the adoring fans?" she asked with a sly grin.

"Didn't you hear? I'm a great big hero. Rescued a couple of princesses and helped save the kingdom, they say. The ladies are practically throwing themselves at me." Roen smiled roguishly. "It's lucky I'm so used to it. Otherwise, I might let it go to my head."

They stopped at some wooden lockers, and he put away his fencing mask and sword. Memory stared at the roll of his shoulders as he pulled the jacket off and put it away as well. He ruffled his hair again and Memory found herself needing to catch her breath. *Yeah, I can understand the fan club.*

"Those masks make my hair feel awful," he explained, noticing her watching.

"Girl."

Roen laughed loudly. "I'm finished for the day, how about you? Want to ride back to the castle with me?"

"Best suggestion ever. Let's get the hell out of here."

A line of carriages awaited their passengers beside the school grounds and like a true gentlemen, Roen helped Memory into one marked with the royal crest. He tapped on the front to the driver, and the carriage started to rumble and bump about as they made their way back to the castle.

"The fencing, was it for something particular or just to show off your moves to the ladies?" Memory leaned back and put her feet up on the seat across from her, next to Roen.

"A friend offered to catch me up on proper technique, as I haven't had many formal lessons. I don't want to be too behind when fencing classes begin." Roen tilted his head. "And maybe just a little to show off."

"You have classes for *sword fighting*? This is so unfair! Men get to do all the cool stuff. I hate to talk down on my kingdom, but there are some funny ideas here about the positions men and women should have."

"Don't look at me, I think women should be able to take any position they want." Roen paused a moment then laughed. "That was a little risqué even for me."

Memory made an exaggerated kissy face. "You're just ahead of your time, ladies' man. Meanwhile in Memoryland, I'm seriously considering magically changing myself into a boy just so I can get into some politics lessons."

"You know, if you really want to do some classes outside of the finishing school curriculum, I have an idea for an easier way to go about it." Roen leaned toward her like they were sharing secrets. "It's not the sort of thing a girl of Avall would normally do, but then, you're no normal girl, are you?"

CHAPTER ELEVEN

Eloryn hadn't seen Memory since they stopped to watch the fencing. She'd missed all of the afternoon's classes. Eloryn sat through them alone feeling an equal share of anger and worry. The gossip that Memory had left the school early with Roen reached her as she boarded her carriage to return to the castle. Her stomach ached every time she hypothesized on why they left early together, and so after walking to Memory's door three times only to return to her seat again, she finally knocked.

"What's the secret password?" came the reply, followed by giggling.

Eloryn frowned. "I don't know the secret password, but I am your sister. Who else would be knocking at our adjoining door?"

"The correct answer was 'Not by the hair of my chinny-chin-chin,' but come in anyway."

All anger fled Eloryn when she walked in on her sister trying on clothes in the middle of her sitting room. She looked as if she had been struggling to put on a pair of boy's trousers that were still around her ankles, the rest of her covered in a shirt that was far too large. Clara lounged in a nearby arm-chair, red-faced from barely suppressed laughter.

"Mem," Eloryn began, slowly stepping into the room. "What in Avall are you doing?"

Memory paused for a moment and then laughed.

"Clara got them for me. Ugh, so many buttons." Memory did a twirl when she finished putting the trousers on. "What do you think?"

"I think I'm confused and a little concerned for my sister?"

"It's an idea me and Roen came up with. I was all 'I'm gonna zap myself into a boy,' and he was all 'it'd be easier to just dress like one' and I was all 'duh, Mem!' and then here we are!"

Eloryn tilted her head. "You… want to be a boy?"

"Sort of, yeah. Just so I can attend the classes that I want, and not attend the ones I don't. Roen's enrolling me as one of his brothers, Tristan. He said he had so many brothers people would assume one had just come out of the woodwork. As *Tristan* I'll be able to learn whatever I want." Memory looked genuinely enthusiastic as she worked on tucking her shirt in. "And *Memory* will be unwell for a while and unable to attend her lame girly classes."

Clara wheezed a squeaky laugh. "You should tell the teachers you're having women's problems."

Is this all just a joke to them? Eloryn wanted to be supportive of her sister, but Memory was making it hard. Eloryn had no way out, no freedom to skip the classes she'd been assigned. Even if she wouldn't

be missed, she had a duty to make her appearance, to do and be seen to do her part. Who was being supportive to her, the sacrifices she was making? Her next words took on a spiteful tone that she didn't like. "And why are you getting dressed out here? If you did so in your bath or bed chamber where there are some mirrors you'd see you've got that shirt on inside out."

Clara burst into tearful laughter and hid her head in a cushion, as though she'd just been waiting for someone else to notice.

Memory frowned and shrugged. "I'm a bit over seeing myself at the moment."

Memory pulled off the shirt and mock-whipped Clara with it while standing in just a bodice and trousers. "You, Giggles McLaughsalot, these shirts are way oversized. How big do you think I am?"

"You're just a teeny tiny little thing." Clara got up and headed to the door, still chuckling. "I'll go and see if I can find something smaller, but I'm really not sure any of the men I know are quite that small. Alack, now she's making me steal clothing from boys!"

Memory pointed sternly at the exit. "Just walk away before I make a comeback so awesome it will explode you."

The door closed after Clara and Memory looked at Eloryn, her expression changing from mirth to concern.

"Okay. What's up, Lory? We were just having a bit of fun, but I am serious about doing this. I should be able to learn what I want to learn." Memory sat down in front of her and Eloryn took a seat as well.

"I know. I'm sorry." She paused, lowering her head. "I'm simply tired and upset. It's been such a long day, and I just bumped into Hayes. He told me he's received intelligence that our uncle is plotting to amass an army against us, to make his claim on Caermaellan."

Memory stood back up again. "What? No way! Why would

somebody do that? After all this place has been through?"

"Power is the worst kind of motivator. There is no sense to what it makes people do." Eloryn stood up as well and started pacing, fidgeting her fingers. "I just… I feel like if I could speak with our uncle I could make things right, but Hayes says he's refusing to even see me. He says we need to act aggressively to show a firm hand and stop any voices of dissent against us or the Council."

Memory looked as overwhelmed as Eloryn felt. "I'm sorry. I had no idea you were dealing with stuff like this. What are you going to do?"

"For now, I'm going to keep sending requests for a meeting. But everyone is pushing me to take a firmer stance. There are just so many decisions to make and changes to oversee." She'd been queen for not even a week and it already wore her down more than she wanted to admit. "I appreciate everyone's opinions and advice, and Hayes has been so helpful to me, but I worry that he's too aggressive when it comes to diplomatic policy. He wants to have more control over the courts and sentencing, to catch and question conspirators and stop issues like this from arising."

Memory frowned as she picked up another shirt and started buttoning it on. It was slightly smaller than the last men's shirt, but masses of excess fabric still draped over her small frame.

"Hayes seems to be taking on a hell of a lot of responsibilities. You know, I don't trust the guy. He outright said to me that ruling isn't a woman's job. I feel like you're giving away too much power to a man we don't actually know that much about."

"He's just trying to ease my burdens."

"Then why is it taking so long for him to establish the proper government instead of taking all those burdens on himself? Hayes might seem like he's looking after you, but he's not Alward. It's like

Hayes is trying to step in and take Alward's place, but you can't assume Hayes has your best interests at heart."

Alward's name felt like a slap to Eloryn's face. Hayes could never replace Alward. They were nothing alike. But that didn't mean she couldn't look to him for guidance. Eloryn straightened her back and stopped pacing. "I have to trust Hayes and my other advisors to take on some responsibilities. I have to delegate to get things done. And who would you rather have in power? Some noble who we've never even met? Neither of us know who we can truly trust in this time, but at least with the Council we know that they support us for rule and are doing as much as they can to help us, even if Hayes's behavior may seem firm at times."

"And you're not worried at all about the Council running *everything*?" Memory kept pushing, but Eloryn had run out of any energy. Her reply had no attitude, just honest curiosity.

"Do you think you could do a better job, Mem?"

Memory pouted, looking at the ceiling. "Not right now. But maybe one day, if I learned about the right things. That's what this is all about," she said, tugging at her trousers. "They don't even want me to have the chance to be able to do it."

"That may be so, but I've had all the training and teaching I'll need for a lifetime from Alward, but only experience can teach me who I can actually trust. That isn't something you can learn at school."

"Maybe you're right," Memory conceded, standing to leave. "But at least I can admit that I do have a lot more to learn, and I'm doing something about it. There's also something to be said for instinct, and it sounds like you're ignoring the heck out of yours." Memory grabbed a bag from a table and strapped it across herself, then loaded it with bread rolls from a tray nearby. "I'm going to see Will."

Eloryn raised an eyebrow. "Dressed like that?"

Memory looked down at herself. "Sure. Will doesn't care what I wear." She paused, as if considering something. "I might pop by to see Roen on the way, to get his approval on my costume. Want to come? I think he was sad you didn't stay after the fencing."

Eloryn's hand went to her neckline and wrapped around her jade pendant. She took a moment to compose herself, to give the answer she should instead of the one she wanted. "No, that's probably not a good idea."

Memory sighed audibly. "When will it be a good idea? Why are you avoiding him?"

"It's just… easier this way."

"Look, Lory, I know you're shy, but you have to get over it." Memory paused at the door on her way out, thoughtful for a moment. She put a bowler hat on then turned back again. "I can tell you two make each other giddy around the knees, but do you really think he's going to wait forever? You saw the girls at fencing. I don't see how it's going to be easier for you when you see him in the arms of someone else."

Grateful to be in pants instead of a massive gown, Memory climbed out the tower window onto the old castle walls. She looked forward to seeing Will. They'd dubbed their meeting place the Ivy Room. *Our secret place. My safe place.* The thought made her smile. She gazed out over the battlements at the view of the city in the distance, a grey forest of steeples and smoking chimneys. Swallows swooped around her chasing tiny insects in the waning light. The temperature

chilled quickly as the sun dropped. It was fresh, and despite having an emotionally draining day, Memory was in a good mood.

Until her path was blocked by Hope, standing right in front of her.

Memory stopped and blinked a couple of times, trying to rid herself of this vision of how she used to be. When it refused to vanish, she forged on ahead, hoping it would just fade away. It didn't.

Hope followed closely beside Memory as she marched along the ramparts.

"I wouldn't bother. He's not there."

Memory ignored her.

"I said Will's not showing. He's off with his fairy friends."

Memory put her fingers in her ears and hummed, looking the other way. Hope grabbed her hands and tugged them out, shocking Memory at her tangible touch.

"Stop being so childish!"

"You're not real, go away."

"Yeah, I am real."

"I know the clothes you're wearing are put away in my cupboard, so they're not real at least."

Hope gave an exasperated groan. "Really? My clothes are probably the least weird thing about my existence."

"Fine, I'll bite. What is the whole thing with your existence?" *I ask a figment of my insanity. Break with reality - complete!*

"I told you, I'm you. Not Memory you. I'm who you used to be."

Memory shook her head. "Still not getting it."

"It's crazy, I know. The best I can figure is that I'm the missing parts of you. The bits that got lost when you cut off Thayl's hand."

"Right. So his brand new stump gave birth to you?"

"Of course it's going to sound dumb when you say it like that.

But all my, your, memories and soul, were caught up in all that magic, and ta-da, here I am."

They arrived at the Ivy Room, and Memory lifted the leafy screen that concealed it.

And Hope was right. Will wasn't there. This was the third day he'd missed meeting up already, and he had only dodged Memory's questions about why.

"I'm not going to say 'I told you so,'" Hope said.

"Just did."

Memory sat down on one of the small benches and blew a raspberry. Hope sat on the seat opposite, her legs crossed the same way, looking so similar but different. The two watched each other, like sitting in front of a twisted carnival mirror. Memory realized the whole scene was creepy, but somehow it comforted her. If a magical ghost of her past self insisted on following her around, she might as well take advantage of the company. Part of her longed for Hope to be real, desperately curious to get to know who she used to be.

"I really wanted him to see," Memory said softly.

"To see what? You dressed as a boy?" Hope scoffed.

"No, I wanted him to see you. For one thing it'd prove you're real. And also, I thought that maybe he'd be happy to see you, to see the girl he waited so long for. He must be so disappointed. He finally found me, and I'm not that girl anymore. Not you. He doesn't talk to me much, and he avoids touching me like I'm a leper or something. But if he saw you-"

"He can't see me. You can't let anybody know about me. Promise me you won't tell." Hope stood up, agitated, staring Memory in the eyes. "If you do, they'll work out that your soul is broken. We don't want that, do we? I want to be with you, and I bet you want to be with me too. We're meant to be together, but it has to be our secret, just the two of us. Secret best friends, okay?"

Memory looked up at Hope. She was right. She couldn't let anyone know how broken she was. "Okay."

Come back, I can't keep up.

Will ran ahead of her. Scrawny little boy version Will. So small, she should be able to keep up. Her legs glided in place, aching from effort, not moving anywhere.

Wait for me. Don't leave me.

Wind gusted and slammed against her chest. Will got farther away, running down a long corridor of squeaky Formica and grimy beige walls. Memory called out again and realized her voice wasn't working. The words just jangled in her head. Will was big now. Bare-chested, beast-like. How could such a small boy grow so big? The hallway stretched on forever, and Will ran out of view, so far away.

She checked in each of the small rooms she ran by, looking for him. All the rooms were the same. Her room from the children's home. Wind swirled again, and her feet smacked the ground, finally able to move again, bare feet slapping on the artificial coating, slippery with water. She wasn't alone.

The man up ahead of her now wasn't Will.

He carried a mop and grinned at her. Memory reversed, smacking her back against a cart full of cleaning equipment. The janitor dropped the mop and came after her, saying something she couldn't hear over the sound of rushing wind in her ears. Her feet skidded on the wet floor. Her body exploded with panic as she broke into a sprint, pushing past dangling tree roots, stumbling down stairs and around dark cavernous turns. The wide-set man remained just steps behind her, no matter the breakneck speed she moved at.

The janitor's cart blocked her way, and she wondered how she'd done a complete loop. She slipped past it and came to a dead end, dark and rocky. Fumbling through the cart, all her instincts turned to self-preservation. She grabbed a box cutter and held it out.

The figure loomed in front of her like a giant made of nothing but shadow.

Memory awoke, sweating, half fallen out of her bed. She struggled to extract herself from tangled sheets, and her hand pressed against something sharp and stung fiercely.

Her knife lay on the sheets, spotted with blood dripping from the gash on her hand. The knife she'd left at the underground lake.

Did I really leave it there? Sleep hazed her thoughts. Maybe she didn't. Maybe she just remembered wrong, and the knife had been here all along. Either that or some of the dream was real, and she'd Veil doored again without meaning to, this time in her sleep. But if some of the dream was real, how much of it and which parts?

Memory closed her knife and tucked it carefully under her pillow like it used to be. Wide eyed and sleepless, she slouched out of bed and into her bathroom. She washed her bleeding hand down in the sink with a sigh then looked up at herself in the mirror. Her shoulders shook as the image startled her. Some blonde girl in a lace-edged sleeping gown.

That's me now, Memory reminded herself. She stared at the mirror, trying to hold onto what was real. But the lines between real and dream, new and old, tangled in her head.

CHAPTER TWELVE

"I'm not sure I'm fooling anyone," Memory said, walking out of her first class as Tristan. She felt at home in pants, but the stiff-collared coat, hat, and tie felt clunky and uncomfortable. Clara had even found her a wig of bowl-cut mousy brown hair for the disguise.

Roen walked beside her down the second floor hallway of the finishing school. The sun shone warmly in through the arched windows, disguising the fact the wind that buffeted the glass was brisk and chilled.

Roen stopped walking for a moment and made a show of eyeing her up and down. "I don't know. I think you make a fairly convincing boy, albeit a twelve-year-old one."

Memory punched him playfully in the stomach. "Yeah and you'd

make one pretty lady."

"Watch it, Tristan. Don't you know it's wrong to hit girls?"

Memory started walking again, grinning back at Roen. The sunlight hit him from behind, making his golden hair glow. *He really can be beautiful sometimes.*

"Are you sure you don't mind me using your brother's name? I feel like I'm somehow shaming his legacy."

"Not at all. It's an honor, and I'm sure if Tristan were alive he'd be very fond of you. He was my closest brother, not in age, but in every other way."

"Which one was closest in age?"

Roen looked away from her, out the windows at the treetops swaying in the wind, rasping against the glass. "We… don't talk about him."

"Oh, that one."

Roen shook his head and when he looked at her again he was still smiling. He stopped at a door and bowed to her in a flourish. "Delivered safely to your next class."

"You're coming in with me, right?"

"Sorry, you're on your own for this one. I'm not enrolled for magic classes."

Memory looked at the floor. "Can you come in anyway? I'd really like someone I trust to be there. Given my history with magic, I'm…" Memory took a deep breath, her nerves shaking her up. Her magic was explosive at best. Even the only spell she could really cast, the Veil door, was going wonky on her. "I'm scared," she admitted.

"You'll be fine. Tristan is tough," he said, reaching out for her hand and giving it a squeeze. "But Memory is even tougher."

A group of girls walked past, giggling hysterically to see what appeared to be two boys holding hands in the hall. Roen and Memory looked at one another and laughed as well.

"I don't think you can hold my hand while I'm being Tristan. People will begin to talk, and I genuinely think that Avall isn't ready for it if it's not even up to women's liberation yet."

"That's a shame."

Memory smiled as Roen loosened his grip, but instead of letting go completely he quickly, and surreptitiously, kissed her hand.

Memory blushed. Roen didn't let go of her hand.

"So, what are you going to do now?" Memory asked, pretending everything was normal and her heart wasn't racing. "Oh! You should totally dress up as a girl and go to my etiquette classes for me."

"I should. I agree, I'd make a good-looking girl." Grinning wickedly, Roen looked down at himself and nodded as though he liked what he saw. "I'd call myself Roena. She and Tristan could court."

Memory laughed loudly in reply. *He's just joking, right?* She and Roen always joked around, but she started to wonder if it was something more. The way he looked at her was warm, his eyelids half closed, smiling widely.

Then he let go of her hand as though she'd burnt him.

Memory turned around to see Waylan, Hayes, and Eloryn heading their way. Eloryn looked stunningly feminine in an A-line, dusty pink gown with her long hair loose and set in neat curls. Memory felt increasingly self-conscious in boy's clothes. *I really am just one of the boys to Roen, compared to her.*

Eloryn blushed and stared at Memory and Roen, but Waylan and Hayes were engaged in an argument and didn't notice them.

Waylan puffed as he waddled, the effort of debating and walking at the same time clear from his flushed round cheeks and beads of sweat on his bald head.

"I think all this talk of Sir Ewain building an army is drummed-

up nonsense," he said.

"Are you questioning the reliability of my intelligence contacts?" Hayes replied.

"Yes, frankly," Waylan said with confidence.

Memory smiled. Waylan had been one of the few people to back her up in meetings, and she loved seeing someone stand up to Hayes.

"From what I've heard," he continued after a pause for breath. "He's just gathering support to get the Wizard's Council back to their normal role and hasten the reestablishment of proper government."

"A proper government with himself on the throne. My contacts are reliable, Waylan."

The trio reached the doorway Roen and Memory stood beside. Hayes barely glanced at Memory, not recognizing who she was enough to care, and instead scrutinized Roen and the look he shared with Eloryn. Memory whispered a goodbye to Roen and ducked into the classroom before Hayes could work out who she was.

"So you say." Waylan stopped and gave a short bow to Eloryn. "I want to talk to you more on this, but have a class to run now. Your Majesty. Councilor Hayes."

Waylan followed Memory into the room, and she could see Hayes lead Eloryn away without a word to Roen who left in the other direction.

There were already a dozen students sitting quietly in the classroom. They ranged in age from about thirteen to twenty-five from what Memory could tell and were all finely dressed. Even the youngest of them wore neat suits with stiff-collared shirts, ties, and tailored coats. Everyone sat at attention and seemed keen to be there. She imagined it must be a big deal to be allowed into this level of education after having it unavailable for so long. There was something snooty about their manner, and Memory wondered if she just thought

that because she knew they were all from noble families. Some of the boys whispered and stared at her as she entered. She took a seat at the back with a sense of satisfaction. *Even if I'm not fooling anyone, they're all too chicken to do anything about it.*

The room shared the same pale limestone walls seen in most of the university. Waylan had made his way to the front of the classroom where a grand wooden desk was piled in a large collection of weighty books. A few crates were stacked to the side, full to the brim with more age-yellowed texts, but a seamstress dummy still stood in the corner as a reminder of the room's previous assignment.

Waylan put on some glasses that pressed into the chubby sides of his face, then looked over a note on his desk. "I see we have a new student, Tristan Faerbaird." He looked up, pulling the glasses down his button nose to inspect the room and nodded briefly when he confirmed his new addition. Memory gave a timid smile back, but he barely glanced at her. The glasses went back up and he started talking, scrawling illegible words on a blackboard as he did.

"We'll continue on from where we were, Tristan. We can catch you up if needed, but this is all very basic theory thus far. We're starting simple, considering the last sixteen years, you understand."

Waylan underlined something on the board that looked like "The Spork of Cowchicken."

"This Spark of Connection-" Waylan said.

Oh, that makes more sense, thought Memory.

"-was granted to those in Avall at the time of the Pact and has been passed down ever since, becoming a hereditary trait of humankind so that everyone in Avall can connect to magic."

A boy in the row in front of Memory whispered to his friend, "Not *everyone*."

Waylan didn't seem to notice and continued drawing a rough body shape on the board with a star in the center, then energetically scribbled lines directing out from the person. Memory smiled to herself at the comparison between his artistic merit and his enthusiasm. "The Spark of Connection doesn't give a person power unto themselves. It simply allows a man – or woman – to become a conduit for magical energy. We all understand behests, that the words of the magical language must be correctly spoken to make requests from a required object or natural force. But the request isn't always enough. An object can have a will to fulfill your request, but not the power to do so. I can say the words to ask this desk to shatter into a thousand pieces, but it needs something more. The Spark of Connection becomes a channel for pure magic to enable these requests."

Memory thought over the times she'd seen Eloryn use magic. A body may want to be healed and respond to the request, but of course it would need something more, something to give it the power to do so. Same with clothes shaking themselves clean or objects flying through the air.

"But where does that magic come from?" she muttered to herself.

"Good question!" Waylan barked, surprising her that he heard. He looked overly pleased at having a student interacting with him.

"There is an energy that flows through us all, the energy of life. It moves through the blood of all living things, through the blood of the very earth. It is a powerful force and that is what is channeled to harness the behests we speak. It is also the lifeblood of the fae. It is speculated that this energy does not exist in the fae realm, Tearnahn-Ohg, which is why they require an earthly home."

Waylan looked at her expectantly like she should respond to his answer. "So magic is from living energy, and it channels through blood, but isn't blood also full of iron? Wouldn't that be poisonous to the fae?"

The same boy in front that had talked before spoke up. "Only *forged* iron, pure iron changed by the hand of man, is poison to the fae. Everyone knows that." He didn't turn around completely to speak to her, and she figured he had no idea who she was. Some of the other students looked at him shocked, like a battalion of guards was about to appear and arrest him for being sassy to the princess.

"That's right." The prospect of a class debate had Waylan grinning ear to ear. "Otherwise we would not be able to call a wisp for our lights, as they are beings of fae energy. They would not come close to forged iron, although that point is purely theoretical since the Purge."

Yeah, theoretical. Memory did a mental face palm. So many times she'd tried in vain to cast the light spell, all the while having her iron knife nearby.

"Any more questions before we continue?"

Memory raised her hand hesitantly. She felt like she was taking over the lesson, but had so much she wanted to know, and Waylan nodded for her to speak up so she asked her question.

"Behests are just meant to be requests, right, and requests that can be denied. So how can behests that kill people work?"

Some of the boys at the back who were chatting shut up. Everyone stared at her. Waylan looked at Memory, more with concern than anything else.

"And why would you ask that, young man?"

"I don't want to know how to do it. I just want to understand how it's possible. I mean, it's not like you could use a behest that would *ask* someone to die."

"Yes, clever of you to realize that." Waylan didn't look pleased and answered through thin lips. "No, one could not ask another's body to simply die. But your body is not all your own, you understand. There is a behest that calls upon disease, bacteria, and life forms on and within the body to attack and kill the host. They rapidly degrade internal organs and shut them down, causing the person to die almost instantly. Such magic exists, but only members of the Wizard's Council are allowed to learn that behest, and then it's only to be used in extreme and dire situations."

Waylan took no more questions, and instead read aloud from one of his books for the rest of the lesson. Dull was an understatement of the quality of the text, but Memory already felt as though she understood magic far more than she had before.

When the class finished and the boys left, Memory hung back to speak with Waylan, another question nagging at her that she hoped Waylan could answer, a question she couldn't ask as Memory. As Memory she felt like an anomaly to be studied, but as Tristan she was just a normal Avall student, eager to learn. It surprised her just how eager she was. She wandered to the front of the classroom.

"Thanks, that was an awesome lesson," Memory opened with, wincing at how stupid she sounded.

"I'm glad you enjoyed it." Waylan nodded as he cleaned the blackboard, small clouds of chalk puffing under his hand. "I can tell from your constant questioning in class that you're going to be a clever and challenging student."

"I actually have another question, is that okay? I was wondering if there was some way that something, like some spell, could change a person's Spark of Connection?"

Waylan stopped clearing up and peered down at her over his glasses. "Princess Memory, there's no need to keep up this pretense."

"Oh." *Busted.*

"Don't worry. I'm not going to turn you in. It is a sincere pleasure to have you as a student. I am already impressed by your insight and curiosity."

A strange sensation struck Memory. *Is that what pride feels like?* Memory looked at her feet.

"Rest assured, young princess, you are always welcome in my classroom. It's wonderful that you're making an effort to learn more, regardless of where some may consider your place to be."

"Right? Man, I thought I was only one to think Hayes is getting a bit pushy about where a princess's place should be."

Waylan shook his head. "Hayes may seem harsh sometimes, but we do follow him for a reason. It was his diligent leadership that saved us and kept us hidden all those years. But I must admit, I do have my concerns with how he is running things. I find myself challenging him more and more during Council meetings, and not just over matters pertaining to the school. I'm afraid that it goes far deeper than that."

Fired up by finding a co-conspirator against Hayes, Memory had to cut off her next comment regarding things that go far deeper and Hayes's ass when another Councilor walked in.

Waylan stood and gave the man a hearty embrace. They looked similar, both bald and wearing glasses, but while Waylan was round and chubby, the other Councilor was stocky, solid, and tall enough to make his weight intimidating rather than endearing. She'd seen him at some Council meetings but didn't know his name. He always stayed quiet and looked grumpy.

The wizard glanced at her and bowed briskly. "Princess."

"I'm really not convincing anyone, am I?"

"Memory, this is my brother, Bedevere."

"Taking some interest in exploring your magic ability?" Bedevere said. By his tone, Memory didn't think he expected an answer, and he continued too quickly for her to give one. "If you've become amenable to investigating your powers and past, I would be very interested to assist. I've many questions I'd love the chance to direct to you."

And there it is, back to being the lab rat. Memory tried to keep the groan out of her reply. "What kind of questions?"

"I know you must be keen to study your own powers, but to be honest I'm more interested in learning about the technology of the lands you grew up in. I'm in possession of some fantastic schematics, brought in as imports from a fae supplier last century. My colleagues tell me they are fakes I paid too highly for and that there couldn't be such fantastical devices existing outside Avall, but I feel theoretically they should work."

Memory blinked a few times as she tried to understand the stream of information.

Waylan cleared his throat. "My brother has somewhat of a fascination with the world that we left behind. He has some rather… controversial views on the matter."

"Like maybe I didn't grow up in Hell after all?"

Bedevere smiled for the first time. "Indeed."

Memory smiled back.

Eloryn and Memory took the aerial walkway that connected the newer palace to the old keep on their way to the Round Room, trailed by Eloryn's usual entourage. Eloryn had read all about Caermaellan Castle as she grew up, studying its floor plans and dreaming about what it really looked like. She knew all its history and admired how her family and architects had worked to preserve the ancient stone keep at the heart of the palace when they came to expansions. The gray slabs of stone were at odds with the decorative grandeur built up around it, but somehow it worked.

Rain washed the windows on both sides of them, making the view streaked and blurry. Barely mid-afternoon, Eloryn felt ready for bed rather than her fifth meeting for the day. The crinoline cage under her scarlet gown felt too heavy and her bodice too tight. She rubbed her eyes and tried to keep pace with Memory, who skipped ahead, full of energy.

"The meeting isn't even to start for a while yet. I never thought I'd see you so keen to be there," Eloryn said.

"I don't care about the meeting," Memory laughed like the idea was crazy. "Waylan said he'd be there early, and I wanted a chance to talk to him."

The twins stepped out of the walkway into a hall that lead up to the Round Room. Roen was walking toward them and Memory ran up to meet him. They whispered together, and Eloryn didn't catch what they said as she caught up.

At the end of the hall, Waylan could be seen through the entryway into the Round Room. Memory waved to him. She gave Roen a soft punch in the shoulder. "You two kids stop and have a chat. I'm going ahead to see—"

A thunder crack of sound shook through Eloryn's skull.

A powerful explosion blew outwards from the Round Room. The rumble of flame deafened Eloryn as her mind caught up with the situation around her. Shards of exploded furniture and stone shot toward them.

"Beirsinn fair nalldomh!" Eloryn yelled, unable to hear her voice over the ringing in her ears. Tapestries flew off the walls, creating a barrier that the projectiles thudded against like hail. Small, sharper fragments of wood and glass cut against the fabric, some pieces piercing through. Air rushed past the barrier, hot and pungent, filled

with chokingly thick smoke.

One of her guards grabbed Eloryn from behind and tackled her to the ground softly. Others shouted around her.

"I'm fine. Off me," Eloryn ordered, but the smoke made her voice raspy. She cleared the vapor from the air with a behest and the guard helped her to her feet.

Beside her, Roen had Memory shielded in an embrace. A rage of jealousy fired through Eloryn, until she realized that Memory was forcing herself forward, trying to push past Roen who was holding her tight to keep her from running into the Round Room, or what remained of it.

"Is everyone all right?" Eloryn called out, her voice muffled in her ears.

"We have to help Waylan," Memory said, desperately trying to get out of Roen's grasp.

"I don't think you can," he said.

The guards tore down the tapestry barrier and hobbled over the crumbled landscape to assess the damage. Red splashed the stone entryway to the room, and Eloryn looked the other way.

When she did, she met the gaze of a man watching from further up the hallway. He wore a servant's uniform and had terror all over his face. The man backed away, breaking into a run. His escape was blocked by Hayes marching toward them, walking cane held out like a weapon in front of him. She heard the words of Hayes's spell with a grim realization.

"Guidhe beag lugha ob ciorram greim-bàis..."

"Stop, hold your words," she cried.

Eloryn dashed toward them. The shining bolt of Hayes's behest hit the man as he ran and he fell to his knees, then face, his life twitching away.

Eloryn stopped, stunned at the action. Hayes reached her and gave her a firm embrace.

"Your majesty. Thank the fae you're unhurt!"

"Hayes, what have you done? Who was this man?"

"A traitor against you. I was informed of a plot – an assassination attempt. I tried to come as quickly as I could." Hayes stared at the damage down the hallway. "Evidently not quickly enough."

Hayes knelt beside the corpse, patting the man down and searching pockets. He produced a piece of paper folded into a small square. He stood and read it, glaring at the note.

"This man was just a tool, and here is the proof of the man who wielded him. This is a writ, your majesty. A payment letter, signed by your uncle."

Eloryn's head drifted slowly side to side. Her ears still hummed, and a weight of sadness settled on her, making the whole world feel underwater. "He would do this?"

"Forgive me, Majesty, but I warned you he was dangerous. Still, you are safe. It's a mercy that the room was not occupied."

"Waylan. He was in the room." Eloryn looked back up the hall. Memory was hunched down against the wall with her head in her hands. Roen sat next to her. The ground shook slightly, and Eloryn worried the building had become unstable, but it passed quickly.

Hayes ran a hand over his mouth, face taut with grief. "There will be justice for this."

Eloryn noted that Peirs and more soldiers had arrived. Peirs jogged up beside her and bowed. "Your Majesty, I vow I will discover the cause of this."

Hayes sneered. "We already know who caused this. That you don't is an added sign of your incompetence at this position, along with even letting this occur to begin with, right in the heart of Caermaellan castle."

Peirs stepped toward Hayes, squaring up his shoulders. "I'm confident the guard has done everything warranted to protect the Queen. We could not have foreseen this."

"I've told you numerous times of the threats being made. I instructed you to increase patrols."

"It is not in your power, respectfully, to order an increase in patrols."

"Please stop," Eloryn said. "This is not the time for bickering. This is a time for mourning, for the loss of a good man, and that one I call family felt driven to such extreme action."

Peirs lowered his head deferentially. "I cannot believe that Sir Ewain is the cause of this, but I will investigate every lead to discover the truth here."

"We already have proof," Hayes said, thrusting the writ at Peirs. "Had you acted sooner on my information this wouldn't have happened."

"Or if I had. Have I handled this so poorly?" Eloryn asked Hayes. She should have dealt with the threat from her uncle. Instead she delayed the process because she didn't want to make a difficult decision. It felt like the only decisions she had been making were to delay making decisions. In times like this, they needed someone who could make a decision at the right time. Waylan had died on account of her inertia. She blushed from grief.

Hayes put his hand on her shoulder. "Any hesitation on your part was only brought by your tender, if misguided, feelings for your family, your Majesty. But now is the time for action, swift justice for this crime."

"I need to see the damage." Eloryn turned away from Hayes and made her way slowly into the Round Room.

Peirs stepped in ahead of her, taking one of the torn tapestries from the ground. He laid it over Waylan's body before she could see and gave her a solemn nod, which she returned as a thank you.

The room itself was in passable condition. Ancient walls of stone built to withstand sieges had been charred and scratched, but not broken. The furnishings, however, had been torn asunder. The leadlight above had shattered and fallen, creating a multicolored carpet of razor-edged jewels. The wide round table where important decisions had been made for centuries had been reduced to kindling by a single act. Even Thayl hadn't dared touch these treasures of Avall history. *Perhaps they could be repaired over time. Even if I have to spend every day speaking behests to splinters, I will repair this.*

"Gunpowder," Peirs said, sifting through the debris.

"Obviously. Set up by a paid off servant and triggered by a simple behest." Hayes studied the scene further, turning over broken furniture. He looked over to Waylan with deep regret. "Though it is tragic indeed, it is fortunate that Waylan was the only one in the room. The assassin must have panicked at your approach and set off the blast too early. Imagine had this occurred mid-meeting. This is what I warned of earlier. This is why we need greater power to investigate, imprison and sentence anyone who threatens us and the stability of Avall. The current system is too slow. If the roles of Grand Bailiff and Legate of Civil Defense were held by a single dignitary, the process would be greatly expedited."

Eloryn felt like crying but held it back. Her hair had come loose from its pins. She pushed the blonde strands from her face and turned to Hayes.

"You're right. I need someone in those positions who can prevent tragedies like this from occurring. Someone I trust. Councilor Hayes, will you take the ranks of Grand Bailiff and Legate of Civil Defense?"

Hayes bowed briefly. "I would be honored to take these roles, your majesty, if you see fit to bestow them upon me."

"I should have done so sooner." Eloryn felt defeated, as if she had failed by handing more of her responsibilities to Hayes, but she knew someone had to take action. Actions she was loath to take.

"Your majesty, you have made a wise decision," Hayes bowed low. He straightened back up, then turned and pointed at Peirs. "And as my first act, you are to be stripped of your rank as Captain of the Royal Guard on the grounds of your complete incompetence and negligence of duty."

Peirs's jaw worked, but he made no reply. He bowed low to Eloryn and paused, looking at her for a moment with a worried frown, before being escorted from the castle. Eloryn turned away, unable to watch him go, or look anyone in the eye.

CHAPTER THIRTEEN

Memory sat on her pillows with her head against the quilted backboard of the bed. She ran her hands through her hair over and over, trying to soothe herself to sleep. Too many thoughts rushed through her head. *So much death.* Her balcony doors were open, and she stared out into the night but no-one came.

I'm never going to get to sleep if I keep staring at the forest, waiting. Memory pushed herself off the bed and went to close the doors.

She looked out across the tree tops. The rain had stopped, but the trees still sparkled in the moonlight. Flashes of darting sprites matched the shining leaves. She thought she could hear singing, somewhere distant, mingling with the sounds of night. A bittersweet song with a strange melody, somehow familiar.

"It's embarrassing," Will said. He wore old army pants and a dirty t-shirt that said "Not It" and they sat together in a vacant lot, down the street from the children's home.

"I know it is, that's why I want to see you do it." Memory cackled. "Look if I'm going to protect you from the other boys, I at least want to know why they love to beat on you so hard."

"Fine, just, close your eyes, okay?"

Memory groaned dramatically and made a point of rolling her eyes as she closed them.

Will began to sing. Something classical, in another language. Something Memory had never heard before. It was strange how her heart reacted to the sound, aching sweetly and beating just slightly faster. His voice was so beautiful. He was still a boy, but his voice was deeper than she'd expected.

Memory's eyes opened to watch him sing. He quickly stopped.

He frowned and stabbed an empty drink can with a stick. "My parents made me take lessons."

A gust of wind rattled the balcony doors and swirled Memory's ivory nightgown and hair about her. She grabbed the doors and pulled them closed. When she turned around, Hope had taken her spot on her pillow.

A small smile appeared involuntarily on Memory's lips. "Hey."

"Hey. Need someone to talk to?" Hope patted the pillow next to her.

"Really do." Memory sat at the foot of the bed, face to face with her other self.

"I know about the explosion."

Memory looked away for a moment, getting her emotions under control. "Waylan died. He was nice to me, and I thought he could help me with my magic, and now he's just gone."

"Who cares about him? What about you? You could have died, too."

Memory shrugged. "I guess the prospect of not existing isn't so scary for me since I only feel like I've existed at all for a couple of months. What I can't handle is how everyone I grow close to is taken away from me."

"I'm not going anywhere. I'm the only one you can trust to stay by you."

Hope's intensity made Memory feel strange, knowing that was her, how she used to be. *Is that the friend Will knew? That he'd waited so long for?*

Memory tilted her head and glanced back at the balcony doors.

"Thinking about Will?"

"Yeah. I didn't make it to the Ivy Room today, with everything. I'm worried about him. Usually his 'Mem is in danger' sense tingles, and he's here like a flash, but he didn't come. Again."

Hope rolled her eyes. "Will is probably too busy with Mina. You can't rely on him. He's not that little boy anymore, following you like a puppy. I think you should spend more time with Roen. He doesn't hang around with slutty sprites. He's there for you and, well, he makes you happy, right?"

"Yeah, but Roen likes Lory. Fact."

"Maybe, but he *could* like you more. I mean, you're basically the same thing as Eloryn on the outside, and as for the inside, you guys get along great. Eloryn doesn't want him anyway, right?"

"I don't know." Memory leaned against one of the bed's posts and played with the tassel that tied the canopy back. "Do you think that you being around is what's bringing back my memories? Is that how it works? Do we share them or something?"

Hope stared at Memory for a moment. "Would you want them back if you could have them?"

"For sure. I would have got them back before, but Eloryn had to reject them to save me from Thayl."

"Did she? Did she *have* to? Think about it. What if Eloryn did that because she wanted to keep you confused and unsure about yourself, keep you unable to know or control yourself? I mean, that is what she did, after all."

Memory frowned skeptically.

"Don't look at me like that. When Eloryn connected with you, when your spirits joined she must have seen that your soul had bits missing. She *knows*. She can never really treat you as family. Why do you think everything's played out like it has? Her becoming queen instead of you?"

Memory focused on the tassel again, unwinding the weave of the threads. "No. That just… made more sense."

Hope crawled down the bed and took the tassel from Memory, making her pay attention. "Did it? The only sense it made was keeping you from power, from the title that should be yours. Hayes and the others treat you like garbage. You were meant to be queen, you should be queen. Just imagine how people would treat you if you were."

"I don't want to be queen. I just want my friends…" Friends she already barely saw. *I see Eloryn so rarely maybe she is avoiding me on purpose. Could this really be why?*

Hope threw the dismantled remains of the tassel onto the floor. "You think you're making friends here. You think you're starting a new life. But eventually they'll all turn on you or leave you. Every last one. Trust me. I'm the only one here for you. You think they like you? How could they? They don't know you. *You* don't know you. You're not even a whole person."

The morning after the assassination attempt, Memory found herself on complete lockdown. No school and no way out of the castle, not even with Clara's help. Hayes had ordered a new guard detail to keep an eye on Memory. These guys treated the job like they were imprisoning Memory, rather than stopping others from getting to her. Memory glared at them from the window seat in the palace library.

Memory had been moaning to Clara about missing lessons when Clara pointed out the palace had its own library that she could keep studying in. Memory decided to check it out and quickly ended up walled into the window seat by piles of books on history, law, and economics. She'd hoped to continue reading up on magic as well, but apparently all of those books were kept by the Wizard's Council.

Memory wriggled her legs around trying to find some comfort amongst her layered skirts. She ended up taking her slippers off, hitching the skirts up and sitting cross legged on the velvet-covered cushions. Some of the guards looked at her funny, and she hitched her skirts up higher in response - daring to show her thighs - until they turned away in shock.

Memory smiled, satisfied and picked up a fistful of small pastries from the tray beside her, popping them into her mouth as she read.

"Look at you. One week of school and you're already burying yourself in texts and tomes." Roen walked up to her, carrying the Avall history book that Eloryn had given Memory for her birthday.

"I sent Clara to get that for me. What have you done with her, you scoundrel?" Memory said with dramatically widened eyes. She wiped the pastry crumbs off her hands onto her skirt so she could take the book off him. The flakes showed starkly against the black velvet.

Roen held his hands up innocently. "I ran into her up at your chambers and gave her the rest of the day off. You've got the poor girl working triple shifts."

"Oh, she loves it. Besides, it keeps her out of trouble with the guards."

"She's in trouble with the guards?"

Memory wriggled her eyebrows.

Roen laughed. "I see. But you do have servants you could call on other than her, you know."

Memory looked up with a sinister smile. "Nope. I finally got rid of all of them."

"Mem, what did you do? Also, remind me not to get on your bad side."

Memory shrugged innocently. "They kept buzzing around, like it was my job to find work for them—"

"It is," Roen interrupted.

"So I did. I've sent them down into the city. I figured I could find better use for them than tightening my corsets and brushing my dresses, because seriously, why do dresses need brushing? They are helping out with the homeless kids I've been taking alms to, while I'm on lockdown and can't do it myself. It's pretty exciting actually. Maeve has found a building to set up base in."

"And Maeve is?"

"One of the older orphans. She's helping me get things organized since she knows a lot of the kids on the street. She's awesome. You've got to meet her. I just wish I could get away from this goon squad and

go check the place out. But I'm just going to have to buy it unseen. Apparently I can do stuff like that because I'm some rich princess."

Roen laughed and sat down on the window seat next to Memory, his shoulder up against hers and head back on the glass. "Look at you."

"What?"

"Never mind."

Memory took another fistful of the delicate bite-sized pastries. Pushing them into her mouth, she pointed at a book across the seat from them with her bare foot.

"Can you chuck that one over here for me?" Memory said through a spray of pastry flakes.

Roen laughed as he passed the book to her. "When you're allowed back to school, perhaps you should reconsider skipping your etiquette classes. You could stand to learn to be a little more ladylike."

"Ladylike your face."

Roen grinned and reached for some of her pastries. Memory play-swatted his hand then let him have some.

He popped them into his mouth one at a time, and Memory couldn't help but stare at his lips. Between bites he said, "Honestly, though, I prefer your current schooling arrangement. It means we get to spend more time together. I feel like I'm getting to know you all over again, and it's amazing seeing you get to know yourself."

Memory shrugged bashfully. She could feel the warmth of Roen's arm up against hers. He smelled like soap and cookie spices. Next to him, she felt comfortable, content, and at home, but she hadn't thought she really wanted Roen in a more than friends way. He was funny, handsome, brave… Why shouldn't she want that? Maybe she was just stopping herself because of some notion of Eloryn's feelings, but all Eloryn did these days was avoid Roen. Maybe Hope was right.

"It's been nice getting to know you more, too," Memory said softly, unable to make eye contact.

"Roen, Memory, good morning to you." Eloryn's voice made them both jump. Memory shifted away from Roen, so they were no longer sitting against each other, then wondered why she felt so guilty. *We weren't doing anything wrong.*

"Lory, what's up?" she asked, as innocently as possible.

Eloryn stood in front of them, clutching her hands together and clearly trying hard to seem cheerful. She also wore all black in mourning, and the stark shade played up the pale quality of her skin and hair. Behind her were twice as many guards as she normally had following her around.

"I had some spare time and thought we could all lunch together."

Roen stood up, brushing crumbs off his pants. "I'm afraid I have to pass."

Memory pouted and Roen gave her a smile. "Some of us are considered expendable enough to still be expected in classes."

Roen's smile dropped when he turned to Eloryn. He seemed about to say something, but then left awkwardly without saying anything else.

Eloryn flinched a little then turned to Memory with a smile. "Just you and I then? I've barely seen you since the incident. And I wanted to say I'm sorry about Waylan. I know that you'd grown close to him and enjoyed his classes."

Memory nodded, looking over her shoulder. The window looked out onto a rose garden, one she found familiar from a dream she once shared with Thayl. The roses bloomed in a rainbow of shades throughout the courtyard. The world outside seemed too bright for this topic.

"You know, I finally managed to cast that damn light behest

thanks to Waylan. I thought he could teach me so much. But now he's not here anymore."

"It was a great loss. He'll be missed by a lot of people. I really hope that you can get back to magic classes soon."

There was something in Eloryn's tone that didn't sit right with Memory. It sounded more like a warning than an encouragement. "What do you mean?"

"Just that I know there's a lot we still need to understand about your magic and what Thayl did to you." Eloryn's sympathy sounded strained. She was overdoing it.

Memory felt her lips curl, defensiveness building. "What do you know about what Thayl did to me?"

"No more than our existing theories. The Council has tried to decipher the rune scars on Thayl's hand, but it's an ancient language, the very basis of the magical language we use today."

"I'm sorry, *what*? They kept *his hand*? You didn't think that would be important for me to know? How could you keep something like that from me?"

"I hardly kept it from you. Had you been at all co-operative with the Council I'm sure you'd have known. I don't have time to tell you every little detail myself." Eloryn became flustered. "You know how full my time is. It must be nice spending your time frivolously, dressing up like a boy and lounging about eating pastries, but some of us have duties that must be performed."

"Duties my ass. Don't go getting angry at me because you're jealous I'm spending more time with Roen. It's not your duties stopping you spending time with him, it's you."

Eloryn's mouth shut, and her back straightened like she'd taken a huge breath and held it.

Memory made a show of picking the last pastry from her plate and popping it in her mouth as she stood to leave. "I'll skip lunch, thanks. I've already eaten."

Memory paced in her chambers. A grandfather clock in the corner read a quarter past six, and she fretted that she wasn't going to make it to the Ivy Room for a second time. Not that Will hadn't missed more than his fair share of meet ups.

Memory knew the minute she stepped out of her chambers her new guard escort would be on her heels again, and she didn't exactly want to take all of them with her to her secret place. She briefly considered opening a Veil door to get there, but it seemed like overkill, and scary, especially when her magic still felt so unstable.

Memory opened her balcony doors, hoping Will would just come to her. But he hadn't, not since her birthday, not even when she missed their meet up for the first time last night. He probably didn't make it himself and hadn't even noticed.

The sun was setting, and being on the eastern side of the castle, the shadows were already dark and cold. Memory brushed a hand over a blood-red rose bud on the vines around the balcony. The tower that led to the Ivy Room was right near her chambers, and one of the windows on her side was open. The vines grew across to it, but much more thinly than the way they rambled up to her window.

Memory knew it was dangerous, but something inside her didn't care, almost dared her to try. She quickly changed into her jeans and t-shirt and stepped onto the balcony edge. A brief glimpse down at the ground shook her, and coldly she wondered how Thayl must have

felt, as he fell.

She reached across and grabbed a strong ivy vine stuck on the wall, grateful that the ivy had grown further and faster than the roses, so her hands wouldn't get cut up this time. Clinging to the vine, she stepped out onto the small ledge that ran from her balustrade across to the tower window. Edging along it, she kept herself stable and upright with the vines. It was easier than she thought it would be.

The vines grew thinner as she went. Just a few steps from the window, one of them tore under her hand. The vine pulled off the wall like tape, tearing a long strip off before it snapped. Memory swung backwards, her other hand slipping from where it still held a vine. Her center of gravity pulled away from the wall. She tumbled.

With a push of her legs, she jumped through the open window and landed inside the tower.

Memory sat on the floor in the Ivy Room. She was barely aware of how she'd made it there from where she'd landed on the tower steps. She still felt in shock, replaying what would have happened if anything had gone differently, if she fell. No one would have known what happened. She wondered how long it would have taken for her to be found, or missed, or who would miss her first.

Memory rubbed the goose-bumps on her arms and her breath blew puffs of mist. Will hadn't shown up yet. She stood up to see how long she'd been waiting. The clock tower across the courtyard read nine o'clock. Memory blinked. She could tell she'd been sitting there a while based on how numb her legs had gone, but hadn't realized it was so late. Will wasn't coming. He'd broken their promise, again. He'd probably be the last person to miss her if she was gone. She was about to leave when the vines rustled.

Will pushed through and half stumbled into a dark corner. Even in the low light, he looked dirty, and the shirt she had got for him was

missing.

He shifted, and seemed surprised to see her standing there, staring at him.

"I didn't think you were coming. Do you know what time it is? I know you haven't got a watch, but there's this ginormous clock, like, right there," Memory said, flinging an arm out to point at the clock tower.

"Sorry," he said. He stayed curled in the corner, seeming shyer than usual.

Memory's gaze kept returning to Will's bare chest, and the ripples of muscle just visible in the darkness. She should be used to him being topless by now, but the act of having seen him in a shirt seemed to highlight the bareness now it was gone.

"And what happened to your shirt?" she asked.

"Got ruined."

"If you didn't want it in the first place you should have just said." *Just like our promise for meeting here every day,* Memory thought. He'd probably made that promise thinking of how she used to be, wanting to see the old her, not who she was now.

Memory sat down again across from Will and sighed.

"I'm sorry I'm being snippy. There's just so much going on, and I feel like I'm losing it. Seriously, seeing things style losing it. It's hard enough trying to fit in around here without being crazy."

"It's okay. You're not snippy. You're honest." Will spoke softly, barely a mumble. "You can tell me what's happening."

You can't let anybody know about me. Promise me you won't tell. Memory bit her lip. She couldn't tell him about Hope. The bombing, Waylan, even what happened on her way there tonight, it all felt like too much to put into words.

"It's just confusing, all this crap with me and Roen and Lory. I

mean, I'm just friends with Roen, and Eloryn barely even acknowledges the poor guy's existence anymore, but I'm supposed to feel bad for spending time with him? We're just good friends."

Will grunted but said nothing else. It was so dark Memory couldn't see any expression on his face. She could barely see him at all in the dark corner he sat in. She might as well be telling her woes to the empty corner.

"Oh hey, check out my new mojo." Memory spoke the words to the light behest, remembering she could actually do that now. "Àlaich las."

A small wisp cast a glow in the room, its light shining off the glossy leaves that enclosed them.

The light also reflected off wet blood on Will's arm, which he kept pressure on with his other hand.

"Jeezus. What happened? Why didn't you say something?"

"It's nothing." Will turned his head away, like he was embarrassed to have been seen.

Memory crawled across the floor to him. Up close, she saw there were also fresh scratches on his chest, torn over much older scars.

"Is it bad? Damn, it looks bad."

Will didn't reply or move. Memory grabbed his chin in her hand and turned his face back toward her.

"I'm not kidding around, Will. Tell me what happened."

Will growled. "Just hunters, in the forest. An accident."

"Hunters in the forest?" Memory lifted a hand to her face in disbelief. "It's the royal goddamn hunting grounds. Why didn't I realize there would be hunting? Will, you shouldn't be out there. I'm going to put a ban on hunting, but you've got to move into the palace. I know I've asked before, but maybe now you've been shot by a damn arrow you might have to admit I'm right."

"Can't."

"Of course you can."

"No," he said firmly.

"Why? So you can stay closer to Mina? Is she why you won't live in the castle?"

Will didn't answer. His eyebrows were low over his eyes and his jaw set.

Memory moaned in frustration. "At least, let me heal you? You can't be running around in the dirt with a hole in your arm."

Will shook his head. "Better not."

Memory poked his arm, right above the wound. "Really?"

Will flinched away. She poked him again.

"All right!"

"I thought so."

Memory moved in closer to Will. He kept his eyes on her and remained still. Memory could smell the blood on him, mixed with mossy earth. She placed one hand on his forehead and one on his muscled chest. Her heart hiccupped.

Memory cleared her throat, but her voice still cracked. "Okay, here we go."

Memory tried to make a connection like she had when she healed Eloryn. In her mind she ran through the theory of healing, but nothing happened. She took her hands back and shook them, then rubbed them together like they needed charging up. Trying again, still nothing worked. The only person she'd ever healed before was Eloryn, her twin. In magic, like calls to like, so healing her twin was easy. Maybe she wasn't skilled enough or focused enough to heal anyone else.

"I don't think I can do it."

"I thought you were supposed to be all powerful at this stuff?"

Will's tone was gentle, joking, but in Memory's fragile state the words stung.

"Why don't you just go back to your fairy lover and get her to fix it for you? And while you're there you can report back to her about me and my lack of ability. That's what you're supposed to do, isn't it? Spy on me and tell her what I'm up to?"

"Do you really think that's why I'm here?" Will's voice remained stable and soft, infuriating Memory even more. "I don't report back to them. They don't need me to. They keep track of what you do themselves."

"Then why are you here? You only show up when you feel like it."

Will pushed to his feet and Memory backed up, out of his way and stood up as well. He looked hurt, but he still didn't raise his voice. "You haven't tried to understand what my life is like, has been like. You just expect me to fit into yours. You're here a month, and you're a *princess*. I've been here a lot longer, and some things… can't just change. It's too complicated. It's easy for you, but I can't be what you want."

"You think things have been easy for me? If you were around you'd know they aren't." Memory was nearly crying, but the reckless energy of her sadness found its way to her voice instead and she screamed at Will. "How am I supposed to understand your life when you're never around, never tell me anything. You didn't even tell me you'd been shot by hunters! You haven't even tried. Just go back to your fairies."

Memory tore the vines away and ran along the old castle wall back to the tower, not caring how close she came to the edge.

She sprinted down the tower steps, round and round, grazing her elbow against the wall in her rush, trying to expend all of her emotions in physical form. The fires in her chest burned bright hot. A rumble built within her. She ran hard, trying to escape herself.

She stumbled out into the eastern entrance yard, having blindly made wrong turns and run too far. She bent over, her hands on her knees, to catch her breath.

Hayes's voice reached her, and she ducked back through the doorway again. She loathed the idea of him seeing her like this, running wild and dressed in otherworld clothes. Marching feet and another man's voice, crying accusations and pleas, passed by right in front of her. Peering out, she saw her uncle, Ewain, being lead bound and under armed escort toward the main keep. The guards wore a strange uniform, something new that Memory hadn't seen before. The symbol of the Wizard's Council, a stylized mouth with a star inside, was embroidered on the sleeves.

"I did nothing. These are lies." Ewain spoke to Hayes, to the guards around him, trying to get the attention of anyone but no one responded. "I wanted the twins off the throne, of course I did. But I have no army in my control, and I'd be a fool to attempt their assassination! I only voiced my wish to remove them from power because it is the right thing to do. They're an abomination, a corruption of the Maellan line. My brother and Loredanna never consummated their marriage."

Memory found herself running toward the small group, and she skidded to a stop on the gravel right in front of her uncle. "What are you talking about?"

Hayes stepped between them, putting his hands on Memory's shoulders. She flung them away.

"Princess, what are you doing out here at this hour? This is no time-" he began.

"What is he talking about? Tell me."

Memory couldn't see Ewain behind Hayes blocking her way, but she could hear him.

"My brother wasn't your father. He told me your whore mother never opened to him."

Hayes turned and hit Ewain across the face with the back of his hand. "How dare you speak of the beloved Loredanna like that. For such disrespect, I'll make what is ahead for you all the more worse."

Hayes clicked his fingers and the guards picked the man up, dragging him up the stairs into the building.

Memory chased after them, half jogging to keep pace. "Then who? Who was my father?"

"As if you don't know." The prisoner spat at her feet.

Thayl? The burning inside her, already alight, roared and her vision blurred, the world flashing grey. The idea crumpled Memory's heart. So much was wrong, everything about their lives broken from start to end. She thought Thayl had just been some sick father-figure in her life. *Did I watch my real father die? Did I cause it?*

"No, you have to tell me more, I need to know for sure." Memory tripped as she tried to keep up and keep talking to Ewain. She yelled at the guards. "Stop. Stop walking. I order you to stop!"

They continued. Hayes paused briefly to look down his hooked nose at her. "You have no authority here. These men are under my orders, as Grand Bailiff I am in control. Do not listen to this lunatic. He is lying, trying to sow the seeds of mistrust to weaken you and your sister. You must not tell anyone of this fabrication. Go back to bed, princess. The truth will be revealed under duress."

Memory shook her head, incredulous, and followed the group down the stairs into the dungeon. The rooms on the first level looked different to the last time Memory had been through there. Vicious contraptions filled the space, and the tables were laid out with all manner of unkind tools. Memory clutched her chest, wringing her t-shirt in her hands, the heat inside her torso unbearable. The room shifted, contorted. It became beige walls in a small space, tall shelves on either side filled with plastic chemical bottles. Shelves with knives, pliers, hooks. The back wall had mops propped up in a messy pile. The back wall had chains hanging down, manacles on the ends. The floor was wet and smelled of detergent. The floor was stone, rough, spotted red.

Memory didn't know what was happening.

She didn't know where she was.

She ran.

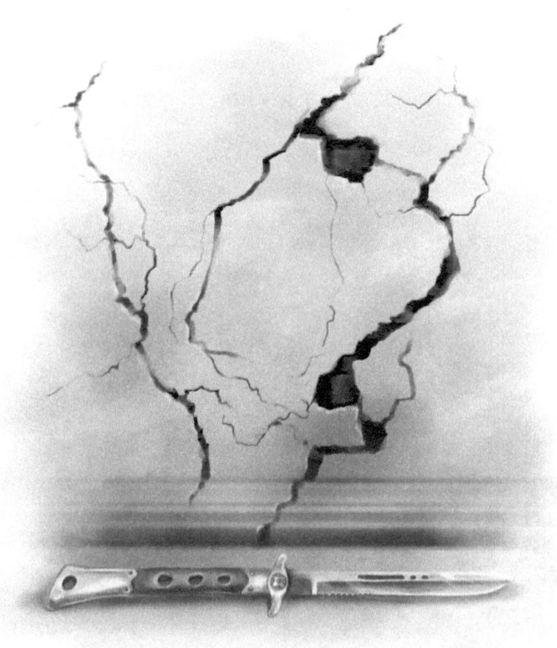

CHAPTER FOURTEEN

Roen sat up in bed and rubbed his face. He could have sworn he just saw Memory step through his room. The way she used to look, in her strange otherworldly clothes, but her hair was its current natural blonde. She seemed distressed, careening past then blinking out of existence.

He pushed the covers back and grabbed the pants and shirt he'd worn that day. He tugged them on, not bothering with shoes in his rush to leave the room. He might have just been imagining things, but it shook him up so much he thought he better check on Memory to be sure. He hadn't been able to sleep anyway.

The chambers he and his parents had been housed in were smaller guest quarters just downstairs from the old royal chambers Memory and Eloryn were in. Given the time of night Roen was grateful it wasn't far to go.

Up the stairs in the corridor leading to the twin's rooms, Roen was surprised at the complete absence of guards. He assumed Eloryn was working late in the queen's office as she often did. Maybe Memory also wasn't in her room, but he still went to check. No guards meant no gossip, for which he was grateful.

Roen knocked at Memory's door and heard whimpering and the rattling of furniture. He pushed the handle and it clicked open, so he slid inside. Armchairs and desks were tipped over throughout the sitting room, and the floor seemed to tremble under him. He pushed through urgently into Memory's bedchamber.

The room was dark, but he could see Memory curled against the far wall, between her bed and a knocked down wardrobe. Tussled gowns tumbled out around her like she was a castaway in a sea of lace.

She muttered to herself, shivering. She flickered in and out of sight.

The wall behind her had cracked and grout shook from it when the room trembled again.

By the fae, what is happening?

Roen knelt beside Memory and brought her into his arms. At first she pushed back, her hands in fists, rigid around her folded iron knife. He held her tighter.

"Mem, it's me, it's okay," he said, using the word she'd taught him.

She dropped the knife and grasped at him, pulling in close.

The tremors stopped. *Was she causing them?*

Memory cried hard in his arms. She mumbled into his shoulder, the words jumbled and incomprehensible. Memory always seemed on the verge of both laughter and tears at any moment, but he'd never seen her like this. He could make no sense of what was happening.

Roen ran his hand over her hair, trying to calm her, reassure her. He kissed her softly on the forehead.

Memory jerked away and looked up at him. Her eyes were fierce and questioning. With a sob, she leaned in and kissed him hard on the lips. She pressed her body into his and he tasted the salt of her tears.

The kiss was so desperate Roen didn't dare push her away, and it stirred confusing feelings in him.

Roen knew he loved Eloryn. He knew it since the morning in his family's old ramshackle home, when she'd charged in, interrupting his father, demanding to know the fate of her guardian. Seeing so much affection and bravery changed something in his heart, and he was hers. He still longed for her, dreamed of her, but he had no hope to ever be with her.

Memory meant so much to him. She was a summer storm, with passion and intensity that awed him and at the same time she was the flower caught within that storm. He would do anything for her.

Memory's lips broke away from Roen's, and she buried her face in his chest. He held her on his lap until she fell asleep, leaving him with nothing but questions.

Memory's whole body ached. She woke slowly, hating the idea of moving, doing anything other than lying still, half-conscious.

She'd gone right off the deep end last night and a dark apathy spread within her. Even opening her eyes was more effort than she liked.

Hope sat on the end of her bed and poked her feet through the blankets. She smiled widely.

Memory pulled one of her pillows over her face and mumbled through it. "What are you happy about?"

"This time I will say it. I told you so. Didn't I say you could have him?"

Memory bolted upright, her heart kicking into life again. *Roen. Frotz.*

"Don't freak out. This is a good thing. Forget about Eloryn, you and Roen can be happy."

Memory's head spun like a killer hangover. Still in her old jeans and t-shirt, she tripped out of bed, her feet getting caught in the sheets. She wobbled to the doors to her sitting room.

"I need some water. I need to think this out."

Swinging the doors open, she saw Roen, looking disheveled in one of her armchairs, his caramel hair falling over his face. Memory cringed and hoped he was asleep but didn't get lucky. He stood up and walked to her, looking her over as if checking for injuries.

"Morning. I thought I heard you talking to someone?" he said.

Memory glanced over her shoulder, her bedroom empty. "Just myself."

They stared at each other, both unmoving.

Roen coughed quietly. "About last night-"

"Assbuckets." Memory covered her face with her hands. "I am so sorry. I was freaking out and not myself and it was just a mistake. I didn't mean it. It didn't mean anything. We can just forget it ever—"

Roen put his arms around Memory, gently pulling her in and kissing her lips over her rambling. Memory froze, stunned, then softened into him. He lingered just a moment before pulling away, his arms running from her shoulders down her arms to hold onto her hands. He stared at their joined hands instead of looking in her eyes.

"If this is what you want, then it is what I want."

"It's what I keep telling myself I want. Maybe I should start listening."

Roen smiled, but somehow it looked sad. "What I was going to say, however, was about last night and the scary magical cracking of walls and flashing out of existence business."

"Oh. That." Memory sat down on a turned over desk. Books and papers littered the floor under her feet. The whole room looked like a tornado hit it. Clara was going to kill her.

"Was that… you?" Roen asked.

Memory nodded. Roen was the closest friend she had at the moment, other than Hope. Maybe she could talk to him. "Things have been happening to me. Some of my memories are coming back, but other bad things are happening too, like the Memory-localized-tremors when I get upset. I'm also kinda slipping through Veil doors without meaning to."

Outrage spread over Roen's face. "You haven't told anyone about this? Mem, you need help and this is far from my field of expertise."

Memory kicked at the papers on the floor. "I wanted to work it out on my own. Promise me you won't tell Lory, okay? She's just too busy right now. I don't want to worry her any more with this."

"Mem," Roen shook his head.

"No, I don't want her to know. I just can't trust her right now, to not freak out I mean, with all the other stress she's under. I'll work this out on my own."

"All right. But you don't need to keep secrets, not from me at least." Roen shrugged and sat on the tipped over desk next to her. He pulled her iron knife from his pocket and handed it to her. "You dropped this last night. I thought you'd purged it."

Memory cradled the knife in her palm. "Yeah, I thought so too. I should probably get rid of it again. Speaking of secrets, do you want

to see something cool?"

"I suppose?"

Memory grinned. "Can you give me some time to clean up and meet up again after lunch?"

Roen gave her a deadpan look. "It's already past midday."

"So I slept in!" Memory pouted. "You were in here all night? I don't think our reputations can take that."

"It's all right. No one saw me come in. I don't know where your guards were, but they are back at your door again now," Roen said.

Memory thought back to her climb to the tower and encounter with Hayes. The guards must have known she wasn't in her room and been looking for her. "Okay, new plan. You hang out until I'm decent again, then I'll leave first and draw the stooges off. You can get out when the coast is clear. Then we'll go and get rid of this nasty iron again."

Memory stood up, wafting her t-shirt and longing to get into clean clothes. Roen grabbed her hand and pulled her back to him, kissing her temple. He frowned as he looked at her.

"Last night, it wasn't a mistake, at all, but we should still keep this between ourselves. There's just too much politics involved. You understand, right?"

"Yeah. Of course."

Memory slipped into her bedroom and closed the door between them. She took a deep breath to steady herself.

The kisses made her feel wanted, warm and real. Alive again. But Memory kept spiraling to the same black thought. *He doesn't really want me. He's just taking the look-a-like runner-up prize.*

Hope's voice came from over her shoulder, whispering, echoing her thoughts. "He just doesn't want precious Eloryn to find out and be upset. If you don't do something, you'll always be second to her."

Memory wore the dress Isabeth gave her, since it had managed the journey well last time. Her bodyguards followed close behind when she left her chambers, and Memory realized her own escape would be trickier than Roen's. She strolled the halls as boringly as possible, hoping they'd leave her be, but they remained diligent. Trying a new tactic, she took a seat and hitched her skirts up to sit cross-legged. When they turned away as they had before, Memory jumped back up and slipped unseen into the servant runs.

Roen waited there for her, and met her with a light kiss on her cheek.

Memory put her finger to her lips and motioned for Roen to follow her. She ran her hand along the stone wall in the narrow tunnel until she felt the waxy lump of her candle stub that she'd left as a marker. Feeling for the door, she tugged and it swung open. Roen followed her in, and when the door closed, she lit a candle for both of them.

"I thought you could cast the light spell now?"

Memory patted the purse at her side. "Not with my knife on me. And for other reasons, you'll see."

"What is this place?" he asked.

Memory led the way, skipping down the stone steps. "Something Will and me found. I don't know if anyone else knows about it. Just wait till we get to the bottom."

The permanently damp state of the tunnel made the steps

slippery and Memory's foot skidded. Roen caught her hand and held it tight. "Slow down, you'll fall and break your neck."

Memory blew a raspberry back at him, but kept holding his hand. It made her feel strange, both comfortable and wrong, adding to the reckless emotions that had grown inside her. Like there was a voice telling her to break rules and take risks and that didn't care about the consequences. *What does it matter if I'm not even a whole person?*

Roen lifted their joined hands and held his candle near to look at her wrist.

"What is that hideous thing you're wearing?"

"It's not hideous! It's cute." Memory defended the bracelet of splintery, chunky, wooden beads she wore.

"I'm a little worried about your taste now. You don't consider me cute, do you?"

"Not at all. If I had to describe you, pretty is the word I'd pick. And this *is* cute," Memory said, shaking her wrist and making it rattle. "Little Edele gave it to me last time I visited the orphans in town, just before the bombing. She made it herself. I can't wait to get back into town and see them all again."

Roen laughed softly. "That's really sweet. I'm not surprised they like you so much."

Memory smiled wryly. "Yeah, it's because I hand out cash."

Roen laughed and squeezed her hand, but Memory didn't feel like she was joking. It felt like there was always some reason that people liked her that wasn't anything to do with who she really was.

They walked in silence until they reached the bottom of the tunnels. With a grand flourish of her arms Memory showed Roen the stacked crates and artifacts.

Roen let go of her hand and lifted the lids of a couple of boxes. "This is all…"

"Iron, yep. A dirty little secret under the capital of Avall. I figure some items missed the Purge and they've been collected here, but I haven't found any official records or acknowledgements of anyone doing that. Will says the fairies have avoided these tunnels since the days of the Pact, so it must have been happening a long time."

Roen ran his hand over the crates. "Have you told anyone about this? Have you told Eloryn?"

"No, if I tell her, she'll tell Hayes, and the Council will be all over it. I think this place is secret for a reason." Memory took her knife and added it to the collection again. "Hey, do you think you can find your own way back? I'm not ready to go just yet. Being down here helps to shake a few memories free."

"I can stay with you if you like."

Memory stared out over the glittering black water that seemed to go forever. "No, I'd like to be alone."

Roen frowned, but nodded. He paused, then kissed her forehead and walked away.

Memory sat down on a wooden crate and played with a dented spearhead with a hole in its base. She wondered if any other memories would come to her, or how long it might take, when warmth rushed through her.

The frail boy stood in front of her, a tiny soldier at attention. Unrecognizable otherwise, his wide blue eyes told her it was Will. The children were never officially informed of how others ended up in the home, but the gossip always managed to get around. She heard that this kid lost his parents and rest of his close relatives in a landslide while they were all on a family vacation together. He was the only one to survive. Some kids said he was stuck under rubble with dead bodies for days before he was dug out. Maybe that was why he was so scrawny.

It had been a week since she'd stepped in and stopped some of the kids beating on him. It wasn't the first time he'd been in fights. It was his fault, taking arty classes and reading books in public. The kid had no survival instincts. She'd ignored it like she ignored what happened to everyone else, but that time the bullies went too far, drawing blood, so she drew a bit of their blood back and warned them off the boy.

He'd been trailing at her heels ever since, saying she'd saved his life, that he owed her.

She tried to shake him off, but as much as she hated to admit it, she liked having him around. Her little minion. He did anything she asked.

Will stood silent, waiting for her to speak.

"Okay, kid," Memory said. "If you're going to keep following me about, then we need to establish some ground rules."

Will nodded. She leaned in close to him, staring him right in the eyes, almost cruelly.

"First rule – no touching. Break that rule and I break your wrists."

He nodded again.

"Second rule – That thing that happens? No talking about it. Ever. Nothing happens. So there's nothing to talk about."

"Third rule–"

Memory found her face wet, tears spilling down her cheeks. Will still followed her rules. Stupid rules from so long ago. And what had she done for him?

She had to find him. She had to apologize. Again.

Memory took the other exit from the tunnels and ventured up through the dried-up well and into the hunting grounds.

The late afternoon sun was a rich orange tone, shafts of light shining through the last few blood-red leaves clinging to branches above. Memory called Will's name, and a flock of birds startled and flew from a tree nearby, up into the golden sky.

But Will didn't come.

She wandered farther into the forest, meandering slowly, watching her footing for pesky toadstools. She called his name again, and he didn't come.

The forest grew dark and Memory came to a small pool, lush with ferns and water lilies, the flowers all closed for the night. Her eyes felt sticky from her earlier tears, so she wet her hands and wiped her face. When she stood up from the water's edge, Mina appeared in front of her.

Memory had never been so close to Mina before. The sprite hovered just above the water, her pointed toes occasionally dipping in and causing ripples. There was an almost faded quality to the way that she looked, translucent and glowing like milky glass lit from behind. Her flame red hair, the one splash of color on her, lifted and swirled around a pretty face marred by a scowl.

"Stop looking for him," Mina ordered.

"Why? Doesn't he want to see me?"

"You can't be with him. He doesn't belong to you." Mina flew up closer to Memory, bobbing from side to side. Her wings, like tattered dragonfly wings, fluttered and shimmered.

"Listen, lady, I know Will doesn't belong to me. I'm not trying to take your boyfriend off you. I'm just trying to find him to talk to him."

"No. I said you can't be with him!"

Mina lashed out, swiping at her, scratching her arm, tearing through cloth and skin. Memory recoiled in pain and shock. "You did not just do that!"

Mina hissed, "Stay away from my boy."

Before Memory could respond, Mina vanished.

Memory touched her arm. She was bleeding. The pattern of the scratches was familiar, similar to the ones on Will's chest the last time she saw him. An angry worry filled Memory. She thought Will actually

liked Mina, that they were together with whatever mutual emotions that involved, but now she was concerned. *Just what kind of relationship do they have?*

Whatever it was, it was Memory's fault. It was her fault he was here at all. If only she could send him home, back to the other world. She'd tried for Thayl and couldn't, but there must be a way. She just had to try harder, learn more. She hadn't even asked Will what he wanted. She shook her head. *Of course he wants to go home.*

Memory dropped to the mossy ground with a thud. "I have to make this right," she said aloud.

Hope squatted down next to her, plucking leaves off a fern stem. In the darkness of the forest, the bright pink heart on her t-shirt seemed to glow.

"Did you see that?" Memory asked her, fuming.

"Jealous fairy attack? Yeah. All the more reason to keep away from that lot."

Memory groaned and threw a pebble into the pond. "There's got to be a way to get home. To help Will go home, away from that she-beast."

Hope dropped the fern and put her hands on Memory's knees, looking into her eyes. "You're not thinking of going back too, are you? You can't. You have to stay here with me. You don't remember what it was like there."

"No. But Will deserves a chance to choose." Moisture had started wicking through Memory's dress from the damp ground, chilling her. She stood up, feeling like she should go back to the castle, but not really wanting to. "I guess I don't really have any home. There, here, nothing feels right anymore."

"You can make here work. I'm here with you, and if you were queen everything would be better. You wouldn't have to be second to

Eloryn anymore. You'd have the power to make everything how you wanted it."

"It wouldn't give me the power to help Will. Are all fairies so horrible? And Mina is a seelie fae. I thought they were the good guys." Memory's breathing became ragged. The encounter had upset her more than she knew why. "I don't like the idea of Will being around her."

"From what I've seen, all the fae are nasty, untrustworthy and better off extinct." Hope stood up and looked in the direction of the old well. "I don't think you should have gotten rid of your knife."

CHAPTER FIFTEEN

At Memory's instruction, the chef placed the top of the bun on the stack of food. She picked up one of the creations and took a bite.

"It's close, but still missing something. Probably the special sauce."

Memory had woken up that morning craving something she hadn't remembered until now. A burger. She'd come with Clara to the kitchens and commandeered one of the chefs to help with the process, and they ended up with a large tray full of burgers. Apparently making just one of something wasn't the way they worked in here.

A small creature crept up the edge of the marble-topped bench. It looked like it was made of twigs and had huge aqua blue cat eyes. It made a grab for some leftover mince.

The chef shooed it away. "Cheeky boggart."

The kitchens were hot and busy, filled with gusts of smoke and steam, sizzles and clanging pots. Memory's bodyguards remained outside, unable to fit into the chaos, which made the experience more enjoyable for her. She sat up on the kitchen bench overseeing the chef's work and Clara leant next to her. They'd taken over a small worksite, but the rest of the kitchen still bustled with staff preparing meals for an entire castle of nobles, servants, and guards. Even the pets had meals prepared here, Memory learned, when she questioned where a plate of raw meat was being taken and learned it was for the falcons in the mews. *Mews*, thought Memory. *Sounds like something a cat does, not a house for birds.*

Although Memory had managed to find most of the necessary ingredients for her burgers, the cheese wasn't the same sort of rubbery processed slice she remembered, the ketchup was fresh and chunky, and the bread was heartier and crustier than the sponge soft bun she wanted.

Clara took a bite of one. "I think they're brilliant. These are sure to become popular in Avall. I'm going to see that my favorite tavern starts serving these. If I tell them the princess invented them they will have no hesitation adding them to the menu."

"That would look great in the history books. Princess Memory Maellan, Inventor of Hamburgers." Memory smiled as she chewed her burger. It wasn't how she remembered them, just close enough to tease her senses.

A large man approached through a gust of steam, kitchen workers scurrying out of the way of his imposing presence. His suit was black and purple. Memory smiled when she saw who it was.

Bedevere stopped in front of Memory and bowed. "Your Highness, I was told I would find you here. I'm sorry to disturb your

meal." He held out a folded piece of paper, without seal or envelope.

"No probs. Is that for me?" Memory wiped her hands on her apron. It had been forced on her by Clara and seeing the sauce smear she'd just made across it she was thankful she hadn't just done that to her ice-blue dress.

"Yes. From my late brother." Bedevere kept his usual steadfast expression, but Memory could see that Waylan's death was still too fresh for him, just as it was for her. "I discovered it on his desk. It was addressed to you, but he hadn't yet sealed it before his untimely death."

Bedevere looked at the row of burgers with interest. "What are these?"

Memory lifted the tray for him. "Something from the other world. Try one."

"Then there will be less for me," Clara said with a playful sad tone.

"No way you could eat that many," Memory scoffed.

"True indeed. That is something you would do." Clara poked Memory's stomach. "Councilor Bedevere, ignore my poor humor. Do try one. They are delicious."

Bedevere, who had been holding a key in his free hand, placed it down on the kitchen bench next to Memory.

"I will take that offer indeed." He reached for a knife and fork.

"That's not how you eat a burger. This is how you eat a burger," Memory said, and demonstrated grabbing a burger in both hands and stuffing it into her mouth. Juices ran down her wrist.

Bedevere raised an eyebrow, but picked a burger up as directed. He didn't begin eating right away. "It is nice to be away from the meeting chambers for an intermission. So much organization still to do for security concerns. The Council fails to agree upon a proper magical security system for the Council's most important works. We're storing such important books and documents in an archaic safe room that uses mundane keys of all things. Very primitive, if you ask me. The only failsafe is that the door requires two keys."

He glanced at Memory with a serious expression then took a bite of the burger. As he chewed, Memory thought she almost saw him crack a smile before his normal dour expression returned. "Yes, delicious. Since the fae ceased bringing imports of food and technology into Avall over a century ago, I fear there must be much we are missing out on. If you don't believe, as most do, the reason they ceased importing was the complete fall of the rest of the world into Hell. At some point, your highness, I'd be appreciative of your co-operation in mapping and comparing timelines, from what you may remember, of course."

Bedevere placed the burger back on the plate, having only eaten one mouthful, and gave Memory another swift bow. "I had better be back to work. Thank you for sharing some of the other world with me. I hope to learn more from you soon."

Bedevere's gaze dropped for a split second to the key beside Memory then back to meet her gaze before he nodded and left.

Understanding the message but not entirely sure why, Memory tucked his key into the palm of her hand before anyone else noticed it.

"What an odd gentleman," Clara said.

"Yeah." Memory looked at the letter he'd given her. For her from Waylan, not long before he was killed. She looked up at the ceiling until her eyes stopped watering.

"Are you having any more of these? I'd like to take the rest to some friends around the palace," Clara asked. Memory took the one she'd already started off the tray then shook her head. Clara took the tray and left.

Memory opened the letter and read while eating the rest of her burger.

The letter was, as Bedevere had said, addressed to her. It explained that Alward's magic books, which had been prohibited from going to Eloryn under the grounds of them being Council property, had already been catalogued and dispersed into the Wizard Council's library. However, the filing of Alward's personal research had been delayed due to short staffing and the time it was taking to catalogue the rambling studies. It had fallen to Waylan to catalogue the work, and while examining the notes he realized much of it was pertinent to Memory. Waylan noted that he had set these papers aside in the storage safe, out of the way on the back table beside other unsorted documents. In the letter he expressed that he believed these studies should belong to Memory and that he would be lobbying the Council to release them.

Then he died before he could.

Memory took a deep breath, a small smile shaking onto her mouth. She realized Bedevere had read the letter before handing it to her. His dead brother's intent was for her to have Alward's research, and Bedevere had left her with information on their security and a key to the safe they were kept.

Memory didn't need to think too much about stealing the documents. In her mind they belonged to Eloryn, and if there was anything in them to help her understand her magic better, then she needed them. She just had to get another key.

Her first thought was of Roen, but asking him to help her steal seemed cruel, given the way he felt about his past. She'd just have to wait for another opportunity.

The window seat in the library was piled in soft pillows and lush upholstery, and made the perfect refuge from the gray weather surrounding the palace. It was becoming one of Memory's favorite places, and the sound of rain on the glass helped keep her calm when thoughts confused her and emotions became dark and volatile, as they did too frequently these days.

She had just wriggled into a comfortable position when Eloryn approached. Her ever-present guard duty kept a distance, planting themselves like suits of armor along the walls.

"Might I join you?" Eloryn's voice wavered. Memory hadn't seen her sister since their argument the last time here at the window seat. She looked perfect as ever, and Memory wondered how her hair always looked so stunning. Rivers of jealousy inducing pale gold. *Does she say her magic words to it and make it do what she wants? Seems like cheating, but then, who'd want a hair straightener when you have magic?*

"You're reading the book I gave you?" Eloryn asked, sounding even more nervous and making Memory realize she hadn't replied.

Memory had the Avall history book balanced on her lap. She offered her sister a small smile. "It's pretty good actually." She tilted her head to the vacant opposite end of the window seat. Eloryn sat down with a look of relief.

Eloryn clutched a couple of books against her chest, but didn't immediately start reading any. Memory wondered if they were for study, or for an excuse. She smiled a little more. She regretted the words she'd said to Eloryn when they'd fought. Memory wasn't

entirely sure what to think about Eloryn right now, but could tell Eloryn was trying to mend their relationship. Memory decided to try as well.

"This book has taught me a lot. Also, the pictures are really pretty." Memory demonstrated by flicking to a portrait of a white-haired wizard, surrounded by archaic chemistry equipment.

Eloryn leaned forward a little and smiled "Lauphmer the Wise, one of the most powerful wizards of Avall history. It always was one of my favorite books of Alward's collection when growing up."

Memory ran a hand down the slightly worn but well cared for binding. "This was one of Alward's books? I didn't realize. Are you sure it's okay for me to have?"

"Of course, that's why I gave it to you."

Memory couldn't look her sister in the face. She'd been so ungrateful when she'd first received the book as a present. She stared at the illustration instead. Something caught her eye, and she frowned in recognition.

"Just how accurate would you say these pictures are?" she asked.

"Quite. Most are portraits the wizards would have sat for personally."

In the portrait, a small object hung from a chain about the wizard's neck. An arrowhead, the same she'd seen in the iron stash beneath the castle.

Memory started flicking through pages, back to other portraits, examining them.

Eloryn moved closer to see what she was looking at. Memory poked the page hard, pointing to another powerful wizard from Avall history who sat beside the hoe she'd also seen in the stash.

"This is iron."

She flicked back to Lauphmer and pointed out the arrowhead.

"This too."

Something twigged in Memory's head and she turned the book right to the front.

"And, of course…"

Arthur with Caliburn.

"Mem, how do you know? They could be silver, or bronze. Caliburn is the only cold iron artifact."

Memory shook her head and chewed her fingers. "No. No, this makes sense. Is it possible?"

"I'm afraid you've lost me," Eloryn said with a confused giggle.

"All these great wizards with their iron tidbits. Me with my magic and my knife. That's not a coincidence."

"If indeed these wizards did carry cold iron, which I doubt they would have as there should be no iron in Avall."

Memory looked up from staring at the illustration of Arthur. "Why do they call it *cold* iron? It always feels warm to me. Doesn't it feel warm to you?"

"That's what the fae call it — cold iron. And yes, the one time I have held your knife it did warm me. In fact it relit my Spark of Connection after it had been shut down." Eloryn bit her lip, staring intently at Memory, her eyes and eyebrows twitching with thought and the edge of a smile on her lips. "It's only forged iron that harms the fae. Raw iron is like a conductor of magic, of life, in our blood and the composition of our earth. What if when iron is worked by man, it somehow becomes affiliated to man, and becomes a magnet for magic?"

Memory's eyes grew wide. "Drawing magic into humans?"

Eloryn nodded in return. "And out of the fae. Magic is their life force. And if forged iron also steals that from them, that's why it hurts them."

"So I've had my knife for who knows how long, just soaking up all this magic?"

Eloryn's eyes sparkled as she paused to think. "For at least sixteen years within the Veil. That we know."

Memory smiled, enjoying bouncing ideas back and forth. They were getting somewhere, assuming they were right, and Memory was happy to assume.

"And that's why my magic's all messed up. I'm not accessing magic like others by using the Spark of Connection. I just use the magic within me that I'm full of." *A vessel too full, ready to spill and spoil everything.* Memory scowled. *The damn fairies already knew.* "What if it wasn't just my knife? There might be more iron in the rest of the world. Why wasn't everyone over there all magicked up? Will said there was no magic there."

"No Spark of Connection. Maybe you need that, to attract the magic into you through the iron, like calling to like." Eloryn looked away for a moment then back to Memory. She'd grown serious. "If this is the case, it explains the ritual. Thayl sent you to the otherworld, to build up all that power, so he could steal it and use it for himself. That's why he had to twist time to find you when you were sixteen, when you'd had those years to absorb so much power."

The air huffed out of Memory and she stared out the window. The rain splashed onto the roses, knocking loose petals to the ground. "It was never about me. I was just a tool, a battery to charge up and steal the power from. And with the magic, my memories." *My soul.* "Why? Why did I lose them too?"

It was Eloryn's turn to shrug.

Memory kept pondering out loud. "What if it all just gets jumbled up together?" *Like Hope, created from my magic and memories and soul all messed up.* "When he took all that magic out of me, it took everything else? Then why don't I lose memories now when I use my magic?" Memory clutched the book on her lap, pulling it up like a shield. "What if I am and I just don't know it?"

Eloryn shifted closer to her, putting a hand on Memory's knee. "If Thayl took nearly everything you had, we could surmise all the magic you have now was channeled into you while you were within the Veil, when you formed no new memories for the magic to become attached to. But I'd have to say it might be best to be careful when and for what reasons you use your magic, just in case. As you form new memories now, we aren't to know the magic within you won't become tangled with those, and be lost as you expend it."

Memory put her head back into the pile of pillows with a prolonged groan. "Yeah, like I can control when and for what reasons my magic splurts out. You've got so much control and power. You can ask anything of anything and just, bam, done. My magic is more bam, HAHAHA DID SOMETHING YOU WEREN'T EXPECTING LOLZ."

Eloryn blushed. It was all too easy to make her blush. "It's not really that powerful. I can talk to animals or speed up natural processes, but not a lot more. To be honest, the most exciting thing I ever did was have some wood rot and break under a guard's foot when fighting Thayl."

"But that's cool. That was being creative. I bet if you thought about it, you'd have the power to do almost anything if you're creative with it. Like doing your hair." Memory eye-balled Eloryn but didn't get a reaction to prove her suspicions so she continued. "Me and Thayl, we're just human-shaped blaster-guns. Okay smart girl, here's one for you. How come Thayl didn't run out of magic after all those years blasting stuff?"

Eloryn looked like a kid who finished her exam before everyone

else. "The basic rule. Like calls to like. Having that much magic within may have made him a powerful magnet for more. The growth would be exponential, almost uncontrollable at times."

I know that feeling. All the information swirled in Memory's head, picking up more and more details as it went, a tornado sweeping up debris. Each time she'd had a memory come back to her she'd been near iron or holding iron. If her magic and memories were out in the world, lost when she cut off Thayl's hand, tangled together still, maybe some were coming back into her through the iron? *But aren't they in Hope now? Or is Hope just made from my soul?* Memory's theories started colliding and getting confused, and she started to lose confidence in them.

Eloryn sighed and half smiled. "But this is all really just theory, based on your wild notion that those items were all iron."

Memory opened her mouth and almost told Eloryn everything, but something held her back. Not quite her own voice, the voice of Hope, warning and whispering. She'd gotten so caught up exchanging ideas with Eloryn, but even now what was Eloryn doing? Telling her not to use her magic.

She closed the book and stood up, the desire to leave taking her. "I guess we all believe what works best for us, right?"

Eloryn stood up right after her. "We have made a start though. The theories are promising. I swore to you once I would help get your memories back, and I still wish to uphold that. But only if it is what you still want."

"Of course it's what I want," Memory snapped. She rubbed the bridge of her nose and looked away. Eloryn genuinely seemed to want to help, but Memory's defenses had gone back up. She felt like a wild dog, at once ready to snarl and attack and yet desperately wanting affection, unsure which direction to run. "Is it what you want? Do you even want me to get my memories back?"

"If I had the power I'd have done so already, I would give you back everything that was taken from you."

Memory's eyes narrowed, and she walked away without another word. *Everything that was taken from me. Everything... She knows. She does know my soul is broken.*

CHAPTER SIXTEEN

When Roen opened his door, his hair was tussled like he'd just woken up. He squinted at Memory and tugged a shirt on.

"Did I wake you up?" she said.

Roen panted like he'd run to the door. "What's happened? Are you all right?"

"I just came to ask a favor."

Roen winced, looked into his room and back at Memory. "At two in the morning?"

"What? Really? Sorry, I haven't been sleeping much lately. I didn't realize." Memory wondered if that was why all the bodyguards that followed her down from her chambers were looking so amused. *They could have said something.* She glared back at them where they stood out of earshot down the hall.

Roen shook his head and chuckled. "I thought there was some danger, or, at the very least, hoped for a more entertaining night call."

Memory stuck her tongue out at him. The joke made her feel awkward, but the favor she was about to ask felt even worse. She'd decided to ask for Roen's help to steal after all since she'd made no progress on the heist on her own. With her recent breakthroughs about her magic, she needed to know more and felt Alward's notes might hold more clues.

Memory took a deep breath and spilled out all her words with the next. "I want to get Alward's notes off the Wizard's Council, but to do it I need two keys and two people to turn the keys, and I have one key but still need to get another one and I'm just not as good at that stuff, you know, as you are."

Roen frowned as he buttoned up his shirt. "Alward's notes? They're important to Eloryn aren't they?"

"Well yes, and to me. A lot of the research was about trying to find me through the Veil. I'd try and get it myself, but I haven't seen the inside of the safe room, so I can't Veil door in, and if I try and use my magic some other way I'd probably just blow everything up. I know it's asking a lot from you, and I didn't want to—"

"I'll do it, Mem," he said, cutting her off with a warm smile. "For you."

Memory nodded, looking at her feet. *For me, or for her?*

"I've got a plan and it shouldn't be difficult. But, um, maybe I'll tell it to you when it's not two in the morning?"

"I wouldn't mind, if you wanted to come in." Roen opened his door a little more.

To hear my plan, or…

Roen's shirt was still only half buttoned, his hair mussed, and a

sleepy smile on his lips. The whole look was undeniably sexy, and a flush of warmth ran down Memory's back. Even if it started with planning, she didn't think it would end there.

Memory gave herself a mental cold shower and pointed with a thumb at the guards watching from down the hall. "The walls have ears, and eyes, and great big gossipy mouths."

"Your faithful protectors. I didn't see them down there." Roen nodded solemnly. Then a smirk cracked the expression and he grabbed Memory around the waist and pulled her two steps back into his room. Out of sight of the guards, he bent and gave her a long kiss on the corner of her lips, then let her go again.

"Sweet dreams, princess," he said, and smiling cheekily, closed the door between them.

Memory touched the place he kissed her with her fingertips. *He always used to call Eloryn 'princess.'* Even without the risk of a scandal, Memory wasn't sure she'd have gone in. She wasn't sure what she wanted at all.

Late in the evening Memory left her quarters, telling her bodyguards that she wanted to go to the kitchens again for another culinary experiment.

"I'm going to cook up some doughnuts even if it takes me all night."

Memory strolled into the hazy, clanging kitchens and frowned when one of her guards followed her in. A chef soon chased him back out again to wait at the entrance as he had last time. Memory

smiled wickedly.

Dodging the cooks and kitchen hands, she made her way into one of the larger pantries and pulled the door closed behind her. On a shelf lay her boy's clothes, delivered there earlier by Clara. Memory quickly wriggled out of her night gown and tailored robe and dressed in her Tristan disguise.

Memory stepped back out and grabbed a cupcake decorated in delicate sugar roses. She winked at one of the chefs who watched her, the one who'd helped her make burgers. He winked back in return and went on with his work. A couple of servants were leaving with silver trays of food and Memory slipped out of the kitchens with them, straight past her bodyguards who didn't look at her twice.

The plan is rocking so far.

Memory had to resist the urge to skip, she felt so free. It was the first time for a while she wasn't being trailed by burly soldiers. But skipping while dressed as a boy would probably draw too much attention.

When she reached the meeting point, Roen was there waiting for her.

He held up his hand, dangling a key on display.

Memory high-fived him. "Nice work. I hope it wasn't too hard to get."

"For me? It was a piece of cake." Roen said, ducking past Memory and revealing her half-eaten cupcake stolen in his hands. She grabbed for it, but he popped it in his mouth.

Memory smiled, relieved Roen was in a good mood. She always thought his skills were something to be proud of. Maybe he didn't mind so much anymore.

"The hardest part is next though. The old safe room is at the top of the western tower, but there's a guard at the bottom of the stairs."

Memory pointed with her thumb around the corner to the arched doorway down the hall, blocked by its sentinel.

Roen looked quickly. "I could probably sneak through while he's looking the other way. But getting us both through without a distraction could be difficult."

Memory put a finger on her chin, pretending to think. "A distraction you say?"

Giggling fluttered down the hall to them, and they both peeked around the corner again. Clara leaned against the wall next to the guard. The maid's uniform she wore was a size smaller than usual and the guard leaned in toward her. He stepped out of the doorway, sliding an arm around her waist.

Memory whispered dramatically, "The dove has taken position! Go, go, go!"

She dashed down the hallway, keeping as quiet as she could. She grimaced whenever her feet hit the ground, still sounding so loud. She expected the guard to hear her at any moment and started to reconsider her tactic. Memory couldn't even hear Roen behind her and was worried he hadn't followed when she made a run for it.

Roen's hands wrapped around Memory's waist and lifted her. She silently squealed. Carrying her, Roen slipped passed the guard without a sound. He put her down just up the stairs, out of sight around the spiraling column.

Standing a step up from him, they were nose to nose. Her heart raced and her face felt flushed.

Roen lifted his chin and looked up the stairwell. Memory nodded and they continued to the top. A small antechamber opened up, revealing a massive door of solid metal, bronze banding and studs reinforcing its strength. To each side, further apart than a normal human could reach, were two keyholes.

Memory pulled Bedevere's key from her pocket and Roen took his, and they turned them in the lock simultaneously.

Gears clicked and rolled, and with a push, the door swung open. The room was small, just enough to fit a couple of tight rows of bookshelves and tables which overflowed with badly sorted and stacked volumes.

Memory punched the air with a silent woot. "That all went surprisingly easily! Let's grab these notes and get back out before that poor guard proposes to Clara and has his heart broken."

Roen pushed the door closed until it was just slightly ajar. He threw Memory the second key, and she pocketed them together, then they went seeking Alward's documents where Waylan's letter had said he left them.

"Which ones are they?" Roen asked, stepping over stacks of books on the ground. The room smelled of powdery paper.

Memory had made her way to the back and stared dumbfounded at the table there. *Papers*, Waylan had called them. *Notes*. What she had imagined as a journal or two to snatch and run with turned out to be crates full of hand-bound tomes stacked one atop another amid mountains of loose leaf parchment and scrolls.

Memory blew out a sigh. "We might have a problem."

"They can't all be his, surely," Roen suggested, whispering.

Memory checked through some of the unsorted papers and books that were strewn amongst the more regimented ones. All had the same handwriting, the same topics, same style to the scratchy diagrams. Sixteen years' worth of research.

He must have been trying so hard to get me back. Memory felt guilty about assuming there would be so little.

Memory kicked the table leg. "We're screwed! We can't exactly do multiple trips to carry all this out."

"I'm sorry. I know this was important to you." Roen moved next to her and put his hand on her shoulder. "Could we remove it all some other way? Could you use a Veil door?"

Memory twitched, the thought of using her magic giving her goosebumps. She wasn't sure whether this research would have any of the information she really needed, but if it did, it was worth the try. She had to, for her, and for Will.

"You'll have to do the heavy lifting, Roen. I need to concentrate." Memory imagined her own chambers, and pinched the fabric of reality with her fingers, opening a door through the Veil. "I'll keep it open. You take everything through."

Roen nodded and moved fast, loading up an armful of books and carrying them through. Even this way, only moving the books a few steps, it would take a lot of trips.

As Roen went back and forth through the door, he took a moment to catch his breath and balance. He started to look gray from the effects of the Veil. The books weren't so much placed as dropped onto the floor in Memory's living room.

Memory focused on keeping the door open and tried to shuffle the remaining books around on the desk to hide what had been taken.

Roen gathered up the last few books when they heard men's voices on the stairwell.

"I hear movement. Someone is in there," one man cried.

Roen froze, a look of terror on his face. Memory looked from him to the door as the footsteps grew closer. The agitation in the approaching voices was clear. Memory and Roen were going to be caught. They could both go through the Veil door, but then there would be no answer to what had occurred there. There might be an investigation, and the Wizards had magical ways of finding out who did what and where. Memory had dragged Roen into this, and the prospect of being caught here, stealing, had left him looking shattered.

Memory charged him, pushing him through the Veil door into her room. She let the door close between them. Grabbing the nearest book, she hopped up onto the desk and shook herself into a casual expression just as Hayes burst in, followed by Bedevere and another Councilor.

"And here we have our culprit," Hayes declared.

Memory looked up from the book she pretended to read. "What brings you all up here? I was just doing bit of light reading, myself."

Hayes marched up to her. "Madoc here discovered his key missing, and when we checked around it turned out Bedevere's had also gone astray. And here we discover – 'Tristan,' is it? – at the scene of the crime."

Hayes pulled her cap off her head, throwing it to the floor. Her blonde hair that had been tucked up in it tumbled down around her face. Memory jerked back away from him and sneered.

"If I weren't locked away in the castle, if you actually let me go to school, and I mean *real* school, with magic classes, maybe I wouldn't have to sneak around to read this stuff myself. Or dress as a boy."

"Nothing excuses your outrageous behavior. I thought you'd been keeping your nose clean, and then you pull this stunt? How on earth did you manage to acquire the keys?"

Memory looked at Madoc, red faced and seething, and then to Bedevere who watched the proceedings with the same lack of expression he always showed. He met her eye, and she was surprised by a tenderness there that seemed to invite her to give him up.

Memory stood up and reached for Hayes's ear. "You mean this key?"

She made a show of pulling a key from his ear, then reached with her other hand to his other ear and pulled out the second key. "Or this key?"

Hayes swiped his walking cane across her arms, knocking the keys from her hands. Madoc skittered forward and chased after them, picking them up.

"Childish games. You have broken the law, and we must administer a suitable punishment. *Tristan* will be expelled from lessons. When you return to school, you return as Memory only. You need to understand that acting out like this is no way to get what you want."

No more Tristan? Memory had only used the excuse of needing to attend magic lessons as a boy to cover up what she'd really been doing. But to have that taken away from her hit her hard. She leaned back against the desk, needing its support.

"But I need to go to magic class. I need to learn more," she said, her head shaking side to side.

"To do what? Cause even more trouble than you currently do by adding magic into the mix?" Hayes scoffed.

In just one class with Waylan, so much understanding had opened up in Memory. She had been looking forward to little else like she had returning to magic class, even without Waylan teaching. She couldn't lose that. She just couldn't. She had to do something.

"I have to because I'm scared." Memory let all defenses drop. She addressed Hayes, but then turned to Bedevere, finding his calm gaze more comforting. "I'm losing control, of whatever is happening within me. I've Veil doored without meaning to. I'm worried about what else could happen. I need to learn about this stuff."

Bedevere's expression changed ever so slightly, a bend of the eyebrows, a softening of the eyes.

Hayes spoke first. "If you would just let us examine you as requested—"

Bedevere spoke over him, his deep voice easily covering Hayes's.

"How about this: rather than attending classes with the male students, which is of course unseemly for a girl of the royal family, I can offer to privately teach the princess. As a tutor."

Memory stood up straight again, leaning forward hopefully. "You'd really do that for me?"

Bedevere grunted softly. "I can probably work my schedule around to find the time."

Memory tried hard to act chastised still and not let loose a toothy grin. She looked to Hayes for approval.

"Fine, so be it. If Bedevere has time to waste on such pursuits, he is free to do so. But this leniency is on the understanding that there will be no further incidents from you. If you step wrong again, a much more dire punishment will need to be found."

Memory jogged briskly all the way back to her chambers. Running in, she found Roen still there, biting his thumbnail and pacing back and forth around the stack of Alward's research. When he saw her he stopped short then strode up to her, grabbing her hands tight. "Are you all right? Why did you do something so foolish?"

Memory rolled her eyes and smiled. "I'm fine. A little slap on the wrist was all. And I threw them off the scent. I doubt they even noticed this stuff was gone or that I had an accomplice."

"I can't believe you took the blame like that. If I were found, if…" Roen's words stuttered away to nothing.

Memory could see it on his face. It would kill him. It almost did in the past. He was more willing to be hung than be known as a thief.

I was stupid for asking him to help me with this, thinking he'd be okay with it.

"Forget about it. Tristan took the brunt of it, but things worked out okay. And hey, check out our haul," Memory said.

Roen didn't turn to look. He stared at Memory intensely and bent in to kiss her lips.

Memory shied away and cleared her throat.

Roen remained still, his cheek beside hers. "Thank you," he whispered.

Memory slid her hands free of his and crouched down beside the sprawling papers, beginning work sorting and stacking them. She remembered sitting surrounded by books in Eloryn's room, holding her sister as she wept from the pain of missing her guardian, wishing for something so small as to just see his handwriting again.

These belong to her, Memory thought. *Just like Roen does, and I'm taking both from her.*

"Change of plan," Memory said, standing back up. "Let's give these to Lory. Don't you think she'll like them?"

Roen just nodded, staring at Memory. She stared back and an awkwardness rose.

"I know you like her," Memory blurted. "I mean, I know you like her more than me. And that's okay. This thing, you and me, I'm not so sure it's working."

Roen's lips moved into a very small smile. "To be honest, I'm not sure either. It was nice, to try, but I would not risk our friendship by forcing something that doesn't want to grow. I love you, Memory. You are the best friend I've ever had, and could I have anyone as a sister, it would be you."

"Or brother, right?" Memory joked, waving at her clothing.

Roen chuckled and gave her a tight hug. "You're truly something special."

"Just not quite as special as Lory?" she said into his shoulder.

Roen pushed her away again and dipped his head a little to look seriously into her eyes. "You and El, for all your similarities, are very different. Don't forget that."

"I know. It's just difficult with her being so perfect all the damn time," Memory admitted.

"That she is. Unobtainably perfect. I want to be better for her, to deserve her, but whenever I try to act up it makes me feel worse." Roen moved back and looked down at their steal. He bent to start clearing it up, but Memory waved him away.

"Leave it. I'll deal with it all in the morning." Memory took Roen's hand and led him from the room. She paused at the door and gave him a stern look. "Roen, take my advice. Just be yourself around her. Your flirtatious, sexy self."

Roen smiled back but his brow was furrowed. "And what if she doesn't like that me?"

"Terrifying, isn't it?" Memory grinned wryly as she let him out the door. "Maybe it's not best to take any of my advice. I wouldn't know how to be myself if I tried. But it's important to be loved for who you really are, right?"

CHAPTER SEVENTEEN

Eloryn sat on a garden bench in the center of the rose garden. Entering her office for the day had caused an abrupt anxiety attack, so she made an excuse that she wanted to spend some time outside and would do her work there instead. A wooden desk and a lacy white canopy had been carried out by servants, and she flipped through her paperwork in the wan sunlight. With a sigh she noted that it was the job itself she wished to escape, not just the office.

She focused on her surroundings and a small wistful smile grew on her lips. Pebbled pathways ran between neat rows of well cared for roses, blooming in shades of peaches, pinks, and behested purples, within a courtyard framed by the tall palace. Something about the space reminded Eloryn of the high-walled courtyard in the home

she'd shared with Alward and her time stealing slips of sunlight there. The sweet smell of the roses hung in the air. With the aid of magic, the roses there were always in bloom, even now when the weather grew steadily worse.

Eloryn's usual guard detail accompanied her, some manning the perimeters of the courtyard, with one always standing directly beside her. She was distracted from her work when another soldier arrived and with a few quiet words, dismissed the soldier closest to her and took his place.

He nodded to her meaningfully. His sandy-colored hair and densely freckled skin highlighted bright blue eyes.

She gave a polite smile and nodded back, meaning to return to her paperwork, when he cleared his throat.

"Your majesty," he said in a boyish voice and bowed to her. "My name is Erec. I am here to protect you."

"Thank you." Eloryn tried to sound grateful and hide the truth that having these bodyguards around smothered her every breath. Despite knowing the reality of the situation, she couldn't help but be nostalgic about her time in the forests with just Roen and Memory, running for their lives.

Erec cleared his throat again, and Eloryn raised an eyebrow at him. He looked around as if to check for listeners and leaned in slightly.

"Majesty, I am the younger brother of Peirs. My brother is concerned about your safety, even though he's no longer captain of the guard. So he has sent me to watch over you."

"Peirs? Why is he so concerned as to my safety? As you can see my safety is being managed," Eloryn said, gesturing to the other guards.

"With respect, my brother feels the guard isn't being properly managed."

Eloryn's eyebrows squeezed toward each other and she forced them apart. "I know I have little experience in this role, but it should no longer affect the guard as it is now under Hayes's control."

Erec's head dropped and he spoke quietly. "It is Hayes's management that concerns my brother. Hayes is removing many good men from important positions, saying they were in league with your uncle's plots. The people he is replacing them with have little to nothing to recommend them, save their complete loyalty to Hayes himself. I'm not sure that—"

Erec immediately fell silent and at attention beside Eloryn as Memory and Roen approached. Memory had her arms behind her back and a smirk on her face.

Eloryn stood to greet them, smiling warmly and taking a deep breath to fight the painful shivers she seemed to get every time she saw Roen.

"Your Majesty," Memory said, giggling slightly as she did a terrible impression of a curtsy while keeping her arms hidden. "I have been feeling bad that I missed getting you something for your birthday," she continued, with an exaggerated shrug. "But what could I possibly get this girl who has it all? Well, dun-uh!" Memory revealed the wad of papers she held and waved them in front of Eloryn.

Eloryn took them, her first thought being to the prospect of more paperwork, until she saw the handwriting on the top sheet and knew it instantly. "Are these…?"

Memory grinned. "They're all yours. Happy late birthday, sis."

Eloryn grasped the notes to her chest. Her voice was small and choked. "Thank you so much. I can't express how much this means to me."

"And there's more. Lots more. Like, 'you'd better come and get it all out of my living room because it's blocking the whole place up'

more," said Memory.

Eloryn's heartbeat grew strong, warming her through. She'd felt horribly at odds with Memory lately. And Roen, what he must think of her, how she's behaved. But here they were bringing her this gift, this amazing gift. She pulled them both into a tight hug, not caring if it wasn't a proper thing to do.

She whispered into the gap between the three of them, "I definitely won't ask how you managed to acquire these."

Roen bowed his head and his hair fell over his face, but Eloryn could see he smiled. "That is indeed very wise."

Pulling away from the group embrace, Eloryn grinned at her sister. "Mem, I hope Alward's notes will have usefulness for you, too. I will study them to help you, like I promised."

Memory tilted her head and smiled softly. "Sounds great. Well, you two have some catching up to do so I'm off!"

Memory dashed away too quickly for either of them to object.

Eloryn and Roen both turned and looked at each other, then at their feet.

Memory left her bodyguards in the hallway and ducked into a bathroom with a window. She stood up on a white pedestal basin in order to peek out the small window and spy on Roen and Eloryn. After an embarrassing start, they sat down together and seemed to be having not the most awkward conversation ever. The small smiles they shared now and then made Memory feel both fluttery and sad. She scrunched her nose up and fanned it with a hand to cool her emotions.

"I can't believe he chose her over you. What was he thinking? You are so the better catch." Hope stood in front of a mirror and picked at a floral arrangement on the side table. The effect of seeing them both in the mirror, like there was four of her, dizzied Memory. She hopped down off the basin.

The deep grimace on Hope's face made Memory smile. It touched her that Hope was so defensive of her feelings. "I just didn't feel that way about Roen after all."

Hope pulled petals off the flowers and flicked them into the air. "Why the hell not? I'm you, and I'd wife him straight up."

A petal landed on Memory's nose, tickling her. She batted it away. "I guess I've known him longer. He's just a good friend."

"Sure he is. He was probably just trying you out while he built up the courage to go for the real thing. And her, with that innocent-little-me act. She's just a tease, stringing him along, and you're just going to let her?"

Hope's words were like every guilty thought Memory couldn't bring herself to say, even when she prided herself on being blunt. Were those dark thoughts true? They didn't feel right. Her sister, hugging her and Roen among the roses. That felt right. She wanted her friends and wanted to shut away her nasty paranoia.

"Hope, enough. Try to be happy for them. I just want things back to how they used to be. Me and Lory and Roen and Will as friends. I feel like we're getting there again. Except for Will." *I miss Will.*

"And what cost has this regained friendship been to them. Admit it. Everybody else gets what they want and you just get spurned. You shouldn't have let him go. You shouldn't have let Alward's notes go." Hope pulled the whole arrangement from the crystal vase and threw it on the floor. Water and green stems splattered on the tiles. "We'll see soon, what kind of friend Lory really is. She has all that research now, knowledge you could have kept, that you needed. We'll find out how genuine she is about helping you when she provides you no help at all."

"You're wrong." Memory had to trust Eloryn would help her if she found anything in Alward's studies relevant to her. She had to trust that Roen and Eloryn were a better match than Roen and herself. If she started to doubt, she had to face tough realizations. That maybe Roen didn't want her because he sensed something wrong within her. Something broken and lost, and at the same time so overfull it could explode.

"Eloryn has helped. I already understand more, about myself, about magic, and iron."

Memory stared at the piercings around Hope's face, the silver-colored buckle and studs on her belt, on her jeans, on the cuffs and bracelets she wore.

"In the world we grew up in, just how much iron was there?"

Hope rolled her eyes. "I told you to forget about that place."

Memory continued, her voice strong. "Tell me. There was a lot, wasn't there?"

"Yes. A whole stinking world of iron."

CHAPTER EIGHTEEN

After three sleepless nights, Roen found himself waiting outside the Council's chambers for an audience. *If I dare to try for her, I have to do it properly.*

It took some time before he was ushered in, and only Hayes and a small handful of Councilors were in attendance, but it was enough to make a decision.

None of the Council members seemed happy to see him. They put down the paperwork that they had been seeing to.

Roen swallowed hard and bowed deeply.

"How can we help you, your grace?" Hayes asked. "I'm afraid that we're very busy, please be brief."

Roen still wasn't used to the title, now that he was the son of a duke once again in good standing. He wasn't sure he'd ever feel worthy of it.

Standing tall, Roen delivered the speech that had chewed away his ability to sleep through its repetition in his head. "Esteemed Council, I have asked for your time today in the hope that you will sanction my courtship of her majesty, Queen Eloryn."

The Council said nothing at first, merely looking at one another. One of them smirked before correcting himself.

"For what reason would we grant such sanction?" Hayes asked, his eyelids lowered.

Roen bowed again, and spoke from his bent position, the words too hard to speak to these stern men face to face. "Because you can trust me to always be there for her. To protect her as I have done and to love her truly as I forever will do."

Roen stood up straight again, awaiting their answer.

Hayes paused, his face hardened and eyes twinkling, as though he relished what he was about to say. "In short, the answer is no. Did you seriously believe we could allow such a thing? Negating the fact that you have been dashing court protocol by seeing both the queen and the princess whenever you so desire, and putting aside your questionable behavior in general, you are the seventh son of a seventh son. Your connection to magic is null, and your offspring will have the chance to carry the same burden. What good would you be to our queen? What semblance of an heir could you provide?"

Hayes stood, walking down the long table toward Roen, thumping his walking cane with each step.

"Hayes, if you would—" Roen attempted to interrupt, but wasn't sure what argument he could give. It was all true, and he had known this would be the outcome. His mouth spoke of its own accord, trying to give some miracle reasoning in his defense that his brain couldn't find.

Hayes reached Roen and looked down his nose at him. His voice had grown soft, a friendliness in it that mocked him. "No, Roen. No. You're young, handsome, and I know you do well with the ladies. Forget these foolish feelings for the queen and find someone else. And do it soon. Need I remind you where an obsession with someone you cannot have can lead? Of Thayl's path to revenge over someone he was never worthy to possess?"

Roen lifted his chin. "No matter what I am, I am not Thayl, and would never take an action against the queen or the Wizard's Council."

"Or the man we choose to be her king?" Hayes's voice dropped lower, threatening. "Remove yourself from the queen's company. That is not a suggestion. It is an order."

Roen turned and left the room, unable to say or hear any more.

He made it back to his chambers where he sunk into a seat, his hands shaking.

At least now he knew that nothing could ever be. Even if he were lucky enough to woo her to love him in return, it could never be. But at least this way, knowing that was the case before declaring his feelings to Eloryn, it would only be him who suffered.

Between the blast and the clean-up, the Round Room looked like it had an inch of stone-work scrubbed off its walls. What had been ancient grey rock had been sheered away, leaving pale limestone. All the original furniture had been removed, replaced with one long, straight table. Hayes sat at one end and Eloryn at the other, with the rest of the Council spread along the length.

Memory had the seat closest to Eloryn and shot her sister a smile.

"You're excited to be here?" Eloryn observed.

"You can tell?" Memory whispered back while the rest of the Wizard's Council arrived for the meeting.

"You are bouncing in your seat."

Memory chuckled. "This is my first official invite to a meeting I've received since longer than a lying puppet's nose. And I actually know some things now. I might be able to contribute, worthy member of society like!"

Bedevere arrived and took his seat, and Memory smiled warmly to him. He appeared to be the last of them, and Hayes began the meeting.

"Thank you for attending," Hayes said, indicating Memory particularly. "We have a number of important agenda items to discuss, beginning with the matters of marriage for the queen and princess."

Memory's seat felt suddenly unsteady. "Matters of ma-what?"

Eloryn had turned pale beside her and looked down at her lap.

Hayes continued as though Memory's outburst hadn't happened. "Both of you are of a suitable age to be married, and given the current political climate, it's been decided that the process be given a high priority."

"Okay, slowing down here." With all the reading and studying Memory had been doing, marriage had not been anywhere on her radar. "For one thing, some might not agree that seventeen is an appropriate age to get married. And what the hell process are you talking about?"

Eloryn spoke softly from beside her. "Memory, for hundreds of years it has been the responsibility of the Wizard's Council to select a suitable partner and arrange marriages for the Maellan line."

Memory spoke mostly to Eloryn, wanting her guidance and not

wanting the rest of the room to hear her ignorance on the subject. "I thought that was just some weird thing with Loredanna and Thayl because those guys didn't like him? You mean they pick the husband for every Maellan woman?"

"And man. The royal line flows through Maellan blood whether it be a male or female heir. It has simply been the case that there have only been female heirs for the last few generations. And it is the role of the Wizard's Council to…" Eloryn's voice grew scratchy and she stopped, paused, then looked up at Hayes at the other end of the table. "I knew this was coming, but I hadn't expected it so soon."

Memory shook her head, staring at everyone around the table. "I hadn't expected it at all. I want it known that I am not cool with the idea of arranged marriages. Not cool at all."

Hayes quirked an eyebrow up. "Your temperature is duly noted. Understand, while we want to begin taking action on this straight away, we will not force you hurriedly into anything. Taking into consideration your unique circumstances, and the considerate upheaval of both your lives recently, we have made a plan that we believe to be acceptable. We're providing unprecedented leniency in allowing you to court and select from a list of pre-approved candidates."

A few of the Councilors nodded like this was some kind of grand charity on their behalf.

"Thank you for this considerate clemency, Hayes. Council," Eloryn said.

Memory hissed, "Don't thank them! You're encouraging their backwards ways."

"Mem, please don't," Eloryn whispered. There was something desperate in her tone, something exhausted. She knew this was coming. The way she'd been avoiding Roen made sense now to Memory. She doubted she was going to find Roen's name on this list of approved dates. But even if the list was filled with steamy hotness, it didn't sit right with her.

"Why should I have to date who you say? What if I don't want to get married at all?" Memory challenged Hayes with a stare.

"The reason this needs to be done, your majesty and princess, is because after all they've been through, the people of Avall need assurance that the royal line will be stable and ongoing. There has already been an increase in civil unrest, with the flurry of vagrancy and the amount of beggars ever increasing." Hayes scowled at the notion. "This, in itself, is a massive risk. Our political opponents will rally the poor and the discontent and they will target the queen – she is unmarried, female, and inexperienced as a ruler." He motioned to Eloryn who listened with a blank face. "That is what they will say. Marriage is merely a way to smooth this all over."

Memory shook her head. "If you're worried about the discontent rising up against you then maybe try and make them, you know, content? I don't think a wedding is going to do that. What they need is assistance to get their lives back together."

Hayes thumped his walking cane on the floor. "What we really require is to increase the town's police force and clear out the undesirables. We should be establishing a stronger, more robust militia under the control of the Wizard's Council throughout the city in order to resolve this issue. The middle and upper classes who support us will think better of Eloryn should we clear the streets of the poor."

"The poor need help, not clearing off the streets!" Memory said.

"Some action needs to be taken, whether it be the wedding of our queen or a display of military force." Hayes turned his attention to Eloryn. "Your majesty, would you put this issue to rest and give the Council authority to build a militia, so that we may handle it for you?"

Eloryn seemed to think for a moment and her brow twitched. When she spoke, her voice was empty. "At this time, I do not think it is the correct option for control of a military to be within the purview of the Council."

Memory nodded encouragement to her sister.

"Very well," Hayes sighed. "Then that leaves us with marriage as the only recourse. The matches, of course, will have to be the most appropriate, so that we can establish the strongest channel of magic. You are the very last of Maellan blood, and it must be kept strong."

This Memory did know. Her reading of history texts revealed one scary thing — those of Maellan blood didn't live long lives. Accidents, illnesses, disappearances, it was like they were cursed. Memory and Eloryn were the last little twigs clinging to their family tree.

Memory rubbed her forehead. "So you think you need to match us up with someone who has lots of magic going on? I don't see the point. Thayl supposedly had little magic, but Eloryn and I seem powerful enough."

"You are a fool if you believe everything you hear, princess. It was just a vicious lie that died with your treacherous uncle," Hayes said.

"Why aren't I surprised that he's dead?" Memory said.

"Mem, what are you talking about?" Eloryn asked.

Epic face palm. Memory realized what she'd let slip. She hadn't told Eloryn yet, hadn't told anyone. Didn't know if it was true enough to tell, only that it was too hard to tell.

"Our uncle, before he was *killed*," Memory threw a harsh look at Hayes, "told me that Loredanna never, you know, did it with the king."

Eloryn's voice was tiny. "And you think that means our father was Thayl?"

"I don't know if it was the truth. Even Thayl didn't know, but I'm leaning towards it." Memory paused. "I'm sorry. I didn't want you to find out this way."

"Hayes?" The way Eloryn looked to him for reassurance made Memory queasy.

"Lies, your majesty. A desperate man will say anything to survive," Hayes declared.

Memory stood up, slowly, firmly, in control. "I'm just trying to make the point that there are other ways to be powerful, rather than forcing people into relationships that ruin lives. Like Caliburn, both a metaphorical and physical tool of Maellan power."

Hayes stood, matching her. "You're speaking of things you know nothing about. Caliburn has been lost since the days of Arthur. An arranged marriage is the only way to solidify the support and strength of the people of Caermaellan."

Memory slammed her palm on the table. It rattled beneath her, flimsy, nothing like the ancient, sturdiness of the round table. She was about to continue her argument when Roen and his parents entered the room.

Eloryn stood up, a confused look on her face that bordered on hopeful. She greeted Roen's parents formally. "Your highnesses, so lovely to see you all."

Hayes met them with a bow, but his expression wasn't pleasant. "You're early, but never mind. If we could postpone what we were discussing, my ladies." He looked to Memory and Eloryn. Eloryn nodded.

There weren't any seats left at the table, so Bedevere offered his to Isabeth, and Brannon and Roen stood behind her. Roen's parents looked very much as they had when Memory first met them. Even in their falling-down cottage they dressed like royalty and held that

bearing. And still Memory couldn't help but look at Brannon's missing arm, which made her think about Thayl even more.

Memory, Eloryn, and Hayes returned to their seats.

"How can we help you, Councilor Hayes?" Roen asked, awaiting the reply with a frown.

"It's more about how we can help you," Hayes began, opening his arms wide in a giving gesture. "I have arranged for those who took over your family's duchy to be relocated. As the estates of Sir Ewain have recently become available, those who had been occupying your family's lands have agreed to move and return your ancestral home to you."

Brannon put his only hand on his wife's shoulder and squeezed, and she reached up and took his hand in hers. She said, "We can go home? After all these years? We will have our home again?"

Hayes simply smiled, and so did Roen's parents. Roen's frown remained.

Does that mean he'll have to go, too? Memory turned to get a reading from Eloryn, but she looked like a statue, a polite smile frozen in place over a sickly white pallor.

"This is fine news indeed," Eloryn said, her voice almost robotic.

Brannon strode up to Hayes and shook his hand. "We are in your debt. We had thought our home was as lost to us as our other sons."

Hayes's eyes closed slightly and he smiled. "Come, we will adjourn this meeting so I can begin your arrangements to move. As the Lafaettes have occupied your estate for ten years, there will be some management required to organize the change. We will, of course, strive to have you home as soon as possible."

As if everything had been resolved, Hayes concluded the meeting, and everyone dispersed. Roen and his parents followed Hayes out. Memory sat stunned for a moment, then ran to catch up with Eloryn, who was exiting under the supervision of her guards.

"Lory, I'm so sorry. About, jeez, well, that whole meeting," Memory pleaded, trying to keep up with her. "Particularly about Thayl. I was going to tell you. I was just waiting for the right time. That *totally* wasn't the right time."

Eloryn stopped walking and looked at Memory. There were tears in her eyes, but her voice remained strong. "It's not that you didn't tell me. For all we know, it is only a lie. That is what upsets me. I don't understand how you could believe it. How could you accept him as a father after everything that he did to you?"

Because I'm not right, because my soul is broken, because I don't fit in anywhere with anyone else, because of all these reasons too painful to say.

Memory turned her face away. "We've all got something dark in us, Lory."

Roen met Memory at the entrance to his chambers. She flourished her hands around herself.

"Notice anything different?" she asked, her mouth edging into a smile. She looked much the same as usual, wearing a wide-skirted gown he'd never seen before, her pale hair pinned into a simple yet elegant style with a braid running across the front.

Roen looked Memory up and down and then laughed. "You've lost some weight."

"Boy did I," Memory said, looking over her shoulder. "About six men plus armor worth of weight."

Roen smiled and stepped out of his doorway. He'd been in a low

mood since Hayes's announcement that his family could return home, but Memory always seemed to get a smile from him. The two of them began wandering along the corridor through to the main wing of the palace.

"Finally convinced them you don't need protecting?"

"Hayes has calmed down a bit, thank the god of all that is cute and fuzzy," Memory said. She opened a delicate silk purse that hung around her waist and pulled out a cream bun and started eating it. Roen laughed. Memory continued through a full mouth. "He's letting us go back to school again soon, and I get free run of the castle without getting trailed. Lory still has a few guards with her all the time though, being the all-important one, poor thing."

Roen wondered if those guards were also being ordered to keep an eye out for him.

Memory finished the bun and licked her fingers. "But the going back to school part is turning out to be a mess. I have to go to all my stupid etiquette classes now but have to restructure them to fit some time in to be tutored by Bedevere. Got to talk it through with the headmistress and see what will work, which is why I need this mirror whatsit."

"The Speaking Mirror," Roen said.

"Yeah, that. What's the story with it?"

Roen thought back to the fairy tales he'd known as a child that explained the magic of the mirrors. "The story is that a powerful Maellan queen created it. She was very vain and enchanted a mirror to compliment how she looked and talk back to her when she asked questions. Things went bad for her, and the mirror was shattered into a number of pieces. A wizard discovered that the parts of the mirror could still communicate with each other, in a fashion. Alward had two, one from the Wizard's Council and another taken from Loredanna's estate the night after she died. Eloryn used one to speak with Lanval before we confronted Thayl."

Memory squinted, looking at the ceiling as she walked. "Gah, something there seems so familiar, but I can't pick it. Something from my past. I bet Will would know." She sighed. "You haven't seen him at all lately, have you?"

"No, not except his late night visits to my balcony every night," Roen said in a dreamy voice.

Memory punched him. "Has Clara been talking? I'm going to kill her!"

Memory looked across at Roen a couple of times then finally asked, "Do you think that you'll move back to your home, with your parents?"

Roen kept walking, chewing his lips, a deep frown over his eyes. It took a moment for him to answer. "No. I will stay at court. When Eloryn was dying I promised her I would never leave her, and I won't. Even if I hadn't promised, I couldn't leave her. Even if it hurts to be by her side, I won't leave her."

Memory seemed saddened by his response but reached out and squeezed his hand briefly. They passed through the main entrance hall and were about to climb the grand staircase when a man cried out.

"Stop! Thief!"

Roen froze. He shook off the fear and turned to see what was happening.

A very short, older man pointed his way and marched toward him and Memory. Roen's fear returned.

"Stop right there, thief."

Roen felt as though all blood had drained from his body. He smiled, but it didn't feel convincing. "Good sir, you must have me confused with someone else."

"Don't 'good sir' me, scoundrel. I recognize your face. You're the one who stole from the Guthrie estate just months ago. Jumped out the window with the mistress's finest gems." The man shook a finger as he spat out his words. He wore a servant's uniform bearing the Guthrie crest and was old, wrinkled, but his eyes were clear and sparkled with disgust.

The night I tore my shoulder from its socket. No, I was sure I got away clean. Roen's breath came hard like his chest was being crushed. He couldn't say anything. His worst nightmare was being enacted here, within the walls of Caermaellan palace.

A few other nobles in the entrance hall had stopped to see what was happening.

Memory stepped between the old man and Roen. "Chill out, mister, you've made a mistake."

The servant looked her up and down. "Your highness?" He bowed, spluttering, becoming flustered. "Your highness, I have made no mistake. We must call guards to protect you from this criminal. Guards!"

He looked about frantically and spotting some guards across the hall, started heading to them. Memory grabbed the back of his shirt, trying to slow him down.

Roen felt a hand on his shoulder and waited to be shackled and imprisoned. Instead, he heard Hayes's voice.

"You have a complaint?" he said. He had come down the stairs behind Roen and continued down toward the servant.

The servant clearly recognized Hayes, and looking triumphantly at Roen, opened his mouth to loose his accusations.

Hayes held up a hand and the man stayed quiet. Turning back to Roen and Memory, Hayes said, "I'll handle this."

Hayes led the servant away to a private chamber, speaking quietly to him.

Roen realized he'd been holding his breath, and let it out in a rush. Nobles around the room went about their way, and Roen tried to convince his legs to keep holding his weight.

Memory hovered around him. "Are you okay? I mean, you know, with the stuff, and things."

Roen looked at her and grinned, relief spreading through him. "I can't believe you tried to tackle an old man for me."

"I wouldn't call that a tackle, just a bit of shirt pulling." Memory smiled back at him, but frowned when she looked to where Hayes and the servant had exited. "Hayes better be looking after this properly. I'm not sure if I like the idea of how he handles things."

Roen leaned on the cold, marble banister, pushing his hair back from his face. "I'm just glad it's being handled. The fact it is something that has to be handled is too much of a shameful imposition already. Hayes has been more than kind."

Memory snorted. "Hayes? Kind? Doubt it. Everything he does gives me the squeams. Like the fact Hayes announces arranged marriages and tries to send you away on the same day. Co-incidence? I think not."

Roen shook his head. He was so grateful for having so narrowly avoided the shame of his crimes. He wouldn't question the man who had saved him. "Let's get you to the mirror."

CHAPTER NINETEEN

The rain and winds that shrouded Caermaellan for weeks had eased, and the sunlight had everyone outside. The ringlet-topped girl with too much enthusiasm from their classes had recommended they all spend their break sitting on the grass in the large courtyard of the finishing school. In an attempt to cultivate friends and some sort of normal life, Memory and Eloryn agreed.

A half-dozen other girls from their classes came along, and they all sat on the ground, the fluffy fabric of their skirts puffing around them, like a field of marshmallows.

Memory wriggled in hers, trying to sit comfortably on the grass in a corset and hooped skirt. She looked at the pagoda across from them longingly. "There are a bunch of benches, right there!" she whispered to Eloryn.

Eloryn rolled her eyes and smiled. "Hush, this is nice. And you've never been one to worry about the risk of staining your gown."

Laudine, with her ringlets, practically bounced in place as she stared at Eloryn, starry eyed. "How many suitors have you met with so far?"

Eloryn blushed. "Two." She didn't elaborate, but Memory knew her feelings about the dates without hearing more. Unfortunately, Eloryn's suitors and marriage were all the other girls wished to discuss.

Laudine sighed. "It must be so wonderful. You must have the pick of the best nobles in Avall."

Eloryn screwed up her mouth then dropped her shoulders as though giving up. She pulled a piece of paper from her binder of notes. "Here, you can see for yourself."

Laudine's eyes nearly popped from her head. "Is this *the list*?"

Eloryn nodded and Laudine reached for it reverentially, but another girl grabbed it first. A huddle of giggles and lace formed around the paper.

Memory frowned. That list becoming public could be a political disaster. "Should you really have given…" One look at Eloryn's expression, so distant and tired, and Memory's warning faded to nothing.

Memory sighed and lay back on the grass to watch the clouds and take some strain off her corseted chest. Clouds were building, and it seemed the sunshine they enjoyed would be brief. Beside her, Eloryn smiled, but Memory could easily see through her expression.

Eloryn glanced at Memory a couple of times then asked, "Have you spoken with Roen recently?"

"A bit. Not a lot, I mean." Memory swallowed. She still felt guilty for what had gone on between her and Roen. What little there was. "I

haven't been seeing him as much since Tristan got expelled."

Beside them their classmates remained enthralled by the list of Eloryn's approved suitors, gasping their opinions at each selection.

"Ew. Too old, too old."

"Oh no, not him, frightfully dull witted."

Their commentary didn't fill Memory with confidence in the Council's choices.

Eloryn looped her finger around the necklace she wore and pulled her jade pendant from where it was hidden under the neckline of her dress. She rubbed it between her fingers in what seemed like an unconscious action. Memory knew where she had gotten the pendant from. She gave Eloryn a knowing look, and Eloryn tucked it away again.

"Did he say when he was leaving?" she asked.

Memory shook her head. "He's not going with his parents. He's going to stay here."

Memory could see Eloryn take a deep breath. Feeling mischievous, she said, "You know he's staying because of you."

Memory only had a moment to appreciate the look on Eloryn's face before they were interrupted by a few young men who joined the group, formally introducing themselves. Memory forgot each of their names instantly.

The huddle of girls broke up, passing the list between them when the guys showed interest in it, like a flirty game of keep-away.

Eloryn and Memory's guards watched the group carefully, but the male additions to their group kept a respectful distance from the royal pair anyway, except for one who came and sat close to Memory.

Memory stole a few side-long glances at him as he laughed at the escalating game with the list. He was gorgeous. His blue eyes reminded her of Will's, but he had wavy blonde hair that was tied back into a short nub of a ponytail. He was dressed formally, but didn't wear the puffy tie almost all other men wore, and the top buttons of his shirt were undone.

He caught her looking and smiled.

Damn it.

Memory tried to casually cover her ogling. "Sorry, I didn't catch your name."

"I'm Dylan."

"Memory," she said, and shook his hand.

He gave her a sly grin, then pulled her hand up and kissed it. "Your highness, I did recognize you."

The kiss made Memory's hand twitch. She wasn't sure if it was pleasant or unpleasant, but the situation was getting out of her comfort zone, so she began the process of standing up to leave. Doing so gracefully proved difficult. She managed to step on her own skirts in a way that meant she couldn't straighten her legs and fell back on her butt.

Dylan hopped to his feet and offered her a hand up.

"Thanks. Lory, I'm heading off," Memory said, then looked back to Dylan. His good looks caught her off guard, as though she didn't believe it until she saw him again. The slight pout to his bottom lip was a thing of beauty. "It was nice to meet you, Dylan. But I'm off to the library to do some research for the afternoon."

"Might I join you?" he suggested.

"I'm not sure you'd be interested. It's just econom-er-etiquette. Etiquettey things, girly stuff. Yep."

"Econom-er-etiquette is one of my specialties," Dylan said, his eyes sparkling.

Fine, you win this round.

Memory gave him the okay to follow her with a flick of her head.

Memory sat across the desk from Dylan in a small private room adjoining the school's library. Her ink pen splotched over her work, and Dylan laughed at her. She scrunched up the paper and threw it at him, causing him to chase her round the table. The librarian walked by the doorway and gave them a look. They both sat back in their seats with suppressed giggles.

The daylight shining through the broad window grew dull, and Memory wondered if she should head back to the palace soon. She had enjoyed her afternoon with Dylan so much she didn't want it to end.

Memory relished the chance to grill him about economics, law, and politics, and it turned out that he was very well studied. He was funny and had a deadpan world-weariness that appealed to Memory. He also made for a pleasant, if distracting, view across the table.

Roen appeared in the doorway and came in as though he were looking for her. Memory prepared to introduce him to Dylan, but it seemed like they already knew one another.

"How dare you show your face here?" Roen shouted. He ran at Dylan, grabbing him by the coat and pushing him into the bookshelf behind him, knocking books to the floor.

Memory had never seen him so angry. "Roen, stop it! What are you doing?"

"Do you have any idea what you did to our family?" Roen shook Dylan with each word, bashing him against the solid wooden shelving.

Dylan spoke behest words and light flared around Roen's face.

Roen gasped, letting go and backing away. He rubbed at his watering eyes, blinking. With a grunt he lunged back toward Dylan.

"I will use the behest again," Dylan warned.

Roen grunted and stepped back. He ran his hands up into his hair, pacing in front of Dylan like a lion penning in its prey.

Dylan reached a hand out to Roen. It was ignored. "What I did, was only to protect myself, Roen. All of our brothers were dead, and I didn't intend to end up the same way."

"You could have come with us! But instead you chose to serve yourself, and Thayl, over your family."

"You're making it sound like I supported him," Dylan said.

"You supported him by not opposing him."

"What would you do? Punish everyone in Avall who did not fight to the death against Thayl? Half the court would be included. You can't punish everyone who complied with a new ruler in order to survive."

Memory looked between the two of them. She should have seen the resemblance before. "Roen? This is your brother?"

Roen turned away. "He is no brother of mine. He is a wretched coward, and he's just leaving."

Dylan's jaw worked like he had more to say, but he bowed to Memory and left. Roen watched him until he was out of sight then turned to Memory.

"Are you all right? He didn't hurt you at all, do anything to you?" He ran his hands down her arms as though checking for injuries.

Memory shook her head, confused. "Of course I'm all right. We were just studying together."

Looking at Roen, Memory could see the similarities between the two brothers more now. Both so handsome, with strong jaws, and golden features.

"Be careful, Mem, he's not to be trusted. He's always been the most selfish person I've known. You shouldn't spend time with him," Roen warned.

Memory stepped back, his words hitting a sore spot. "I can spend time with whoever I want. Especially since your time is better spent uselessly pining over Lory."

The wild electricity in Roen's eyes scared Memory. He grunted. "Is this what you want?"

He grabbed her, pulling her in roughly and kissing her.

The kiss was full of passion and anger, his lips hard.

Memory cried out, pushing at Roen, his arms stronger than hers, imprisoning her. A sick feeling swelled in her, and books around them started rattling on the desks. The glass in one of the square window panes cracked.

Roen let go of Memory. His eyebrows were low, confused, appalled.

Memory backed away from him. Her chest ached, and she took a moment to gather herself.

"No," Memory said. "It's not because I know it's not what you want. Be with Eloryn," she said, looking into his eyes. "Stop letting anything get in your way."

"I'm… Memory, I'm so…" Roen put a hand to his mouth.

Memory knew that he hadn't been in control, that he had lost himself for a moment. She knew what that was like. But it didn't make her feel any better about it.

"You should go," Memory said.

And without saying a word, he did.

Memory flopped to the floor. Thin arms wrapped her from behind and held her tight. She held them back, clinging to the black and white striped sleeves.

"I know how horrible it feels," said Hope.

"Something specific, or just everything, always?" Memory asked with a dull laugh.

"The pain of having someone choose somebody else over you," Hope whispered in her ear.

"I don't even want Roen, I just—"

"It still cuts."

Memory nodded and put her head down on Hope's shoulder. "How do you know how it feels?"

Hope paused. "Just part of our life that you can't remember."

Had I been in love before?

"Tell me about it," Memory asked.

"All you need to know is that the people you care about will only hurt you. Love is a poison that has no antidote."

After receiving a note from Memory to meet with her, Roen waited in the private gardens of the palace, pacing near the entrance to the hedge maze. It had been freshly trimmed and the rich grassy smell of the cut leaves brought back memories of his early childhood in his family's estate, playing in the garden with his brothers. He didn't know why she'd ask to meet there, of all places, but his thoughts were too occupied to care. He ran through wordings for his apology in his mind over and over. He hated that Memory had seen him behave so venomously. Seeing his brother had unleashed years of pent-up rage. He couldn't believe that Dylan had the audacity to speak with the princess, after everything he had done. It made his blood boil, and he

had projected some of that onto Memory. Words could never undo that, but he had to let her know how sorry he was.

Some staff arrived, putting out a table with placements for high tea. He approached, thinking it was for his meeting with Memory, when Eloryn and one of her suitors appeared, trailed by a procession of guards. Roen ducked back behind a hedge as the couple made their way up the path and took seats at the table.

Memory… Roen knew that she must have set him up to see this. Was she punishing him, making him be a spectator to Eloryn's courtship?

Watching from within the entrance to the hedge maze, Roen wondered how he could get away without being seen. The maze itself only had a single entry and exit, and if he stepped out he'd surely be noticed. He had to stay, and he couldn't stop himself from spying.

Servants in formal dress and white gloves solemnly poured tea from silver teapots. Roen found small comfort that Eloryn didn't appear to be enjoying the other man's company. He was tall, and fairly good looking, but he controlled the conversation in a way that left few gaps for Eloryn to speak. His arms swung in grand gestures that came close to knocking over the tall tower of cakes, and he laughed frequently at his own jokes.

As Roen watched he saw Eloryn move from tolerance at the banality of her companion to pure boredom. Fake smiles of humor became commonplace and pained.

When her partner stood up to enact some anecdote, faux fencing and barely paying attention to Eloryn, she reached a hand to her chest. Her fingers grasped at something, and she looked longingly into her palm before squeezing her hand closed.

Around something small, green, a pendant the color of her eyes.

Is this what Memory meant for me to see?

Roen's heart split. He knew he owed Memory a heartfelt thank you along with his apology for what she had tried to do for him, but the outcome for him brought only pain.

Staying here in the palace, so he could at least be near Eloryn, if never being with her, had only been tolerable on the notion that it was merely him whom would suffer. He had assumed that Eloryn didn't have feelings for him. But having seen this, the hint that she may feel the same for him — he couldn't cope. He would have to leave.

CHAPTER TWENTY

Memory waited at the foot of the palace steps for a carriage to be prepared. Now they were being allowed out of the palace again, she was desperate to go and visit her shelter. Maeve had been sending her updates, but Memory hadn't been to see them since before the bombing.

It had taken her all morning to find a suitable dress to wear. She was nervous and all her fancy gowns seemed too over the top for visiting the homeless. Clara set out on the mission and had returned not long after lunch with a simple day gown of charcoal-colored linen, with only a modest bustle and long, fitted sleeves.

Memory wondered how Roen was enjoying her little trick with Eloryn. It made her nervous too, but she couldn't help meddling. The two of them were silly over each other. Eloryn had been dutifully, mournfully, working through her list of suitors, but Memory had flat out refused to go on any dates.

How long did it take for them to get a damn carriage out here? Are they building one from scratch? Memory rubbed her hands which felt shaky. Thick, low clouds were keeping the world blanketed and warm, so she couldn't blame the cold. It felt like everything that had happened recently kept building inside her, wringing her emotions. She needed some kind of emotional holiday, but wasn't sure how.

Memory heard someone walk down the stairway behind her. "Is standing on the steps your new pastime, your highness?"

She turned and saw Dylan. "Call me H… Mem, please."

She eyed him warily. The time they'd spent together in the library had been fun, but it was clear how Roen felt about him. Yet he kept showing up, and Memory couldn't say she hated that. "What are you doing here?"

Dylan gestured back at the palace. "I live here."

Memory raised her eyebrows and Dylan chuckled. "I've just moved into a guestroom, temporarily."

Memory's eyebrows rose further. "You're staying in the castle? Is that wise, with how Roen feels about you?"

Dylan hopped down two steps below her, so they were the same height. "It is my foolishness either way. I requested to be able to take a room here in order to reconcile with my family before they return to our lands. Once they're back home, I doubt they will open their doors to me."

A carriage rolled up in front of them. "Finally."

"It was lovely to speak with you again, Mem." Dylan bowed to her and began walking back up the steps.

"Do you," Memory started talking before she thought it through. *Too late now, spit it out.* "Do you want to come into the city with me?"

A handsome grin split across Dylan's face. "I thought you'd never ask."

Three guards had been waiting with Memory to escort her into town. Dylan lifted his chin at them, which they seemed to take as a signal they weren't needed anymore.

Typical, like I'm safe as long as I have a man around to look after me.

Dylan took her hand and helped her up into the carriage then sat beside her on the same seat.

"Where are we heading?" he asked.

The carriage started rolling, the gravel of the driveway grumbling beneath them. "I'm going in to visit my homeless shelter. Sorry, it probably won't be very interesting for you."

"If it's interesting for you, I'm sure it will also be for me. Although I don't for the life of me know what a homeless shelter is."

Memory rolled her eyes. People in Avall just didn't seem to understand dealing with poverty. Maybe it was their prosperous history that left them so unprepared. "Well, you take homeless people, and you shelter them. It's pretty simple really." Memory sighed and looked out the window at passing terrace houses. "Actually it's not that simple at all. I was so focused on these poor little orphans, right? I wanted to help the kids, but then I realized how many more people there were who needed help. So the shelter is turning into a bit of a training school as well. Not only does it give a home to the orphans, it's giving jobs to a lot of other people who've lost their way. There's so much to be done, from repairing the building, to cleaning and cooking, and if they don't know how to do it, I have to find people to teach them."

Dylan whistled like he was impressed. "Where do you get the funds for this?"

"Pawn shops mostly," Memory laughed. "Also asking a lot of favors. Most of my servants work there instead of in my chambers, and a few other people I know are helping out." Peirs was enlisted straight away after Hayes fired him. Memory trusted Peirs. She liked him from the moment he made a pun about how she defeated Thayl. His dismissal from captain of the guard came at a good time for her when she'd become torn about how to run the shelter. She wanted to let everyone in, to help everyone, but kept getting scared someone would abuse her trust somehow. She worried so much for the kids in her care. The amount of responsibility terrified her, so Peirs was there to make sure everyone was safe.

The carriage stopped, and Memory was about to jump out when Dylan moved first so he could help her down. She took his hand, but it felt odd when she could get out of the carriage fine herself.

The building Memory had purchased for her project was huge, if old and dilapidated. Four stories tall, it had once been an inn, so it had the perfect layout for her needs. Memory had bought it only seeing the plans and a sketch of the front, and seeing it now made her smile. Its architecture was of an older style than many buildings around it. Made of gray bricks with diamond shaped windows and pointy gothic features, it had an imposing presence. Stepping inside, Memory was pleased to see how the place was cleaning up.

A skinny girl with brown hair so long, curly, and thick it seemed larger than her body, jogged up to them, holding layers of old skirts out of the way of her legs.

Memory lifted her hand in a fist, and the girl bumped it with her own. "Yo, Maeve, this is Dylan."

"Good day to you," she said, holding up her fist.

Dylan lifted his up as well and laughed when she bumped it. "Is this some kind of secret handshake?"

Maeve just winked at Memory. "Would you like the grand tour?"

"Why yes indeed," Memory said and linked her arm around

Maeve's.

Dylan followed close behind as Maeve showed them the building. Lots of kids came out to watch them pass, and some ran up, just to touch Memory's hand briefly then run away again. Memory was pleased to see they were happy, their rooms clean, and some of them putting on weight.

"You're a hero to them," Dylan said.

"She's done a fantastic job, sir," Maeve agreed.

Memory blew a raspberry. "Nah, my money is the hero here."

"Not at all." Maeve directed them through the kitchens. A cook offered Memory some food, but for some reason she didn't feel hungry so she declined.

Maeve pointed out some women who were learning from one of the palace chefs. "It's more than just money. The way you're able to come up with ideas about how to help us. It's almost like you know this world, these troubles. Nobody else in Avall knows how to help us, but you seem to understand."

Dylan looked at Memory with pride. "She spends her time studying such matters."

Memory just shrugged. Their praise made her feel awkward. *Coming from a group home myself helps too. From what little I remember.*

Maeve slowed her pace and let go of Memory's arm. She gripped her hands together nervously. "I'm afraid I have some bad news for you, though. There have been some of the orphans leave us."

"Don't they like it here? Is something wrong?"

"No, it's more like… they just vanish. We aren't sure where. Peirs has men looking. Maybe they are leaving to go somewhere else, but I thought I'd bring it to your attention, especially since Edele is among them, and I know you were fond of her."

Memory reached for the bracelet she still wore. "Edele? Little

Edele is gone?"

Maeve nodded. She looked far more worried than she was saying.

Memory spent the rest of the afternoon talking with the guests at her shelter, from youngest to oldest, to Peirs and the staff from the palace. No one seemed to know where people were going or why. No one had any idea where Edele had gone. She was only six, where could she have gone? Memory refused to consider all the alternatives. She couldn't bear to lose a single person more from her life or discover those in her care weren't safe.

Dylan waited patiently as she made her rounds, but it was clear he'd become tired of the place. Memory also grew frustrated with the lack of information and the worry that lacking caused. It was dark by the time she gave up and apologetically told Dylan they could leave.

The carriage waited for them on the street just outside, but Dylan took Memory's hand, holding her back. "It's a beautiful night, let's walk a little. You look like you need to relax a bit."

"So obvious?" Memory let him lead her by the hand along the cobbled pavement. It had rained while they were inside, and the stones glistened in the light of the streetlamps. The lamps seemed to have wisp lights in them, and Memory wondered whose job it was to come along and behest them all each night.

"I hope it is not too forward of me to say, but on a night such as this, your skin is comparable to the moon," he said while keeping a straight face.

"Gray and full of craters?" Memory laughed. Dylan winced. *Aw, the poor boy was trying so hard.*

He stopped and twirled her around to face him.

"I picked this for you." Dylan revealed a single red rose bud, which he handed to Memory. She had no idea where he had been keeping it. Maybe he had some qualities in common with his brother.

"Nice trick," she said, sniffing the flower because she thought it was the polite thing to do. It didn't have any fragrance.

"Do you like magic?" he asked.

"Complicated question. Let's just say yes for now."

Dylan bent forward and Memory tensed, thinking he might kiss her. Instead, he whispered a few words of a behest to the rose and the bud spread and bloomed, its petals unfurling large and silky.

Memory gaped. "You're good with magic, aren't you? It's funny. I've never seen Roen do anything like what you can do."

Dylan seemed disheartened that his trick resulted in a discussion about his brother. "You don't know? My brother is the seventh son of a seventh son. It means that he has no Spark of Connection at all. My father, knowing rumors of the curse and that he was already a seventh son and had six of his own, never intended to have Roen. It's sad, really. The Faerbaird lineage is actually quite strong in magic."

Now she thought of it, not once had Memory ever seen Roen use magic, but she never realized that he outright couldn't. "He's never said."

"Well, he wouldn't. It is his most shameful secret."

Maybe not his most shameful, Memory thought, considering how Roen felt about his thieving skills. Memory felt a strange burst of pride for Roen with the way he lived and coped, without any magic at all, with the prejudice that must come with that. And to have known his parents never meant to have him for that reason, and be left as the last son they had, all their wanted children dead or gone. No wonder Roen was angry at Dylan for abandoning them. Memory shook her head internally at herself. *No, Roen's parents love him no matter what. I can see it.* They were proud of him for how he looked after them despite his handicap, just as she was. She wished Roen could feel that pride, too.

Dylan offered Memory his hand again, drawing her from her thoughts. "If comparisons to the moon do not please you, then let me compare you to that rose, although the rose will surely come off second best."

Memory rolled her eyes but couldn't fight the bashful smile that appeared. Over Dylan's shoulder, in a shadow of a building up ahead, Memory noticed Hope, watching. Memory caught her eye and tilted her head. *Should I?*

Hope gave a distinct nod.

Memory took Dylan's hand.

The shelter was near the center of town, and Dylan walked with her over a stone bridge into the bustling nightlife street. Revelers ambled by and cats stalked in the light fog that rolled along the ground. They came to Beyond the Veil, the pub Memory had been to before, where she and Will had made a scene when he'd come to her defense. Despite the trouble caused, Memory missed the days when he'd come to her defense. Times when he'd see her at all. She didn't even know if he was still around and the thought that he might have gone away made her stomach roll.

"Would you like to go in?" Dylan asked.

Memory realized she'd been staring at the pub for long enough to seem strange.

"Nah, I don't think I'm ready to show my face there again just yet." Having Will dominate her thoughts also left her in no mood for clubbing.

Dylan and Memory were about to walk away when Memory saw a face she recognized. One of the older orphans from her shelter was leaving the pub with a gangly man. Memory focused, and saw the man had the elongated, emaciated limbs of a corpse, and all black eyes. An unseelie fae.

beyond
the
veil

The mousy haired boy with him - Memory searched her mind, his name was Bran - looked dazed as if he'd been drugged.

"Bran?" Memory called out. The boy didn't respond.

Memory headed toward them. "Bran, are you okay?"

The unseelie fae creature led him away completely under its spell.

Memory ran until she could stand in front of them, blocking their path. She waved her hand in front of Bran's eyes, but he seemed to stare straight through her.

She looked up at the fae. Its skin was pale gray, both wrinkly and stretched like pulled taffy. It wore a suit in the human style, but it was dusty and tattered.

"What do you think you're doing? Where are you taking Bran?"

"No concern of yours. He's mine. Get out of our way." Its voice surprised her. For a masculine creature, it sounded almost like an old woman.

Memory folded her arms. "Okay, now I'm really not letting you take him."

"Who do you think you are? Unnatural scum." The creature spat a glob of black goo at Memory's feet. "Think you can order anyone about? You're nothing but a power store created by my master, who'll come to collect soon, you mark my words."

Whoa, what? Those few words from the creature slammed Memory. So much meaning, but what did it mean? Who did it mean? Providence? Could Providence have been a fae?

Dylan caught up to Memory and pushed her behind him.

"How dare you speak that way to our princess?"

The fae leaned down, hissing at them through needle-like teeth.

Dylan reversed, running into Memory who held her ground. His voice was high pitched. "Back down. If you do anything I shall Brand you, unseelie fae."

A crowd of humans and fae emerged from the tavern to see what the commotion was about. Memory frowned at them, willing them to leave. *Great, caught up in another spectacle. I really can't come back to this pub again.*

"Do you think I care?" The unseelie fae howled, wild anger in its cry. "I can feel my life fading from me, ebbing away. Not long and it'll all be gone. I wouldn't mind taking a few humans with me."

Memory gasped when the creature lashed out at them, swinging a long arm and backhanding Dylan across the jaw. It knocked him sideways, and he fell on the pavement hard.

The fae advanced on Memory, and she backed away. Some of the crowd moved in to try and pull her to safety.

Memory saw Dylan spit blood from his mouth. He looked up and spoke through red-tinted teeth. "Bronmarbh Aileadh."

The unseelie fae loosed a cry that drilled through Memory's body, aching her eyes. A rune symbol appeared on its forehead, as though burned into the gray flesh.

But the Brand didn't slow the creature down. The unseelie fae lunged at Memory. She managed to dodge, bumping into a large man who walked into the fray, smiling.

The mark on the creature's face changed everything.

The humans and seelie fae around her were no longer on the defensive. They moved forward, happily turning on the unseelie fae. The creature was seized, and the humans fell upon it, tearing into it.

Three men held down the unseelie fae who screeched and buckled in their hands. The large man she'd bumped walked up between them and started stomping on the creature's head.

Pixies darted about high above to get a good view. Dust and what looked like thick mud started pouring from the unseelie fae. It smelled of ocean winds and rotting mushrooms.

Bran watched blankly from right by its side. Memory ran over to him, unsure whether he was really seeing anything, but covered his eyes with her hand anyway.

She wanted to look away herself, but couldn't.

Some of the seelie fae swooped down at the creature like buzzing hornets. Cries of 'monster' grew in the crowd, cheering on the violence. The large man had succeeded in pulling off one of the unseelie fae's arms. He held it above his head on display.

Dylan stood beside Memory, wiping his mouth. "Stupid monster deserved it."

Memory just shook her head. "I want to go home."

Memory took Bran under her arm and walked him back to the shelter. On the carriage ride home to the palace, Dylan tried to lighten the mood again and failed at every attempt. The violence kept flashing inside Memory's eyelids with each blink. She stared into the black night around them and tried to contain her lurching stomach.

By the time they arrived and hopped out of the carriage together, it had passed midnight. The very few guards patrolling the grounds who saw them eyed them scandalously.

Memory grunted. "Fantastic. More reasons for people to gossip about me."

Dylan paused and caught Memory in his arms. His lips lifted on one side in a wicked smile.

"You know, Memory, if people are going to talk, why don't we really give them something to talk about?"

Still smiling, Dylan leaned in and kissed her on the mouth.

The world spun.

Memory found herself in the Ivy Room.

Goddammit!

Memory gagged out the feeling of the Veil. She hadn't been

expecting Dylan to do something so spontaneous, not after the night they'd had. And she certainly hadn't expected the result.

Memory turned slowly in a circle and found herself desperately disappointed she didn't discover Will sitting behind her amongst the vines.

"At least I've saved myself from the walk of shame," she muttered, making her way off the roof and down the stairs to her room. Her Veil door defense mechanism occupied her mind, and she was glad to let it take over after the earlier events she never wanted to think about again.

Was that twice now? Did the dream count? Or was it more? Memory thought back to when Thayl's magic had killed the wizard hunter with the scarred face, and she was pinned under his body. She didn't know what happened at the time, how she got free. Maybe his body had just been knocked off her, but maybe this uncontrollable Veil dooring had been happening since then. Either way, it was happening too often.

Memory reached her chambers and stepped inside with her shoulders drooped. She was about to close the door when Dylan bolted down the hall with an anxious expression.

"Thank the fae," he gasped. He took a moment to catch his breath then chuckled softly. "I kissed the princess and made her vanish. If I didn't find you, I would have been in trouble!"

Emotionally spent, Memory just mumbled. "Sorry about that. It's just this condition I'm dealing with at the moment."

Dylan held her chin in his hand. "If I do say so myself, it seems I had quite an effect."

Memory thought of the effect and her destination. She wasn't sure exactly who was having an effect on her.

With his mouth close to hers, Dylan whispered, "Would you begrudge me another attempt?"

Part of Memory wanted to pull away, not ready for physical contact, not now. But the lure of Dylan's persistence won out. As though being desired so much could make her feel better, make *her* better. Memory lifted her head and he pressed his lips against hers.

This time she stayed where she was. The kiss left a bitter taste in her mouth and a shiver low in her spine. But he liked her. He wanted her. That was all that mattered. Right now, she needed that.

Memory half smiled when Dylan pulled away. "I'm still here. Disappointed?"

"Not at all."

With a kiss of her hand, Dylan said goodbye and Memory shut the door, closed her eyes and leaned against it. Her head was a mess, and she just wanted to sleep.

After a few deep breaths, she was ready to drag herself to bed. When she opened her eyes, Will stood in front of her.

"Goddammit!" Memory choked. "Will, you scared the ass off me!"

Will stared down at her, breathing heavily, his expression dark. Half naked, ferocious, the way he used to look.

Memory's pulse pounded in her throat, and she felt sickened by the idea Will had watched Dylan kiss her. She spoke softly, knowing just next door Eloryn probably slept. "Did you see… Were you watching me?"

Will growled low in his throat. "You shouldn't be seeing him. He's only pretending to like you."

"Right, because it's so unbelievable someone could like me that way?" The thought that Will couldn't understand someone would like her burned like a scorching sun in her gut. Memory could feel her temper slipping again, but Will had a habit of bringing high emotions out of her. She continued, her voice rising to a yelled whisper.

"Thanks so much for dropping round, spying on me and telling me I'm unlovable."

"That's not what I said. I'm trying to warn you. He's not good for you."

Memory folded her arms across her chest. Staring at his, she saw the scratches there almost healed. She softened her tone. "Is this me we're talking about or you? Why don't you tell me what your relationship with Mina is really about?"

Will turned away, and Memory worried he would bolt. He looked over his shoulder, his blue eyes sparkling under strands of dark hair. He looked cute when he frowned that way, the same way he'd frown when he was a boy, as though his eyes held thoughts deeper than a boy should know.

"It's complicated," he said.

"Don't Facebook answer me. I want to know if you're okay, that she isn't…" *Hurting you. Hurting you. Hurting you.* The words ricocheted in her head, but her mouth was dry and wouldn't work.

Will spoke again, his voice shaky. "You said you've remembered some things. Have you remembered much about where we came from?"

Memory thought of their tattoo, her rules, how they met. It was her fault for letting the kid follow her everywhere, crush on her, making him do what she said. *He must hate me. He must blame me for bringing him here.*

"Is that what you want? To go back there?" Her tone was harsher than she meant, her pain biting into her voice.

Will's only reply was to growl and leave.

Memory collapsed into an armchair, not even enough strength left to make it to bed.

CHAPTER TWENTY-ONE

Memory pulled the curtains to her living room open, but the dim sky didn't offer much light. She'd been unable to sleep, so when the first hints of morning sun appeared she gave up trying and got up. Her mind wouldn't stop, filled with questions and theories and worries about the day before. And the day before that. And the day before that.

The things that fae creature had said haunted her. And Bran, being led away, to who knows where. Memory had already sent out a letter for Peirs, instructing him to investigate 'Beyond the Veil' and other fae hang-outs to stop more abductions. Memory kept imagining little Edele being taken as well and what might have become of her at the hands of a monster like that.

And then there was Will. Another life she'd destroyed.

Memory stretched and shook herself out. It was time to start finding answers. She stared at the spread of notes on the floor, all in Alward's handwriting. They'd been left in her room while she was out the night before. There was a note on top from Eloryn, apologizing that she hadn't had time to study them herself and how she thought Memory might like a look.

Hope picked up the note and scowled. "Didn't she give you every bit of help I told you she'd give you?"

"Lory is busy, that's all. And she could have kept all this, but she gave it to me instead. That's something."

"Like she could have given you the crown, but kept it instead?"

"Not even the same thing." Memory knelt down and shuffled through the papers. Alward's notes were rambling, but well annotated with clear subjects and headings. Memory focused in on his theories on the other world, and ways to travel there. *If Will really wants to go home, it's the least I owe him. I have to work out how.*

"Semi-permeable membrane," Memory read aloud.

Hope squatted down beside her, looking concerned. "Are you having a stroke?"

Memory pointed at the section of research that had caught her eye. "That's how Alward describes the Veil, as a membrane between dimensions, between the human world and the fairy world. He seems to think what the fae did when they separated Avall from the rest of the world was bring it into some kind of bubble within the Veil."

"Stop changing the subject. Eloryn isn't to be trusted, didn't I tell you?"

Memory didn't reply, too caught up in her epiphany. She considered the knowledge the dragon had left with her, the way she pinched and pulled at the Veil to open doors. Moving within Avall was like bending that membrane, skimming the surface of the bubble holding Avall. To get through to either the rest of the human world or the fairy world would require punching a hole right through.

"When I tried to open a door to the other world for Thayl, it felt like pushing against stretch fabric. I was trying to do the same thing I normally do, just skimming the membrane, and I just ended up pushing against it when I needed to pierce through."

Memory flicked to the next page. Alward had spent sixteen years trying to write a behest to get to the rest of the world, find her, and return them both safely to Avall. The return seemed to be the hardest part in his opinion.

But Memory didn't need a two-way door. She doubted Will would want to come back for visits. "I think I can do this. It's just a different mindset." Memory chewed her lips, reading and absorbing the information.

Hope stood back up and kicked at the papers, messing up the rough order Memory had laid them out in. "Why are you wasting your time on this stuff? You don't want to go back there. You don't remember what it was like. Your place is here. As queen. That's the way to solve your problems, not this stuff."

Memory slapped at Hope's foot. "Quit it. It's not my problems I'm trying to solve here."

Hope blew a raspberry and dumped herself in an armchair across the room. "Then who is going to solve yours? It's not going to be Eloryn, too busy. Not Roen, he's only interested in her. Not Will, off with the fairies. There's just you and me. Don't think otherwise. Except maybe Dylan, but he's just a bit of fun. Why don't you go get some of that right now instead of this garbage?"

Memory ignored her. She was absorbed in Alward's curling handwriting, and the knowledge it contained. The idea of seeing

Dylan again after last night also left her cold and uncomfortable.

You're nothing but a power store created by my master, who'll come to collect soon.

The dark fae's master. The fae were able to travel between worlds. They only didn't anymore because of all the cold iron in the rest of the world. Providence was able to open a doorway to the rest of the world. *Opened one and sent a human through to do her work for her,* Memory realized.

"Do you think Providence is a fae?" Memory asked aloud, even though she was already certain.

Hope stared at Memory for a long moment. "Makes sense. Let's face it, only a fairy could be that cruel, right? Should be exterminated, the lot of them, if you ask me."

Memory scooped up a few key papers then stood up. "I'm going to see Bedevere."

"Bedevere? Really?"

"What? He wasn't on your list of people who wouldn't help me. I trust him. He's been helping me so much in our private lessons."

Hope blew another raspberry and turned away to look out the window. Memory left her behind.

It was only when knocking on Bedevere's door that Memory noticed she was still in her night gown. She'd been up too early for Clara to have come and readied her for the day. In her mind a dress was a dress, but her appearance forced a crack in even Bedevere's stoic expression when he greeted her.

"Yeah, yeah, I know," Memory said. "What I want to show you is far more interesting, trust me."

Bedevere let her into his chambers, which were plain and immaculately kept. A tray on his desk had a steaming pot of tea and a plate with nothing but some crumbs. She was glad he seemed to be a morning person.

Bedevere pulled a seat out for her, but she remained standing.

"I want to open a Veil door to the rest of the world." Memory said.

"Straight to the point." Bedevere poured himself a fresh cup of tea, carefully straining the golden liquid with a strainer and putting three spoonfuls of sugar in. "Do you believe you are able to?"

Memory nodded and explained her new understanding of the Veil. "I want to try it, but I wanted someone around, you know, just in case."

"Wise. It hasn't been unheard of throughout history for wizards to attempt to travel between worlds. And a few have succeeded. At least we can assume so by their absence. Unfortunately, wherever they went, they never returned."

Memory nodded again. She was getting jittery, nervous of what she was about to attempt, and her head felt like it was bobbing up and down of its own accord. "Thayl said the same thing, that Providence said it's pretty much one way, unless someone is holding the door open, like she did for Thayl."

Bedevere put his tea down without having drunk any and leant against his desk, as though the enormity of what they discussed required some support. "If you succeed, is that what you would do for me? Hold the door open, so I can confirm what you have done?"

"Only if you want to go through. I know it could be dangerous, and I'm asking so much."

"Not at all. To even take a step into the other world would be an incredible experience. It would prove so much of what I've theorized. I trust you to help me return home again."

Memory wasn't sure she liked the answer. It meant she had no reason left not to try, and Bedevere's faith in her only made her feel worse. *What if something goes wrong?*

But she had to try. For Will. "No time like the now, I guess. Shall I?"

A single nod marked his approval, and Memory focused her thoughts. She considered locations, and picked the vacant lot from one of her returned memories. Instead of pinching the Veil she placed her hands palms together and jabbed them forward like a thrusting blade, then spread them, widening the hole, spilling the heat of her magic into it. Before her eyes, the Veil tore and opened, swirls of smoke whipping about.

Bedevere said nothing, just looked at her for approval and then stepped through.

Memory held her breath, and just a moment later, he returned. His face had turned an off-green tinge, and he walked straight to the lounge across the room and sat down.

Memory let the doorway fade.

It worked. She could tell just by the look on his face. Memory sat down hard in the seat Bedevere had offered her before. She had opened a door to the rest of the world. Will could go home. He would go home. He would leave her.

Memory's hands shook, and her throat felt blocked. The pot of tea rattled violently beside her. Bedevere put his hands on it to keep it still and looked at her, concerned.

"Deep breaths, in, out, in. You have just achieved something incredible, but you have to keep calm. When your emotions overflow, so does the magic inside you. Like a pot boiling over." Bedevere spoke a few words in the magic language, and the pot bubbled and steamed, spilling tea from its spout. Memory sympathized with his demonstration. "I believe that's what is causing your accidental Veil door events also. The Veil is of magic, and like calls to like. The mass

of magic within you is unstable, and when you aren't in control, that magic tries to flow through the Veil as well, taking you with it. You just need to keep calm."

"I just need to keep calm," Memory repeated like a mantra. Her inner voice laughed maniacally at the idea.

"The other world, the rest of the world, even the brief glimpse…" Bedevere's jaw shook. "I would love to go back, for longer, again, anytime you would let me. But of course we must learn if a way to return to Avall is possible, in case the door closes."

Travel between the worlds would change Avall forever. It would change the rest of the world forever as well, to discover Avall, to discover magic was real. It was too much to consider, too large of a responsibility. At least for now, as far as they knew it was one way only. Just enough for Will to go home.

"No one else can know. Not yet," Memory said, looking at Bedevere.

The pleading expression on her face must have been obvious.

"Of course. It is too early," he said.

"Thank you," Memory said and stood up. Bedevere stood as well and put a hand on her shoulder when her center of gravity failed and she almost fell. Still shaky, she thanked him and headed to the door.

"Memory?" Bedevere said.

She looked back.

"You are a wonder," he said with a bowed head.

She left.

Back in the hall to her chambers, she found Roen, pacing in front of her and Eloryn's doors.

"Hey you," Memory called to him as she approached.

Roen looked up, startled out of thoughts that had him frowning. Those frowns turned into a smirk at one look of her outfit.

"So sometimes I get distracted and forget what I'm wearing! Honestly, I am actually making an effort at my etiquette classes now. And still I end up like this." Memory tried to laugh casually, but wired nerves made it sound like a snort.

Roen chuckled silently and dropped his head, looking at the floor. When he looked back up his smile had faded slightly, and his eyebrows were twisted.

"I'm leaving," he said. "I'm going home with my parents, back to our duchy."

Memory stopped in her tracks. She had in no way prepared for any craziness today aside from her own. "Why? You said you'd stay? Is this, because of me, what I did sending you to see Lory?"

Roen shook his head but his lack of voice made Memory second guess his response.

He put his hands in the pockets of his coat and shrugged. His hair was a mess and gray smudges marked his bottom eyelids. "I wanted to tell you and El first, before letting my parents know. And then the Council, since they seem keen on my absence."

"Have you told her yet?" Memory asked, tilting her head at Eloryn's door.

Roen looked at the door for a long moment. "No. Soon."

Roen bent forward and kissed Memory softly on the cheek then walked away.

She watched him go then stood in the hallway, numb, for a long while after.

Hope is right. Soon I'll have no one left.

Roen felt sick and empty. A cold fear grew in his stomach, and he didn't really know what he was doing. He had the vague notion that he was leaving, but sometimes he found himself asking why. His whole self felt torn between surrendering to the truth he and Eloryn couldn't be together, and the desire to deny that, to fight it, to do anything to make it happen. But fighting could hurt more than just him. He would not follow Thayl's path. He had to leave.

It was hard telling Memory. He hoped he would survive telling Eloryn. He'd put it off long enough.

He knocked on the door of her office and exhaled slowly.

"Enter," called a man's voice. Roen opened the door and found Hayes working at the queen's desk, papers spread on every inch of the surface except a small plate of fruit in the corner.

"Councilor," Roen greeted him, confused. "I was hoping to see Eloryn."

"*Her Majesty* is busy, Roen, and I thought we had come to an agreement about your relationship with her?" Hayes's voice was calm, and he only barely glanced up from the documents on his desk.

"It is not a social meeting I seek," Roen said.

"Of course not. You won't be swayed will you?" Hayes put his pen down and looked up at Roen properly. His gaze wasn't aggressive, and he let out a loud sigh. "You're young, and for what it's worth I do understand. But never mind. You've come at an opportune time, as I have a favor you could assist me with. Could you run an errand in the city for me?"

"An errand?" Roen repeated, not fully understanding, but glad not to be on Hayes's bad side.

"We've discovered some rare magic works that survived Thayl's reign, and I need someone I trust to collect them so they can be safely stored in the Council's collection. I'd go myself, but I'm stuck here with this paperwork, and it really is quite urgent. "

"And you'd like me to collect them?"

Hayes eyed him critically. "I can trust you, can't I?"

"Of course. I can go right away."

"Very good," said Hayes, taking a slow bite from an apple. He scrawled an address on a scrap of paper and handed it to Roen. He already looked back at his documents and waved Roen off with a wiggle of his fingertips.

Roen felt odd doing a job for Hayes, but the distraction was welcome. A way to put off telling Eloryn for a little longer.

Or so he thought until he ran into Eloryn on the castle steps.

"Roen, are you on your way out?" she asked. She wore a more casual dress than usual, and her hair had been left loose and natural, tumbling down to her hips. The soft rose fabric of her dress played up the ever present flush in her cheeks. Roen swallowed and reminded himself how to speak.

"Just a quick errand in the city. And yourself?"

"I, well I wasn't feeling very well, so Hayes offered to let me have some time off today."

Roen bowed his head to her. "I'm sorry to hear you are unwell."

Eloryn shook her head and looked to her side. "It's something that has been troubling me for a while. But I feel I may find a remedy if I try harder to do so instead of avoiding the issue. I think a change of scenery would be nice to try. Could I join you on your errand?"

Roen took a deep breath and forced a return smile. "I would be honored to have you accompany me. As long as you are feeling well enough."

Eloryn's smile widened into her blushing cheeks. "I am. I'm feeling much better already."

A carriage took Roen and Eloryn into the city, with her bodyguards on horseback surrounding them. Roen looked across the cabin to her. The small bumps rattling the carriage made her hair dance and shimmer.

This might be the last time I ever spend with her, thought Roen. He planned to treasure it.

"Would you walk with me?"

She agreed with a quick nod and Roen stopped the carriage and helped Eloryn step down onto the street. Eloryn's guards dismounted and secured their horses then gave the approval for Eloryn to proceed. Erec, as usual, remained closest to Eloryn, just a few paces behind

them. He smiled, unlike the other guards with their stern expressions, and Roen didn't like how attractive he was. He felt a pang of jealousy at how much time Erec must have with Eloryn and would continue to have when he was gone.

Roen extended his arm to Eloryn and she took it, walking by his side. He hoped she couldn't feel his trembling.

It was a dull day. The sky was a mass of low lilac clouds and a mist of rain curled up the fine strands of Eloryn's hair, making the edges glow like a halo in the filtered light.

Few other people were braving the damp, and the stone streets were eerily empty, with just a few city folk around to gawk at the queen and her handlers.

Roen led Eloryn into a small square filled with the cooing of pigeons. They lined every eave and sill on buildings around the square, sheltering from the wet. He smiled down at Eloryn. Looking at her, he could forget the weather, the trailing guards, or the fact he soon would be leaving. His nerves threatened to take over and he panicked about how to behave. Memory's voice came to him. *Just be yourself around her. Your flirtatious, sexy self.*

"Thank you for coming with me. It makes me look good, having a queen on my arm," Roen said in a mock haughty tone.

Eloryn raised her eyebrows slightly, her lips pursed. "It has been my greatest aspiration to become an attractive accessory," she replied with a straight face, followed quickly with a small smile and blush. Roen swallowed. He'd miss the way she blushed so easily.

"Well you do, make an attractive accessory. Not that I consider your beauty to be your only asset." Roen smiled wickedly at her. "You are also very rich. If only you weren't so terribly intelligent, you would be the perfect catch."

"Such a shame." Eloryn lifted her palm to her forehead

dramatically. "A shame I had thought you a better man than to want for such a lady."

Roen slowed his pace and grew serious. He enjoyed these last few moments with Eloryn more than any other time he could recall, but their last day together couldn't be filled with jokes alone.

Sincerity made his voice rough. "If I may, I would have to admit that it is your mind, and your heart, which I value above any of your many other qualities."

Eloryn squeezed his arm in hers. He almost thought he could feel her trembling as well.

"I'm sorry I've not been able to spend more time with you, Roen," she said softly.

"You owe me no apology. I understand the demands of your position. In fact I should be the one apologizing. I have to tell you—"

Roen got cut off by a young girl with bushy, carrot-colored hair running to clutch at Eloryn's hand, sending her guards into a flurry.

The guards tried to push the wide-eyed waif away, and Eloryn raised her voice in a commanding tone.

"Step back, men. Can you not see she's but a child?"

The girl seemed confused and looked from Eloryn to the guards and back again, then gave Eloryn's hand a fluttering kiss.

"Thank you, m'lady," she said.

Another child ran up beside her, hair the same color, suggesting she was a sibling. Both wore scrappy, dirt-stained clothes.

"Thank you so much, your highness."

An older girl with rivers of brown hair followed the children, grinning widely. When she was closer to Eloryn, her grin failed, and she hassled the two children into deep bows, their chests lowered almost to the ground. She dropped herself into a curtsy.

"Forgive them, your majesty," she said. "They mistook you for

Princess Memory."

"That's not their fault. We are twins after all. Although her hair is somewhat shorter than mine."

The girl stammered. "We've never seen her with her hair down before, majesty."

Eloryn gestured for the three of them to rise. "You know my sister well? What is your name?"

"Maeve, your majesty." Maeve stood back up but remained bent slightly at the waist, her head down and eyes lowered. "Yes, your majesty, from her shelter she runs not far from here."

Maeve bobbed a small curtsey to Erec as well. He nodded in return, and Roen wondered how they knew each other.

Roen thought back to the clunky bracelet Memory wore all the time. "Is one of you little Edele?" he asked the two red-headed girls. They looked at each other nervously and then to Maeve, who frowned and shook her head.

Eloryn turned to Roen to continue on their way. Maeve took a step forward again, her mouth open, then lowered her gaze again.

Eloryn stopped. "You have something you wish to speak to me about? You can do so freely, please."

Maeve nodded seriously. She tried to talk, but it looked like her effort to overcome her nerves enough to speak with the queen would take a while.

Roen squeezed Eloryn's hand and let go. "If you'll excuse me, I will continue on. I'll only be a moment to pick up these items for Hayes and meet you back here."

Roen left them talking and checked Hayes's address again. It directed him down an alleyway just across the square. He glanced back at Eloryn and smiled before heading in. The gutter ran with grayed water and the tall stone buildings either side left the narrow

alleyway heavily shadowed.

"Looking for something?" A burly man seemed to appear from nowhere. His nose looked like it had been broken more than once and his face was marred by scars, some which ran up onto his bald scalp.

Roen shook his head. The bruiser didn't look like the kind of person that would be the owner of magic documents. A second man stepped up behind the first. If possible he looked even rougher, wiry and wearing a makeshift eye-patch.

"We've been looking for something, haven't we?" the new man said.

He held up a crumpled sheet of paper. Even in the low light, Roen could read the word 'wanted,' and see the rough drawing of his own face.

Roen spun around, straight into the sights of another two men. They already held daggers in their hands, their intentions clear. The alleyway was only the width of one man and Roen could see no way past them, and no way back. A battle on two fronts.

On instinct Roen felt for his own blade in the seam of his pants, but he never carried it anymore. He held out his hands innocently and smiled. "I really think you have the wrong person. I am friends with the queen."

"Yeah and I'm buddies with the lusty queen of the seelie fae." The bald man laughed, groping crudely at his crotch. His expression turned vicious as he drew a bronze sword. "We know exactly what you are. Go on, run. Run like the street rat you are."

Before the man even finished speaking, Roen kicked off against the grimy wall beside him, bounced off the other, launching himself higher in the narrow space between the buildings.

Reaching a point well above the men's reach, he suspended himself there with outstretched arms and legs, looking for a window or some other exit.

"They always run, but we always catch 'em," said the bald man, laughing. He picked up a block of wood from some refuse beside him and hurled it at Roen.

Roen twisted his torso and the block flew past, cracking on the bricks beside him.

A second object flew at him before he could recover from the first assault and a blinding sting in his thigh made his knee buckle. Just a scratch, but enough to make him lose the tension he needed to stay suspended between the walls. A dagger clattered on the ground behind him, and he slipped.

He hit the ground hard, landing with a splash in the gutter. The block of wood lay just near his head, and he snatched it up, knowing it would be his only weapon, his only defense.

The third man, missing an ear and most of his teeth, lunged at Roen before he had a chance to get on his feet. Roen swung the wood at him, blocking the dagger and with a second hit, knocking away a few more of the man's teeth. The man stumbled and slumped against a wall. There was only one man left on that side who'd already thrown his dagger. Roen rolled to his feet and ran at him, trying to break past.

Roen barged through and made a run for the end of the alleyway. Almost there, his leg gave out beneath him. It bled freely and hurt too much to keep his weight on. The wound was worse than he first thought.

Roen managed to turn around in time to block the sword aimed for his back. The three men were right behind him. The bald man walked leisurely, matching Roen's hobbled attempts to flee. He jabbed his short sword playfully at Roen. Roen blocked and parried with the piece of wood, but every movement seemed to tug and tear at the cut in his thigh. Sweat ran onto his lips and he breathed hard to try and stay focused.

The bald man fumbled his sword. Roen took the chance to knock it away with the wood. He realized his error too late. The man had bluffed, letting his weapon go so Roen would over extend. The block of wood was snatched from Roen's hands and smashed into his face.

"We're going to enjoy this," was all he heard before he lost consciousness.

Eloryn knew nothing about the girl who stood in front of her, working up the courage to say something. Something important, it seemed.

"Maeve, really, it's okay," Eloryn encouraged.

The word, Memory's word, made Maeve smile and seemed to give her the courage to speak. "As you know, the princess has been doing so much for us. I don't know what we'd do without her and her shelter. So I wanted to ask, your majesty, respectfully, with apologies, whether it is true, the rumor I've heard?"

Eloryn was lost. "Rumor?"

Maeve looked distraught at being pressed to give details. She lowered her head some more. "That you and Master Hayes are going to shut down the shelter."

Eloryn shook her head. She'd heard nothing about it. She hadn't even known what Memory was doing in the city for these children, let alone anything about closing down the shelter.

She wanted to give her assurances that she'd want nothing of the kind to happen, but she didn't know enough, about what Memory had set up, or whether Hayes truly had some objection to it. She looked around to see if Roen was returning yet since he seemed to know at least a little more about it.

Her eyes found Roen at the entrance of an alley across the square, stumbling backwards. Her heart launched into a gallop when she saw he was fighting off a group of rough-looking men.

Eloryn tried to run to him. Her guards, seeing what she saw, held her back. Maeve gathered the younger girls to her side and rushed them away protectively.

Eloryn cried out in frustration at her guards, ordering them to release her.

"You must return to the castle, majesty. This is not safe," one said, grabbing her around the wrist.

She knew they were only trying to protect her, that was their job, but she had to help Roen. He and the men had disappeared, back into the alleyway.

Erec, at the front of the group, tripped and fell, taking the other guards down with him. Eloryn took the chance to break free. She spoke a behest to weave the guards clothes together, one guard's to another's until they were caught tied in a mess. She swore she saw Erec wink at her as she lifted her skirts and dashed after Roen.

Reaching the alley, there was no sign left of him or his assailants. Words fell from her mouth, the same behest she'd used to track Memory when she went after Thayl. The wet ground glittered, a group of footsteps forming, leading away at walking pace.

"Deann-ruith," Eloryn said. *Faster.* The glowing steps increased their pace and Eloryn followed at a jog. "Deann-ruith!"

Eloryn ran through the streets, into the long shadows of a cluttered warehouse district. Ankle-deep mud covered the road, sliced into by cart tracks. Half of the buildings appeared disused, closed up and cold. The buildings backed the river and a moldering fishy smell tainted the air.

The footsteps led Eloryn to the side door of a smaller warehouse. She ended the behest there, to not alert those inside to her presence. Peeking through a crack in a boarded up window, she could see four men circling Roen.

They had him hanging by the wrists in the center of the room. He'd been stripped of his jacket, which one man held, searching through the pockets, and his shirt had been torn down so it hung about his waist.

The men laughed and mocked Roen. Eloryn heard every second thing they said.

"Let's see if he lasts till the money arrives."

"The bounty does say alive *or* dead."

The bald man lifted his arm, and the crack of a whip echoed.

I have to help him. How can I help him on my own? Eloryn put her palms on her forehead, trying to still her panic and think. *Memory would know what to do. I just have to think creatively, like she said. Then I can do anything.*

She assessed the room to see what could be used. Shafts of light from just a few high grimy windows broke the darkness. A desiccated pig corpse hung not far from Roen, and Eloryn guessed this must have once been a butcher's storehouse. On the sawdust strewn floor, rats moved about without concern for the men. There was plenty throughout the space she could use. She hoped it wouldn't come to that. She was queen. That should be enough.

Eloryn pushed the door open without knocking and strode in with her chin raised. Sawdust stirred under her feet, tossing rancid odors and dust motes into the air. It took a while before they noticed her. Another strike with the whip, before they turned to take in her presence. Eloryn seethed.

"I am your queen, and I demand you free him," she announced.

Eloryn caught Roen's eye. He frowned hard but gave her a short nod which she returned. Red welts marked his chest and blood ran from one of his legs, dripping onto the floor at a speed that worried Eloryn.

The men stared at her then looked to a wiry man with an eye-patch for direction, whispering amongst themselves.

"He weren't joking about knowing the queen after all," said the man in the eye-patch.

One man tried to run, and the largest of them put a firm hand on his shoulder and said, "You think she's just going to leave us be after this? Think she and her kind won't hunt us down wherever we run?"

The men shot anxious glances around their group, gauging their options. Eloryn thought to tell them she'd let them be free if they left now but saw the bloody whip and knew it would be a lie. A place deep in her churning stomach wanted them to fight.

"Not matter what we do, they'll hunt us down," the skittish man said.

"She's here alone. I say we finish them both off before anyone else knows what's happened. Get rid of the bodies." The large bald man snapped the whip between his hands.

The man in the eye-patch nodded and drew a sword. "No one left that seen our faces. No one won't even know where to start looking."

The four men circled around her, penning her and closing in.

Eloryn narrowed her eyes. She breathed a deep breath then spoke her words of magic, behest running into behest, commanding help from her environment.

Her very first spell meant the men had time to draw closer, but it had to be made first before she dealt with them. Seeing it done, she turned her attention to the cruel bounty hunters.

The bald man struck the whip at Eloryn. It crumbled in the air, brittle as old bone.

Chains with hooked ends like the one Roen hung from grew long, catching up the man with the eye-patch and one other, wrapping them tight. Eloryn made no effort to make their bonds gentle.

The coward with missing teeth who thought to flee at the presence of the queen tried again. He found the hinges on the doors had fused shut. His terror multiplied as the floor beneath him became spongy, sucking him in up to his neck.

The dried pig carcass swung across the room and slammed Eloryn hard into her chest, winding her and knocking her down. Her words became useless gasps.

Someone wrenched her up to her feet. The large bald man dusted the remains of the whip from his hands menacingly. Eloryn's breath returned, but she barely managed a syllable before the man wrapped his hands around her throat and lifted her off her feet, crushing her neck. Eloryn's eyes watered.

A wet crunching sound was followed by a shudder that ran up the man's arms and into his hands around Eloryn's throat. His grip loosened and Eloryn landed back on her feet.

The man crashed to the ground.

Behind him stood Roen, half a brick bloodied in his hand.

Her first behest had been to free him. She had to free him first. No matter what happened to her, he had to be freed.

Roen took a step toward her around the fallen giant then crumpled to his knees. Eloryn dropped into the sawdust beside him and started checking his wounds.

Roen raised an arm slowly, stopping her, then put that arm around her waist and rested his head softly on her shoulder. He pulled her into his chest. She could feel his breath on her neck.

"El," he whispered. "You came for me."

"Of course," she whispered back.

"Of course," Roen repeated in reply, laughter in his voice. He winced then stilled again.

"You were amazing," he said.

"The fear of losing you proved to be great inspiration." Eloryn tried to chuckle lightly, but it sounded a little like a sob.

"It's okay, I'm not going anywhere." Roen gave her another squeeze. "Back at Elder's Bridge inn, when I'd been caught and called out, I had been ready to die. I told you and Mem what I really was because I wanted you to hate me like I hated myself. I wanted you to leave me there to my fate. At the time, I thought I deserved it."

Eloryn's head shook in fierce denial.

"Today, I could only think about how much I needed to live. Even if everyone knows the truth of my past. It seems as though at some point I have stopped hating myself. I don't know when, or how, but I suspect it has more than a little to do with you and your sister." Roen's mouth lifted into a half smile and he pulled back to look to her fully. Eloryn reached for his hands and he continued.

"There are things I've done I'm not proud of, things I must make amends for, but everything I have done has shaped who I am now, and I value that. I'm not just… a thief. I need to live long enough to show you who I really am."

Eloryn touched his cheek lightly. "I can already see."

Eloryn had seen the skills of Roen's criminal trade, she'd seen him play the flirt, and she'd seen him behind a formal polite façade. She'd seen his courage, his shame, and his passion. He was not any one of those things, but all of them and more. There was not one part of him that Eloryn didn't love.

Her head tilted back. She lifted her mouth to his. A look of confusion, relief, desperation, and desire, all rolled together, flashed across his features. He bent his face to meet hers.

Their lips didn't meet.

The sound of thudding footsteps and guards calling for their queen broke them apart.

Eloryn quickly got to her feet to meet her escort. "Take these men into custody, for hunting an illegal bounty and attempted regicide."

The men she'd caught were all watching her. She flushed, angered and embarrassed they had been present during her moment with Roen.

Erec tied a quick bandage to apply pressure to the gash in Roen's thigh until he could be healed magically, then pulled Roen to his feet and gave him his guard's jacket. Eloryn bit her tongue to try and slow her heart and remind herself there was more occurring of importance than Roen, shirtless, in uniform.

The other guards extracted the mercenaries from their bonds and dragged them from the building.

Erec ran his hand through his hair and laughed breathily. "It is a great relief to see how well you can handle yourself, your majesty. Otherwise I might have been in real trouble. I am supposed to be protecting you, not hindering your protectors."

Eloryn smiled warmly at him. "Thank you, for your help. I won't forget it. Rest assured you would have been in no trouble from me or my sister if it came to that."

Erec smirked. "It's not you and yours I'm worried about. It's my brother that'd kill me if I let you come to harm."

Roen got Erec to help him across to the man with the eye-patch and took a piece of paper from the man's pocket. Eloryn followed and stared at the poster with the etching of Roen's face

"The bounty?" Eloryn asked. "Who set it?"

Roen scrunched the paper in his hands and dropped it to the floor. "People I have wronged. I was recognized not long ago by someone from an estate I once robbed. Only that was supposed to have been dealt with." Roen paused, putting his thumb against his lips and shaking his head. "Maybe the man who spoke with Hayes wasn't the only one to have seen me."

Eloryn bent and picked up the crumpled poster, squeezing it tight in her hands. She didn't want anyone else to find it. "I'll make sure they are appeased, anything to keep you safe."

Roen put his hand over hers. "No. It's time I faced my past."

CHAPTER TWENTY-TWO

Roen spoke well, when faced with the formal gathering of Avall's nobles, wizards, legal authorities, and his parents. Eloryn had never been more proud of him and nervous for him.

"Know that I am ashamed of my thieving. For myself, and for my family. But also know this. I would never change my past because without it I would never have had my path cross with that of the Maellan twins. They are a treasure in my life, as they are to all of Avall."

The confession was followed by his promises to try to repay those he wronged, then Eloryn took over and offered Roen an absolute and unconditional royal pardon. She spoke heartfelt words of how Roen had given himself to her cause. From the applause of the crowd, it seemed they agreed that everything Roen had done to help the Maellan twins and to defeat Thayl outweighed any crimes from his past. Memory cheered for him in a boisterous and decidedly unladylike manner, which made Eloryn grin wider than she knew was proper for her station.

When the meeting ended, Eloryn amazed herself that she held in her tears when Roen's parents both brought him into an embrace. She watched from a distance as the three of them held each other for a long moment.

Erec leaned in to whisper in her ear from his usual place by her side. "I've had a few men scouring the city, and all bills and mentions of the bounty on Roen have been removed."

"Thank you," Eloryn whispered back. She breathed out shakily. She'd been more scared than she wanted to admit. Crime of any kind was treated harshly in Avall. She could still see some of the guests gossiping amongst themselves, enjoying the scandal of it all. But now it was public and officially forgiven Roen should be safe from further reprisals.

Erec cleared his throat and spoke even softer. "Those from the estate named on the poster are denying having any knowledge of the bounty."

"Has there been any further information from the bounty hunters on who they were to meet with, or who tipped them off as to where to find Roen that day?"

Erec set his jaw and stepped back in line behind Eloryn.

Hayes appeared, looking stern and sympathetic. "Those cutthroats knew nothing more than what was on the bounty poster and have since been disposed of as they should be."

Hayes put an arm around Eloryn, directing her to a quiet corner of the room. "Your majesty, I know you had your qualms before,

but when even a close friend of the queen can be attacked in broad daylight, surely now you have reason enough to grant me, as Legate of Civil Defence, the use of military force. The streets are filled with criminals such as those men. If you had given me control earlier, this entire, almost fatal mess could have been avoided."

Eloryn looked across the room to where Isabeth fussed over Roen. By the time they'd gotten him into a carriage and Eloryn had begun healing him, he'd lost a dangerous amount of blood. Now he had not a mark on him to reveal what he'd suffered, but Eloryn could almost still feel the wounds herself. Her hesitation had killed Waylan, and again her hesitation almost killed Roen.

Hayes paused to lick his lips. "Illegal bounties have become more commonplace with the increase in poverty. There simply isn't enough authority to deal with it all, and so a lot of the victims of crime will turn to illegal bounties and rough mercenaries for help. If we were granted a larger police force, or militia, we would be able to clean up the streets of those who would hang and whip a man for money."

Eloryn held her hand up to silence Hayes. "Yes. I've heard enough. Yes. Please do what you must to make our land safe."

Hayes bowed and then gave her a modest hug. "You are a wise ruler, my child. Sometimes the best thing someone in power can do is hand that duty over to someone who will be more capable in the role."

The kitchens of the shelter were smaller than those at the palace, but just as busy. The food being prepared was also much simpler fare, but Memory was amused to see that her hamburgers were becoming popular on the shelter menu. She knew she had Clara to thank for that. Workers in white aprons loaded trays for delivering lunch into the mess hall as Memory finished discussing the meal planning with the head chef.

Clara leaned on a bench next to Memory and scrutinized her. "I don't like this at all."

Memory wiped her forehead, the heat of the kitchen making her sweat. She was tired and feeling dazed at everything she'd taken on. She second guessed her every decision. "Do you think I'm budgeting for food wrong?"

"No. I don't like this, seeing all this food pass under your nose and you not taking a bite. Who are you and what have you done with my Hope?"

"I'm Memory, for starters. And I'm just not hungry."

"No, that doesn't sound like you at all. You've barely been eating anything lately. You're acting so differently, I may have to do some tests to make sure you've not been replaced with a changeling," Clara joked and picked up a small bowl of pudding.

Memory took a small bite out of some bread and choked it down. She didn't really feel like eating. Food had become tasteless for her. "Satisfied?"

"Only if you finish all of it, and then another, and maybe one more, then I'll be convinced you're really you. And you can let me know what's happening with you and that fine gentleman of yours while you're at it," Clara grinned and popped a spoonful of pudding in her mouth.

Memory's heart seemed to clamp shut. "I haven't seen Will for ages. And also, really? Will? A gentleman?"

Clara raised an eyebrow. "I meant Dylan."

"Oh." Memory felt her face grow hot. *Why did I think Clara was talking about Will?* He had been on her mind a lot since she managed to open a door back to their home world. But it should have been obvious she meant Dylan.

"I'm just studying with him. That's all."

Memory still wasn't sure how she felt about Dylan, but there had been more visits, and more kissing. He was the one person she could be around and feel completely wanted, but she didn't feel like their relationship was developing, despite Dylan's enthusiasm. Memory wondered if her inability to be enthusiastic back was due to her broken soul. She certainly blamed that for her allowing things to continue despite her lack of feelings. She was already broken, already a monster, and Dylan was the only person who seemed to want her anyway, so she'd take it.

A commotion broke their conversation, and Memory could hear Maeve yelling a stream of Avall curse words. She ran to the front door to see what was happening, Clara on her heels.

A squad of armed men had entered the shelter, facing off with Maeve and Peirs. The men wore guard uniforms marked with the symbol of the Wizard's Council that Memory had seen before.

On spotting Memory, the men stepped back and stood at attention.

"What's happening?" Memory asked, coming to stand beside Maeve.

Maeve swiped a punch through the air, directed at the men. "They are here to close us down, but I won't let them."

"Under whose authority? You know who I am, right?" Memory asked the men.

The men nodded. "Councilor Hayes has classified this building as a house of ill-repute, and a beacon for undesirables. He requires it be emptied and closed immediately for the betterment of the city."

"That's ridiculous. This is a solution to the problem, not the cause," Memory said.

The guard just shrugged. "Orders are orders."

I'm arguing with the wrong person. Memory stepped between her friends and the militia men. "You'll have to go back and say I wouldn't let you carry out your orders then, because unless your orders allow dragging me out of here kicking and screaming then you're getting nothing done here today."

The guards looked at each other as though assessing their options, then bowed and left hurriedly.

Memory rubbed her forehead with both of her palms. Everything she tried to do, everyone she grew close to, everything she wanted. She would lose all of it. The inevitability turned her blood to cold sludge.

When she turned around she saw that both Peirs and Maeve had their hands on hilts of daggers. Clara just looked stunned.

"They will be back," Peirs said grimly. "Hayes has been taking action all over the city to remove vagrants, but that's not all. I've also heard rumors that he's using his militia to gain control of the trade guilds through force."

"Why hasn't Eloryn done anything about all this?" Memory questioned.

"I doubt she even knows," Maeve said, her hands on her slim hips.

Clara spoke, her tone scandalous and low. "I see his control even at the palace. Since your uncle was arrested there has been a steady stream of prisoners coming into the castle. Anyone who questions the queen or the Council is arrested, and a lot of them don't come out again." Clara made a delicate swipe across her neck with one finger.

"You mean anyone who questions Hayes." Memory looked at the three of them before her. "Damn it. Guys, you can talk like this to me, but watch yourselves, okay?"

They nodded seriously. Memory looked around the shelter. From every doorway leading into to the entrance foyer, from between the bars of the stairway banister, little eyes watched. Memory couldn't let anything happen to them, but she couldn't be here all the time.

Memory was suddenly glad she'd let Clara dress her up with more accessories that day. Memory unclasped her necklace and started slipping rings off her fingers. She placed them down on a side table, along with her purse and the gold it contained. She stripped brooches and jeweled buttons off her dress and the ornate buckles off her shoes. She took off a heavy gold bangle, leaving just Edele's wooden bracelet on her wrist. Her hair had been pinned up using golden filigree combs which she removed, letting her hair fall free, still short above her neck at the back. Maeve put a hand to her mouth as though the sight of the cropped hair shocked her.

Memory pointed to the pile of valuables. "Maeve, Peirs, get all the kids together and find somewhere to lay low while Hayes is on his rampage. Use this stuff to get you through until I work something out. I'll try talking to him or Eloryn. They can't shut us down."

Memory said it but didn't believe it. *If I believed it I'd be letting them stay.*

Memory stared at the wealth on the table for a moment, then picked out the three most beautiful pieces and presented them to each of her friends. "I want you each to have something as well, to say thank you for being there for me, and to keep you safe."

Her companions were speechless as Memory made her goodbyes and beckoned Clara to begin their ride back to the palace.

Memory fidgeted with the bracelet from Edele. A symbol of one of the many lives taken from her. It was as though her broken self was a repellant to life, and anyone to come close would soon be lost, die, or be so repulsed they'd simply leave. She knew it wouldn't be long before another person she cared for would be gone from her world.

On their way out to the carriage, Memory said, "Clara, could you do me a favor?"

"Anything, Hope."

"Could you get me some hair dye?"

Memory took one step at a time, walking in slow motion. She ran her fingers along the rough wall as she circled up the tower stairs on her way to the ivy room. Her face ran with tears that she couldn't seem to stop. Her mouth trembled, but she made no sound.

Hope walked backward a couple of stairs ahead and stared at her. "Why with the waterworks?"

"I don't know." Memory hesitated through tears. The words collapsed on themselves, imploding, as if she didn't have the breath to utter them. "I'm… happy, for Roen and El, that they have finally started to sort their lives out, and I'm happy that Will can go back to where he belongs."

"Yeah, you look sooo happy."

Memory shook her head, and a tear flicked off her cheek. She'd put this off since she'd proven she could open a door to the other world, but she knew, no matter what, Will deserved to have the choice. She imagined that Will would probably just want to go back on his own, but she began to toy with the idea that they could go back together. Neither solution seemed right, but nothing seemed right to Memory anymore. Memory grew increasingly anxious about everything around her, her shelter, Hayes, her magic and lost soul, even Hope, and depression ached in her bones.

"Are you going to start believing me yet? That you're never going to just fit in, the way you are? That the only way to command respect is as queen?"

It made sense. She wasn't even a complete person. How could she hope to fit into a world full of people who were beginning to make sense of their lives?

"You shouldn't be crying," Hope continued. "You just need to fix things, that's all, become queen, and everything will be better."

Memory climbed out through the window and onto the roof,

letting the light breeze dust away her concerns, trying to think clearly. "Being queen hasn't seemed very easy for Lory."

Hope kept in front of her, in her face. "If you were queen you could control everything. Eloryn just lets everything, and everyone control her instead. She's not right for the role. You are."

Memory shrugged. "That's too bad then, isn't it, because she's queen and I'm not, and I can't see any way that could change."

"There is a way, if you're strong enough. I can help you become queen, where you'll be loved and wanted and never treated badly, but when you are, you have to do something for me, okay?" Hope stopped and blocked the way, forcing Memory to pause and look at her. "It's simple. You would become queen if Eloryn wasn't around anymore."

Memory pushed passed her into the Ivy Room. Her head spun with dark words and pain and confusion. She barely noted the time on the clock tower or the bareness of the space around her.

"He's not here," she mumbled.

"When is he ever?" Hope said.

Memory nodded. She had expected this. She pulled an envelope from her purse and propped it on one of the stone benches. It had taken her three hours to get the wording of the letter right. Eventually she left it simple.

I can send you home.

Hope followed Memory for a little of the way back to her chambers, but Memory was completely unresponsive, so Hope vanished. Memory was at a loss for what to think or do.

Sleep would be good. Sometimes she imagined that she could sleep forever. It seemed easier that way. She approached her chambers and could hear the crashing of a brawl inside. She swung the door open.

Dylan and Will were locked in a brutal fight. Will was on all fours with Dylan pinned underneath him on the floor, slugging him in the face.

Both were spattered with blood. Bruises already swelled on their skin.

"Stop." The word was barely a breath. Neither man heard her. Dylan tried to shield himself with an arm, and Will shook him against the ground.

Memory put both hands to her head and screamed, "Stop it!"

The room rumbled and Dylan and Will were thrown apart by the invisible force of her magic.

Dylan slid along the silk rug. Will hit the side of the fireplace. He immediately got back up and rushed Dylan.

Memory stepped in between them.

Will's fist froze a hairs-breadth from her face.

He bared his teeth and looked for a moment like he might vomit. With a roar he ran off, practically throwing himself from the balcony and disappearing.

"Will!" Memory stepped toward the windows and felt Dylan's hand close around hers, pulling her back. It was slick with blood and Memory shuddered. She looked down at him where he lay on the floor.

"Stay. I need your help," he said, his lips red and swollen.

Memory nodded slowly.

She knelt beside Dylan. The damage to him was brutal.

"That savage should be caged," he said, wiping his mouth.

Maybe he's right. Maybe the Council was right all along.

"How hurt are you, can you stand?"

He nodded and Memory put an arm around him, helping him into her bedroom and laying him down on the bed. She grabbed a hand towel and dampened it, and came back to wipe away some of the blood.

"It's insane, allowing a brute like that to run wild," Dylan said.

Will. Memory remembered the boy who sang so beautifully. She'd done this to him, turned him into what he was now. So much anger, so violent. He'd never seemed that way to her before, but maybe she'd just refused to see it. Dylan groaned and Memory wondered if she should try healing him with magic but was worried about hurting him even more. All she did was hurt people.

"It's lucky you showed up." Dylan grinned wryly in a way that reminded her of Roen.

"Dylan," Memory said. She sat back, holding the stained towel in her lap, frowning as her mind worked through events. "Why didn't you defend yourself with magic? Like with Roen?"

Dylan ran a finger down Memory's cheek. "I'm worried about you. Promise you'll keep your window locked from now on."

Memory twitched away from his touch. "Is my brain skipping? Did I not say that out loud? Why didn't you defend yourself? Will can't use magic, just like Roen can't."

"It doesn't matter. I'm all right, see?" Dylan sat up so he was closer to Memory. His voice was low, gravely, and he pushed his lips against hers. Memory tasted blood and her stomach churned.

Stop, stop, stop. "Stop." Her voice was lost under his mouth. He placed his hands over her shoulders, pulling her in closer.

A frantic shuddering built in her limbs, and Dylan flew off her and was pinned against the headboard of the bed. He cried out in pain. Memory fought to calm herself, letting him go.

Dylan slumped and looked at her fiercely.

"What are you doing?" he shouted. "You bring me into your bed after your creature beats me and then you carry on assaulting me? Do you have any idea how difficult it's been with you?"

"What do you mean?" Memory moved off the bed, stepping

away from him. He stood up and followed her.

"I deserve better than this. Hayes should have given me the good twin, not you." Dylan spat blood on her floor. "You think I came into your life by accident? When you refused to even look at the suitors the Council offered you? I was chosen for you to keep you busy and out of trouble. And the lengths I've had to go to."

Memory's lips curled, her whole body jolting with disgust. The one reason she liked Dylan was that he desired her, to have someone around that really wanted her, and it was all a lie. The truth was nobody wanted her. How could they?

Dylan made his voice gentle again and reached to touch her. "You should be grateful and just take what you've been given."

Memory felt the ground shaking under her feet. The whole world felt unstable and ready to topple. She had to get out of there.

Memory smacked his hand away from her and ran to the door. She bumped into Clara who was staring at the messed up room and sprays of violent crimson.

Clara gasped at Memory. "Hope, are you—"

"Call the guards," Memory said to her, not stopping. She pointed back to her bedchambers where Dylan followed. "Just get rid of him."

"Highness," Clara said in confirmation.

"Guards? Whose side do you think the guards are on?" Dylan called after her as she ran. She could hear his mocking laughter chase her all the way up the stairs.

CHAPTER TWENTY-THREE

Please be there, please be there.

Memory ran all the way to the Ivy Room. She didn't know what she was going to say to Will, but she needed to see him.

Memory burst through the screen of ivy, and the sight of Will in front of her almost stopped her heart. He stood still and tall. His reddened hands shook and his cheeks were marked with the tracks of tears, but he didn't move, didn't cry.

He looked her in the eyes, both staring at each other for a long moment, before he flinched and looked away.

"Did I hurt you?" he mumbled.

Memory mouthed the word "no," but no sound emerged.

Will started pacing, like a caged lion. His voice grew louder. "He just… you didn't hear the things he said. That he could tell you didn't like to be touched. That he'd force you anyway."

Memory just stood there watching, like she had no energy left to move or talk. Dylan provoked the fight, and let Will beat him, let Will be the animal. But why? Just to get Will out of her life? It was going to happen anyway. She looked over at her letter to Will and saw the envelope torn open. Bloody fingerprints marred the cream-colored paper.

Will saw her look and scowled. "You don't believe me."

"I do. I know Dylan was a fake, just like you said."

"But you still want me gone."

I just want you to be happy and safe.

Memory reached out for him. Will growled viciously at her.

Memory let out a soft cry, not from fear, but from the pain of Will turning on her. Her Will.

Breath tore through Memory like daggers, and she gritted her teeth and opened the Veil to the other world. She held the door open.

Will looked at her with those blue eyes, and a single tear ran down his cheek.

"Just go," she said.

Memory turned away to hide her own tears that ran, closing her eyes, unable to look.

No. She curled her hands into fists. *Look at him. It will be your last time.* She turned around and opened her eyes. "I… I'll miss you."

He was already gone.

"Will? WILL?" Memory screamed.

A rumbling built inside her. She clutched at her chest to hold it in, sobbing. The leaves of the ivy trembled, gusting like a strong wind took hold of them. Memory tried to grasp any scrap of calm within her, but it all flew away, anguish tearing her raw. It spilled out, burst from her. The vines around her were shredded, charred, every last leaf and tendril disintegrated. The ivy that hid and protected the room, that gave it its name, was gone. Memory's knees cracked as they hit the ground.

Will. My safe place. Everything is gone.

Memory wasn't sure when it had gotten so late. The moonlit courtyard was empty and through the windows of the palace she only saw the odd servant passing in the halls.

Her gown was marked with blood and ashes, and she just walked, wherever her aching feet would take her.

"Of course Will left you. What did you think he'd do given the choice?" Hope said.

Memory walked so slowly that Hope circled around her, doing laps.

"I'm sorry about Dylan though. Who could have known that would end badly?" Hope kicked at the pebbled path. They came to a large marble fountain, and Memory focused on the sound of the running water, trying to drown everything else out.

"But it was just like I said, wasn't it? No one can like you how you are. But if you were queen, things would be different. You could save your shelter. You could just get rid of Hayes. You could do anything you wanted."

Could I? "What about my sister?"

"Don't go getting sentimental. She's not your friend. Her and Hayes are working together, on everything they've done. Eloryn knew about Dylan, and about your shelter. Eloryn's seen inside you. They are cruel to you because they know you're barely human. I told you this would happen. They're not you real friends – I'm your only friend. The only one you can trust."

"I can't… do anything to Lory."

Hope grabbed Memory by the arms. "You can. You don't remember yourself, what you have in you, what you're capable of."

"Stop it, I don't want this." Memory tried to pry Hope's hands off her, but her grip was tight and Memory had lost all strength.

"We have to get rid of her," Hope hissed.

"Shut up! Shut up, shut up, shut up!"

Memory threw herself at Hope, pushing them both into the pond around the fountain. Hope disappeared out from underneath her as they splashed in. Memory sat staring into the water. The ripples stilled and she saw her reflection. With a snarl she smashed at her face on the water surface, hitting it over and over. The water was icy and she let it numb her.

"Mem?" Roen called her. She could hear him running over the pebbles. "What are you doing in there? I heard you screaming."

His arms wrapped around her and pulled her out of the water. "It's okay, calm down. Let's get you back to your room."

Memory pushed out of his arms, shaking her head roughly.

"No, not there, I can't go back there. Dylan could still be there. The blood."

"You're soaked through. We have to get you warm. Come on."

Roen put his arm around her again, and she let him lead her into his chambers nearby. Roen held up a blanket around her while she unclasped her dress with shaking fingers and let it drop. They left it in a puddle and Roen wrapped her in the blanket. His chambers were only a single room, unlike hers, and he sat with her on the bed, keeping her in his embrace, rubbing her arms. Memory could tell she was shivering but felt nothing.

"Can you tell me what happened?"

"Dylan." Memory's breath came hard and she had difficulty expressing herself. "He was… working for Hayes."

"I'm sorry. Would you like me to break his knees for you?"

Memory's mouth twitched, lifting a little.

"You know I'd be more than happy to. Just say the word."

Memory frowned again. "I don't know what I want. I don't even know who I am anymore. So how can I know what I want? Everything about who I was got stripped away. Everything that was Hope: my memories, my clothes, my hair, even my piercings, all taken or lost until I was Memory. Memory, Hope, I don't feel like either of them anymore. I need a new name."

"How about Mope, it'd suit you the way you've been lately," Roen said.

"Har-dee-har-har."

"It's okay, to not know who you are. I don't know who I am, and I'm not facing half your obstacles. You have time. You'll work it out," Roen said.

She sat tucked right in under his shoulder, and she snuggled against his chest, seeking warmth and life. Roen gave her a small peck on the side of her head.

"You almost didn't flinch that time," Roen observed.

"What do you mean?" Memory asked.

"You flinch, you know, every time someone touches you. Even me. I see it. Maybe it's only a little, but I still see it. Actually, Will's the only one you don't flinch at."

"Yeah," Memory groaned, "but now he flinches at me. I think…" *He's gone.* "I think…" *He's left me. I'll never see him again.* "I…" Memory couldn't even get the words out.

They sat together in silence as Memory focused all her being on keeping calm. It was starting to come more easily to her now, like she had no energy left for her emotions.

"I'm sorry I'm such a mess. The worst thing is I keep having to see Eloryn, every day, being so bloody perfect. And it's like… she's everything I could have been. I hate her for that sometimes. That's terrible isn't it? I shouldn't. I shouldn't have even said…"

Roen just squeezed her tight.

Memory looked up at him and could see a distant look in his eyes, a deep sadness.

She asked, "How are things, with you, and her? Is something wrong?"

Roen smiled but the sadness remained. "I asked the Council if I was allowed to court Eloryn and they vehemently refused, told me I shouldn't be seeing her at all. And I thought I could get by, hide my feelings, but I can't."

Memory thought of Will, and how she'd been told she shouldn't see him. She wondered how much of Dylan's provocation was his idea or how much was Hayes's. It didn't matter anymore. Memory squinted to hold in tears.

"What are you going to do?" she asked.

"The usual. Cry myself to sleep each night. But at least now I'll have someone to blame other than myself," he said, smiling wryly. "You don't want to try again, you and me? We could both do with some comfort."

Memory shook her head but stayed in his arms. "I know you don't really feel that way about me. I might look like her, but I'm not the girl you love. Besides, if she's too good for you, what are you saying about me?" Memory dug a thumb into Roen's ribs playfully. Although she

spoke lightly, the words cut into her. Maybe Roen only ever wanted her around because she reminded him of Eloryn. Another person who didn't truly want her, or care for her. Not for who she really was. Memory tried to shake off the dark thoughts. *No. He's still my friend, maybe the only one I have left.*

A hectic banging at Roen's door startled them and before they could move the handle turned and Eloryn stepped in. "Roen, have you seen Memory? Something has happened in her chambers and she's—"

Eloryn froze when she saw them on the bed together. Her nose twitched and she lifted her chin.

Memory realized how it must look, with her in just undergarments and a blanket, wrapped up in Roen's arms.

"El, I can explain," Roen began. He got off the bed and walked to Eloryn.

Eloryn put her hand up and he stopped. "No, I want to hear it from Memory. Have you two been seeing one another? Can you deny you've never been intimate?"

Memory stuttered. "It's not how it looks. We kissed once, ages ago, but that's it."

"You kissed her?" Eloryn asked Roen.

"I kissed you first," Roen said.

"You what?" Memory blurted.

She and Eloryn spoke in unison. "How does that make it better?"

Eloryn pushed her hands against her stomach, her face twisted, staring at Memory. "I try my best, I try to do things correctly, stay positive, but you just wade in, not understanding anything and do whatever you want. Take whatever you want. I could almost have accepted this if you'd come to me. I could have been happy for you both. But you," Eloryn's voice wavered and she turned her face away from Memory. "You taunt me with tales of how Roen feels for me. You tell me to share my feelings, to risk everything to allow myself to care for him, only to take him for yourself?"

Eloryn ran from the room.

Roen ran after her, without even a glance back at Memory.

Every dark thought inside Memory felt confirmed. She felt completely, helplessly alone.

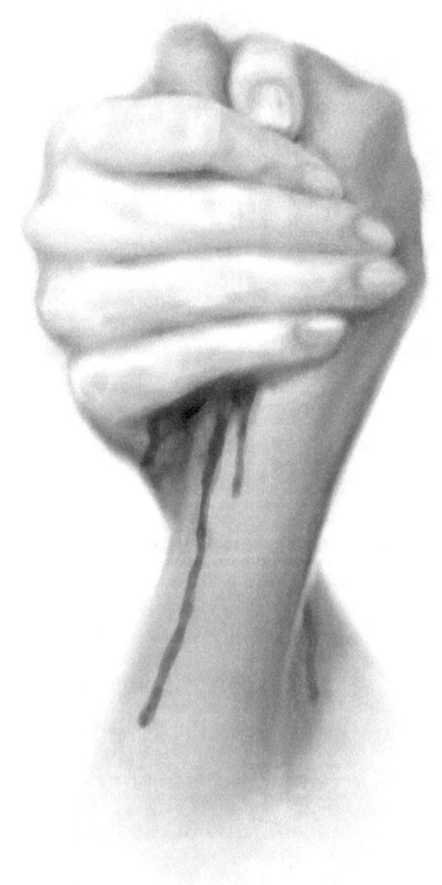

Memory let loose her churning emotions, opened herself to the Veil, daring it to take her away, somewhere, anywhere better than this. She found herself back in her room. Disappointed, Memory crawled into bed in her still damp underclothes.

"I've lost everyone," she whispered.

"You still have me," Hope said. She laid her head down on the pillow next to Memory.

Memory turned to face the other way. "It's your advice that keeps screwing everything up. I should never have messed around with Roen or Dylan."

Hope groaned pointedly. "No, it was my warning all along that everyone would reject you. It was you who wanted to play happy families like you're a real girl. It was my advice all along that the only way to make people treat you right was to be the queen, so they had no choice. Let me help you."

Memory rolled back over, face to face with her old self. "Can you help to stop everything from hurting?"

Hope smiled sympathetically. "I can help you become queen, and then it will be better, I promise. You can pay me back later. We just have to kill Eloryn."

A chill ran up Memory's back. "There has to be another way. I'm not a murderer."

Hope pursed her lips as though thinking. "Sit up. I want to give you something. Something that will give you the strength to do what needs to be done."

It took all her energy to sit up. The blankets felt like lead. "What?"

"Your memories. I've been learning too, and I think we can do it. And once we do, then you'll see. Then you'll know who you really are, what we're capable of."

Memory exhaled sharply. "My memories? What about my soul?

Can you fix it? Make me better again?"

"Your soul is kind of *me* now. I don't know how to put that Humpty back together again. But I think I can share our memories so you have them too."

Memory stared at Hope, at who she used to be. If she could at least have all her memories back, would she feel more whole?

"What, you don't want them?" Hope's voice was teasing.

"Do it."

Hope grinned, and pulled a small, unfamiliar knife from her pocket. She cut the palm of her own hand harshly, letting blood seep out. She took Memory's hand and did the same. Memory flinched but made no sound when the blade sliced her skin.

Hope took Memory's hand and pressed it into hers, their blood mingling, and began speaking words of magic.

The world faded as Memory fell into her past.

She ran out of the children's home, running blindly up an alley strewn with trash bags. Her body ached all over, and she felt sick in a way like she could never get better. A man in an old-fashioned suit stood there, reaching a hand out for her.

Thayl, Memory realized, her thoughts overlaying the memories. *This is the last moment, last memory, before he took them all from me.*

Time jumped backwards, and she stood in front of a charred body. A corpse. Nothing burnt so badly could be alive. A choking stench like burned rubber and pork fat filled the small space, murky with smoke. She bent to pick up her knife from the floor as though she still needed protection. Horror coiled inside her. *I was wrong. Make it stop. I don't want to see more.*

Back again and a wide-set man grinned at her as he unbuckled his belt. She wouldn't let it happen this time, enough was enough. She drew the knife she'd stolen the day before and told the man to back off. She'd always thought he wasn't quite all there, mentally, and the confusion on his face confirmed it for her then. As though he couldn't understand her defiance. As though he thought she wanted this and couldn't believe she'd turn on him. It angered him in a way she'd never seen before and he struck her. Her knife fell uselessly from her hand, and the man beat her and beat her until she thought he'd knock the life right out of her. She curled up on the floor, trying to shield herself. A bubbling pressure built inside her. She tried to hold it back. She knew how dangerous it could be. The man cracked her chin with his boot. She couldn't hold back. She exploded and the man burned.

Back again and she's drawing tattoo designs with Will in her room when the man comes to get her. Small, frail Will stood up like he wanted to do something, but didn't.

Back again. Each vision played faster than the next, hopping backwards in time, playing through her whole life, faster and faster, flooding her.

An entire life in rewind. Every scene scarred by the vision of the burned man. Every scene silenced by the repeating words, *I'm a murderer.*

CHAPTER TWENTY-FOUR

Eloryn felt surrounded by lies. She wanted to trust people, to give the world the benefit of the doubt, believe in the goodness of those around her, but she felt repaid with betrayal. Like Memory and Roen, together, behind her back, despite everything they said. At least they had made one part of her life easier, allowing her to reach one decision.

First thing the next morning, Eloryn went to find Hayes where he worked in her office. *Can I still trust him? What if he is all lies as well? No. I can't think like that or I'll have no one left to trust.*

Hayes scribbled notes down on a stack of pages bound in string.

"Your majesty?" He looked up, seeming surprised at her presence.

"Hayes," she said. "I'm sorry I have delayed progress on approved courtship and marriage plans. I wanted to let you know I'm now ready to do my duty as queen. I'll marry whomever the Council deems most appropriate."

Hayes put down his pen and rose to his feet. "That is wonderful news. I shall call a meeting this afternoon for the announcement." Hayes put his hands on her shoulders fondly. "Do you mind if I ask what prompted your decision?"

The image in her head was still too clear. Roen and Memory, holding each other on his bed, wrapped in each other's arms. "I would prefer you didn't."

Memory awoke. She last remembered it being late in the night, but now sunset shone through her window, the pink glow tinting the room. It had become a different day, and she had become a different person.

Her eyes closed again, but a knocking on her bedroom door made her sit up. She could hear Clara calling through it. "Hope, please, open the door."

I finally am Hope again. The thought didn't bring her much happiness. Memory looked around. The doorway was barricaded with

furniture and Memory wondered who did it. The other Hope sat on a chair that blocked the way in.

"Welcome back," she said.

"How long have I been out?" Memory stood up and wavered a little before steadying herself.

"All of last night and today. How do you feel?"

Memory paused and looked at her hands. She needed some nail polish. "Like me."

Clara knocked and called, but Memory ignored her pleas. Memory went to her wardrobe and pulled out the box of her old clothes, taking the whole lot into the bathroom. Standing at the mirror, she worked on putting all of her piercings back into place. Some of the holes had started to close and she forced the jewelry through. The slash on her hand stung and bled as she screwed in the labret. Memory examined her face then tugged at her hair. It had grown an inch or two, trying to be more fitting for this place that no longer felt like home.

"It's all back?" Hope asked, trailing beside Memory as she returned to the bed and retrieved the knife Hope had used to cut their hands. Clara seemed to have given up and gone away. Memory went back to the bathroom.

"Yeah. Still a bit messed up. It's definitely there though. Everything makes a lot more sense now," Memory said. She sawed at her hair, cutting the back short again.

"Of course your head will be a bit busy at first. You've just had a life's worth of memories injected into your brain. I think we can forgive it a little."

A life's worth of memories. A life's worth of pain.

Her insides were raw, like a scab picked away to the mess underneath. Memory began to feel sick and the mirror rattled against the wall. She felt like an emotive proximity mine. *Keep calm. Keep busy.*

Memory threw her t-shirt and jeans on over the old fashioned bodice she wore.

"It's not right," she said, looking herself up and down in the mirror.

"I like it. You look like you," Hope said.

"No. I look like who I used to be." Memory started changing back out of her old clothes. She slipped on a plain underskirt. She meant to put a proper dress on over the top, but lost motivation half way, left in her t-shirt and the flowing layers of silk that dropped from her waist. *Still not right.* She picked up a make-up brush off the dressing table and started blackening around her eyes.

Hope groaned. "Enough dress up. Now you know what we're capable of. Are you ready to take what belongs to you, become queen?"

"You're asking if I'm ready to murder Eloryn?"

"You don't have to be so blunt about it, but yes. It's what needs to be done. Eloryn is heavily guarded. But you've got the best chance to get close to her. Remember it's got to look like an accident. The point is to get you to be queen, not executed for regicide."

Memory said nothing and continued lining her eyes. She wondered if she could go back to the other world. Maybe find Will again. The thought of the other world left a deep nausea in her bones. She couldn't go back, especially now she knew she was a murderer there. The floor shook, and the exposed pipes running to the bath and sink groaned like they could crack.

Memory centered herself, considering her options. She couldn't go back. What she had to do to stay here seemed impossible. What else could she do?

An eerie calm fell over her.

The room stilled.

Memory stared at herself in the mirror, then down at the cloth bag on the dresser filled with the coarsely ground powder that Clara assured her was hair dye. It looked worse than the cheap packet sachets Memory used to steal from the drugstore.

I'm calm. I'm in control.

Memory closed her eyes and breathed deeply, imagining the result she wanted, "Change it."

She opened her eyes. Her ivory blonde hair had become a rich royal purple, the bottom halves of the longer front sections tipped black.

Hope stared. A faint look of concern flashed on her features before she punched Memory in the shoulder and smiled. "Fancy stuff. Getting those emotions locked down, huh?"

"Something like that."

"Good. It's all forward from here, 'kay? And you know what the next step needs to be. I'll do what I can to help you, just give me the go ahead."

"No." Memory took the knife and headed for the door. "She's my sister."

Eloryn was passing time within the Round Room, waiting for the meeting Hayes had scheduled for later that day that would seal her fate. A messenger had told her that Roen's parents were preparing to leave and everyone was making their goodbyes. She wasn't able to bring herself somewhere she knew Roen would be.

She ran her hands up one of the pillars that stood around the room and found a crack in it still from the explosion. She spoke a behest to fix it. If only she could repair everything so easily.

"Eloryn?" A friendly voice came from around the corner.

"Isabeth," Eloryn greeted her with a smile. "What are you doing here?"

"I understand it might be asking a lot, but I came to see why the queen hadn't come to see us off."

Eloryn worked hard to keep the smile on her face.

Isabeth frowned. "My child, what's wrong?"

The obviousness of her emotions caused Eloryn to lose control, and she began weeping.

Isabeth took her in her arms, gently stroking her hair. "You surely can't be that upset to see me go," she joked softly.

Eloryn put her hand to her mouth in an attempt to hold back her grief.

"It's all right. Don't hold it in. Tell me everything."

Eloryn had never known the comfort of a mother's arms. She found every one of her doubts and worries falling from her mouth. "I feel I'm making so many mistakes. I owe the Council my trust and loyalty, but find my trust given to men with misogynistic, antiquated, hard-line views. And even knowing that, I've handed so much power to them because I couldn't use that power myself. I'm just not a ruler. But I'm worried. So worried that I've done the wrong thing. I don't know if I can keep going along with their wishes, but don't know how to challenge them." Eloryn pulled back. She dried her face with a handkerchief but desperation still filled her voice. "What if you try your hardest to be strong, and do your duty, but it's simply not who you are?"

"Sweet child, let me tell you something," Isabeth put her hands on Eloryn's shoulders and looked at her straight. "Your mother had

all the same complaints. And if she had stood up for herself, then things would never have gotten so bad for so long. I'm not blaming your mother, dear, I'm only saying… don't make the same mistakes that she did. Follow your heart."

But the one my heart wishes for has already chosen another. "I can't. I can't have what I want. Even if I could, would you still encourage me to follow my heart if it meant I would no longer be royalty? That I and the one I chose to be with would not hold this power?"

Isabeth laughed softly. "Power and duty be damned. You are sad to your core, and it makes me sad to see you so. You should do whatever makes you happy, and if that's serving your kingdom then so be it. But if it's not what you want, then why can't someone else do it? Shouldn't a prerequisite to rule be the passion and desire to do so?"

Eloryn had already given Hayes so much power, but the thought of handing over what remained gave her chills. "I cannot let Hayes rule. I… I just don't think he's right for it."

Isabeth looked at her like she was a dullard. "Of course he isn't. I said passion and desire, child. Not greed."

"I've been so foolish." Eloryn put her head on Isabeth's shoulder and held her tight. "Thank you. It feels like an age since someone has been so honest with me, Isabeth. I'm so used to lies and duplicity and spending wasted effort on making myself trust and believe. Even from family. Even my sister…"

"If there is one thing that I have learned you can trust, it is family." Isabeth said. "And I am no hypocrite to say so, despite having just learned how my son kept us fed and clothed all these years. His words were lies but in his actions, every coin he brought home, every sack of flour or new dress spoke clearly, 'I love you, I care for you, I would do anything to keep you safe.' And all those years I lied to myself, saying the weight we placed on his shoulders was not too much, that he had not such a hard road."

Isabeth squeezed Eloryn tight. "For whatever has come between you and your sister, have you looked at the truth in her actions or just seen what you wanted to believe?"

To follow my heart, to be with Roen, has terrified me at every turn. I've sought every reason not to, and in Memory and Roen's intimacy I gave myself the ultimate excuse. Was it just what I wanted to believe?

Maybe she over-reacted. Maybe she should have trusted Memory more. Eloryn gave everyone else the benefit of the doubt. It was the least she owed her twin. In her heart, if nothing else, she desperately wanted to believe Memory's insistence that said she and Roen weren't in love.

CHAPTER TWENTY-FIVE

The entire Wizard's Council gathered in the Round Room. Fifteen of them. All that remained, who'd lived in fear of their lives for so long as all their brethren were hunted. Those who had lived in complete isolation from the world for sixteen years, even more than Eloryn had.

Eloryn's partner for the rest of her life would be decided by these men. It didn't seem right. She'd requested it, but her talk with Isabeth left her mind spinning, unsure. The meeting came upon her before she could clear her dizziness and find clarity.

Only the Council was in attendance, although Memory had been sent an invitation to the meeting. Her absence concerned Eloryn. There was more they should have said to each other. Apologies to be spoken and forgiveness to be given. To know for sure, before she recklessly sealed her fate.

Hayes stood and waited until he had everyone's attention, then sat and nodded to Bors. Hayes smiled in a way that unsettled Eloryn. Something greedy in his eyes twisted the expression. Did he always look that way and she was just seeing it now?

Bors cleared his throat. "Your majesty, we hear that you wish to expedite the arrangement of your marriage?"

Eloryn found she couldn't speak, so she nodded.

"In order to accommodate your request, we have been carefully reviewing the candidates for your partner. In light of recent events and changes, we've reached a somewhat untraditional conclusion, but we feel it is now our best option."

A number of the Councilors were frowning, but nodded in agreement.

Could it be? Eloryn's heart beat like a voice, *Roen, Roen, Roen.*

Bors gestured to Hayes at the head of the table. "We have come to the agreement that the most suitable candidate is one of our own, Councilor Hayes."

"It is my most humble honor," Hayes said, bowing his head slightly.

Eloryn's jaw dropped. A few Councilors offered muted applause and congratulations.

"I don't understand," Eloryn said. "What about the list of other candidates?"

Madoc grumbled from next to Bors, "The list, unfortunately, somehow made its way into public hands. It has been trouble enough quieting the furor that entailed, with families demanding to know why their sons weren't selected, and those who were selected suddenly receiving proposals from across the land. I'm afraid every one of those candidates had to be removed from selection."

Eloryn felt the breath knocked out of her. She'd so flippantly handed the list to a group of giggling girls. She didn't even consider the consequences. She was thinking of nothing but the name that wasn't on the list.

"But a member of the Council?" she said.

Bedevere, who rarely spoke up, grumbled from beneath his frown. "Believe me, we debated this decision at length. We had very little choice. I'm sorry, your majesty."

Hayes left his position at the head of the long table and paced down to stand by Eloryn's side at the other end. He held his walking cane horizontally in both hands.

"My peers are all in agreement that I am the most magically powerful contender and thus the most obvious choice for king."

Eloryn felt sick to her gut. Should this go ahead Hayes would have more power than her. Not only would he be king, but should they have children - Eloryn swallowed rising stomach acid - his children would be heir to Avall's throne, before Memory, before anyone.

Is that what he was after all along? Every foothold of power she'd given him over the past weeks had been begged and manipulated from her, and now he would have it all.

Her own indecision and naivety had brought them to this juncture. She couldn't let it continue.

"No, I can't. I won't," she said. Her words felt clumsy in the face of this man's arrogance.

Hayes frowned sympathetically, and put a hand on her shoulder. "This is the decision of the Council and we must go along with their wishes. Your majesty, we must do this for Avall."

"No, for Avall, for myself, I deny you." Eloryn tried to stand, but Hayes pushed her firmly into her chair under his grip. He bent a little

and whispered in her ear.

"You cannot go against the council's decision, girl. Even if you would, here's something else to consider. I have full control of the military. Control of Avall's police and militia is in the hands of those loyal to me, and I have complete domination of the trade guilds. Should you refuse to marry me then I will simply cripple the economy of Avall, punishing her people, and force control through a coup."

Eloryn winced then set her face firm. She did this. She gave him the power to force her into this position. She had to find a way to undo it. Even if she stripped him of his power now, he had armed militia under control of his loyalists who would wage a war to take it back. But there had to be a way.

Hayes squeezed her shoulder as if consoling her, but his words were venomous. "Keep in mind, you're not the most popular monarch or figurehead at the moment. Even your dim-witted sister is more popular than you. You're much too young and weak willed to rule a kingdom on your own. I deserve this position." Hayes straightened back up and addressed the whole room again.

"The Council recognized the leadership I have displayed as we suffered and survived Thayl's rule, the cunning that saved us. I vow to devote that same ingenuity to my role as King. I vow to do anything required to save Avall." Hayes pounded his walking stick on the floor with each intonation. He moved away from Eloryn and she stood up, but made no move to run from the room despite it being her greatest desire.

Hayes bowed to her, but the look on his face remained cruel. "You must do this for your kingdom, your majesty. You cannot simply marry some Sparkless thief." Hayes rumbled a deep, mocking laugh that some of his allies echoed. "That fool had the audacity to come to us, the Wizard's Council, to ask for your hand. A seventh son of a seventh son asking for the hand of a Maellan?"

The pounding in Eloryn's chest seemed to wake her from the numbness of what was happening. *Roen formally asked to be with me.* It shouldn't have been the most important piece of information she'd taken in so far, but it was, to her. It was all she cared about, and that realization gave her the hunger to find a way to make it happen. And she would find a way to destroy every greedy goal of the man in front of her with the same act. *I know exactly what I can do.*

Eloryn spoke, making her voice loud and firm. "Very well. I will marry you, Hayes."

Hayes looked like a wolf who'd just had a lame goat cross its path. Eloryn smiled sweetly and spoke over him before he could say anything in reply. "On the condition that upon signing of a behest-bound pre-nuptial agreement, you hand all control of the militia and trade guilds to the ruler of Avall and to not use them against myself or our heirs."

Hayes smirked. "For what difference it will make, being as I shall be king."

"I want it drafted and signed now." Eloryn lowered her eyes and bobbed a short curtsey as though signaling he had won.

Bors unfurled a roll of parchment and began scrawling the words in large flourished script. As he worked, Eloryn heard a small scuffle from the corner of the room and saw Erec holding Roen back. The sight of him almost chased her resolve away. Eloryn caught Roen's eyes and warned him with the tiniest shake of her head. *Trust me*, she mouthed. He bared clenched teeth, but nodded.

"I am now binding the agreement with the required magic," Bors said, and uttered a few behest words. "It is ready to sign."

Without delay Hayes moved over to the contract and signed it.

Eloryn stepped over to the paper and also signed.

Eloryn turned to the Council, purposefully ignoring Hayes.

"Good sirs, I hereby formally announce my abdication as queen."

All around the table voices grumbled, outraged and confused at her announcement. She could hear Hayes breathing hard behind her.

She turned her head, barely looking over her shoulder at him. "Someone once told me, that sometimes the best thing someone in power can do is hand that duty over to someone who will be more capable in the role. I trust we will find my sister to be more capable."

"You can't do this," Hayes hissed. She knew he'd calculated what she'd done. Since they were not yet married, Memory was still the legal heir and through abdicating Eloryn ensured Hayes would never be king through marriage to her. With the contract, she'd stripped him of any power he'd accumulated through control of his militia. They were now under Memory's control, and he was behest-bound to never use them against either of the twins.

"No one will support your halfwit sister in power," Hayes warned, salivating at the mouth with rage. He looked around the table, but all other voices remained silent. Bors kept shooting panicked looks at Hayes.

Eloryn still refused to turn and face him. She made her case to the rest of the Council. "Memory will make a better queen than I ever could. She has been diligently studying the laws of Avall and has consistently made better decisions than I have. She has always stood by her own instinct, rather than what I did, which was almost handing the kingdom over to a greed-driven warmonger. I was never made for this. It was never truly what I wanted." She flicked Hayes a sparkling glare. "Besides, I have recently heard that my sister was a more popular choice than me anyway."

The Council looked back and forward between themselves and her. They muttered to each other as though she were barely there.

Hayes snatched Eloryn's arm and spun her to face him. Bedevere and two other Councilors jumped to their feet. Erec and Roen appeared by her side, and Hayes snarled and let go.

"Is that all who would stand with me against this man, who would threaten our land with military might for his own ends?" Eloryn said, daring each man around the table. "I will no longer be queen, and he will not be king through me. He will be punished for what he has attempted, and do not doubt that any who stand with him will be as well."

Bors joined the other Councilors on their feet. He licked his lips, eyes darting. "I cannot remain silent any longer. Hayes's crimes exceed what any of you may imagine."

"Bors," Hayes growled.

Eloryn raised her hand to Hayes. "Not another word from you. Bors, please tell us everything. You are safe."

He nodded, his voice lifting with each word as though fearful excitement drove it louder. "The entire threat from your uncle was a fabrication. Hayes killed Waylan for challenging him too much. He dressed it up as an attack on you in order to also remove your uncle. And Hayes was the one who put the bounty on the Faerbaird boy. These were all things he did to get what he wanted and to remove who he didn't."

As Bors continued, the words Eloryn heard behind her lifted the hairs on her neck.

"Guidhe beag lugha ob—"

Eloryn turned and slapped Hayes across the mouth, stunning him silent. He stumbled back a few steps, fury dripping from him.

There was chaos in the room. Every other Councilor got to their feet, calling accusations and demands to each other, to Hayes, Bors, and Eloryn.

Eloryn finally looked him in the eyes again. "I trusted you, Hayes. I freely gave you all my trust, and this is what you've done with it?"

Hayes yelled across the clamor in the room. Everyone drew quiet. "Everything I have done was for the kingdom, and I would continue to rule as I have begun, doing anything that needed to be done for our kingdom! You, foolish thing, should reconsider your abdication."

Hayes lifted his hands in an offensive manner.

Some of the people in the Round Room moved clear, anticipating danger. Roen remained near Eloryn, but she stepped away from him, toward Hayes.

"Strike me with what you have, Hayes. You cannot touch me." Eloryn stood defiant, ready for him. "I am Maellan. *You bred me for this.*"

In a roar of words, Hayes cried a behest as though each word would physically strike her.

Eloryn's voice, calm and focused, was lost under his shouts. She spoke with the world as though they were oldest friends, every element understanding her, knowing her intentions, on her side. She smiled and waited.

Hayes's spell echoed through the room. Everyone tensed. Nothing happened.

Hayes growled and repeated his behest.

"Give up, Hayes. You are done," Eloryn said.

Hayes stuttered and drew a scroll from his pocket to read from. Eloryn recognized the intention of the behest and watched as Hayes seemed surprised when the air did not solidify around her.

Desperation filled his words as he turned to his vilest spell. "Guidhe beag lugha ob ciorram greim-bàis eucail spad eug!"

Eloryn's body did not turn on itself. She did not retaliate. She watched silently and waited as every attempt Hayes made failed him.

"The world will not listen to you, Hayes. I have asked that all your behests be denied."

Hayes reached to his side again, and Eloryn shook her head at his stubbornness. He grabbed at his walking cane and twisted it apart in his hands, pulling the handle from the length. The zing of metal filled the room.

She barely realized what was happening as the concealed sword swung at her neck.

An inch from her beating veins the blade stopped, blocked by another. Erec held his sword firm, and Roen burst passed him. He grabbed Hayes's arm and wrenched the thin sword from his hand.

"I may have no Spark of Connection, but I believe we're now even in that regard."

With a second strike at the wizard's chest, Roen knocked him to his knees.

Roen lifted his chin, daring Hayes to keep fighting. Hayes remained on the ground.

Behind them, guards, Councilors, and servants all moved forward to defend Eloryn. Everyone stood with her, and she knew she'd made the right decision.

Eloryn had Erec and men he trusted take Hayes to the dungeons. He shouted curses and blasphemies as he was dragged away.

The room was in turmoil. With their leader gone, and their queen abdicated, the Council were at a loss, arguing amongst themselves. Bedevere's voice cut through the chaos, trying to get his bewildered companions in order.

Eloryn caught Roen's hand in hers and dragged him from the room. He followed without a word. The two of them slipped away silently, not missed by the crowd they left behind.

In the quiet hallway, Eloryn stopped and turned to him. She kept his hand tight in hers. He looked at her with the golden eyes she loved.

"I'm sorry, Roen, for not doing everything in my power to be with you sooner. I doubted how you felt, I doubted my place in this kingdom, but I never doubted how I felt for you, and I should have acted on that. I'm sorry I'm so bad at the relationship I have with you, and that I'm not impulsive like Memory. I won't object if you want to be with her, or leave, or do whatever you need to in order to be happy."

"El," Roen's forehead creased but a smile sat on his lips. "I have tried to love others, but could only love you. I have tried to deny it, and only loved you more. I love you in a way that should make me a poet, but instead leaves me speechless. If you love me but a hundredth of how I love you, then I am happy."

Eloryn's hands reached for Roen's collar, but she couldn't feel the movement, could feel nothing but tingling nerves. Fingertips brushed his neck and sent a flush of warmth through her as she pulled him down to touch her mouth gently against hers.

She could feel his smile under her lips and kissed him again before letting go.

She blushed triumphantly as he looked down at her, shaking his head like he couldn't believe what was happening.

"I hope that felt like a little more than one hundredth," she said.

"Hard to say. I think I may just need to try..." His words became breath, disappearing to nothing as he walked into her, pressing his body against hers. Roen scooped the back of her head into both hands and kissed her cheek and neck.

Eloryn wrapped her hands around his shoulders, and he lifted her off her feet, spinning her in the air.

CHAPTER TWENTY-SIX

The knife had warmed to body temperature in her hands. Memory wasn't sure what she intended to do with it but couldn't let it go.

Servants gave her worried looks as they saw her walk by, but Memory barely noticed. People always stared at her wherever she went. It came with the hair colors and piercings. They made people judge her on first glance and that was how she liked it. It meant people left her alone. She felt shut off from the world, too busy struggling with herself. She'd already made her decision, but the options kept rattling around like loose change, tempting her. Would taking Eloryn's life solve her problems? No. Not even in her darkest fantasy. But she had to see her one more time.

Memory knew they would all be at the meeting Eloryn had called. The meeting didn't matter to her, but she was surprised that she had been invited at all, or that they even remembered she existed. She felt like she was already gone and couldn't understand that others didn't think the same.

Memory heard giggling and slowed down. At the end of the hall, she saw Eloryn and Roen. They looked utterly happy, wrapped in each other's arms, kissing again and again.

Memory looked away, squeezing her dry eyes closed, holding the image of them together like a snapshot in her mind.

Hope's familiar voice whispered from behind her. "If you want Roen, then you can have him once Eloryn is gone. You can have everything you want."

"No. I want Roen *and* Eloryn. I love them both. I love them and want them to be happy." Memory turned and headed back the way she'd come. The knife dropped on the floor, tumbling into a dark corner behind an ornamental suit of armor.

Memory didn't know if Hope still followed her, but she spoke aloud anyway. "I already know the problem that needs to be removed. It's not them. It's me."

"What a fun trick we played." Mina laughed, making a sound like tinkling chimes. She lay on top of Will in long, lush grass, spotted with wildflowers. The overwhelming fragrance of the blossoms added to the sick feeling in Will's gut.

She'll think I went home without her. I have to get back.

Mina had snatched Will away right at the worst moment. He'd been avoiding her, and this was how she punished him. He knew the

more he wanted to go back, the less likely it would happen. He tried to seem relaxed, carefree.

Mina rolled over him into the grass, and the blades lit up from within where she touched them, glowing golden, and sprays of petals danced as she giggled. Even now, Will ached at her beauty, that dangerous beauty he wished he could deny, like being lured by poisoned honey.

Will stretched casually and carefully picked his words. "Wouldn't it be a good trick if you sent me back now? She must think I'm gone. She'll be surprised if I show up again."

"No." Mina flipped onto her stomach and put her elbows under her, lifting her chest up like a sphinx. "You'll go back when I'm bored of you."

It had already been all night and most of the day Mina had kept him with her. He wasn't sure where they were. Somewhere deep in the hunting grounds, but he wasn't as familiar with this forest as he was with his last home. The small meadow grew dim and shaded, and a pair of deer wandered in, grazing. Mina sprung up onto her knees, reached out a hand, and the deer cantered over to her.

Will shifted in the grass, off his back and into a crouch, eyeing the elegant creatures. Recognizing the look on his face, the form of his body, the deer changed course. He was a predator, and they knew it. They bounded off into the darkened woods.

Mina smacked her hands onto the ground, shrieking. "I wanted to play with them."

"They're gone now." Will shrugged and lay down again. He yawned and closed his eyes. "You could probably catch them if you want. But I'm tired."

Mina threw handfuls of torn-up grass at him. "Horrible boring boy."

She floated up into the air, shimmering dust falling from her, and zipped away through the trees.

Will remained still for a few moments more, waiting to make sure she had gone, then pushed up to his feet and started running. He ran west, following the setting sun until he started to see familiar ground, then ran until he reached the palace walls.

Will climbed the vines to Memory's bedroom. The window was locked, for the first time Will had ever known.

Will knocked hard on the paneled glass, and a figure rushed to open the doors for him.

The red-headed maid stood in front of him, worry all over her features.

"Where is Memory?" Will asked, stepping into the room. It was still a mess from his fight with Dylan.

"Will, I'm so glad you're here. I don't know what to do." Clara handed him an open letter, written on the same cream-colored paper as the one Memory had left for him in the Ivy Room.

Clara rambled, almost hysterical. "She locked herself in her room earlier. I could hear her talking to herself. And now this."

Will only needed to read the first word. *Goodbye.*

"How can we find her?" Will roared.

Clara squeaked, "Maybe her sister, or—"

"Take me. Now."

A fear Will hadn't known since he was a boy in the other world gripped him. Back there he'd often worried, often thought it could happen. But he hoped here Memory had found a new life, had escaped her past. Something must have changed.

Clara led Will at a run through the palace. Will didn't care what he wore or the looks he got. He only cared about reaching Memory in time.

They found both Eloryn and Roen together, smiling despite the turmoil of wizards and messengers rushing about them. Will didn't understand what was happening. The castle seemed to be in chaos.

"We have to help Memory," Will said.

"Where is she?" Eloryn asked, her expression of joy slipping away to concern.

"We hoped you could find her," Clara said. "She may be planning to do something awful."

"She has no one with her? No guards or servants?" Eloryn asked.

Roen shook his head. "You know what she's like. She'll be alone."

Clara nodded and began to cry. "She only has me, and I wasn't there for her. It's my fault. I shouldn't have left her like that. The things she was saying, things she was doing. I'm so worried."

"It wasn't just your responsibility. If she's in danger, it's all our faults," Roen said.

Will's breath grew rough, each exhalation a growl. "We have to hurry."

They started moving, and a handful of guards that had their eyes on Eloryn followed. Will stopped. "Just us. It has to just be us, no one else."

Eloryn gave the guards a signal. One in particular nodded.

The guards remained where they were and Will, Clara, Eloryn, and Roen ran to find Memory.

What am I doing?

Memory felt more broken than ever. Regaining her memories had made things worse, not better. She hurt in a way that she didn't know how things could ever be better again.

She found solitude in Thayl's old quarters. The whole wing was still closed up, and she could wander freely without anyone staring at her. Only Hope was with her, ever by her side, as Memory wound her way around the tower stairs, up and up.

Memory paused along the way, drifting through the piles of junk in storage in the tower. She ran her hands over the stack of mattresses and their moth-eaten covers. A rolled tapestry on the floor showed burn marks. Paintings with cracked frames were stacked haphazardly. Splintered pieces of the round table had been piled in a corner.

This is the place for broken things.

She didn't belong in Avall with Eloryn and Roen. Maybe they thought so at first, but as the jigsaw of their lives came together, it became clear that Memory was a spare, broken piece that didn't fit. No one really knew her. No one accepted her for who she really was. Not even herself. Now she remembered her past, she knew she'd always been trying to be something she wasn't, someone different, running from herself.

Memory wondered whether Thayl felt like this as he made his way up this same tower, that there was no place in the puzzle for them.

Memory stood at the balcony and looked down.

Hope pulled her away by the arm. "What do you think you're doing? I've told you how to solve your problems. Why won't you believe me and just get it done?"

Memory looked out the window into the distance. "My own screwed-up brain is telling me to kill my sister. I don't deserve to live."

Hope shook her. "I'm not your brain. I'm real."

"Prove it."

"I knew things that you didn't. I knew you killed that guy before I showed it to you."

Memory snatched her arm from Hope's grasp. "Yeah, thanks for that."

"I just wanted to prove what you were capable of doing."

"And now I know." Memory headed again toward the edge.

Hope grabbed her roughly, dragging her back into the room and slamming the balcony doors closed behind her. "I'm sorry if your memories weren't all puppy dogs and picnics, but you have to snap out of it, we have things to do."

Memory faced Hope. She snarled and the room shook.

Hope smiled uneasily. "I thought you'd gotten yourself under control?"

"I have." The tower shook, and Hope was knocked to the floor.

Hope looked at Memory with genuine fear in her eyes. "I know it's a lot to ask, to kill your own sister, but it will work, I promise. If you want I can do it for you. Let me do it for you, and you can owe me a favor in return. Just give me the all clear."

Memory turned her back. "Shut up, Hope. Whatever you've got to say, whatever experience you think you're calling on for this advice you're giving me, it's all in me again now too. There's nothing anymore you can offer me. You've given me everything I needed to end up here."

Memory pulled the balcony doors open again, a soft breeze rushing in past her. The last sliver of orange sun kissed the horizon. She watched until it dropped from sight then stepped up onto the balustrade, balancing on the thin marble edge. "Later, Hope."

CHAPTER TWENTY-SEVEN

"Memory?" Eloryn's voice reached her. "What are you doing?"

Eloryn, Roen, Clara, and Will ran up into the room, and the sight of them almost made Memory slip and fall. Her heart thundered and feet tingled until she steadied herself.

What am I doing? What the hell am I doing?

Memory simply looked at Will, confused.

"Will?" Memory asked. She sounded inebriated and didn't know if it was her voice or hearing that was faulty. The whole world seemed to swim in her senses. "I thought you left me."

Will edged toward her. "Why would I leave?"

Because of all the horrible things I said, and do, and am.

Will shook his head as though she'd said the words aloud. *Did I?*

"Mina took me away. I didn't go through the door."

A small fire of jealousy lit in Memory, a spark of passion in a body she'd thought had already lost all life. "You stayed for her."

"Mem, please get down. What are you doing?" Eloryn pleaded.

Clara just watched with her hand over her mouth.

Memory couldn't look them in the eyes, so she looked down at the ground so far below. "I'm removing a problem."

"You're not a problem." Roen said, moving closer to her. "You've done so much good, inspired so much good, in me, in Eloryn, in Avall."

Clara nodded. "And the lives of the poor in the city. I've never seen such caring."

"You're both wrong. I'm a bad person. I don't belong – not here, not anywhere. Any good you've seen me do? Fake. I'm just trying to fit in but all that isn't the real me. The kids at the shelter only like me because I give them money. Why do you think you like me, Roen? It's because I look like Eloryn. Clara's only around because looking after me is her job. The Council just wants to study me. Dylan was just following orders." Memory ran her hands up through her hair, tugging at the purple strands. "The real me? I hurt people. I… kill people. *My soul is broken.* I might as well die. I know I murdered someone, and that was before Thayl's ritual stole my soul. How much of a monster does that make me now?"

Eloryn seemed confused. "Your soul isn't broken, Mem." She smiled like that solved everything. "If it were, I would have known when I joined spirits with you. How do you think that was even possible? Thayl was wrong – he never understood magic. He just assumed the power he stole was your soul. It was just magic he stole, just pure magic tangled with your memories. Not your soul."

Memory's shoulders fell. She felt thin as paper. "This is what I am *with* a soul?" *No.*

If this was all there was to her – the complete package – her actions were always hers. The way people reacted to her, the wrongness of her, she had nothing to blame but herself. There were no excuses, no get-out clauses. No getting better.

Memory's legs gave way beneath her. Her skirt billowing out behind her like a parachute trying to hold her in place. She could hear footsteps like thunder behind her as she fell into the wind.

Hands clutched at her, but she was already falling.

She could still feel arms around her and opened her eyes. The ground rushed up toward her, and dark brown hair blew into her face. Will tangled his limbs around her, trying to protect her from the fall, as though his own body would be shield enough to save her. His ice blue eyes remained fixed on her face.

Will. My Will.

Adrenaline flamed through Memory's limbs, making her gasp. The deadly ground flew at them. She ripped a hole into the Veil. The two of them fell through.

Will landed first, still holding Memory above him. They crashed down hard on the stack of old mattresses. The top three mattresses split and burst on impact, spraying dust and downy feathers into the air.

The stuffing fell around them like snow, and Memory cried out as she tried to sit up. Her hand stung like fingers were broken. Will lay still beneath her, and she put her good hand on his chest, trying to stir him. The second she touched him, he opened his eyes and pulled himself up, dragging her into his lap and holding so tight her bruised limbs ached more.

"You're an idiot to think I'd leave you. I would always be with you, if I could." Will's voice trembled, stopped and started, like each sentence was a struggle. "You make me so angry, but… but I could

just die I love you so much. I've always wanted to be with you, when things are good or bad, no matter what color your hair is or where we are. My home is where you are."

Memory clung back to Will, sobbing. The only person who knew her, that knew Hope and Memory, before and after, good and bad, and still accepted her.

He whispered into her neck. "I know you're hurting. It would be insane if you weren't after everything you've been through. There's no quick fix, but I'll be there for you. And you will be there for me, too, like you always have. You can't take yourself away from me."

And if he could accept her as is, maybe someday she could too.

"Will, I got my memories back. I remember it all. Everything."

He shifted back to look into her eyes, searching. "Are you… okay?"

Memory giggled softly, shaking her head. She pointed to the balcony. "See exhibit A."

"You will be. You will be okay." Will brought her back into his arms.

Roen, Eloryn, and Clara stood watching them. Roen held Eloryn as she stared at Memory, crying. Memory tilted her head back as a welcoming gesture and they came to join the embrace.

Memory let the warmth of her friends bodies soak into her, bringing her back to life.

She'd failed them by refusing to believe they could care for her. She knew how wrong she'd been when she could feel it now in every tear that fell on her.

Even Hope, in her own way, cared so much.

Memory shook her head. *Hope.*

"Hope," she whispered then spoke louder through the muffle of her friend's embrace. "Then who is Hope?"

Eloryn, Will, Roen, and Clara let her go.

Memory wobbled her way off the mattresses, her legs shaky and sore. “Hope, come out. I know you’re out there!”

Clara looked at the others, confused. “Aren’t you Hope?”

“No, there’s another me. I didn’t tell you all because she said she was made from my broken soul, and I didn’t want you to know. But if that’s not true…” Memory looked around the circular room. “Then who are you? What are you?”

She didn’t appear. Memory groaned in frustration.

“Is Hope who you’ve been talking to?” Roen asked. He and Eloryn looked at each other with clear concern.

“Don’t tell me she isn’t real, that I really have been crazy all along.” Memory squeezed her hand into a fist. The cut across the palm still stung. “It can’t be. A hallucination couldn’t have cast the spell to bring my memories back. She knew things, about my past, before I did. Game’s up, Hope, come out!”

A movement flashed in the corner of Memory’s eye. Hope stepped out from behind the stack of paintings. Memory’s friends gasped, and she sighed in relief that they were seeing her too.

“You spoiled everything,” Hope pouted. “It was just meant to be you and me, but now they all know, things will have to change.”

“You’re not me, not made of my soul, so what are you?” Memory demanded.

Hope picked her way through the unwanted furniture in the room. She lifted her palms upward, the vision of innocence. “Hey, I only knew what you knew, right? Maybe I’m just made up of your memories after all?”

“Don’t bullshit me. The things you told me to do, that isn’t me. It never was.”

“What, you really wouldn’t do this?” Hope cocked her head to the side. "Cuir aerlaith, briseadh cloich, séid goath."

Hope's words of magic bent the air around them, flinging a gust of wind that pushed Eloryn toward the open balcony windows.

"What are you doing?" Memory screamed. Eloryn was yelling her own magic words, but nothing seemed to stop the gale forcing her to the edge. She looked to Memory for help.

"I'm doing what you should have done. Such a shame your sister would die from a tragic accident." A few more words from Hope, and the balcony Eloryn slid toward crumbled away. Eloryn fell to her knees, clutching at the ground, trying to hold herself still. Roen ran to grab her and was caught in the rush of air himself.

"Ah yes, unfortunately this time, there are also witnesses that will have to go." With a look from Hope, the air seemed to wrap Clara and Will, pushing them the same way. Clara shrieked, crying.

The sound of the wind rushed through Memory like a river. Memory roared over it. "Stop it!" She let her magic loose, forcing a bolt to strike Hope.

The wind stilled. Memory's friends scrambled for stability.

Hope didn't even sound human when she screamed back. The whole tower rumbled, and the stones beneath Eloryn's feet fell away. Clara pulled her across onto a solid piece of ground then looked surprised at herself. She barely had a moment before the floor under them started breaking away.

Memory threw more magic at Hope. Even with the new control she'd found, it was all she could do. Each burst of magic knocked Hope back, disrupting her for just a moment. Memory wanted to Veil door her friends to safety but was worried if she let up her assault on Hope for even a second it would be too long.

Memory pummeled Hope back across the room, but it barely seemed to distract her.

Memory yelled. "Stop this!"

The floor kept crumbling on its own, too little left of its structure to stay intact. Furniture and old frames slid into the gaping pit. The stones under Memory dropped away. She almost fell backwards into the spreading hole. Will grabbed her and dragged her to solid ground at the edge of the room.

A wooden beam dislodged itself from a wall, throwing itself across at her friends. Memory managed to deflect it, but it still clipped Roen on the back when he stepped to block it from hitting the girls.

Memory gritted her teeth, staring at her twisted twin. "Why are you doing this? I didn't give you permission, I didn't…"

Hope had said she'd do it for her, if she'd just give the word. She should have known then, should have realized.

Hope only showed up after Thayl had died. Appearing at will, manipulating her, wanting debts and bargains and asking permission to harm those she loved. Just like Providence. Just like…

"Bronmer… Bron… Shit. Eloryn, I think she's a fae, Brand her!"

Eloryn cried, "BRONMARBH AIL-"

Hope was gone. Vanished in a flash, just the way a fairy would.

Memory breathed, liked it was the first time she had in weeks.

But the tower still roared like a crumbling stone dragon.

"The tower's coming down," Roen yelled over the sound.

"Can you try and hold it together?" Memory asked her sister.

Eloryn already spoke her words and nodded so as not to interrupt them with her reply. A sudden jolt shifted all of them a foot across the floor.

"Loreee?" Memory sang. "Whatcha doing? Can you hold this?"

Eloryn shrugged, shook her head, kept speaking words of magic anyway.

"Time to run, then."

Everyone nodded. Clara remained still, terrified, and Memory grabbed her hand and they ran first down the stairs. Eloryn, Roen, and Will followed close behind.

The roof of the tower flattened the room they had been standing in just as they hit the stairs. Memory let go of Clara who kept running and paused to check everyone was out and okay. Roen and Eloryn passed her on the stairs.

Dust and shattered slate pelted them from the destroyed roof. Eloryn stumbled her steps, and stumbled her words. The tower lurched, tipping to the side. They all slid with it and hit the wall of the stairwell.

An explosion of noise cracked around them and the stairwell split. Eloryn and Roen looked back at Memory, and she looked down at them from across the chasm where the stairs had been.

Will grabbed her hand, a question on his face.

Memory nodded.

He scooped her up, and at a run he jumped the gap, running along the wall and hitting the landing at the bottom on his feet. Memory bounced in his strong arms and tucked herself tight into his body.

Sprinting down the last flights of stairs, they slid out into the adjoining corridor atop an avalanche of crumbled masonry. All that was left of the tower.

They all sat there coughing, checking over each other with silent looks.

It was Eloryn who spoke first.

"Mem, are you okay?"

Memory wafted dust from her face. "Yeah, in one piece."

"I mean, really okay?"

Memory felt like laughing. She was full of relief and wanted to express it through that unstoppable sort of laughter that hurt your belly. But her sister stared at her so seriously, she worried her relief was misplaced. Maybe she had a metal pipe sticking through her chest and didn't know it yet, like those dumb chicks in gore flicks.

"Why?"

"Because you're going to need to be." Eloryn bit her lip and tried to smile. "I've abdicated. You're now the queen of Avall."

TO BE CONTINUED IN PROVIDENCE UNVEILED

MEMORY'S
WAKE
SELINA A FENECH

HOPE'S
REIGN
SELINA A FENECH

PROVIDENCE
UNVEILED
SELINA A FENECH

SELINA A FENECH
BESHADOWED
DARKNESS
UNKNOWN

SELINA A FENECH
BESHADOWED
BLOOD
BOUND

SELINA A FENECH
BESHADOWED
SHADOWS
AWOKEN

SELINA A FENECH
BESHADOWED
EVERDARK
CURSED

EMOTIONALLY
CHARGED
1
SELINA A FENECH

EMOTIONALLY
UNSTABLE
2
SELINA A FENECH

EMOTIONALLY
POWERFUL
3
SELINA A FENECH

ABOUT SELINA A. FENECH

Whether it's painting artworks or writing novels, creating fantasy works is Selina's biggest passion. She lives in Australia with her husband and daughter and loves food, gardening, geekery, and all things fantasy.

Find out more about Selina at her official website-

www.selinafenech.com

www.ingramcontent.com/pod-product-compliance
Lightning Source LLC
Chambersburg PA
CBHW020914310726
48980CB00011B/887/J

* 9 7 8 0 6 4 8 7 0 8 0 7 0 *